Last Bird Singing

Jane Holland

ISBN: 1517693276
ISBN-13: 978-1517693275

Other Publications by Jane Holland

Fiction

GIRL NUMBER ONE

KISSING THE PINK

MIRANDA

Poetry

THE BRIEF HISTORY
OF A DISREPUTABLE WOMAN

BOUDICCA & CO

CAMPER VAN BLUES

THE WANDERER

ON WARWICK

FLASH BANG: NEW & SELECTED POEMS

Jane Holland also writes fiction as:

Beth Good
Victoria Lamb
Elizabeth Moss.

i

ACKNOWLEDGEMENTS

My thanks as always go to my husband Steve and children Kate, Becki, Dylan, Morris and Indigo for bearing with me despite my craziness.

.

CHAPTER ONE

Newcastle, late 1980s

When she was small, Keely used to wake in the mornings to the sound of her mam singing. Her mam was beautiful. She had long blonde hair and smiling eyes. She used to bend over the bed in a smell of flowers and clean hair and tickle Keely until she wriggled.

'Time to get up, sleepyhead.'

Dad had a job then. He wore white overalls covered in paint and drove a van. He would go out to work before Keely got up for school and come back every evening just before teatime. He used to wink at her as he came through the door, handing Keely an acorn or a fallen leaf he had found on the way home.

'It's a magic leaf,' he would tell her. 'You have to make a wish on it, but don't tell anyone what you wished for.'

'Why not, Dad?'

'Because it doesn't work like that, princess.'

Sometimes it would be a packet of sweets or a lollipop from the corner shop though her mam used to shake her head and say it would rot her teeth. But Dad only slipped it to her later while Mam was busy clearing the table.

'Don't tell your mam, okay?'

Whenever he came in from work, Dad would wash his hands with soap and hot water and then give Keely's mam a big noisy kiss, and her mam used to giggle and tell him to 'Stop it, Malcolm!', but sometimes they would go into the bedroom and shut the door for a while.

One evening when Keely was nearly seven, her dad didn't come home from work. His tea went cold on the table but he still didn't come in. Keely's mam sat there tapping her fingers and looking at the clock.

Then a policeman came to the door, and Keely's mam started crying. Keely ran upstairs to find her shoes and coat, feeling very excited, then they got into a police car with the man.

'Where are we going?'

'Not now, love,' her mam said, squeezing her arm. 'Your dad's had an accident.'

Dad was lying pale in a high bed and Keely wasn't allowed to sit beside him, but she could see his eyes were closed. Keely's mam told her that he had hurt his back falling off a ladder at work. She sounded very angry. Keely was scared because she had never seen her mam that angry before, but she didn't say anything, she just held on to her mam's hand and wouldn't look up at her dad again in case he was dead. Sometimes that happened to people. They went to sleep and never woke up again.

Dad stayed asleep for nearly six weeks but he woke up on a Thursday morning. When he came home from hospital they had a party with streamers and sausage rolls. Keely's mam wrote 'Welcome Home, Malcolm' on a sheet with red paint and hung it out of the front bedroom window. Lots of people came to the house and they played loud music.

Keely was given a glass of something sweet that made her feel sick and she had to go to bed early, but she lay down on the landing in her new nightie and watched through the banisters. When everyone had gone home and it was quiet, her mam helped her dad upstairs but he got angry and told her to stop fussing. Keely hurried back to her room before they saw she was still awake.

Later she woke up and heard shouting, and then her mam crying. The moon was a cold face at the window. Keely knelt up and looked out at the rain until it stopped falling.

The only place Keely liked in their house was her own bedroom. Her bedroom wallpaper had red poppies on it. She had chosen it herself ages ago, and even helped her dad to put it up before his accident. He had smoothed the paper onto the wall and Keely had held the ladder steady.

Some evenings, before her mam came home from work, Keely would press up against the headboard in her school uniform and stare at the wallpaper for ages, tracing the shape of the nearest petals with one finger. The poppies stared back at her. They were like huge scarlet eyes with yellow lashes and black centres. When she moved about the room the scarlet eyes followed her curiously. They liked to know what she was doing.

'Keely, love? Your supper's ready.'

But if her mam called up the stairs, Keely froze on the spot and the poppies froze with her.

Her mam always seemed to be tired those days. She would sit in front of the telly after tea, rubbing her calves and ankles because she'd been on her feet for hours. Her long blonde hair was always tied up in a bun and she wore lipstick that made lines appear around her mouth. 'You have to make an effort, Malcolm. We can't live off what I bring in.'

'Take a look at this leg, you stupid cow. No one wants a man who can't walk properly.'

'But you're not even trying.'

'What's the matter, Anne? Did you get lumbered with a cripple? Is that what you tell the lads on your nights out?'

Those were the arguments that went on for hours. Sometimes her mam would run into the kitchen and her dad would follow her, slamming the door behind him. Keely would hear breaking glass and other horrible noises, as if they were having a fight, and the muffled sound of her mam crying afterwards. 'Malcolm, please ...'

'I don't even know if she's mine.' The sound of a blow and her sharp cry. 'How can I be sure, with a whore like you? You even did it behind my back on your hen night.'

'I told you, that wasn't my fault.'

When they fought like that, Keely used to hide behind the sofa with her hands over her ears or run upstairs and slam the bedroom door, leaning her hot face against the cold flat poppies.

No one ever came after her.

One night, after another evening of shouts and thuds, the front door slammed shut. Keely was up in her bedroom. When she raced to the window and stared down, she saw her dad limping away down the street in a winter overcoat, leaning heavily on his stick.
She pressed her face up against the glass, but it was raining and she couldn't see him properly. Then he turned the corner towards the pub and disappeared from sight.

Her mam came into the bedroom. She had a bruise on her cheek and she was crying. Wiping her face on her sleeve, Keely's mam grabbed some clothes and toys and packed them into a suitcase. 'Get dressed, sweetheart. And put your best shoes on.'

'Where are we going?'

'Hush.' Her mam led her downstairs by the hand. 'Wait by the front door, Keely. I won't be long.'

When they left the house, it was raining and there was a taxi waiting outside. Keely climbed into the back with her mam, still half asleep. The driver had a grey beard and moustache. He drove them through the dark streets to

Aunty Jean's house.

Her cousin Jess was already asleep, so Keely had to creep into bed next to her without making a sound. She could hear people talking downstairs in loud angry voices. Feeling a bit less scared now, Keely tried to shrug herself further into the middle of the bed, banging Jess in the ribs.

Her cousin sat up yawning. 'What's happening?'

Keely shrugged.

'I know why you're here,' Jess said.

'Why?'

'Because your dad hits your mam.'

'He does not.'

'Suit yourself.' Jess turned over, kicking her lazily on the shin. 'Shove up, Kee. There's no room to breathe.'

'Don't breathe then.'

Her cousin made an angry noise but didn't bother hitting her. Instead, she turned over and dragged the duvet violently over her head.

It was hard to settle down. The bed smelt funny and the sheets were rough against her skin. But when she finally fell asleep, Keely had a strange dream. She couldn't remember it properly in the morning, except that she had been sliding down some hole in the ground, hands stretched high above her head in the darkness, racing down a water chute forever.

They didn't stay long at Aunty Jean's. Her dad came round every day for a week and hammered on the front door and windows until the neighbours called the police.

Uncle Trevor went round to the housing office and a few weeks after that Keely and her mam moved into a flat in one of the high-rise blocks. The lifts were always out of order there. Bloody little hooligans, the neighbours would say, and tell them to take the stairs. There was graffiti on the walls of the stairs, and they smelt of wee. Some of the lights flickered on and off, trying desperately to work. Others were broken, wires hanging down, or the glass covers all smashed up and the bulbs stolen. They had to turn those corners almost in darkness.

'Stay close behind me,' her mam would whisper. So Keely always hung close behind her mam, watching her heel move up to each step. The steady clack-clack of her mam's black shoes was comforting, and her perfume smelt nicer in the dark too.

When the holidays were over, Keely had to start at a new school. On her first day, a boy called Tommy threw a paper aeroplane at Keely. It whizzed past Keely's ear and she stared at it as it landed, close by Miss Harrick who was writing on the chalkboard. Then Miss Harrick thought she had done it and gave her a black mark.

After class that day, Keely walked home alone, wiping her face on her sleeve. It was cold and her feet hurt in her stiff new shoes.

Tommy came thudding down the road after her. He had his friends with him. They stood over her with their hands in their pockets. 'How did you get to be so ugly?'

'Leave me alone.'

'You're horrible skinny. Doesn't your mam feed you? If you stood sideways, you'd disappear.'

'Go away.'

But Tommy came closer, staring at her and opening his jacket a little. He was big and hot and she could smell peppermints on his breath. 'See what I've got here?'

He had a bird under his jacket. A baby bird. It was tiny and black with a yellow beak. It opened its eyes and looked at her, blinking. Then its beak moved slowly, as if it was in pain, and there was a thin squeaking sound like nails on a chalkboard.

Keely gasped. 'Let it go.'

'Bog off.'

'Where's its mam?'

'She's dead. I killed her.' He looked at Keely. 'Want to hold it?'

The baby bird was cold and small in her hands, and it

wriggled. Its beak kept opening and shutting on the thin squeaking noise. Its back wasn't made of proper feathers but stuff like damp cushion covers. She put out a finger and touched its beak. It turned its head towards Keely, as if it wanted to know who was there, but it couldn't seem to see anything and it kept making that squeaking noise. There was a white thing like an inside lid that kept dropping over its eyes as if it was tired.

'It needs looking after,' she whispered.

Tommy snatched it back from her. He dropped the wriggling baby bird to the floor, raised his boot and crushed it. There was a snap as its bones broke. The body lay there unmoving. Blood and grey-black stuff oozed out onto the pavement and ran into the cracks. It hadn't made a sound.

'That's what it needs.'

She broke away from them and started to run. She didn't know where she was running, but she tore down the nearest alley behind the houses and kept running until her face was red and she could hardly breathe.

Exhausted, Keely leant her cheek against the cold brick of a wall for a few minutes. It had started to rain. Her hair and face were damp with drizzle. She closed her eyes and put her hands over her ears, but she kept hearing his boot coming down on that wriggling body.

SNAP.

CHAPTER TWO

Some nights, sitting alone on the sofa, Keely could hear people arguing in the other flats or down on the ground. At the weekends, people often banged on the window as they passed but she ignored them. They were just drunks, on their way home from a night out. If she opened the window after midnight, she could hang out and watch the lads in the car park, kicking the dustbins around and throwing bottles at the walls.

Once or twice she would see a faint glow from outside and hear a big shout go up from the lads. When she went to the window, there would be a car or a dustbin on fire down below. After a while, the police would come and look at it, then go away again. There never seemed to be anyone left in the car park by the time the police showed up.

Her mam always had magazines lying around the flat, so Keely started a scrapbook of pictures. She enjoyed cuttings things out with scissors. She had to be careful not to make a mistake. She decided to collect pictures of animals instead of people because they were more interesting. There weren't many pictures of animals in her mam's magazines but whenever she found a good one, she would fetch her scissors and cut it out for her scrapbook. She liked pictures of birds best. Sometimes she drew round them with crayons afterwards or tried to copy the pictures onto paper with a felt tip. She showed Jess her scrapbook once but her cousin only laughed and said it was babyish. So Keely didn't show it to her again.

School started again in September and her mam complained because Keely had nearly grown out of her uniform. Some of the girls at school laughed and called Keely a tramp because she was wearing secondhand clothes. She hung around near the bushes at break times. No one else ever went there so she could be alone and watch the sparrows hopping in and out of the bushes without having the others laugh at her. Keely would sit like a statue by the bushes and sometimes a few of the sparrows came really close to her before flying away.

Her dad was allowed to see her some weekends now. He would come up to the flat and knock, but her mam always made her answer the door. 'I don't want to see that bastard,' she would say.

He took her to the pictures and the park, and sometimes they went on a bus into town and he bought her a few things. He would always ask how her mam was treating her but Keely just shrugged. Her mam had told her not to say about being left alone in the evenings. She had said she could get into trouble with the police and Keely might be put into a home if they found out. She didn't want her mam to get into trouble.

Whenever he brought her home, her dad would leave her at the door and give her a quick hug. He smelt strange and his face prickled her cheek like the men who came to her mam's flat sometimes, but she never said anything in case it made him angry. She would go inside instead and shut the door without looking at him again.

But often her dad didn't bother coming round to see her at all. More and more often.

'Bed by nine o'clock sharp tonight,' Keely's mam said, opening her eyes wide to put her mascara on in front of the mirror. 'Understand, pet?'

'What if someone knocks at the door?'

'Sit quiet till they're gone.'

Once her mam had got all dressed up and gone out into Newcastle, the flat was always really quiet. They couldn't afford a telly, so after Keely had done her homework she used to sit and stare out of the living room window instead, watching the cars zoom across the dark city like ants with teeny torches on their heads. They made wobbly ribbons of light all the way in and out of town. Sometimes, Keely would make herself toast and jam, and if there was any pop left in the fridge she'd have that too. When she was tired, she went to bed.

Her mam never came to bed as soon as she got in. Keely would sneak out to go to the loo sometimes and her mam would be crying. Lying there on the sofa, all hunched up in her short skirt and tights, with her high heels kicked off on the floor beside her. Keely never knew what to do, so she'd go to the loo real quiet, then tiptoe back into bed. Then she'd cry too, hot-faced under the covers. But her mam was usually okay again by the time she slid into bed next to her - except for her mascara, which used to run and make her look like something out of a horror movie.

One night, her mam didn't come back for hours and hours. Keely fell asleep waiting for her.

When she finally heard the key in the lock, Keely sat up in bed and blinked at the luminous hands of the alarm clock. It was just after four in the morning. She heard footsteps, then a crash, and muffled laughter. She stared at the light under her bedroom door. She could see shadows moving about in the living room.

After a few minutes, her mam said something quietly and a deep voice replied. There was a man in the flat.

Keely leapt out of bed and banged the bedroom door open in her excitement. 'Dad?'

But it wasn't her dad at all. It was a young man in

jeans and a denim jacket, long dark hair tied up in a ponytail. He stared at Keely, standing in the bedroom doorway in her PJs. 'Who the hell is that?'

'What, baby?' In white high heels and a short black dress, her mam stumbled out of the kitchen with two glasses in one hand and a bottle of wine in the other. Her pink lipstick was smudged. She gasped when she saw Keely was awake. 'You naughty girl. Get back into bed this minute.'

His voice was angry. 'You never mentioned her.'

As Keely started to close the door, she saw her mam rub herself against the stranger with a pleading smile on her face. 'Don't be cross. She's only eight, she doesn't understand. There's no problem.'

'I don't like it. Kids make me nervous.'

'Hush, sit down and have some wine.' After kissing him on the lips for a few minutes, her mam glanced back over her shoulder and saw the bedroom door wasn't shut properly. Her face stiffened and she moved towards the bedroom angrily. There was that high sharp note in her voice that meant trouble. 'Close that door right now and get into bed, Keely. I'm not going to tell you again.'

Keely tried really hard to get to sleep but she kept hearing noises from the living room. In the end, she buried her head under the pillow and lay there in darkness, listening to her own heart beating instead. Everything went all hot and hazy in front of her eyes. She must have fallen asleep at some point, because next thing she knew there was a strong pair of hands lifting her gently out of the bed and carrying her through to the living room. Her feet were cold without the duvet.

Keely opened her eyes, shivering. The man with the ponytail was laying her carefully down on the sofa. He covered her with his denim jacket because she was so cold. 'Go back to sleep, darling,' he said, stroking her hair. 'There's a good girl.'

But she blinked, trying to open her eyes against the

bright light. She could see her mam now, standing behind him. She was barefoot and her dress straps were falling off her shoulders. But she was clinging tight to him and smiling. Then somebody put the light out in the living room and they went into the bedroom together. The door closed softly behind them.

Keely drew her toes up under the denim jacket and closed her eyes again, trying not to listen to those noises whimpering through the darkness like animals in pain.

On Keely's birthday, her mam let her have the whole day off school so they could go into Newcastle together and buy some clothes. But her mam kept looking at the price tags and shaking her head.

She came up to Keely with a blue skirt from the sale rack. 'How about this one?'

'That's rubbish, mam.'

She put it back and picked out another one. It was plain black with a pleated front. 'This is nice. It's good value too.'

'I hate it.'

'Okay, which one do you want?'

Keely reached for the shiny blue skirt she'd seen first. 'This.'

'That's too dear. I can't afford it.'

'Oh forget it, mam.' Suddenly angry, Keely threw the shiny blue skirt down on the floor and walked away. 'I wish I'd never come out with you. What's the point?'

Her mam called after her but Keely ignored her. She walked towards the big glass doors at the shop entrance and stood next to the accessories display, arms folded and her mouth shut tight. The kids on the estate already laughed at her for wearing second-hand clothes. What would they say if they saw her in one of those funeral skirts?

When her mam finally spotted her, she grabbed hold of Keely's shoulder and gave her a right shake. 'Don't you ever do that to me again. Come on, we're leaving.'

But as they went through the doors, an alarm went off in the store and her mam started to run, pulling Keely after her.

Keely screamed. 'What's going on, mam?'

'Shut up and run.'

They ran through the freezing air for a few minutes, Keely dragged along by her coat sleeve, dodging people as they pushed their way down the street. There were elbows and shopping bags slamming into her face, but her mam was holding her so tightly that she couldn't do anything but desperately try to keep up.

There was a man in a dark suit running alongside them. He caught at Keely's mam and pulled her down to the left. She almost fell, struggling to get free. Breathless, the man blocked their way forward. 'Can I see what you've got under your coat, madam?'

'Get lost.'

He wrenched at her mam's coat and the shiny blue skirt that Keely had chosen fell out onto the pavement. The man in the suit stooped to pick it up, still gripping her mam's arm. 'What's this? Forgot to pay, did we?'

'You put that there.'

'Come along, madam. You're going back to the store with me and I'm calling the police.'

'Let go, you're breaking my sodding arm.' Her mam struggled but the man in the suit wouldn't let go. He was smiling now as he dragged her back along the street. Keely followed slowly. Her mam was wriggling and kicking. 'You're really enjoying this, aren't you?'

'Save it for the police.'

'Look, it's her birthday and I couldn't afford it, all right? What did you expect me to do? Poor little cow.'

He glanced over his shoulder at Keely but didn't say anything. When they went back through the glass doors, all the other shoppers stopped to stare and whisper. The man took them down the back of the shop to the manager's office. The manager wasn't there so they had to wait while someone called her. While they sat down and waited, the man in the dark suit stood beside the desk without taking his eyes off Keely's mam. It was as if he was afraid she might try and run away again.

Her mam squeezed Keely's hand and started crying. 'I only did it for you, love. I didn't want to see you disappointed.'

Keely didn't know what to say. Her stomach was hurting like she was going to be sick. They seemed to be waiting forever while the man in the dark suit stared at them without speaking. In the end, she couldn't help herself. 'Will they put you in prison?'

Before her mam could say anything, the door opened and a woman came in. She was very smart with glasses and short blonde hair. She listened to the man, and she looked at the blue skirt. She didn't smile.

Keely's mam explained about the birthday present and the money. She even opened her purse and offered to pay something towards the skirt, and more later when she could afford it. She kept crying and wiping her face with the back of her hand. Her mascara was running down her cheeks and her ponytail was all messed up from struggling with the man.

The smart woman looked at Keely and then at her mam. Suddenly the man in the suit was opening the door for them, and they were free. Her mam kept saying sorry, but the smart woman waved her away, speaking in a stern voice. The man took them to the glass doors and watched them leave. Outside the air was very cold and people knocked into them as they stood there on the pavement.

'What's happening?'

'Just walk,' her mam said, pushing her forward. She fumbled for a tissue in her handbag. 'Those bastards.'

'You're not going to prison?'

She shook her head. 'Just keep going.'

They sat right at the back of the bus on the way

home. Her mam stared at the steamed-up windows without speaking. Keely buried her cold hands in her pockets. She could feel her eyes getting wet. Hurriedly, she wiped her face with her sleeve, keeping her head down so her mam wouldn't see the tears and get angry.

She didn't need her mam to say anything about what had happened back there in the shop. Keely already knew it was her fault.

It was nearly Christmas. Keely was fast asleep in bed when she felt someone lifting her. She opened her eyes and it was a dark-skinned man she had never seen before. He was big and smelt of leather. The man winked when he saw Keely was awake, then he carried her easily through to the living room and laid her on the sofa.

Her mam leant against the door, watching him. She was smoking a cigarette. 'Cover her with the blanket.'

'What's her name?'

'Keely.'

The man ran his finger along her cheek. 'Okay, Keely, this is the deal. My name's Zal. I'm going to turn the light out now and you're going to sleep in here. No trips to the loo and no glasses of water. Your mam and me don't want to be disturbed. Do you understand?'

Keely nodded silently.

He leant forward and kissed her on the forehead. She could smell alcohol on his breath. 'Now remember what I said. Not a peep out of you till morning. You wouldn't want to make me angry, would you?'

With his arm wrapped tight around her mam's waist, the man gave her another warning glance and went into the bedroom. Keely turned over on the sofa and stared into the darkness, listening to their muffled laughter and the other noises. Keely wasn't stupid. She knew why the stranger was there and what he was doing to her mam. He was just another one from the night club where her mam worked. It wasn't important. Those men never came back to the flat again. Sometimes she saw the money they left next to her mam's bed in the mornings.

Later, she heard them arguing in the bedroom. The man's voice got louder. There was a terrible crash and her mam yelped like a dog hit by a car. It went quiet for a while. Then they had sex. Soon after he had finished, Keely heard unsteady footsteps along the hallway and knew it was her mam, stumbling out to the loo. From the choking noises and the almost constant flushing, it sounded like she was being sick.

Keely wanted to go out to her mam, but she didn't dare. She just lay there with her eyes squeezed shut, remembering the way he had said to her 'you wouldn't want to make me angry, would you?'

'It's a Greek name,' her mam said the next day. 'Zal owns the night club where I work.'

The new man didn't sound Greek, though his hair was very thick and dark. He always wore an old soft leather jacket and a gold ring on the middle finger of his right hand. He smelt of spice and oranges. He had a little goatee beard and one gold stud in his left ear which made him look like a pirate. And when he smiled, the corners of his eyes creased up like an old man's, even though he was only about the same age as her mam.

Zal didn't disappear like the other men. Instead, he came round to the flat a few days later with a huge bunch of bright yellow flowers for her mam. She put them in a jug in the living room and they lasted for nearly two weeks.

Her mam was in a good mood after that. She even gave Keely some extra pocket money and sent her off into town on her own. She messed around outside the cinemas and shops for a few hours, bought herself some chips from one of the kebab vans, then trailed home in the rain to find Zal on the sofa with his feet on the coffee table and their mam cooking something spicy in the kitchen.

'Hello again,' Zal smiled. 'Had a good day out?'

Her mam came out of the kitchen at that moment, wiping her hands on a dishcloth. 'The meat's nearly done, do you want to....?' She saw them both standing there and stopped dead. The look she gave Keely was furious. 'I thought I told you to stay in town until six o'clock?'

'I got tired.'

Getting up from the sofa, Zal waved his hand to clear the smoke. 'It's okay. I told you, I don't mind kids.'

'She can play in the bedroom.'

'No, let her stay.'

'She's not going to put you off, is it?' Her mam looked worried. 'I know you said you don't mind kids underfoot, but men always seem to vanish once they catch sight of Keely.'

Zal smiled, bending to kiss her on the lips. 'Does it look like I'm about to dash out the door?'

Her mam went round singing for weeks after that and life soon fell into a new pattern for Keely. Whenever she heard Zal's car pull up outside, Keely scrambled back into the bedroom at top speed, knowing her mam would shout if she saw Keely out of bed so late at night.

Sometimes Zal was in a specially good mood and would let her stay up to watch telly when they came in together from the club. On those nights, he would smoke joints and drink large tumblers of brandy while they watched a video together. Then her mam started to smoke as well, though she said she didn't like the taste of brandy.

Zal always kept a block of cannabis in his pocket, wrapped in a little bit of cling film. Keely knew what it was because she had seen Jess and her friends smoking it behind the mobile classrooms at lunch time. Even with the lights off, she could still see what they were doing by the light of the telly. Zal usually had his arm around her mam, as she sat with her legs tucked up beneath her, rolling him a joint in front of the flickering screen.

The sweet smoke would make Keely drowsy, and after a while she would fall asleep in the armchair, but she could always hear their voices in her dreams, murmuring on for hours under the sound of the telly.

'Go on, why not? No one will know it was you,' Jess said.

'Zal would know who did it,' Keely replied quickly, shaking her head. 'And he'd skin me alive.'

'But he's not going to miss a tiny bit, is he? He's a dealer. Everyone knows that. He must have loads of it stacked away.'

They were lying on the floor in Aunty Jean's living room, watching a morning chat show on the telly. Aunty Jean and Uncle Trevor were both out at work. It was a Tuesday but Jess had persuaded Keely to skip school for the day and come over to her place on the bus. Keely was in her school uniform, and her stiff shirt collar kept irritating her, but Jess had stayed in her PJs and dressing-gown because she couldn't be bothered dressing just to sit around the house. They were having a carpet picnic with crisps and chocolates and sticky jam sandwiches.

Keely shivered. 'It's too dangerous.'

'Bollocks.'

'I don't like him, Jess.'

'Then what's your bloody problem? All the more reason to take some of his gear,' Jess said, taking a cigarette out of her pack and holding it out to her. 'Go on, help yourself.'

'You know I hate the taste.'

Her cousin made a face. 'There's nothing else to do round here, is there? It's dead boring if you can't even have a smoke. Come on, Kee. What he doesn't see can't hurt him. Next time he leaves his jacket lying around, just lift a bit for us. Enough for a couple of joints, that's all.'

'Why don't you buy your own? Didn't you get any money for your birthday?'

'Yeah, what a great birthday.' Jess laughed, taking a deep drag on her cigarette and blowing the thick smoke towards the ceiling. 'All I got was a tenner and some Marks and Spencer's knickers.'

'At least your dad's still living at home.'

She looked at her sideways, holding out the cigarette. 'Not for long.'

'What do you mean?'

'They're going to split up, aren't they?' Jess shrugged. 'Mam won't stop drinking. Dad stays out all night out so he doesn't have to watch her sleeping it off on the sofa. And he can't always be with his mates, can he? He must have a girlfriend tucked away somewhere.'

'I don't believe you.'

'Suit yourself.' Jess blew a ball of smoke straight into her face, laughing as Keely started to cough. 'But your mam's doing all right down at Zal's club, even if he is her pimp. My mam says it's better than working on the streets.'

Keely sat up angrily. 'What's that supposed to mean?'

'Come on, you're not that soft in the head. Everyone knows about it. Your mam only works in that night club at the weekends but suddenly she's earning enough to pay the rent on your flat and buy herself all those fancy new clothes. What did you think she was doing there? The bloody washing-up?'

'You're disgusting. My mam's not ...'

'A whore?'

Keely slapped her face.

Jess gasped as if she'd been stung, clutching her cheek for a few seconds, then launched herself furiously at Keely. She rolled her over on the carpet, pinning Keely's arms down with the full weight of her knees, and hit her violently several times in the head and chest. Keely tried to get free but her cousin was too strong. Jess sat on top of her, viciously pushing her neck down against the floor, thumbs squeezing her windpipe.

'Get off me,' Keely croaked, fighting for breath. 'I'll tell my mam what you said. Then you'll be sorry.'

'Your mam's a prozzie, Kee. Face it.'

'Liar.'

Jess laughed, pushing her face right close to Keely's. 'Is that so? Then how come even some of my dad's mates have had her?'

'That's not true.'

'Go and ask her yourself. Zal owns the night club and he owns your mam too. She pulls the punters and he takes a cut.' Suddenly Jess got up, standing above her with a contemptuous stare. 'It's common knowledge. And she's not the only one working for him. He's got other girls there too. You're so bloody thick not to see it. He'll have your mam on smack next, to stop her from going off with another pimp. That's what my mam reckons.'

'Your mam doesn't know what she's talking about,' Keely yelled, rubbing her wet face with her fists. She rolled over, burying her face in the carpet so she didn't have to look at Jess anymore. There was a stink of bitter cigarette smoke in the room. Keely tried not to breathe so fast, resting her cheek against the rough carpet. She felt sick and her stomach was heaving. Her throat ached where Jess had pressed both thumbs into it as if she was going to strangle her. 'I want to go home now.'

'Go home then, you little baby.'

'I hate you.'

'That's fine by me. I was sick of your bloody whinging anyway.' Jess bent and picked up the smouldering filter of her cigarette. 'Fuck, I've burnt a hole in my mam's carpet now. She'll kill me when she sees that.'

Jess stormed out and started banging about it in the kitchen. Keely looked down at the singed black smudge on the carpet where Jess had dropped her cigarette. She rubbed at it with a wet finger for a bit, but it wouldn't budge. She stared at it in silence. The smudge stared back at her like a little black eyeball.

The hot water drummed onto her upturned face as Keely arched back under the shower, rubbing shampoo into her hair. It was a Saturday morning and she wouldn't normally have been up this early, but she was going into town on the bus later with Jess. It was a chamomile shampoo and she closed her eyes, relaxing into the sweet flowery smell of the lather.

Startled by the sound of the door opening, Keely swung round, still soaping her hair under the shower. She knew the lock was broken, but no one usually came in if the door was shut properly. Her eyes stung as she tried to open them against the warm streaming blur of water and shampoo. 'That you, mam?'

But it was Zal standing in the doorway, not her mam. Shock flooded her body and she jumped as if the water had suddenly turned scalding hot.

Handing her the blue towel off the radiator, his voice sounded completely normal. 'Soap in your eyes, doll?'

She nodded, her heart thudding.

'Dry yourself, then.'

Keely felt heat prickling at her cheeks as she rubbed her face with the hand towel, totally aware of her own nakedness. He must be able to see everything, but he wasn't making any attempt to look away or leave the room. His eyes wandered over her without hurrying.

Turning away from him slightly, though she knew it was pointless trying to hide, Keely felt like a collection of naked parts instead of a person. Damp skinny thighs, the round white flash of her bum, straight waist, the half-hidden curve of what would eventually be breasts but were just two tiny mounds of puppy fat right now, each one topped with an embarrassingly pink nipple.

Her shoulders drooped and bent inwards, trying to conceal them. The towel wrapped round her waist, but wouldn't close. Keely held onto it with trembling fingers. 'Do you need the loo?'

Zal was still watching her, completely silent, standing near the bath with a strange look on his face. Keely thought he wasn't going to answer her at first, but then he suddenly nodded, shaking himself like a dog coming out of water. 'Yeah, that's it. I need a piss. I didn't realise you were in the shower.'

'I'll be out in a tick.'

He jerked the door shut with his foot. His hands went to his flies, unzipping his jeans, deliberately watching her expression. 'You carry on, sweetheart. This won't take long.'

Keely swung to face the bathroom wall. Steam was still rising off the white tiles. Her face was burning. She wanted to scream at him and run out of the bathroom, but she was frozen there, standing high on her toes in a draining pool of water, aware that the hand towel must barely be reaching the top of her thighs. He could see everything, probably even the crack of her arse. Keely's long tangled hair was dripping down her spine, she could feel the trickles cooling on her skin as they slipped under the towel and over her buttocks.

She heard the splash as it hit the toilet bowl. Gradually, the stream slowed to a few drops and then stopped.

Zal laughed, zipping up his jeans. Then he was gone, shutting the bathroom door quietly behind him as though he meant her no harm. *I didn't realise you were in the shower.* But she had seen the look in his eyes, and knew he was lying.

CHAPTER THREE

The summer at Skegness was the first time Keely had ever been on a proper holiday. She was so excited she could hardly sit still in the car on their way down even though Jess got irritated and kept snapping at her to sit back and calm down. Her mam had said Jess could come with them on holiday in return for looking after Keely and helping to keep the caravan clean. Jess had brought tons of new catalogue clothes in a suitcase and she told Keely she could even borrow some if she was good.

Their caravan was only a short distance from the beach. Keely had never seen the sea before, except on telly, and she was a bit scared in case she drowned. But Zal just laughed at her and said she was being a baby. He'd bought some new red and black striped trunks specially so he could go swimming. On the very first day of the holiday, Zal pulled the two girls out of their bunk beds before it was properly morning and made them find their beach towels and swimming costumes.

'Look lively, you two,' he said, slapping Keely's bum as she bent to look through her suitcase for a towel. 'It's a nice sunny day out there. No more lazing about, we're all going for a swim.'

'Christ, it's a bit early for that, isn't it?' After coughing violently for a few minutes, her mam rolled over in their double bunk and reached for a cigarette. The caravan rocked like a ship with the movement of her body. Her thin blue smoke coiled upwards and hung against the shuttered windows like mist.

She turned her face to the wall when Zal bent to kiss her. Her voice was muffled behind the duvet. 'I need my beauty sleep, love. Would you take them down there for us?'

'Suit yourself.'

'Mam?' Keely sensed the irritation in Zal's voice and didn't want to get on his bad side, but she couldn't help her stomach clenching at the thought of going into the sea. 'Couldn't I stop here with you? I'll make you breakfast in bed, honest. I don't really want to go to the beach.'

'You'll bloody well go and like it,' her mam snapped.

'But I don't want to.'

'You heard what your mam said. Now shut up whining and get yourself ready.'

Turning away from them both, Keely sat on the edge of her bunk and folded her arms. There was anger boiling inside her. She felt hot and cold at the same time. Her face was sweaty and there were even goosebumps come up suddenly on her arms. She looked sideways at Jess, but could barely bring herself to speak. In the end, her voice was only a hoarse mutter that no one but Jess could possibly have heard. 'I hate him. I hate both of them. I hate the sea. I don't want to go.'

'Well, I don't care what you think. I quite fancy a swim,' Jess muttered, glancing secretly across at Zal as she rolled up her towel and stuck it under one arm. 'I've got a brand new cossie too. It's dead sexy.'

The sea was longer and broader and more greyish-white than it had looked on telly. The smell of salt air hit them as they rounded the corner and found themselves almost on the beach. There was a gate ahead of them, and after that there was nothing but sea for miles and miles. Although it was still sunny, the breeze was much stronger now and Keely's hair whipped around her face like a mad thing. The tide looked like it was on its way out, leaving little pockets of water behind it.

Zal ran down through the pools of water, pulling Jess after him, both of them shrieking with laughter which was carried away on the wind. He stooped to pick up a huge strand of seaweed, trailing it over Jess's shoulders and back. She screamed, grabbing it away from him, and they wrestled there for a moment. Jess leant in towards him, and Keely could see sand glittering on her bare shoulders. After a few moments of silent struggling, Zal managed to get the seaweed again and threw it far out into the moving tide beyond her back. It bobbed there for a few minutes, then came slowly back to them, ripple after green frilly ripple, shining in the sunlight.

'Hey there, Kee!' Zal suddenly yelled, glancing back at Keely as if he'd only just remembered she was there. ' What's up? You scared?'

Keely shook her head, saying nothing.

'You liar.' Zal gave a little laugh as he said that, but he didn't meet her eyes. Instead he seemed to shrug, suddenly letting go of Jess and wading straight into the sea until it was up to his waist. Diving forward, he disappeared under the water for a few breathtaking seconds while darkness and white flecks swirled about the place where his body had been. Beyond that, the sea stretched past the last fingers of land with the light bouncing off the water for as far as Keely could see and blinding her as she watched.

When he surfaced again, Zal was spluttering and pushing the wet hair away from his face. His large glossy shoulders shone in the sun. 'I bet Jess doesn't want to go home without getting herself a bit damp,' he called out to them, winking. 'Isn't that right, sweetheart?'

The water was freezing, but Keely tiptoed to the edge so she could see what it was like. She stood in it up to her calves and let the frothy white waves rush around her. She looked out at the sea and wondered how many fish were living in it. Millions and millions of fish, probably. Billions even. She couldn't see any fish in the water but there were lots of little dark floating things that clung to her skin for an instant and then dashed back out again on the tide.

Pausing at the water's edge in her blue swimsuit, Jess looked across at Keely as if uncertain at the last minute, then she too slowly waded in. The water came up to her knees and then up to her waist. Giggling, she stumbled and splashed forward into the sea like Zal had done. It was almost up to her chest now. Her light blue swimsuit had gone streaky dark up her hips and along her stomach, but the straps on her shoulders were still pale and dry where the water hadn't reached it.

Keely was nervous. 'Be careful, Jess. There might be sharks.'

'Don't be soft. There aren't any sharks in this part of the world,' Jess called back across the roaring hiss of the tide. As if to prove it, she ducked her arms right under the water, shivering with cold as she surfaced again. The dark streaks on her costume spread even further upwards until she was as wet as a mermaid. 'This is England, stupid. You've got to be somewhere like America to find sharks in the water.'

'Or Africa,' Zal added, turning to float on his back for a moment. 'They have crocodiles there, as well as sharks.'

'And alligators. Don't forget alligators.' Jess trod water beside him for a few moments, her arms flailing as she tried to keep still like him and not sink at the same time. The two of them seemed to be locked together by the dark mass of water, thousands and thousands of miles away from Keely standing alone on the beach, watching them. Her cousin's voice sounded distant and breathless above the curving waves. 'I saw some alligators on telly once. They've got enormous teeth and huge scaly bodies. They could take your whole leg off in seconds.'

'I'm not coming in!' Keely shouted, but her voice must have been carried in the wrong direction by the wind because neither of them seemed to hear what she said. They just carried on floating silently on their backs, staring up at the sky. Giving up, Keely turned away from them at last, stamping back out of the shallows and up the beach. Let them both drown if that's what they wanted. She didn't care anymore.

Keely sat down higher up the beach and tried not to think about sharks and alligators. After drying her wet feet and ankles with the towel, she wrapped it around her shoulders to keep warm. It was still only early morning, but there were a few other people already there on the beach. Families with large mothers in tent dresses and striped canvas deckchairs that fluttered and slapped in the breeze. One man in big baggy shorts trying to read a newspaper. There were some loud kids near where Keely was sitting, throwing a bright inflatable beach ball to each other, but the wind kept taking hold of it and suddenly whirling it in the wrong direction. Then the biggest boy would go running after it, while the others just stood there and waited.

Behind them all, the grey-blue sea rolled in and further out each time, leaving a damp stain all along the shore.

They walked over to the disco at seven o'clock, arm in arm. It was crowded in the bar and all the tables were full. The lights in the hall were already turned down and there was a steady dance beat thudding out of the speakers. The dance floor was empty but there were kids standing around in groups at the edge, staring back at the double doors as each new person came through. The disco lights were flashing red, blue, green and orange.

Keely folded her arms across her chest in the cold satiny top, keeping her eyes on the floor. The glittery skirt came up high above her knees and she felt half naked as everyone turned to look at them, stumbling slightly in the heels Jess had lent her.

'Stand up straight,' Jess hissed, gripping her arm.

'I can't walk properly in these.'

'Well, try.' Then her voice changed, getting high with excitement until it was almost a squeak. 'Oh my God, look at that boy over there. The one in the black jeans. Isn't he gorgeous? Christ, if I don't get to snog him tonight I'm going to die. I'm just going to bloody die.'

Some of the other girls and boys moved onto the dance floor. The coloured lights flashed more quickly. They were standing quite close to the speakers and the music was thudding through her body until she could almost feel it in her throat.

Suddenly Zal was standing right next to her on the edge of the dance floor. 'You look great in that outfit, Keely. Very grown-up. How about we have a dance together?'

Keely shook her head, face burning with embarrassment.

'Don't be stupid, kid.' He seemed to brush against her body almost deliberately as he came closer. Bending to her ear, he had to raise his voice so she could hear him over the music. 'You've come dressed for a dance and you're going to have one.'

Zal pulled her after him onto the dance floor. Her heels clacked loudly as she tried to walk faster but without stumbling against him like an idiot. Then they were close together, close enough to make her face red, and she could hear him laughing at her. Keely kept her head down, not daring to look up at him in case he thought she wanted to move closer. But she felt out of place because she didn't really know what to do. She was just moving her feet to and fro in the high heels, letting her arms swing uselessly by her side.

A lad came up to Jess. It was the older boy in the tight black jeans that Jess fancied. He slid his arm round her waist and pulled her onto the dance floor too. She laughed and went willingly.

Zal watched the pair through narrowed eyes. He pulled Keely tighter against him as the music slowed. It didn't feel right anymore. He smelt of alcohol. When she looked up, Jess seemed to have disappeared into the crowd with her lad. Keely wasn't sure what to do anymore. In the end she leant her face on Zal's shoulder and they moved slowly together.

'Get your hands off him, you little tart.' Her mam was standing right there beside them, swaying unsteadily as she looked from one to the other with wild eyes.

Keely ran away off the dance floor like a frightened animal. Outside, the night air was cool against her burning skin. Keely stumbled back to the caravan in the darkness, always hearing the sound of someone following but never once looking back in case it was her mam.

When she reached the caravan door, Keely heard Jess calling out behind her and spun round on the top step, breathing hard. 'For God's sake, Jess. Why did you go off with that lad? Why did you have to leave us alone like that?'

'Calm down, Kee.'

'Now Mam's furious, and it wasn't even my fault.'

'What did you do?'

'Nothing.'

Jess squeezed her hand hard. 'You must have done something. Did you kiss him? Did he kiss you?'

'Cross my heart and swear to die, I didn't do nothing.'

'Jesus, you're burning up.'

Keely dragged herself into the caravan and flopped down on the bed in her short skirt and clingy top. Closing her eyes tightly against the overhead light, she let Jess sponge her face with cold water. Her heart was skittering like a wild thing inside her chest. 'Christ, what am I going to do? Mam looked like she wanted to kill us.'

'Don't be soft. You said it yourself, it wasn't your fault. He was dancing with you, not the other way round.'

'I don't know. I can't think straight anymore. Turn the light out for us. It's hurting my eyes.'

Jess knelt up on the mattress and pulled the light cord above their bunk beds. They were sunk in complete darkness for a few moments and didn't say anything. Then their eyes gradually got used to it and Keely realised she could see the glimmering of the campsite lights through the window shutters. She was starting to feel cold and afraid now. It wouldn't be long until her mam came back to the caravan. That look in her eyes had been pure murder.

'Hold me.'

Jess sat up and hugged her. 'Your mam's pissed, Kee. She'll have forgotten all about it by the time he brings her back here.'

There was silence for a while. In the darkness of the caravan, Jess's arms were warm and comforting around her narrow back. Keely could feel the rapid rise and fall of her cousin's chest against her own. Scooching round a little in order to get more comfortable, Keely stroked her hair in a slow gentle rhythm. It felt thick and clean under her fingers.

'Did you like that lad you were dancing with?'

Her cousin nodded, watching Keely's face. Her eyes seemed to shine in the dark like a cat's. 'He's dead fit, isn't he?'

'What's his name?' Keely asked.

'David.'

'Did he kiss you?'

'Course he did. He put his tongue right into my mouth. He wanted me to go outside with him after, but I said no.'

'Ugh.' Keely shuddered. 'Didn't it make you feel sick, having his tongue in your mouth?'

'Don't you know?'

'No one ever kissed me like that.'

They didn't say anything else for a while, but in the end Jess pulled Keely back down onto the mattress and they lay there together in silence. Their bodies just seemed to spoon together naturally so they stayed there without moving, four bare legs tangled together over the edge of the bunk bed. Then without any warning, Jess turned her head slightly and kissed her. Her mouth was much softer than Keely had expected, and when Jess put her tongue into Keely's mouth, as if to show her how it felt, both girls started to tremble with the excitement of it.

When her cousin tried to pull away, Keely pressed herself hard against Jess to keep her still and felt their skins go prickly with heat. She knew she was probably doing something wrong, but it felt too good to stop. Reaching down with the sensitive tips of her fingers, Keely brushed against the small breasts she had found in the darkness and heard Jess moan quietly. She couldn't speak anymore and she didn't want to look at her cousin. Both their faces had gone hot.

Then Jess pulled away. 'Stop it.'

'Did I hurt you?'

'I don't want to talk about it. Just go to sleep. Everything's going to be all right.'

Without saying another word, her cousin got to her feet and pulled herself up the ladder into the top bunk.

Fumbling with the satiny top, Keely threw it together with the skirt in the bottom of the wardrobe. Her naked body was tingling and she touched it with electric fingers, hardly daring to breathe. Then she kicked off the high heels and crawled into bed, dragging the covers right over her head. Her feet and calves were aching from the dancing but Keely ignored them. She felt hot and tense all over. After a while, sweating in the heat of the lower bunk, she pushed herself against the air like a wild animal. The darkness inside her head exploded into fierce lines of stars, all bursting under her eyelids at once.

CHAPTER FOUR

'How old do you think I look in this?' Keely asked, trying to squint at herself sideways in the mirror.

It was a Friday night in Newcastle, so Zal was taking Keely and Jess to his new club. Her mam had wanted to come too but she was in bed with the flu. It had been Keely's birthday that week. She had got some silvery earrings from her mam and a watch from Zal. Real gold, he told her, and her mam said she mustn't ever forget to take it off when she had a bath or she'd get a hiding.

After they'd eaten supper, Keely took out her sleepers and put in the new earrings, borrowed some of her mam's high heels and a strappy little black dress, and was letting Jess do her make-up for her in the back bedroom. 'Lots of blusher and eyeshadow. I want to look older.'

'It doesn't matter how bloody old you look,' Jess said irritably, tilting her head back under the bedroom light. 'It's his sodding club. The bouncers can't turn you away.'

'I don't want people thinking I'm a kid.'

'But you are a kid.'

'Piss off.' Keely stretched her eyes wide for the mascara brush. 'Is that the new Max Factor?'

'Yes, now hush. I can't do this right with you

jabbering on.' Jess finished the mascara, tongue stuck out between her teeth as she concentrated. She picked up the lash-curling tongs. 'When I say close your eyes, do it very slowly. Right, close them.' After a few seconds, Jess pulled the curling tongs away from Keely's face, carefully releasing her lashes. 'You can open them now. Slowly, remember, or they'll smudge.'

'How do I look?'

'You'll pass.'

Keely stared into the mirror. 'Christ, I look about twenty-one.'

'Eighteen, mebbe.'

'Piss off, I look older than that.'

'Do you fuck as like.' Jess closed her make-up bag with a snap and grabbed her coat. 'Come on then, Cinderella. Prince Charming's waiting downstairs. And don't you show me up tonight. No more sodding pop. You'll have real drinks, or none at all.'

Keely ignored her, scrabbling for her new gold watch in the top drawer of her dressing-table. She slipped it onto her wrist, turning it in the light and admiring the glittery flash.

Jess stared. 'Where did you get that?'

'Zal bought it us.'

'And what does he want in return?'

Keely bent down to fiddle with her heels, suddenly embarrassed. 'It's a birthday present.'

'Oh aye?'

'Shut it. Why do you have to spoil everything by being dirty?'

Jess hesitated. She opened the bedroom door, glancing cautiously up and down the landing as if to check no one was listening. Then she closed it again with a click, lowering her voice. 'I've heard things.'

'What things?'

Her cousin shrugged. 'Don't matter. Just steer clear of him, won't you? I mean, if he comes on to you?'

'Zal?'

'Don't act innocent. You know what I mean.'

Keely looked away, flushing. She knew perfectly well what Jess was saying. But she didn't want anything to ruin her birthday night out. She'd never been to Zal's club before. It was meant to be fun, wasn't it? Going out on the town for your birthday? And she didn't see why Jess had to get so high and mighty about it when she liked clubbing too.

'Don't be daft.' Keely pulled open the bedroom door again, swinging her handbag strap over her shoulder as she walked towards the stairs. 'I know what I'm doing, all right?'

'Okay, seat-belts on,' Zal said, starting the engine with a roar. 'We don't want the law pulling us up, do we?'

They went to the club in his new car with the soft top up because it was raining, Drum 'n' Bass thudding through the speakers so the other drivers turned to stare whenever they pulled up at the traffic lights. Zal had bought himself another BMW only a few weeks before. Keely thought it was dead smart and she hoped some of her mates from school would be out on the town too, to see her driving past in it. Because it was her birthday treat, Zal let her sit up front, where her mam usually sat, while Jess sat in the back, sliding about on the leather seats.

He changed gear fast, watching Keely's face as they cornered at speed through the city. 'You like that?' he kept saying. Then he grinned at Jess in the rear view mirror. Keely reckoned he must have taken a pill or two before he left the house, he was so up. 'Do you like that, sweetheart?'

Jess never said a word.

The club was smaller than she'd imagined but it was packed out to the walls. There was a whole gang of lasses queuing up to get in, shivering in their short skirts and strappy tops, but they just sailed through them and up the steps. It was like magic. Keely was dead nervous when she walked past the bouncers on the door, they were a wall of huge chests in white shirts and black jackets, but none of them said anything because Zal had his arm round her waist.

As soon as they pushed though those dark red swing doors of the club, the music was beating inside her head, it was so loud. Zal got them a table in an alcove away from the speakers so they didn't have to shout. She'd thought everyone would be dead old there and she'd feel embarrassed, but she could already see other girls from her school hitting the dance floor, so she relaxed a bit and asked for a Bacardi and coke, no ice. Her mam drank that sometimes, and Keely liked the taste though it always seemed to make her mouth tingle.

'You getting smashed tonight?' Zal asked, laughing as he put the drink down in front of her. 'That's a double.'

'I'm old enough, like.'

'Almost,' he said, glancing at her legs. Then he sipped his whisky, gazing around the club. 'But not quite.'

Within a few minutes, Jess got dragged off to the dance floor by some lad she knew called Eddy. They danced right at the edge under a revolving glitter ball that caught the disco lights and flashed thousands of silver specks onto their heads. He was a bit older than her, tall and slim, wearing baggy jeans with zips down the side.

As soon as they started dancing, Eddy tried to put his hand on her arse but Jess pulled away, and Keely could see her telling him off. Her mouth was moving angrily against the music. Jess didn't like it when they came on to her so soon. She said they had hands like bloody octopuses. And it happened every time she went out clubbing round here. Just because Jess was on the game, the lads seemed to imagine she must be easy. Keely grinned to herself. There was nothing easy about their Jess.

'Do you want to dance?' Zal asked, leaning forward.

'Na.'

'It's your birthday, doll. You've got to dance.'

'I'm not fussed.'

'Suit yourself,' Zal said. He got up, swinging his jacket off the back of the chair. 'I've got some business to sort out. There's twenty quid, get yourself pissed. I'll be in the back room if you need me.'

The night went dead fast after that. Too many Bacardi and cokes, she thought hazily. She would have been all right though if it hadn't been for Jess, who kept pulling her onto the dance floor for a bop until she was out of her tree, both of them dancing round their handbags with a group of lads watching and cheering them on as they did a two-handed conga round the two main pillars and back, ending up in a giggling heap under the revolving glitter ball. Staring round at the lights as someone picked her up off the floor, Keely thought the club was spinning faster than the ball.

'You're mad drunk,' some lad yelled into her ear, holding her upright by the waist.

Keely ignored him and staggered off for another drink, dragging her handbag by its long strap. 'Can't catch me!'

The walls and pillars and dancers surged up to her face like a dark wave and then rushed away again as she stumbled forwards and sideways and backwards at the same time. The drums were slamming under her ribcage and up through her heels. Her cheeks were flushed with the heat. She was making for the bar, she thought, or maybe the loos, but she wasn't sure which. The club was so crowded, she couldn't remember where their table was.

Jess ran after her. 'Got any more cash?'

Keely dragged her handbag up and scrabbled through it. Make-up, coppers, mirror, tampons. 'S'all gone.'

'What are you like? Go and ask Zal for some more beer vouchers. I'm dying for a drink.'

'He's in the back, talking business.'

'Well, go and stop him talking business. Flash your tits, whatever. Just get us some cash.'

'He won't like me asking for more.'

'Go on with you,' Jess pushed her firmly between the shoulder blades. 'I want a proper dance, you know I mean? There's a bloke over there with some really cheap E's and he'll be sold out soon.' Grinning, she gave her another little push, harder this time. 'So get that skinny arse of yours moving.'

The back room was small and dark, down a corridor past the loos. She headed towards it unsteadily, stumbling in her high heels. There were two bouncers on the door, but they moved aside when Keely nervously explained she was with Zal. He was at the far end, sitting at a table with several other blokes. The air was thick with cigar smoke, coiling up beautifully towards the green-shaded light. The music from the club was just a distant throbbing through the walls.

She immediately recognised Eddy, the lad who'd been dancing with Jess before. He was standing beside the table, bending slightly to listen to what Zal was saying, but he straightened as Keely approached, nodding his head to the others. 'We've got company.'

Zal looked at her sharply. 'What's the matter?'

'Nothing really.' Keely suddenly wasn't sure what to say, glancing at the other men. 'I'm sorry. I didn't mean to disturb you.'

'What do you want, pet?'

'Jess and me have run out of money.'

Zal leant back in his chair, putting the fat cigar back between his lips. Smoke billowed out slowly from the corners of his mouth. She thought he looked like a dragon, breathing fire at her across the table, dark and frightening and watchful. Then he smiled, waving his cigar in the air and glancing around at the others. 'You see what these lasses are like? No matter what you do, it's always money, money, money. No please, no thank you, just give us the money.'

'I'm sorry.'

He got up, slipping an arm about her waist. 'Don't look so scared, pet. I was only kidding you.'

The other blokes at the table laughed, though Eddy was still watching her without smiling. Keely didn't like him much, even though Jess said he was great. He sort of reminded her of Tommy from when she was a kid, the lad who'd crushed the baby bird in front of her. He had the same nasty look in his eyes, like he didn't care who he hurt as long as he got his own way. She looked away from him, shivering. It was horrible, remembering how that tiny bird had lain there on the pavement, its brains all oozed out and reddish-black from his boot.

'How much do you want, sweetheart?' Zal's voice was slurred. Deliberately letting the others see how much money he had, he peeled off some notes from a roll in his back pocket, turning slightly to tap his cigar ash onto the carpet. 'Twenty? Fifty? A ton?'

'Twenty,' she whispered.

'Come on, that's not going to get you very bloody far.' He pressed several notes into her hand. She could smell whisky on his breath. It was sour and dark. 'Take fifty.'

'Cheers.'

'Where are you going now? Sit here with me for a bit. You can keep me company.' Zal laughed, pulling her down onto his lap. His hands were like iron and Keely sat very still, not wanting to upset him. 'These old fuckers want to look at your legs, don't you lads?'

'Jess is waiting.'

'She can bloody wait. You're mine now.'

He slammed his hand down on the table and everyone jumped, but then he just laughed again, finishing his glass of whisky. Keely sensed that he was pissed and enjoying himself, making sure they all knew he was the boss. There was nothing she could do but wait until Zal got bored with playing the game and let her go again. Even Eddy was staring across at her now with a contemptuous sort of smile on his face, as though he thought she was nothing but a dirty little tart.

Keely felt her face flush with embarrassment and shame, wishing that Zal wasn't holding her so tight. She could hardly breathe, his hand was pressed right in under her ribs, making sure she couldn't escape.

'Yeah, the van needs to come from down south. Not London though. One of the little towns. Somewhere quiet, like.'

He was speaking to Eddy really, but he kept looking at the others round the table, jabbing the air with his cigar as he finished. The two older blokes had gold rings and expensive looking shirts. Keely could smell their aftershave, it was so strong and spicy. She suddenly realised his hand was moving upwards along her leg and stiffened. Eddy was staring at her now because the dress had hiked up so much on her thighs. She could feel cold air creeping into her knickers.

One of the older blokes spoke. 'Not in front of the lass.'

'She's all right.'

'Come on now, let her go.' He had a thick Geordie accent. 'Poor little cow wants to dance, not sit on your lap all night.'

'I said she's all right.'

There was a tense silence, then Eddy lit a cigarette. 'I can arrange that for you. When do you want it?'

'Jesus Christ.' The older bloke dumped his smoking cigar into the dregs of a pint glass. It hissed viciously for a second and died. 'Jesus fucking Christ.'

'Problem?'

'Not in front of the lass,' the older bloke repeated, and Keely could see the veins standing out on his neck now, they were like little blue worms bulging under the skin. As he unclenched both his fists on the table, Keely saw the faint red letters E V O L tattooed across the knuckles of his left hand back-to-front. It took her a few seconds to make sense of the word. 'It's your club, you do what you like here. But not at this table.'

Still pulled tight against his body, she could feel Zal's chest swell as he took a deep breath. She thought he was going to lurch forward at the other bloke but he suddenly relaxed his grip instead, shifting his knees so that she dropped easily from his lap.

He didn't even look at her, picking up his cigar and relighting it. 'You heard the man. Run along now, pet.'

Stumbling back down the red corridor towards the bar, walls and floor pulsing with the music like massive speakers, Keely's stomach heaved and she had to dive into the loos. Two girls in the doorway screamed abuse at her as she barged past and into the first cubicle.

She only just made it in time, throwing herself onto her bare knees beside the stinking bowl and puking. She thought the whole of her stomach was jetting out in a series of thin painful watery streams. The black and white tiles danced in front of her eyes as she sat up afterwards, gasping for air and wondering if she was going to puke again.

Grabbing some loo roll, Keely wiped her mouth with it, staring down into the bowl. There were little orangey-yellow bits of carrot bobbing about in the frothing water. Behind the sick coating her teeth, she could still taste Bacardi.

CHAPTER FIVE

County Durham, Northern England

The dog's stillness should have been enough of a warning. But after a cursory glance, Niall thought it was a man blocking the path ahead of them that morning and kept on walking.

He was too busy enjoying his first cigarette of the day to stop and take a proper look. His mother wouldn't allow him to smoke in the house anymore, and he had not had a chance to light up since walking her dog the day before. He'd been on the point of turning back to the house anyway. It was icy down here in the valley and his knuckles, cupped about the thinly smoking cigarette, were already raw from the cold.

So when the dog stopped bounding cheerfully along by his side and froze, Niall didn't bother to wonder why.

The river was deafening at this bend, rough-running with clumsy stones and the occasional splash of salmon or otter, and in the dim autumn light it was difficult to pick out anything except this early mist clinging to the trees and scrubland of rural County Durham. Trails of fallen autumn leaves, frosted into iced over puddles, cracked underfoot at every step and sent birds clattering into the distance.

Niall whistled again to his mother's spaniel, which was standing stock still only a few feet away, as if either too surprised or too frightened to bark. But the dog didn't respond with his usual tail-wagging enthusiasm.

'What is it, boy?' he asked impatiently, then lifted his head properly and caught his breath at what he saw ahead. Tall, broad-chested, the deer stared back at him in silence, poised for flight, its muscular front legs aslant the path not more than a hundred yards from where they were standing. Now that they were face to face, man and deer, Niall could see that the animal was utterly magnificent. In the dim flurry of leaves around them, its dark liquid eyes seemed hooded and unreadable, but Niall caught the sharp flicker of the deer's throat as the great head turned and the massive thighs flexed for action.

The reddish-gold tangle of undergrowth running alongside the water shook slightly, as though a faint wind had caught it. Suddenly, the path ahead was empty. One minute the deer was there, the next it had disappeared as silently as it had come.

Rather deliberately too late, the spaniel leapt after it through the scrub bushes with the ancient instincts of a hunting dog, chest convulsed with excited barking. Niall yelled at him to come back and even tried to follow for a short distance, fumbling uselessly with the lead which he had removed once they were safely away from the main road. He scrambled up a sheer mossed slope beside the river to get a better look, dislodging stones and falling painfully among nettles at one point. But an impenetrable barrier of thorn bushes stopped him going any further and his mother's dog was probably too far away now to hear his shouts.

His heart was unexpectedly racing. He had never seen a deer so close up before and he still felt rather startled. Further up in the hills, perhaps, or running through the fields once or twice during the summer months. But not like that, never walking openly abroad like a man.

The deer had stood there before him almost like a dancer, precise and assured in its stillness. Powerful front legs and the thick-set throat above them. Hooves set apart on the frozen ground, perfectly balanced and ready to leap in any direction. That smooth reddish coat against the falling chaos of leaves.

Niall searched up and down the river path with frustrated whistles until the spaniel returned at last with a burr-infested underbelly, gasping at the air and jumping as if desperate to relate the tale of his pursuit.

'Useless bloody animal,' he said, struggling to clip the lead to the spaniel's collar before he escaped again. 'What's the point of giving you a name if you don't come when somebody calls it?'

When Niall got back to the house, he was surprised to see his mother already downstairs. She sat slumped in her favourite spindle-back chair at the kitchen table, fast asleep. His mother had never been much of an early riser. Today, she hadn't even bothered to get properly dressed. There was only a pink nylon dressing-gown over her nightie and she was wearing her scruffy tartan slippers. But she had combed her hair as always, parted neatly in the middle and dyed now to hide the grey.

He came in on tiptoe and sent the dog straight to its basket in the corner, not wanting to wake her up. The clock on the mantelpiece said eight fifteen. The fire he had set in the grate before leaving the house was still burning, though some of the smaller logs were almost in ashes now.

As quietly as he could, Niall bent to add some more coal to the fire. His mother's head had nodded sideways in the warmth, and her mouth was slightly open. She looked very peaceful.

There was a pot of tea sitting on the warm slate hearth. She had a full cup in front of her. Untouched and going cold now. Niall tested the brown china pot with the back of his hand, poured himself a cup and freshened hers.

It was still hot enough to drink.

He sat down opposite her and glanced rapidly through the post on the kitchen table. It was a pity he'd come back later than usual. It was always dangerous to allow his mother to intercept the post, since she had a habit of unashamedly reading his letters.

She had already opened several of his bills, in fact. There was a letter unfolded in front of her which she must have been reading before she fell asleep.

Abruptly, Niall frowned and put down his tea with a thud. There was something familiar about that formal black letterhead under her hand. He leant across the table and tried to read the print upside-down without disturbing her. No, he hadn't been mistaken. The letter she was reading came from Sallis Road School in Newcastle.

Niall turned over the torn envelope beside it and saw his own name handwritten on the front.

'For God's sake, mam. That was quite clearly addressed to me,' he snapped, dragging the letter towards him from her loose fingers. 'When are you going to stop opening my bloody post?'

She did not stir. Her hand lay on the table cloth, finger and thumb almost touching each other, as if still holding his letter. The skin on the back of her hand looked fragile and parchment-white, threaded with veins like pale bluebells.

'Mam?' Niall touched her hand. It was limp and chill. The fire burning steadily now in the grate seemed to be having no effect on her. 'Mam, wake up. You're freezing. You need to get back to bed and wrap up warm.'

His mother simply continued to sit there in her chair, perfect as a waxwork. Niall felt his heart tighten. He examined the powdery-white furrows around her mouth and eyes that seemed deeper now than he remembered. The silly old woman had probably been up half the night, and now she was too deeply asleep to hear him.

He got up and went round to her side of the table. He

was aware of his limbs moving jerkily, his voice loud and falsely cheerful. 'Come on, mam. You can't sit there like that all day. Open your eyes, it's time to wake up now.'

 He put his hand on her shoulder and the whole body sagged sideways and forwards across the table, knocking over her cup of tea. Its dark brown stain spread like an instant blot across the tablecloth.

Niall caught her under the arms and hoisted the body upright again. He felt hurriedly for a pulse, first at her throat and then at her wrist, but there was nothing.

At first, Niall couldn't bring himself to admit what had happened. He kept scrabbling at her neck for a pulse, eyes closed as he bent to listen for breathing, wondering whether he had missed some faint sign of life. Her mouth was still slightly open, as it must have been when she died, and he stared down at it wildly. Perhaps he should lie her on the floor, breathe into her open mouth and push at her chest, attempt to resuscitate her.

His hands dropped away from her body. There was no point. She was already cold to the touch.

Niall sat down in his chair again. He felt sick and there was a dull pain behind his eyes. She looked so peaceful in her chair, as if she had died without any pain at all. Maybe it had been some kind of stroke, the sudden and irrevocable cessation of blood flow to the brain. Losing consciousness and never regaining it. She might not even have been aware what was happening to her.

'Oh Christ, I'm sorry, mam. I shouldn't have gone out so long this morning, left you alone. If I'd been beside you when it happened ... '

He glanced down at the letter she had been reading before she died, automatically smoothing out the creased edges where her fingers must have tightened on it. Sallis Road School in Newcastle.

> *Dear Mr Swainson,*
> *In response to your recent application ...*

Niall read the letter through once, rapidly, and then stared up at her white shuttered face, feeling his chest constrict with guilt. Could this letter have precipitated her death in some way?

It was an invitation to an interview in Newcastle for the position of Art Teacher at Sallis Road.

He had applied for the job some weeks before, though without much hope. He wasn't really experienced enough for the post and hadn't expected to be called for interview. God only knew what effect reading this letter might have had on his mother. He had promised her in the beginning not to go back to Newcastle, because she couldn't live with the idea of him living and working there again. His mother had hated the place for years. She blamed the city for everything that had gone wrong in their lives.

The realisation that Niall had gone directly against her wishes and applied for a teaching job there would have angered and depressed her, perhaps more than he'd anticipated.

'I'm sorry about this too.' Niall gestured to the letter as if his mother could see it. 'I was going to tell you about it, but I didn't want to upset you. I didn't think you'd understand.'

The clock on the mantelpiece chimed the half hour. Niall was aware that he ought to ring the doctor now, make sure her death was reported to the proper authorities, but he sat there for a little while longer, just watching her face.

It felt comical, unreal. He kept expecting her to stir suddenly, open her eyes and find him waiting. She did appear to be sleeping, even though he knew with his logical mind that she wasn't.

'I saw a deer down by the river,' he said conversationally. 'Walking along the path like a man.'

Later, he picked up the telephone and rang her

doctor. His hands were steady again by then.

'Perhaps you can enlighten me, Niall,' the head teacher murmured, dropping the file and leaning back in his chair. 'You've been teaching in a quiet rural area for the past few years, under very different conditions to the ones we have here at Sallis Road. The board of governors and I have been wondering what makes someone like you apply to an inner city school?'

'I was born in Newcastle,' Niall told the board coolly. 'I grew up not far from here. I feel this is where I belong, that I'm on the same wavelength as these kids. Besides, ever since I finished my training, I've wanted to work in this part of Newcastle. You know, give something back to the area.'

Niall paused, scanning the expressionless faces on the selecting panel opposite as he tried to guess whether or not he had given them the right answer. 'And with such a strong Art Department at the moment,' he added, 'Sallis Road has to be my best opportunity to do just that.'

'But we have many children here with special needs, pupils who need constant monitoring and one-to-one attention. What sort of qualities do you possess as a teacher, Niall, that would support a child like that?'

Niall nodded at the deputy head. 'Again, it's a case of natural empathy. You can't grow up here without developing some awareness of the difficulties of an inner city childhood.'

He crossed his legs and began to run through how he felt about himself as a teacher, all the time watching their faces for any adverse reaction and trying to appear confident without sounding arrogant. But they were a hard panel to read and the place didn't help him feel more comfortable. The interview room they had chosen smelt disturbingly of disinfectant, almost like a hospital ward. Its window looked out on an ugly concrete walkway between mobile classrooms, where Niall could occasionally see the heads of passing kids. But he wanted this job badly enough to overlook the drawbacks of working at Sallis Road. He had been hiding out in County Durham for too long. Now that his mother was dead, he had something to prove to himself, perhaps his own personal ghost to lay to rest.

Niall could feel his hands shaking and kept them pressed firmly against his knees as he spoke. It had been about three hours since his last cigarette, smoked furtively round the back of the canteen with one of the other candidates, and his desire for nicotine was growing stronger every minute.

When he had finished, there was a short silence during which some of the panel scribbled down notes and others stared blankly out of the window. The head glanced around at his colleagues as if waiting for some signal which never came, then cleared his throat ready to speak. MacFerson was a thick-set balding man in his early fifties, looking every inch the institutionalised figurehead that he was expected to be, yet his eyes were surprisingly keen as they watched Niall across the table.

'Your sentiments are commendable, of course,' MacFerson said without smiling. 'But don't you think you might be biting off more than you can chew, coming into such a dynamic and challenging environment before you're ready for it?'

It was only much later that Niall came up with a better answer than the one he gave at the time, but by then it was too late. Their choice had already been made. It was a fait accompli. Niall was sitting with the other candidates, too exhausted after a full day of interviews and trial lessons to keep up even an appearance of enthusiasm, when MacFerson finally came back into the waiting room.

Sweating slightly, the balding older man smoothed down his tie and nodded at them all sympathetically.

Niall uncrossed his legs and threw aside the glossy government brochure he had been pretending to read for the past half hour. The young woman opposite straightened up abruptly and tugged at the hem of her skirt. Her eyes had widened on the head's face. Everyone in that room knew what MacFerson's re-appearance indicated. The selection process was over at last. The panel had reached its decision and the candidates were about to hear who the winner was.

There was a tense silence as MacFerson glanced around at the circle of faces, meeting nobody's eyes for more than a second. Suddenly, the cramped waiting room seemed darker and more claustrophobic than ever before, an insistent rain beating at the windows as if trying to get in.

'Niall?' MacFerson murmured, giving him a smile. 'The panel would like to speak to you again. If you wouldn't mind following me, please?'

'Excellent.'

Niall stepped carefully down from the bath and pulled the light cord, admiring his successful handiwork for a few seconds before bending to unzip the photographic equipment bag at his feet.

He had opened the ancient circular light fitting in his bathroom ceiling, unscrewed the standard bulb he found there, and replaced it with the ghostly red light of the darkroom. Now everything else was ready to go. A cup of coffee steamed gently on the tiled sink surround. The temperature of the water from the hot and cold taps had been checked. He had even remembered to take his socks off in case of any spillage.

It only took a few minutes for the film to be developed, once slipped into the black plastic developing unit. Watching himself silently in the bathroom mirror, Niall tilted the unit back and forth in his hands like a cocktail shaker so the black and white film inside could be bathed in the chemical solutions which would eventually develop it.

As soon as his wristwatch beeped the alarm, Niall

leant forward over the sink and emptied the unit of its chemicals. After a thorough rinsing with cold water, he hurriedly retrieved the wet roll of negatives inside for drying. Using a set of miniature bulldog clips and the bathroom shower rail for support, he suspended the dripping transparent strip above the bath and ran two fingers briskly down its length to remove excess moisture, weighting the end with a clip to prevent it from curling up.

This was the part he loved. Under the red light, these shadows and blooms of white on the negatives always seemed a little out of focus at first.

He waited a little longer, sipping at his coffee speculatively. Then a few faces swam out of the darkness, fixing themselves into clearly discernible images.

Two blonde schoolgirls, linked arm in arm, heads turned back towards him as they passed at the school gate. The older one smiling, long hair brushing her shoulder. He had dropped his cigarette in the school's neatly ordered flower bed in order to take the shot. But it had been more than worth the risk, even if they could probably still see him from the school offices.

The other photographs were less dynamic, but Niall still felt pleased as he trawled down the damp strip of negatives for the most promising reverse images. In spite of the shortness of time, he had managed to capture what he wanted. Heaps of rubble and pieces of twisted metal on a building site in West Newcastle. A gang of small dirty boys pitching stones at each other in the dust of a deserted street. Empty buses rumbling back to the depot with their windows steamed up. Narrow rows of houses on a demolition site, their burnt out shells yawning next to the shudder of a digger. Dust dancing in the air of a golden afternoon.

Leaving the negatives to dry properly, Niall crossed the small bedroom to lift his shutters on the afternoon. It would be evening soon and he guessed there was more rain on the way. Beyond row upon row of dull-walled estate houses stretching into the distance, he could just see that grey slant of sky which was all Newcastle had left of the day's sunshine.

Later that evening, he printed up a few copies of the school girls and sat on his bed to examine the photographs in more detail. His choice of black and white film really worked with the younger girl's simplicity. It was such a rich and vibrant image though.

Her older friend's arm - possibly her sister, their faces were so similar - was linked so tightly with her own. Practically hip to hip, in fact. Like Siamese twins.

The younger one had wanted him to take this picture, almost willed him to do it. Not in a grinning school kid fashion, all awkward braces and freckles, staring straight into the camera lens and blinking at the very instant the shutter closes. This one had invited the shot just by existing, gliding past like some unanticipated muse.

'What's your name?' he whispered.

The small flat on Stannard Row wasn't exactly a dream residence, but at least it was cheap, Niall wasn't sharing it with anyone, and there was a fairly comprehensive view of the housing estate from his bedroom window. It was also fairly near to the school, which would save him a fortune in petrol. A top floor flat with a rusty-looking fire escape from the landing window, the only other room facing the estate was the bathroom, and the frosted glass pane rendered it useless as a vantage point except when propped open after a bath to let the steam escape. Niall took the flat because of the view. That constant stream of people in and out of the housing estate.

It was a strange thing to admit, even to himself, but simply watching those people coming and going in the streets made him feel somehow reconnected to the world, a connection he had missed whilst living in the country with his mother.

Many nights, unable to sleep, Niall would sit by his

bedroom window for hours, watching the streets of the housing estate with their dark orange glow.

Occasionally a taxi would drive slowly past, no doubt looking for the right address. Groups of students linked arm in arm, yelling or climbing over parked cars to set the alarms off. Then there was the odd police patrol car or van, radio buzzing constantly inside, circling the housing estate like a dying bluebottle. Women walking quickly alone or in pairs, hoping not to get attacked this time. Drunks staggering home with their hands in their pockets, leaning as if in a high wind and trying not to look from left to right as they passed the dead mouths of alleyways.

And if Niall sat there long enough in the semi-darkness, he would always see a prostitute or two at some point during the night, presumably on their way home or waiting for another trick.

Alone in the stillness, listening to her heels on the pavement, he would often fantasise about leaning from his window and calling out for her to come up to his top floor flat. Or getting dressed, slipping quietly down the stairs and following her along the street, a handful of notes stashed away in the back pocket of his jeans.

But even looking for company on the streets was pointless. It was no use kidding himself that things would be any different with a professional.

The doctor had told him it was all in his mind. Some sort of mental block. There was no obvious physical problem anyone could find. After all, masturbation was possible, so long as he concentrated hard on blotting out the past, reinventing himself in his fantasies. But faced with a live flesh-and-blood woman, Niall simply couldn't manage to hold an erection for longer than a few minutes. Everything seemed to die away as soon as he began touching her, including his desire. Though there were times when Niall really wanted to have sex. When he wanted to have sex so much it hurt his entire body just thinking about his lack of it. For him, sex was like an intense red tunnel of need, constantly twisting and burrowing deeper and deeper inside his body.

At the end of that tunnel lay his appalling impotence. Whatever Niall did, everything had to come back to that dead end. Every dream or fantasy had to finish with that realisation.

CHAPTER SIX

It had been raining heavily the night before and the school walkways were slick underfoot. Feeling a little cold, Niall slid his hands into his trouser pockets and wandered slowly round towards the back of the science block. Already he was beginning to question his role as a teacher and why he continued to waste his life on such a disappointing and stress-ridden profession. It had become a well-established thing to have these circular arguments with himself on a grey Monday morning, but Niall still felt he had to go through those reasons again and again, trying to remind himself why he was still locked in here and not out there in the real world, doing something more emotionally rewarding, like long-distance lorry driving.

Niall paused, staring out across the playing fields with a blank expression. Water dripped uneasily from the guttering above, slipping down his neck and behind the collar of his jacket. There had to be a good reason for doing this job. It was just that he couldn't exactly remember it. After a few moments of silence, he moved on along the path towards the science block, barely bothering to shrug away the rain.

He was on break patrol duty again, which basically entailed pretending that he hadn't noticed the sixth formers smoking down by the fence or the Year Eleven kids noisily sorting out some quarrel behind the mobile classrooms. Contrary to what they were told in the staff room, there was never any point trying to stop such activities. Sure, he could head down in their direction and move the kids along, maybe even put the odd one on report for misbehaviour, but within minutes the majority of them would be back in place, remorseless and undeterred. They were programmed to it, like robots. Trying to stop their way of life here was rather like re-enacting the stupidity of King Canute. The only thing Niall could possibly do to control these kids was show his face briefly, let them know he was on patrol, and hope that was enough to keep their rule-breaking from escalating to the point where intervention became unavoidable.

It was the sound of whispering behind the science block that jerked him out of thought. Niall stopped dead and listened for a few seconds. He couldn't hear what was being discussed, but the urgency in the kids' voices was enough to make him suspicious.

He knew the signs. That was the sound of kids who knew they would be in serious trouble if caught red-handed.

There was a rustle in the bushes ahead, a startled face peering round at him, then a shout of alarm. 'Run for it.'

Niall reached the corner of the science block just in time to see a small group of kids scattering into the bushes and across the field. They didn't appear to be kids he normally taught. He recognised a few of them, mainly the girls, but not enough to put a clear name to any of the faces.

'Stay where you are,' he called out to their fleeing backs, but it was a futile command.

One of the taller girls, her back to him, had tried cutting across to the main hall but she had stumbled on heels that were too high for the soft grass, dropping the packages she'd been clutching to her chest. She gave a shriek of horror and bent to retrieve them, still attempting to run as she did so. In the shadow of the science block, she scrabbled desperately at her belongings while her heels sank deeper and deeper into the muddy ground.

'Hold it,' Niall insisted as he came level with her. When she twisted away in fear, he caught at her arm. 'You're not going anywhere.'

'Let go, you're hurting.'

Hurriedly he released her. 'What's that you've dropped?'

Niall glanced down at her feet and raised his eyebrows. One of the packages had split in the tussle, and there was a tell-tale shower of strong-smelling green stuff across her right shoe. He was no expert, but it looked and smelt like skunk to him.

'It's not mine. It's nothing to do with me.'

Niall glanced across the field, feeling a real sense of relief that the cavalry was already on its way. MacFerson was hurrying along the walkway from the main hall, large floral tie flapping over one shoulder. One of the other teachers must have spotted Niall struggling with her and alerted the head's office. 'Here comes Mr MacFerson now. You can tell him whatever you like, but I saw you drop that.'

'Please.'

Niall shook his head, frowning. 'It's out of my hands.'

'But I'll get kicked out, sir.'

'You should have thought of that before.'

'Bastard!'

'I'm not the one dealing drugs to kids. Some of them were only Year Sevens. Twelve year olds, for God's sake.' Staring down into her sulkily defiant eyes, Niall felt his anger building and tried not to lose control. 'What's your name? Jess, isn't it?'

She nodded, eyes narrowed and smouldering.

'Don't you have any sort of conscience, Jess?'

'If it wasn't me, it would be someone else.'

Niall increased his grip on her arm as she tried to pull

away. 'That's a fairly pathetic excuse for dealing drugs to kids.'

'I give them what they want. How is that wrong?'

MacFerson arrived, out of breath. His eye fell on the tiny plastic packages strewn across the grass at their feet and he stiffened, glancing round to make sure there were no other children within earshot.

'Dear God. Are those what I think they are?'

'I'm afraid so.' Gingerly, Niall picked up one of the tiny packets and sniffed it. The smell was unmistakable. He had smoked the odd joint at college, after all, and it was not such a long time ago that he had forgotten how the smell hits you in the back of the throat. 'Marijuana. I caught Jess hanging around back there, behind the science block, with a bunch of other kids. She had these in her hands.'

'They're not mine,' she insisted. 'I found them.'

MacFerson made a snorting sound of disbelief as Jess spoke. 'Thank you for sharing that little fantasy with us, young lady. But I think you can leave your explanations until we've been in touch with your parents. Not to mention the police.'

'The police?' Jess echoed, staring at him in horror.

'For dealing on school premises.'

Stooping down, MacFerson gathered together the plastic packages and slid them into his jacket pocket. There was a gleam of satisfaction in his eyes as he took Jess by the arm. Niall watched him in silence; he knew perfectly well that MacFerson had been waiting a long time for this day. From what he had heard in the staff room, the school had been dying to kick Jess out for years, and now this - her final insult in what must seem like a continual stream of offences - probably represented their best opportunity to get rid of her for good.

'I'm not scared of you,' she spat.

MacFerson didn't even blink. 'You're coming with me, young lady. Let's go and find out what your parents have to say this time.'

Niall watched them head back across the field towards the main hall, Jess with her heels still sinking in the muddy ground, MacFerson unpleasantly officious and triumphant as he dragged her along towards a crowd of pupils and teachers waiting curiously in the doorway. It was always a shame to see a pupil on the verge of permanent exclusion, but Niall couldn't imagine there would be any other option available to the governors now.

Jess had quite obviously over-stepped the mark this time. The drugs policy at Sallis Road was strict and non-negotiable, and she knew that. It was her own fault for flaunting the rules so openly.

He was scouring the grass for any other tiny packages he might have over-looked, when a noise rather like stifled coughing - followed by the crack of a branch - alerted him to the fact that there was someone hiding in the bushes beside the science block.

Niall went still, aware that it might be another pupil with drugs on them. He glanced back towards the main school building. MacFerson had disappeared inside and the small crowd of onlookers had already dispersed. There were no witnesses.

'All right, give it up,' he said, raising his voice when there was no further movement from the bushes. 'I know there's someone hiding in there. You might as well come out, there's no point pretending.'

Niall stepped threateningly closer to the bushes, and the prickly branches finally parted. A girl came crawling out on her hands and knees. Her face was dirty, hair dishevelled, uniform rucked up, and she had quite obviously been crying.

There was something vaguely familiar about the girl, but Niall couldn't seem to put a name to the face.

'What's your name?' he demanded as she straightened, wiping dirt from her clothes and still sniffing.

'Keely.'

Niall ignored the shakiness of her voice. These kids were brilliant at putting on the agony to avoid punishment. 'What on earth were you doing in there?'

'Hiding, sir.'

That was surprisingly straightforward. 'Empty out your pockets, then. Let's see what you've got to hide.'

When the girl reluctantly turned out her pockets, he found a small packet of skunk amongst the debris of pens and hairbands, his heart sinking as he realised he would have to report her as well.

Stupid child. This could wreck her entire life.

Suddenly he remembered the photograph he had taken at the school gates after his job interview. This was the younger girl in the photograph, her head turned so invitingly towards the camera.

'I'm going to have to report this.'

She nodded silently.

'Come on,' he said angrily. 'What is this thing between you and Jess? She's much older than you, and she's not exactly a brilliant influence or you wouldn't have that rubbish in your pocket. Why on earth are you always hanging round with someone like her? Haven't you got any friends your own age?'

'Jess looks out for me,' she whispered. 'We're cousins.'

'Some cousin.'

As he dangled the bag of skunk in front of her eyes, Keely stared at it with distaste. 'Jess dropped it when she saw you coming. I picked it up off the ground, that's all. It isn't mine.'

'That's a convenient story.'

'You can ask Jess, she'll tell you the truth.'

Niall hesitated, gazing at her averted face.

'Oh go on,' he suddenly said, thrusting the bag of skunk into his jacket pocket. 'I'll tell MacFerson I found this on the ground. But don't let me see you hanging round with that lot again. They'll only get you into trouble.'

When she still didn't move, Niall found himself forcibly turning the girl around and pushing her between the shoulder blades.

'What are you waiting for? Permission to run away?'

Keely threw him a strange and compelling look over her shoulder, just as she had done that day when he caught her on film at the school gates, then walked slowly back towards the school buildings.

He waited, but she did not look back.

'Can I come in?'

Halfway through choosing an outfit, Keely spun with embarrassment at the sound of her bedroom door being opened, hands darting to cover herself.

It was late Saturday morning and she had only been out of bed a few minutes. He must have been sitting in silence downstairs, waiting for the first creak of the floorboards to let him know that she had finally got up. Standing there before her bedroom mirror in nothing but bra and knickers, she watched his face leer round the doorway and realised she was in trouble.

'I'm not dressed yet,' she said, already beginning to tremble at what she knew was coming next. She knew it was no good trying to stop him, but her begging seemed to have become part of the game recently.

Zal ignored her, coming straight into the bedroom and throwing himself down across her bed.

He smiled up at her lazily. 'What's the matter, Kee? Anyone would think I'd never seen you in your underwear before.'

Keely carefully said nothing in return, simply folding her arms to hide the small mounds of her breasts under the sports bra.

'Put your arms down by your side, Keely.'

She didn't move.

'I said, put your fucking arms down.'

Slowly, not wanting to anger him any further, Keely lowered her arms.

Zal smiled, and nodded for her to carry on dressing. 'That's better. You see how easy that was, Keely? A little bit of politeness goes a long way. Or didn't your mam ever teach you that?'

'No, I don't suppose she would have done,' he carried on when she didn't answer, lighting up a cigarette while he watched Keely dress herself with clumsy fingers. 'But a stupid tart like your mam never knows what side her bread's buttered. She's no good, your mam. She's got no respect for men. I wouldn't want you to end up like her, Keely. That sort of attitude could get you into serious trouble one day.'

He looked her up and down as Keely turned to face him again, safely dressed.

'Good girl. Now, do you want to go down the park with us or not?'

CHAPTER SEVEN

'Fucking hell, what happened to your hair?' Jack laughed, tousling his hair roughly. Then he grabbed Niall's neck in a vice-like grip. His voice was deep and hoarse in his ear. 'You're getting old, man. Maybe we're all getting old. But can you still pull the lasses?'

Flushed, but trying to laugh, Niall managed to struggle free. 'I do all right.'

It was years since they had last seen each other, Niall finally getting a place at art college, and Jack heading off to London with plans to form a rock band. 'Forget that painting shit and join us, man. We're going to be bigger than the Beatles,' he used to say in the pub, drumming his fingers against the table and playing an imaginary guitar. 'You sing and I'll play bass.' But Niall knew he was simply riding on the back of his hash deals, and once that money was gone, he would be back in business, flogging his gear on the streets of London instead of Newcastle.

Jack ordered them a couple of pints, smiling at a passing girl in a short red dress. 'Now that's what I call top totty.'

'How's the band?'

'You know those bastards. It never worked out.' Jack grinned. 'But I've got a few projects on the go. Fingers in pies, you know the score. I've got Sandra to support now and a bloody kid on the way.' His lager arrived and Jack gulped most of it down immediately. 'How about you?'

'Never met the right girl.'

'There's no such thing, man. In this life, you take what you can get. Sandra's okay. Bit of a nag, but she keeps the house tidy. And that's all you need, isn't it? Someone there when you come in, clean towels, shirts ironed.' He shrugged. 'Sweet.'

Niall looked at him, not sure whether he felt disgust or pity. 'You don't love her?'

'What sort of question's that?'

At a sudden burst of applause, Jack glanced across the bar at a raucous crowd of women, probably out on a hen night. One of the younger ones, some petite blonde dressed up as a St Trinian's school girl, had precariously balanced a half pint in her cleavage, and was now attempting to sip it. Someone pushed her and it spilt down her chest and stomach. As the girl leapt up shrieking and swearing, her white blouse now completely transparent, the other women screamed with laughter.

Jack eyed the blonde with evident satisfaction. 'Of course I love Sandra. She's my wife, isn't she?'

'When's the baby due?'

'Three weeks.'

'Doesn't she mind you being away, so close to the birth?'

Jack winked at him. 'Told her it was a funeral.'

'Smart.'

'That's what I thought.' He glanced at Niall's pint. 'You not finished that yet? It's your round.'

'Give me a chance.'

'But you're a teacher now, aren't you? I suppose you have to be careful. Like the filth. Can't be caught stepping out of line.'

'It's not that bad,' Niall said, feeling uncomfortable. It was always the same with Jack. Nothing had changed since they were kids at college. Still taking the piss at every opportunity. He was beginning to wish he hadn't agreed to meet Jack tonight, but he'd been knocked back by the phone call, hadn't been able to think up a good excuse in time. It had come out of the blue, which was Jack's preferred style. It gave people less chance of escape once they recognised his voice on the other end of the phone. Niall finished his pint in three determined swallows. 'Same again?'

Jack winked at the empty pint glass. 'Just like old times, eh?'

'We were crazy.'

'Fucking madmen, we were. Remember that blonde hairdresser? What was her name?' Jack clicked his fingers. 'Beverley.'

'With the bottle of Jack Daniels?'

'And the nutcrackers.' Jack laughed, throwing his head back. 'Christ, she was one mad bitch.'

'Gorgeous, though.'

'Ah, she was all right. But just look at that little babe over there,' Jack murmured, visibly shaking off the memories as he glanced over at the energetic young blonde. Someone had found her a cloth now and she was turned slightly towards the bar, cleaning the beer stains off her white blouse and giggling hysterically as the others jostled about her, laughing. 'Now that is gorgeous.'

'She's just a kid.'

'Fresh and sweet, man. That's how I like them.'

Niall laughed. 'Better find someone your own age. She's way out of your league, you old bastard.'

That was obviously a red rag to a bull. Turning squarely to face Niall, Jack smoothed down his hair and straightened his shoulders. His Geordie accent was becoming stronger by the second, all traces of his time in the   East End disappearing rapidly in the face of hurt pride. 'I can pull any lass in Newcastle and I'll prove it.'

'Don't be ridiculous.'

'Get us another pint in, and a whisky chaser, and if I'm not in her knickers by midnight, I owe you twenty quid. Deal?'

'You ought to be locked up.'

'Is it a deal?'

They shook on it and Jack headed off towards the crowd of girls. Niall was a little embarrassed that he'd have agreed to the bet, but at least it seemed to have lightened the atmosphere. Weaving through the crowd after him, Niall balanced their drinks on his arm. He couldn't fault Jack's style. The ruthless bastard had already installed himself at the table, shaking hands with every woman there and introducing himself unbelievably as a rally car driver. But he appeared to be on old form, complimenting the blonde lavishly on her high heels, and getting a shy smile in return.

Leaning further towards the blonde, he told the girl that Niall was his co-driver, 'though he usually does the navigating. I'm the one behind the wheel.' He smiled and raised his eyebrows, at his most charming now. 'Do you like it fast or slow, sweetheart? Don't worry. I can do both.'

The whole table laughed, happily making room for Niall to join them. With a grin, Jack signalled him to sit down opposite, and Niall found himself squeezing in beside a forty-something housewife and a plump girl in her mid-twenties, whose nose had been pierced in several places. It looked like some sort of hideous disease. But the plump girl gave him a drunken smile, which was better than nothing, pressing her hefty thigh against his every time she leant forward for her drink.

It was a little after eleven when Jack suggested a club. By the time they got outside the pub, it was absolutely pissing down, but Jack somehow managed to hail a cab. The housewife and the nose-piercing girl had obviously decided to go home, the latter weaving away from the toilets half an hour before with traces of vomit on her dress. That left only Niall, Jack, and the petite blonde with the beer-stained blouse, who had introduced herself as Paula.

'Let's hit this town,' Jack roared.

They all fell into the back of the cab, laughing and shrieking as knees hit thighs and heads hit elbows. The taxi driver ignored what they were doing, pulling off into the rain without a single word.

Within seconds, Jack was all over the young blonde. One hand went straight up her skirt, the other was unbuttoning her damp blouse. He leant right over her, pressing her hard against the fur-covered seat. Jack must have had his tongue as far into her mouth as physically possible, but she didn't seem to be protesting. The driver glanced into his rear view mirror, then looked back at the road again, smiling slightly.

Niall stared at them with disbelief, holding onto the door as they sped along the city streets.

Paula was moaning, her legs already open. Jack was whispering to her, his fingers working urgently under her short skirt. Squeezed up beside her, Niall could see the occasional flash of white lace and gingerish pubic hair. He felt himself getting hard in spite of his embarrassment, and glanced at the taxi driver nervously. But the large man carried on driving, whistling under his breath, hands easy on the wheel.

Then the taxi halted at a red light.

Jack leant back, effortlessly lifting the tiny blonde onto his lap. 'Here you go, darling,' he muttered. 'Get a load of this.'

Her knees dug into Niall's thighs, skirt rucked up around her hips, face hidden behind a mass of bright hair. Jumping at the contact, he looked desperately away. There was a gang of noisy girls crossing in front of the taxi, swaying on their ludicrously high heels. The driver honked appreciatively and several of them banged on the bonnet, laughing drunkenly. One of the prettiest must have been absolutely frozen, wearing what appeared to be nothing more substantial than a sequinned bikini. Niall stared, trying hard to focus on her body, but everything was swimming. He knew then that he was very drunk.

The lights turned green. The taxi pulled off sharply, and they all collided with each other.

Niall was so anxious, he felt almost sick with it. 'Jack, we're nearly there. We're nearly at the club.'

Jack ignored him, pushing himself upwards into the young blonde, blue veins standing out on his neck with the sheer physical effort.

Heart palpitating, Niall glanced frantically at the driver, then back again at the writhing figures of Jack and Paula. The whole scene was surreal, like a clip from some blue movie. Yet it was completely real. They were screwing right there beside him, only inches away. He could smell that perfume between her legs over the musky aroma of sweat. Even with the fear that they might get caught and arrested, his own excitement was almost unbearable.

The city lights flashed past their heads, blurry with alcohol. Jack was jerking her like a rag-doll now, long blonde hair whipping his face. He must have known they had very little time left.

'Come on, baby,' Jack kept whispering hoarsely into her ear. 'Faster. That's it. We can make it. Come on.'

There was a queue outside the club, and other taxis were pulling up alongside the pavement. The cabbie slowed down just past the flashing lights of the club entrance, sounding the horn as a group of pissed lads wandered around his cab, jeering and kicking the side panels. One of them dropped his pants as he passed Niall's window, waving a hairy white ghost moon in his face for a second. The driver yelled abuse at them from behind what looked like a reinforced windscreen, and the lads sloped drunkenly off, directing exaggeratedly crude gestures towards the lens of a CCTV camera further along the street.

'Oh yes,' Jack finally groaned, pulling the blonde tight against him for a few more agonising seconds. Then he dumped her unceremoniously off his lap and zipped up his flies, glancing swiftly around himself. 'What's up, man? You're as white as a sheet.'

Niall fumbled for the door. 'You cunt.'

'That's not very nice.' Jack was breathless, but grinning.

When she realised Niall was waiting for her to get out, Paula turned her back slightly with a belated display of modesty. Looking flushed, the petite blonde was adjusting her skirt and blouse. 'Give us a minute, would you?'

Niall held the door and waited, speechless.

Restored to decency with the rapidity of practice, Paula smiled up at him like a public school girl and slid out of the cab with both feet primly together. 'Ta very much.'

'Keep the change, mate,' Jack was saying cheerfully to the driver, rustling a couple of notes through the window.

Stumbling after Paula's high heels, Niall tried desperately to clear his head of alcohol. He felt sickened by his physical response to what he had seen, yet strangely elated too. For a split second back there, Niall had been jealous and ready for a taste of the same action himself. He had wanted to know how it felt to be screwing some blonde in the back of a taxi, with Jack and the driver watching, silently cheering him on.

CHAPTER EIGHT

'Look at my legs, Kee. Just look what Mam did to us.'

Jess lifted her skirt and Keely gasped at the dark purplish-black welts across the backs of her knees and thighs.

'You remember back when I got excluded for dealing drugs on school premises, and my mam threw me out of the house for it?'

'I thought that was all forgotten.'

'Well, she never forgets. Still lays into me every time I go round the house for a sub, says I should have gone to prison, first offence or not. But who's she to act all high and mighty? She's drunk most days and can hardly see straight. That's my mam, mind you, who should love you no matter what. Not some stranger or a sleazebag pimp like Zal who thinks he's God's gift. My own mam did that to us.'

'Hush, keep your voice down.'

'Is Zal in?'

Keely nodded quickly, listening for movement from downstairs. Now that she was older, his moves towards her were getting bolder and more open, like he didn't care if he got caught by her mam. It scared her, how much he thought of her as his possession.

'He'd kill us if he heard you call him that.'

Neither of them moved or spoke again for a while, just in case. Keely could feel her palms sweating at the thought of what Zal might do to them if he knew what they were saying about him. He often slipped upstairs to check on them when they were together, and sometimes even listened secretly at the door before coming in. He told Keely her mam didn't trust the girls to behave properly on their own. But after a few tense moments of silence there was still no sound of feet on the stairs. Gradually, the girls both started to relax again.

Jess threw herself down on the bed and stared across into the mirror, playing with her earrings. 'I'm glad Eddy let me move in with him for the time being. Dunno how you can stand living like this, cooped up here every evening like a five year old. You'll be eighteen soon.'

'I know, I can't wait to leave school. I wish I'd never stayed on so long. I could have been working by now if I'd left school. I could have been earning good money, have a place of my own.' Keely shook her head in disgust. 'You know the latest sick rule? I'm not allowed out in the evenings unless I'm with you.'

'Says who?'

Keely made a face. 'Him.'

'Can't you just slip out? Creep downstairs and do a runner while he's watching the telly?'

'He checks on us nearly every hour.'

'Christ Almighty. The sooner you get out of here the better.'

'I've nowhere to go.'

'But you might have soon enough, pet,' her cousin whispered, turning over and winking at her. 'Don't make that face. I've got it all planned out. Eddy's looking out for a squat. Some empty flat where no one's going to bother us.'

'A lurve nest?'

'Don't be so soft. Eddy's too busy doing Zal's dirty work for that.' Her cousin looked away, not meeting Keely's eyes. 'That's why he wants me out of his place as soon as he's found somewhere else. He does business there, you see, and the punters get nervous when they see a new face. He really wants us to be together, though. He's said so. It's just difficult for him right now.'

'So you're going to live on your own in a squat?'

'Why not?'

'Won't it be dangerous, like?'

'No more than living at home with those mad bastards. I mean, what sort of pervert uses a studded belt on her own daughter?' Jess lifted her skirt again. 'Do you think my legs look swollen?'

'Only a little. Can I touch them?'

When her cousin shrugged, Keely leant forward and slowly ran her fingers down a patch of the horrid purple-black blotches. She thought the most heavily discoloured parts would feel sort of hot, like the beating had only just happened, but the skin was cool and smooth to the touch. The mass of bruises ran along the backs of her thighs from above her knees to a little below her knickers.

'Ouch.'

Keely pulled back and looked at her. 'Sorry.'

'Don't stop.'

'You don't mind then?' She stroked the puffiest area of her cousin's thighs, an inch or so below her bottom. The skin looked red raw.

'You've got cold hands, that's all.'

'Evening girls.'

The bedroom door opened and Zal stood in the doorway, unshaven and with his blue shirt sleeves rolled up. He hadn't bothered knocking. Jess dropped the hem of her skirt, but not quickly enough to stop him seeing the bruised legs and Keely's fingers on her skin.

He came into the room silently, pushing the door slightly closed behind him. The girls moved apart without saying anything else or looking at each other. It was best not to put him in a bad temper by showing any reaction to him coming into the room. Keely had learnt that the hard way. She could hear the low hum of the television from downstairs. It sounded like the news. He must have left her mam watching it alone. For a second, she risked a glance at his face and wished she hadn't.

There was a familiar expression in Zal's eyes that made her want to shrink away from him, though she managed to stop herself in time. That sort of reaction was a sure way to get him in a mood.

But he was smiling easily enough at her cousin. 'What's that you're trying to hide there, Jess? Looks like you've fallen off your bike.'

'It's nothing.'

'Don't be soft. Give us a show.'

'It's not important. I just fell and hurt myself, that's all.'

'Is that so?' He lounged against the wall in the small bedroom and lit up a cigarette. Through the thin smoke, his eyes flickered briefly from Jess to Keely's face and back again.

When he spoke again, his voice seemed a bit sharper than before. Keely shivered and pulled back into her corner. She knew that change of tone was a clear warning sign not to push him any further. As he'd got older, his temper had got worse, until she was afraid to provoke him in case he belted her one. 'I keep forgetting that you're all grown-up these days. Both of you. Right couple of bookends, you two. Tweedledee and Tweedle-fucking-dum.'

'It's just a bruise. Nothing worth seeing.'

'I'll be the judge of that, sweetheart. Come on, you showed your cousin. So why not show me? We're practically related.' Zal gestured at Jess to lift her skirt again. He was still smiling but he sounded impatient now. 'Christ's sake, anyone would think I'd never seen a pair of legs before. What's up, are they deformed?'

Her cousin shrugged and hitched up her skirt again without saying anything. The purple-black bruises gleamed magnificently against the pale skin of her thighs. They could see the lacy white elastic of her knickers under the raised skirt. Skin reddening slightly as if with the embarrassment of it all, Jess turned her face away towards the pillows. Keely thought she'd never looked so beautiful.

Zal whistled under his breath. 'That's no bike crash. Who did that to you?'

'My mam. For doing drugs and getting kicked out of school.'

'Serves you right.'

'But that was ages ago, and besides, everyone at school takes drugs. It's not fair. Why does she always have to pick on me?'

Zal leant forward over her thighs, casually flicking one of the purple-black bruises with the tip of his finger. He laughed when Jess yelped and jerked her body away, obviously enjoying himself.

'Because you're the one who always gets caught. But don't worry, sweetheart. There are plenty of other things you can do with your time. You're far too attractive to be stuck behind a school desk anyway.'

'That's what Eddy says.'

'Eddy?' Zal took another drag on his cigarette, never taking his eyes off her face as he sat down beside her on Keely's bed. 'You're not still going out with Eddy Sullivan? Sounds like it's getting serious. Aren't you a bit young for that loser? He must be at least twenty-five.'

'He's not a loser. He's earning good money at your club.'

'Small-timer, can't be trusted, always fucking things up. Don't look at me like that, sweetheart. I know Eddy better than you. He's worked for me often enough since he left school.'

'What, dealing?'

He slapped her arse, grinning. 'On the door at the club. Nothing else.'

'That hurt!'

'It was meant to.' He laughed at her sulky lip. 'What's up now? Do you want me to kiss it better, like?'

'Piss off.'

'Now come on, sweetheart. I know you don't mean that.' He chucked his cigarette out of the window and leant over her body, both hands sliding up the bruised thighs. It made Keely sick to watch them together. 'Why not come along to the club next weekend, let your hair down? I know a few people who could put some cash your way on a regular basis.'

'She's not interested,' Keely said.

'Keep your nose out of my business, kid. You don't want to make me angry. I was talking to your cousin, not you.'

'Zal?' Her mam's voice had come from downstairs, high and suspicious. 'Is that you up there?'

'Coming, love.' He left the bedroom immediately, not looking at either of the girls as he closed the door and went downstairs, deliberately raising his voice. 'I was just helping Keely with that window of hers. It needs a bit of oil.'

Once he was safely gone, Jess made a face at the closed door and put on a nervous-sounding voice. 'I was just helping Keely with that window. It needs a bit of oil.'

They couldn't help giggling at that, but quietly, hands tightly over their mouths, in case he heard and came back upstairs. It was getting dark but there was still a bird singing somewhere outside in the street.

Jess slid off the bed beside Keely. 'Seriously though, I fucking hate your stepdad. I used to like him but now he gives me the creeps.'

'He fancies you.'

'No shit.'

Keely hugged her knees to her chest. 'I think he

fancies me too.'

'That pervert. Has he touched you?'

'Not really.'

'Not really?' Jess reached out and gently touched her face. 'What does that mean, Kee?'

Niall was huddled behind the wheel of his car in the staff car park at break time, enjoying his first cigarette of the day and idly flicking through the kids' sketch pads for potential works of art. He had wound the window down a crack and his smoke was drifting away on the cold air. In true Nazi fashion, smoking was no longer permitted anywhere on school premises, but for some bizarre reason it had been deemed that a teacher smoking in his or her own car was an exception to that rule.

His fingers hesitated over one page and he frowned down at the battered sketch pad on his knee, then checked the name on the front again.

No, it wasn't a mistake. The pad belonged to Keely Down, one of his top students. But this charcoal sketch of a seagull couldn't possibly be her own work, he was certain of that. Either she had copied it from a book or somebody had helped her. Her work had always been good. Excellent, even. But this was on another level entirely.

Shouts and screams rang out from across the playing fields. Niall narrowed his eyes and watched kids running illegally amongst the clustered bushes down at the wall. He was glad not to be on patrol duty that morning. In spite of some thin sunlight breaking through, the weather was still quite cold and he wouldn't have wanted to struggle across there to flush the kids out. More rules and regulations, designed to keep everyone in line. The kids out there were probably just risking a quick fag like himself. Those who weren't dealing or buying drugs, that was. Which was most of them.

He glanced down again at the seagull in charcoal and shook his head. The whole drawing was superb.

'Unbelievable.'

The charcoal strokes were rough and quick, but deliberately so. He could almost see the air currents holding the seagull aloft. Both extended wings had been sketched in that smoky imprecise way, marvellously reminiscent of flight, and the bird's expression was quite haunting. Its head cocked arrogantly to one side, round eye unblinking, beak open as if about to screech. Even the claws had been perfectly captured. He couldn't fault it.

Niall checked his watch, took one last drag on his cigarette, and gathered the sketch pads together under his arm. It was colder outside as he trudged back into the school, wishing he hadn't left his jacket in the staff room.

He noticed her by the main entrance door. Keely, leaning against the wall with Tracey and a handful of other girls hanging around.

She looked paler than ever, whitish blonde hair draining the colour from her skin. Tracey had her head close to Keely's and was saying something in a low hurried voice. Keely seemed completely silent and expressionless, watching her. The other girls had formed a sort of semi-circle around them, hair hiding their faces and hands on hips as they leant inwards to hear what Tracey was saying.

The girl looked like she needed help.

'Keely?' Niall couldn't stop himself. 'Could I have a quick word before the bell goes?'

He held out his hand and Keely immediately took a step towards him out of the circle of girls around her, breaking the ring and scattering them.

Tracey stopped speaking and straightened up. She seemed irritated by his interference. The other girls slipped silently away through the entrance door and into a grey maze of corridors.

'You'd better hurry up inside, Tracey,' he told her. 'You don't want to be late for your next lesson.'

Once Tracey had shuffled inside after the others and

they were alone on the school steps, Keely pushed her blonde hair out of her eyes and looked up at him. If he had expected gratitude there was none in her face, merely a strange blankness. 'What did you want me for, sir?'

'Is this yours, Keely?'

She glanced at her sketch of a seagull. 'Uh huh.'

'You drew it completely on your own?'

'Uh huh.'

'You're sure you didn't copy it from a photograph?'

Hesitantly, Niall looked down into her pale face as she shook her head. Keely seemed to be telling the truth but it was always difficult to tell with these kids. He didn't want to end up looking like an idiot if it became obvious later that she had copied the sketch and then lied about it.

'If this is your own work, drawn freehand, I'm really impressed by your ability. It's the best thing you've shown me. In fact, it's quite superb for someone your age. I mean, obviously your work has been improving lately, and I know you'll do well in your final exams. But this ... ' He tapped the sketchbook. 'This is outstanding. Do you understand what I'm saying?'

She just looked at him blankly.

'Have you considered a career in art?' he asked impulsively.

'No.'

'Perhaps we could have a chat about it after school one day? The way you've caught the bird's eye so precisely, it's truly stunning for someone your age. Maybe I could arrange for your parents to come in so that I can explain to them too.'

'I'm going to be late, sir.'

This wasn't working. Niall was struggling now with her lack of response, wanting to carry on with the conversation but not sure of his territory anymore. Keely was so completely expressionless these days, he found the kid more than a little disconcerting. But however she felt about it, this talent of hers was too real to ignore and pass by. It was something he couldn't let drop like he did with the others. The ones who would never make it. Everything inside him that was an artist was crying out for Keely to listen to him and understand.

What on earth was wrong with the girl?

The bell rang and she pulled away at once. He thought there might have been relief in her eyes but she glanced away before he could be certain, letting that blonde curtain of hair hang around her face again.

Reluctantly, Niall closed the battered sketch pad and handed it back to her. 'If you ever want to show me other things you may have drawn at home, sketches or paintings or whatever, please don't hesitate to come and see me. I'll always have time for you, Keely.'

'Come on, it's through here.' Jess led the way through the broken gate. It creaked spookily on its rusted hinges as she pushed it shut behind them. The back yard of the derelict house was littered with crap. Pieces of smashed glass, beer cans, planks of rotten wood, empty paint pots, an old mattress with a busted spring sticking out.

It was horrible. Everything was filthy and soaking from the rain. The back windows were boarded up, nailed shut except for the door and one little window. Keely thought the house itself looked like a giant coffin, closed up tight and ready to be sunk into the ground.

'Watch your step, there's glass everywhere,' Jess muttered, lifting her heels carefully over an abandoned plank.

'When are these houses getting knocked down?'

Her cousin shrugged. 'Sometime after the New Year, I think. We've got a good month or two yet. '

'Have they cut the water off?'

'Yeah, bastards.'

'I don't like it, Jess. You won't have any water or electric and you'll freeze to death here over the winter.' Keely shivered, hugging herself. 'What if the police come round?'

'The police don't give a toss. There's squatters all over the estate, they can't get rid of them.' Jess pushed the chipboard aside that had been hanging loosely over the back door. It was freshly splintered. 'Anyway, if the owners didn't want us to get in, they should have boarded these places up properly. It took Eddy two minutes to do that with a crowbar. Not exactly secure, is it?'

Inside the tiny back kitchen, it was damp and gloomy. The chipboard over the window had been removed, so there was some daylight coming in, but the rest of the house was in darkness. Someone had left behind a small kitchen table, one of its legs broken so that it leant drunkenly sideways. There was a blue plastic bin near the door with some foul-smelling water in the bottom.

Keely walked past it and stared down the cold blank hallway. Two doors into other rooms were stood half open, both of them leading into more shadow. She didn't like it here. The floorboards in the hall were dirty and had holes in them, some big enough for a foot to go through. An old bike stood against the peeling wallpaper, rusted to pieces. There was a whole pile of rubbish down the far end, old junk mail and free newspapers snowed up against the front door. The front door itself had been boarded-up on the outside, blocking out the light. Its frosted glass panel was cracked and filthy with dust. There were still pieces of glass scattered on the floor beneath it.

Keely caught a sudden movement out of the corner of her eye and screamed, pointing. 'A rat!'

'Calm down, it's only a mouse.'

'Jesus Christ.' Keely could hardly breathe, her heart was going absolutely crazy. She turned to her cousin, keeping a careful eye on her feet in case there was another one scuttling about in the kitchen. It was pathetic, but her hands were trembling. She couldn't stand the thought of mice and rats in the house, it sent shivers down her spine. 'How can you bear to live here, Jess? It's awful.'

'It's free.'

'But what if one of them climbs on you when you're asleep? Runs over your face, like? Ugh, that's dead horrible.'

'Don't be so soft. They're more scared of us.' Jess lit a candle and placed it on the kitchen table. In the flickering light, she went to one of the wall cupboards and rummaged about inside. The whole red-painted row of cupboards were leaning forward, as if they were about to fall off the wall. None of the doors shut properly and the paint was peeling off along the sides. Jess found what she was looking for and held it up. It was a wooden mouse trap with a vicious metal spring. 'See? You put cheese in this bit, and leave it down for them in a corner. They fancy a nibble and ... snap! End of mouse.'

'I'm going to puke.'

'Shut up, would you? Come and have a skeet at the rest.' Jess picked up the candle, shielding the little flame with her hand. 'I'll have to buy some more candles. We need two or three at least for each room, and they burn down real quick.'

'That stinks,' Keely peered into the water in the blue plastic bin.

'I'm going to clean it out next week and use it to store water. If I take a couple of empty bottles out with us, I can fill them up at the loos and keep the water in this bin for washing and making drinks. It'll be a reservoir, like. Eddy's bringing us round a camping stove with a gas ring, so I can even boil a kettle for tea. He's got it all worked out for us.'

'Clever Eddy.'

'Only problem is, because there's no running water here, you have to remember to use a bucket instead of the loo. Then you chuck it down the drains in the back yard.'

'Ugh.'

'Eddy says you get used to it. This is the living room, that's the bathroom, and that room behind us is going to be my bedroom. It's filthy in there, but the floor's rotten upstairs so I'm staying down here to sleep.' Jess laughed, holding up the candle as she led Keely into the darkened living room. 'I'd get up a lot quicker in the mornings though. Step out of bed and fall straight through into the kitchen, like.'

'So you really not going back to your mam's again?'

Lifting her high black heels, Jess walked through stacks of rubbish to the boarded-up windows. She looked weird with a candle in her hand. It lit up her face and long hair with a flickering orange glow. 'Told you, I'm steering clear of my mam from now on. She can go fuck herself. Anyway, I'm not planning to stay here forever. Eddy's looking for this new flat and then I'll move out.'

'I wouldn't trust him. He works for Zal.'

'I like Eddy. He looks out for us.' Jess said, nearly dropping the candle as she turned at the windows. She put it down on the mantelpiece, rubbing her fingers. 'Ow, that hurt. But at least I can do my own bikini line wax now. That'll save us a bit of cash.'

'Eddy's a greasy little pimp.'

'Shut your face.'

There was a long horrible silence between them. Keely looked away from her cousin, not sure what to say. The candle didn't give much light but she could see well enough from a pale daylight creeping in around the boarded-up windows. The living room wasn't as large as she'd expected. There were old newspapers scattered all over the floor, some of them glued flat to the floorboards like ancient underlay. The room smelt of damp and the wallpaper was peeling down in ugly sagging strips at every corner. Someone had tried to paint it at some point, but the white paint had started to flake away now with the dampness behind the walls, showing little hints of blue underneath. She thought it needed some posters up to hide the crap, or maybe a few coats of dark paint.

Beside the crumbling bricked-up fireplace, there was a heavy metal radiator. Its huge metal pipes were fixed deeply into the wall. Keely kicked it and stepped back. The white-painted metal rang hollow and a few flakes of paint fell to the floor. 'Christ, this radiator's a museum piece.'

'Eddy reckons he could flog that to one of his mates before the demolition gang move in. He says it's worth a fortune.'

'It must weigh a ton. How would he shift it?'

'Dunno.'

Keely shivered. 'It's perishing in this place. And it's so dark. How can you bear to sleep here on your own? It's dead creepy, even with the candles. It's like something out of the Adams Family.'

'I'm not always on my own.'

Keely made a face. 'You and Eddy?'

Without answering that, Jess turned to pick up the candle again as if she was avoiding Keely's eyes. 'Come on, I'll show you my bedroom. I found an old mattress upstairs. Eddy dragged it down for us into the other room so I can sleep there. Bloody thing smells like someone died on it, but I keep spraying the air freshener so you can't tell. I've made it real nice in there now. Brought all my gear and even my duvet from home.'

Keely followed her slowly into the bedroom, stepping in the shadows left behind by her candle. 'You're not back on the game, are you?'

Jess shrugged, flushing slightly. 'It's not for long, babes.'

'What are you like?'

'I need the cash!'

'What for, drugs?'

'For moving out of this shit-hole and getting a real flat for myself, with running water and electric.'

'But Eddy takes a cut of your earnings, doesn't he?' Keely stared at her cousin's face in the orange candle glow. 'I don't believe you, I really don't. That bastard's using you and you can't even see it.'

'You're so wrong about him. Eddy loves us, he only

takes the money for my own good. So I don't spend it on the wrong things, you know. We're getting this flat across the river together, he's promised. After that, it's no more punters and no more drugs.'

'Bollocks.'

'What else am I meant to do?'

'Get a council flat, like my mam did. It's dead easy. You don't even have to go out to work for it.'

'You don't understand. I want to live somewhere decent, not another tip like this. At least this is mine and there's no bastard junkies knocking on the door in the middle of the night.'

Jess held up the candle in the bedroom, showing her the mattress with its duvet and crumpled sheets. There wasn't any rubbish left in the room, it had all been cleared away, but her own stuff was already littered all over the place, clothes hanging out of cardboard boxes, shoes on the bed, make-up and perfume bottles scattered across the old wooden dresser. Her little bedside table was covered in pools of wax and ash and blackened candle stubs with dog-ends crushed into them. The place was an utter mess.

'Sorry.' Her cousin kicked some of her clothes into the corner. 'I haven't been down the laundrette for a few days.'

There was a mirror leaning against the damp wallpaper, with a pair of sheer black tights thrown carelessly across it. It reflected the candle flame eerily through a rip in the nylon as the two girls sat down together on the bed and looked at each other. They didn't say anything for a minute or two. Keely bounced a few times to test the mattress. It was very springy and lumpy. But at least it didn't seem to be as cold in here as the other rooms, and it smelt strongly of perfume and make-up instead of mould.

'You can stay whenever you like, babes,' Jess said softly, touching her hair. 'The back door locks, but I could leave it open for you if I have to go out working. We could share the bed at night, just like old times, or you can bring your sleeping bag and kip on the floor.'

'Sleep here?'

'Why not?' Jess looked at her for a moment in silence, then shrugged. 'You'd be safe enough. Zal doesn't know about this place.'

CHAPTER NINE

'God, I hate her,' Keely muttered.

Tracey was taking the piss as always, flicking her hair back like a right tart and gazing up at Mr Swainson beside the art room sinks. He was showing her how to stretch a canvas. It was pathetic. Everyone doing the A Level course should already know how to do that. It was basic stuff.

Tracey was just taking the piss because she reckoned Mr Swainson fancied her. But he didn't fancy her. Why on earth would anyone fancy a silly tart like Tracey, let alone someone like Mr Swainson?

He finished explaining and turned away, so he didn't see her laughing behind his back and making that gesture like wanking. She thought she was so special. She thought she could pull any man she wanted and then drop him in the shite.

Keely bent her head to the drawing. 'I hope she dies soon.'

Kicker was sitting next to her. He chucked a rubber at her head, but it missed, bouncing off her sketch pad and under the desk. 'You being nasty about our Trace again?'

'Fuck off.'

The red-headed lad leant forward, raising his voice.

'What did you say?'

'You heard me, wank job.'

Mr Swainson was back at his desk now. Keely sneaked a glance at him out of the corner of her eye, pretending to sharpen her pencil. He wasn't dead good-looking, but there was something about him. She concentrated on her sketch pad again. They were drawing onions towards a still life. She had bought two from the shop on her way in that morning. It was really hard, trying to get all the little changes across the brown skin, and then the thinning neck, with its dry curved stem sticking out.

She liked drawing. She was good at it, didn't have to struggle to keep up. Mr Swainson had said she could go on to do an art degree if she worked hard enough and got good grades in her A Level.

Tracey came up and stood right behind her. She laughed, making sure everyone in the room could hear her. 'Fucking hell, Kee. You must be the only person in the world who could draw a square onion.'

'It's not square.'

'I've seen matchboxes rounder than that.'

'Leave me alone.'

Tracey bent closer. 'Aw, what's up, Kee? Have you gone all jealous because lover boy was talking to us for a change?'

'Get out of my face,' Keely spat.

Mr Swainson was behind them suddenly, shutting out the light. It was like a sixth sense with him, he always seemed to know when she was in trouble. Especially when it was to do with that stupid little tart. He'd saved her from Tracey she didn't know how many times. Now Mr Swainson dug his hands into the pockets of his jeans, looking from one to the other. He didn't sound angry though. 'Problem?'

'No, sir.' Tracey smiled, glancing round at the others. 'I was just giving Keely a few suggestions about what she could do with her onion.'

'Well, the fun's over now. I think you'd better sit down and concentrate on your own work.' He raised his voice as Tracey walked slowly back to her own seat, exaggeratedly swaying her hips as if to make sure he was watching her. 'That goes for all of you here. These preliminary sketches are vitally important if you want a coherent idea of what you'll be aiming at in your final piece. You may find the groundwork less exciting than the actual painting, but without it, you're simply not going to get the details right. So heads down, stop chatting and get back to work.'

Mr Swainson was still standing behind her. Keely could almost taste his aftershave, he was so close. It was spicy and expensive-smelling. She tried to carry on with the sketch, but it was impossible with him watching. It wasn't like it had been with Tracey, the straight anger. Instead it was all wrong and confused inside. Pretending to check the scale was right, she lined up the onion with her pencil, glancing down again at what she had drawn. But she wasn't really checking, it was just for show.

He touched her shoulder. 'That's coming along nicely.'

'Ta, sir.'

'Remember, if you have any problems, come to me first.' He was looking at her face. 'Okay?'

'Yes, sir.'

'Even if it's not about school work.'

Keely nodded. That seemed to satisfy him. He said okay and carried on round the class, looking at everyone else's work. But she didn't feel confused anymore. On impulse, she bent to pick up the rubber that Kicker had thrown and chucked it back at him. He wasn't looking and it caught him on the side of the head.

'Ow, that hurt.'

'What did?'

Kicker stared at her, rubbing his head with his fist. 'You're a right fucking weirdo, d'you know that?'

Niall took another sip of whisky. The Jack Daniels burnt the back of his throat, but he welcomed it. It was his birthday, and there was no one to celebrate it with except himself. He had not mentioned his birthday to anyone at work, too embarrassed to deal with their inevitable questions. What you doing tonight, then? Hitting the town? Out on the prowl? You lucky bastard.

The bar churned with drinkers. It was after eleven o'clock now and most of them were pissed, knocking into him as he stood alone with his glass, watching football highlights on the big screen.

There was supposed to be something liberating about not having a girlfriend. He should be pleased. You're single again, you can do whatever you like, you lucky bastard. One of those girls by the bar was even smiling at him now. She had gorgeous chestnut hair, neatly swept off her bare shoulders. She was only in her early twenties, and sexy as hell in one of little black dresses they all seemed to be wearing.

When Niall smiled back and lifted his glass, she looked away, clearly horrified. He glanced around and saw her friends behind him, waving and forcing a path hysterically across the crowded bar. The brunette had been smiling at them, not him.

He finished his whisky, suddenly dying to get out of the bloody place. He felt ridiculous, far too old for this scene. That thought made him angry.

Niall gazed slowly around the bar, narrowing his eyes through the alcohol haze, and finally saw a girl on her own.

She had her back to him, but her legs were very long and slim, short skirt, thigh-length boots, nicely rounded arse. She was looking up at the television screen, twiddling the umbrella in her drink.

'On your own?'

She turned and stared. 'Piss off.'

Niall retreated immediately, falling backwards into

some large bloke in a leather jacket, who righted him with aggressive hands. 'Watch where you're going. You nearly had my drink, you daft sod.'

'Sorry,' he muttered.

The bar doors were open and Niall stumbled through them into the street, avoiding the steely eyes of the bouncers. He didn't want any trouble. He just wanted something to help him forget. The fresh air hit his face and he swayed, belatedly realising he was drunk. He stepped out into the road and a car hooted indignantly.

Well, that was a complete failure, he told himself.

Finding the pavement again, Niall made his way unsteadily towards the corner, instinctively looking for some dark place where he could take a piss without being arrested.

There were bin bags lying in the alley, just past a row of illegally parked cars.

Niall stopped, checking cautiously for witnesses, but the air was still. It was quiet away from the constant traffic, and his head didn't ache so much now. Enormously relieved, he peed generously over the bin bags, admiring the thin golden arc of his piss as it sprayed up and onto crumpled black plastic with a hissing, splattering noise. He supported himself with one hand as the stream came to a gradual end, shaking the drops away as he peered back down the alley.

Niall froze. There was a girl coming towards him. He could hear heels clattering, but her face was in darkness.

Hurriedly, he zipped himself up. 'I was just ...'

'Taking a piss?' she finished for him. It was a strong Geordie accent. An attractive enough girl with long legs, probably about eighteen, but in the dim light of the alley he couldn't see if she was smiling. 'I saw what you was up to there.'

'I was desperate.'

The girl came closer. There was something naggingly

familiar about the way she held herself, but he was too drunk to focus on the memory he needed. It kept slipping away into the slim midriff and long bare legs and that perfume she was wearing.

'You haven't zipped yourself up properly.'

Without losing eye contact with her, Niall checked his jeans. Was this a come-on or what? 'Yes I have.'

'Pity.'

Her smile was encouraging and he felt the beginnings of a hard-on. Maybe his birthday hadn't been a complete washout after all. Then he looked at the girl more carefully, focussing on the clearly visible cleavage, the slim thighs, the glossy parted lips.

She was a prostitute. He felt like a fool. He felt a burst of pure rage, as if she had deliberately tricked him. 'How old are you?'

'Old enough.'

'Don't fuck about. How old are you?'

She blinked. 'Twenty.'

'You can't be, not yet.' Niall had finally worked out who she was. He should have recognised the sultry arrogance as soon as she walked up. Too pissed, he thought angrily. 'I still remember you from school. I took you for art, Jess. Are you on the game already?'

'A girl's got to live. My mam threw me out.'

'I'm not surprised. You were caught dealing on school premises.'

'So what?' Jess tossed back her hair with that familiar gesture of defiance. 'I got my wrist slapped for that. It's ancient history now.'

'And what are you doing now? Selling yourself instead?'

'You going to tell on me, sir?'

'I should do.'

'Take a look at yourself.' She giggled suddenly. 'You want to go down the nick in that state? You'd be done yourself for drunk and disorderly, sir.'

'It's my birthday.'

His voice was suddenly slurred. He had no idea why he'd said that. Perhaps he wanted sympathy. Perhaps he wanted congratulations. Perhaps he just wanted some company on his birthday.

She was still smiling. 'Out drinking on your own?'

'No.'

Jess glanced furtively up and down the alley, moving closer and stroking his groin. 'Seeing as it's your birthday, sir, why don't you let me give you a freebie?'

'Don't be disgusting.'

'You did my cousin Keely a favour, didn't you? Not telling that bastard MacFerson you found drugs on her.'

'Keep your hands to yourself, Jess.' He was too pissed to cope with this, not tonight of all nights, not on top of everything else that was fucked-up in his life. Niall fumbled for the right words, trying to sound in control of the situation. 'Look, I'm not interested.'

But Jess was on her knees. 'Shh.'

Before Niall's drunken mind could click through the gears, she had unzipped his flies. Her fingers were so swift and practised, she must have done this a thousand times. His physical reaction was instantaneous.

Niall pushed her away. 'I don't want this,' he said thickly.

'Happy birthday, sir.'

'I told you, no,' he insisted.

She rocked back on her heels, shrugging petulantly. 'Suit yourself.'

Like a sprinter released by a starting pistol, Niall spun away, groping for the wall and missing it. He fell among the bin bags, slithering comically on black plastic. His left foot came down awkwardly on a tin can, which rolled backwards in a slow ridiculous blur.

Niall collapsed sideways, exploding his head against something grim and unyielding. Probably the wall.

There was a dead interval of what felt like several hours, but was probably about thirty seconds. It was as if his drunken brain possessed some sort of trip switch, designed to stop potentially lethal activity at moments of extreme physical and mental stress. Niall let himself float comfortably in oblivion for those precious seconds, relieved to be somewhere outside the universe, however briefly. Then some age-old warning light must have flickered on inside his head, because Niall found himself forcing his eyelids apart, shakily aware that he had to get out of that alley before somebody spotted him and the police were called.

Gathering the strength to roll over, at first Niall didn't recognise the familiar sweet-sour smell under his cheek. Then he realised what it was. He was lying amidst broken glass and sodden rubbish, face-down in his own piss.

Jess was long gone. He had a memory of laughter and retreating heels, echoes bouncing off the walls. That stupid grin as she knelt before him. 'Happy birthday, sir.'

Niall raised his head convulsively and the world zoomed in and out of focus. He needed to get back to the safety of his flat.

Groping for the wall, Niall stumbled to his feet but instantly heaved, emptying a gutful of Jack Daniels over the rubbish bags.

The head teacher was searching through his filing cabinets, his face flushed, tie slightly askew. 'Really, Niall, can't this wait? I've got some papers to go over before the governors' meeting tomorrow, and it's my wife's birthday, we're going out to dinner tonight. I can't be late. I've forgotten to pick up my bloody suit from the cleaners, Jeff's got piano at six o'clock and I'm meant to be driving him, and if I don't find those bloody papers soon, I'm going to look like a right sodding prat in the morning.'

Niall sat down. 'It's about Keely Down.'

'Who?'

'Keely Down. One of my top students. She did that art presentation last term.'

Another drawer slammed open and shut. 'Oh yes. Pale girl with the long blonde hair. What's the problem?'

'I'm not sure.'

'Christ, where on earth did she put them?' MacFerson slumped behind his desk, staring dejectedly around his office. 'Angela's off today. Flu, if you can believe that. Why the bloody hell does she always have to disappear at the worst possible moments? So what did you say the problem was?'

'That's just it. I couldn't get it out of her.'

'Symptoms?'

'Pale, withdrawn, erratic behaviour.'

The head shrugged. 'Boyfriend, probably.'

'She says she hasn't got one.'

'Hmm. He's dumped her, I expect. It happens.'

'I don't think so. I think it's more serious than that.' Niall sat forward. He placed the two sheets of art paper on the head's desk, spreading them out. 'This is what she did in my class today.'

MacFerson fumbled for his glasses, sighing. 'I'm really very late, Niall. Surely this is a matter for your head of department?'

'Tony's still off sick.'

'What about Frances? I thought she was ...'

'She's on that INSET course this week.'

'Oh yes, I'd forgotten about that. Great timing as always. Okay, maybe just take a quick look before I go.'

There was a silence as the head carefully examined the two sheets of scrawled black handwriting, then pushed them away and shook his head. 'I'm sorry, Niall, but I don't see any particular significance in these. It's just a bored kid expressing normal frustration. Perhaps you should consider pepping up your classes a little, Niall. Keep them more interested.'

Niall ignored the implied accusation. 'Look, Keely's not that sort of kid. She's always been one of my best pupils. There's more to this than mere boredom, I'm sure of it.'

'I doubt it.' Standing up again as if to indicate the matter was closed, MacFerson reached for his creased jacket and shrugged into it. A late sunshine was streaming through the windows behind him. He turned automatically to close the shutters before he left, darkening the small school office so that it suddenly felt chilly. 'Cleaners, piano lesson, dinner. What was the other thing?'

'Governors' meeting.'

'Those bloody papers. I'm going to be hamstrung for this. Either that, or I'll have to come in at six o'clock in the sodding morning and have another hunt round for them.'

MacFerson checked absent-mindedly for his keys, opening the office door. He was a small man - his jackets always one size too big for him as if he felt the need to look more imposing than he was - but the deep Scottish voice had usually sounded reassuring in the past. Now Niall wasn't so sure, suddenly filled with the conviction that MacFerson wasn't really listening to him. Even the friendly clap on the shoulder could mean nothing except that the man was late, and wanted to get him out of his office as quickly as possible.

'I'm pretty sure you're imagining things, but just keep an eye on the situation anyway. Talk to Frances when she gets back.'

'Couldn't we ring the parents, get them in for a chat?'

'Oh, not at this stage. No, no.'

Niall felt a bitter surge of frustration as he collected the sheets of paper from the desk. 'Jim, this isn't normal behaviour for Keely. I'm genuinely worried about the kid. We should do something.'

'You want to do something? Stay detached. Monitor the situation. Bring it up at the next departmental meeting, see what Tony and Frances think before you take it any further. In my experience, these things blow over astonishingly quickly. Another few days, she'll be mooning over some other wee lad, and all this attention-seeking will be forgotten.' MacFerson locked the office door as they went out, pocketing the keys with a weary smile. 'I've been in this game twenty-eight years, Niall. Teenage girls and strange behaviour? I've seen it all before, trust me.'

Their conversation clearly at an end, MacFerson stared down at his watch and shook his head. 'Christ, have you seen the time? The wife's going to bloody kill me.'

Niall turned sharply as the door to the art room opened. 'Where on earth have you been, Keely? You're ridiculously late. The others started fifteen minutes ago. I've marked you as absent now.'

Keely looked pale and sullen. 'Sorry, sir. I felt sick.'

'Have you seen the nurse?'

She shrugged.

'Well, you'd better sit down and start work. We're trying to finish the still life today. Did you bring your sketch pad?'

'I forgot it.'

Niall frowned. It was unlike Keely to be so disorganised. She had always seemed to enjoy his classes in the past. But maybe the kid really was feeling ill today. Forgetting to be stern for a moment, his voice softened. 'Have you brought a pencil at least? Okay, good. Take some spare sheets from the back table. You can do more preliminary sketches instead.'

Keely did as she was told, settling to work in silence, head bent, her long fair hair hiding her face.

Five minutes before the end of the period, Niall wandered idly among the desks, checking to see how much everyone had achieved. It was nearly the end of the school day. His impatience was unusual, but he had actually managed to catch up on his marking that weekend, so he was free to go as soon as the bell rang.

If he reached the supermarket before the rush-hour started, he could still get home in time to catch the football on his satellite television, only recently hired and still something of a novelty for him. It was a big screen with twin speakers, and he had taken to lounging in front of it during the evenings, enjoying a few cans of cold beer. It was a sad existence, perhaps, but anything was better than trawling round the bars and clubs like he used to, another pathetic drunken bastard with his tongue hanging out, hoping for a shag, a grope in the dark, a kiss, even just five minutes of conversation that didn't end with a slap in the face.

Passing Keely's desk, he glanced at her sketches and stopped dead in astonishment. 'For God's sake, Keely. Why on earth have you done that?'

She had covered one sheet with a thick black scrawl, huge capital letters, a string of words making absolutely no sense, HATE WALL FINGERS CHAINS BLOOD SLAP ANGER BED BLACK LOCK.

On the other sheet, still clutched in her hand, she had sketched some sort of rough hangman's gibbet. There was a body suspended from it, the crudely-drawn naked body of a woman with no face. Underneath, she had written ME in block capitals, and underscored the word several times, gauging a hole in the paper with her pencil.

'Just felt like it, didn't I?'

Niall examined the second sheet over her shoulder, trying not to let any concern show in his voice. 'I think you should stay behind. We'll have a chat.'

But the girl next to her had seen the drawing. She gave an incredulous gasp, almost laughing. 'Keely! What do you call that mess? Have you gone crazy or what?'

'That's enough for today, everyone.' He raised his voice as chairs scraped noisily. 'Put your sketch pads on my desk before you leave and don't forget it's pottery on Monday, so bring your overalls. No excuses this time. It's okay, Tony. I'll clear that up.'

Keely stayed at her desk while the others made their way out of the art room, fiddling with the zip on her pencil case. Her face was pale and distant, eyes devoid of emotion.

Once they were finally alone together, Niall drew up a chair opposite and looked at her speculatively. Her behaviour had been a little uneven for some months, though he'd dismissed that as the normal fluctuations of teenage angst. But it wasn't teenage angst on that sheet of paper, it had to be something rather more sinister than that. Niall couldn't help remembering his recent birthday encounter with Jess. Not for the first time, he wondered uneasily whether Keely knew what he had done that night. The cousins must still be in contact with each other. It had been preying on his mind lately, how he could have lost control of the situation so quickly, drunk or not. He almost felt like a fraud now, attempting to mentor this child when his own example was so appalling. But the last thing he wanted was for Keely to turn down the same self-destructive path as her cousin. 'You didn't really feel sick today, did you? So why were you late?'

She didn't respond.

'Is it a boyfriend?'

'I haven't got a boyfriend.'

He hesitated, watching for a reaction. 'Problems at home, then?'

'There's nothing wrong with me. Look, I was just messing about and I'm sorry. I won't do it again, okay?'

But her face had gone cold at his last question. He had clearly touched a nerve there by mentioning her family. She tore a corner off her sketch of the hanged woman and rolling it listlessly between her finger and thumb. When he didn't say anything in response, she looked him straight in the eye. Her tone was unnaturally level for a kid staring down a teacher. He had expected aggression, but there wasn't any.

'Can I go now, sir?' she asked blankly. 'I'll miss the

bus.'

CHAPTER TEN

Keely was trying hard to be alone at lunch-time, hunched up, perched on the wall outside the science labs. She didn't feel like hanging round with the others anymore. They never said anything worth listening to. She was looking at the sports field instead. It was all hacked up where they'd been playing football in the rain. Mr Philips was out there, prodding the grass with his boot and putting back clumps of earth where they'd been kicked out. He had a flashing mac, like the dirty old men wore down the park. The rain had made it go streaky.

Tracey came up to her, grinning. 'Guess what I heard?'

'Piss off.'

'Oooh, I'm so scared.'

Keely put her fingers in her ears, looking away at Mr Philips. He was still plodding about the muddy sports field, pressing down the earth with his boots. She didn't have to listen. This wasn't friendship. Tracey had only come up to her to take the piss.

The others had gathered round. Her cronies. Nudging each other and laughing. 'Have you heard, Keely?'

'Piss off, all of you.'

Tracey shook her head. 'That's not very polite, is it? I was only coming to tell you the big skeet about Mr Swainson, but maybe I won't bother now.'

'I'm not listening.'

'He fancies me, it's official.'

'I don't care.'

'He drew this for me.' Tracey held out a Christmas card and opened it. 'Go on, have a look inside. Nice picture he's drawn for me, isn't it? And he's even signed it at the bottom.'

Keely glanced down at it. *Love to my darling Tracey, can't wait to shag you again.* It was a crap little pencil sketch of a man on top of a girl with big tits. 'That's nothing but shite. You've done it yourself.'

'Mr Swainson drew it.'

'What, he spelt his own name wrong?'

Tracey stared down at the card. 'What?'

'It's not spelt like that, you twat. It's N, I, A, double L.'

'Fuck off, it's not.'

It was starting to drizzle again. Blinking against the rain, Keely jumped down from the wall and snatched the pathetic little Christmas card out of Tracey's hand and ripped it to shreds. The pieces scattered across the concrete like confetti, dampening with rain. That was what she thought of that crap. Keely looked up above their heads to see if the weather was going to get any better or if she should go back inside. There were flashes of blue sky beyond the dark clouds overhead, but the rain was still falling. As she looked down again, she realised that Mr Philips had stopped pissing about on the sports field and was coming towards them in his flashing mac.

'You bitch,' Tracey was shouting, trying to pick up the torn pieces of the sketch. 'That was my fucking property.'

'I told you, it's nothing but shite.'

Tracey pushed up close to her face, almost spitting.

'You can't stand that he fancies me, can you? You're so jealous you're turning green. Do you want to know how he does it? How he shags me every time we see each other? Oh yeah, he's a right porn star, that one. His dick's so fucking enormous, sometimes I can't get all of it in my gob.'

There must have been lightning or something overhead, because it blinded her for a few seconds. Then Keely was walking away, paying no attention to the shouts and chaos behind her.

It was raining more heavily now. She was getting soaked, but she carried on walking. It was probably only a quick shower. Kids were running past her into the buildings with their coats held above their heads, but she didn't bother running. She'd forgotten to bring her coat out at lunch-time anyway. The playground ahead seemed to be nothing but a black sheet of water from a distance. But as she crossed it, she could see bright blues and reds and greens swirling in the little puddles, because of the oil.

Mr Philips was calling after her to stop. Keely turned reluctantly to face him. He didn't actually take her for any subjects, but he was still a teacher so she had to wait.

He hurried up to her in his flashing mac, red-faced and panting like he was going to keel over with a heart attack. But he was quite overweight, so that wouldn't have been a surprise. 'What on earth happened back there?'

'Dunno.'

'Did you just hit that girl?'

Keely looked back over his shoulder. She could see Tracey sitting on the ground near the science labs, all her cronies bent over her in a circle. There seemed to be a lot of shouting and pushing going on. Some of the others were staring at Keely.

'No, sir. I didn't.'

'She claims you did.'

'I never touched her, honest.'

He was looking at her carefully. 'Are you telling me

the truth?'

'Yes, sir.'

'All right,' he said suddenly, turning away. 'Get back inside then, it's pouring. Mr MacFerson will probably want to see you later.'

'I told you, I never touched her.'

But he was already gone, hurrying back to where Tracey was standing on her own now by the science labs, head bent as if she was crying. There was no point standing there to watch anymore. The rain was in Keely's eyes and she couldn't see properly. She went back inside and took a few text books from her locker, though it was a waste of her time. She would not be staying at school much longer.

The large woman in blue, overloaded with shopping bags, eased herself down on the bench next to Niall and smiled apologetically. 'Crowded in here today, isn't it? I hate Saturdays. But you can't shop after dark these days, too dangerous.'

Niall nodded without speaking, then looked away in the hope that his new companion would give up trying to engage him in conversation. But she was right. The shopping centre was crammed with Saturday shoppers: hassled-looking mothers, nauseating kids, grim husbands, the odd bewildered pensioner looking for a shop which no longer exists, and gangs of young girls, walking deliberately abreast through the crowds in order to cause the maximum disruption.

Not for the first time, Niall questioned why he was wasting even a single moment of his life in this hellhole of modern civilisation. He wouldn't normally have ventured into the main shopping centre at all, let alone on a chaotic Saturday afternoon like this, but he had woken up that morning with a frightening and only-too-familiar sensation of deadness and known that he had to get out somewhere that day - anywhere, it didn't really matter where - and connect with the world again. He had got into his car and drifted out into the madness of inner city weekend traffic, following the crowd which had eventually led him here. And now that he was here, sitting on a bench next to this sweating middle-aged shopper with her vast collection of plastic bags, Niall realised it had been the right place to come. For if spending his life alone made him depressed, the thought of having to come shopping here every Saturday with a partner was quite enough to make him count his blessings.

Abandoning the bench area with its towering indoor trees and over-flowing rubbish bins, Niall headed back towards the car park at an unhurried pace.

It was good to feel so relaxed again, especially after waking up in such an appalling state that morning, blank-faced and barely able to rouse himself from under his covers. Not that it was unusual for him to feel like shit in the mornings. It was his own personal darkness which had been hanging over him for months now, rather like a bad dream he was unable to shake off on waking. That emptiness and despair which threatened to engulf him in the early hours were what he dreaded most, followed by the futility of seeking professional help. How could anyone help him, when he was totally incapable of helping himself?

But just at this particular moment in time, for no apparent reason that he could see, Niall felt okay in himself. More or less able to cope with whatever the world was planning to throw at him. Maybe it was simply because the sun was shining somewhere out there, beyond the ludicrous glass roof of the shopping centre. Sometimes the grim black screen through which he habitually saw the world was enough to blot out the sunshine. But not today. Today was going to be OK.

'No. I told you, I'm meeting Jess this afternoon. I don't want to go home yet.'

The rebellious teenage voice was oddly familiar. Niall

stopped and turned to check out the crowd around him.

For a moment he couldn't spot her, then realised Keely was less than a hundred feet away, standing with her back to him outside a travel agency, shoulders hunched defensively forward as she argued with a well-built man of about his own age. From his clenched jaw and dark eyes narrowed on her face, he didn't look like the sort of man anybody would want to argue with, let alone a kid like Keely.

Slightly concerned about what was going on, Niall hung on his heel for a moment, eavesdropping.

'Don't give me that crap.'

'But mam said I could stay out today. What's the problem? We're only going to the park after we've been shopping.'

'You're coming home right now, so don't fucking argue with me.' The man's tone held barely suppressed anger.

'I'm not arguing. I just said ...'

It was probably her father, Niall thought cautiously, about to fade back into the crowd and leave them to their family squabble when the man suddenly grabbed hold of her arm and shook it violently. Wearing a sleeveless tee-shirt to show off several coloured tattoos, it was obvious how well-developed his biceps were. Keely's squeal of pain was not faked.

But the big bloke didn't even give her a second glance, dragging Keely unceremoniously through the crowds. 'I've told you. If you know what's good for you, you'll shut your face and do what you're told. Your mam needs you at home and that's an end to the matter.'

Aware that this was absolutely none of his business but letting his instincts over-ride his brain, Niall kept close behind them as the couple headed towards the car park. It was difficult to keep out of sight in the brightly-lit shopping centre but he tried to look as nonchalant as possible, watching their reflection in shop windows as he let them turn corners some yards ahead of him. He persuaded himself that he was merely checking that this man really was related to Keely, but he knew from the way his blood pressure was singing in his ears that he was furious inside and wanted to take the bloke apart.

Keely was such a slight girl, petite and fragile-looking. Those haunted eyes betrayed her vulnerability as soon as she looked at you, Niall thought angrily. He couldn't believe any man could bring himself to treat her so roughly, except perhaps a bully who got his kicks from threatening girls. What kind of monster was this father?

Now that Niall was looking specifically for the evidence, there didn't seem to be any family resemblance between them at all. Keely was slenderly built, while the man was broad and muscular. His hair was strikingly dark, hers a pale blonde. Even their skin tones were different: his was coarse and sallow, but she had a soft peachy tint.

Unlocking an old BMW, the man threw the passenger door open and ordered Keely to get inside. She refused, still struggling. His face red with temper or exertion, he tried to force her inside. 'Do what you're told, you stupid bitch.'

'I'm not going home with you.'

'Get in.'

'Fuck off,' she suddenly yelled at him. 'I'm not a kid anymore.'

Practically in the same second, like a knee-jerk reaction, his hand flashed up and slapped her hard round the face.

Niall heard her head snap back under the force of the impact. The tumbling blonde hair hid her face as Keely twisted away, letting out a sharp cry, but it was quite obvious that she had been hurt.

She scrabbled at his hands as they fixed on the lapels of her jacket. 'Get off me, I hate you. I'm going to tell mam you hit me.'

'You think she gives a toss about you? Don't be so

stupid. She can't wait to get you out of the house. The sooner you leave that school and get yourself a job and your own place, the better.'

'Why can't you let me go then?'

'You're needed. There's jobs to be done.'

'I know what you want,' she hissed.

He slapped her again, this time much harder. 'Don't you speak to me like that, you foul-mouthed little bitch.'

Niall's temper had been building rapidly to a crescendo as he watched them struggle, trying not to be seen as he stood a few spaces away in the car park, but now he simply couldn't hold himself silent any longer.

The man's behaviour was intolerable. Niall would have stepped in at the first slap, furious and accusatory, but he was only too aware of how well-built the other man was. But that crap didn't matter anymore. He was too angry to pay attention to the differences between them. The only thing Niall could focus on through his rage was that Keely was getting beaten up by a man twice her size.

'Get your hands off her!' He stepped forward, surprised to hear the force in his own voice. 'What sort of man are you? You should be ashamed of yourself.'

The man pushed Keely away immediately, as if he had suddenly lost interest in her, taking a couple of steps backwards so that he could look Niall up and down. The unpleasant eyes came back to his face and narrowed aggressively. 'And who are you?'

'That doesn't matter.'

The man shot Keely a harsh glance. 'You know him?'

She was crying, leaning against the side of the old BMW. Her voice shook, barely above a whisper. 'He's a teacher at my school.'

'A fucking teacher? What do you teach?'

'That's not important.'

'What does he teach?' The man was looking at Keely again.

'Art.'

'You what?' Now the man had thrown his head back and was laughing, visibly relaxing, as if someone had been playing a joke on him and he had only just realised. He leant back against the open car door and cracked his knuckles, watching Niall with contemptuous amusement. 'You're the fucking art teacher? Do yourself a favour and fuck off, would you? This is none of your business. This is my step-daughter and I'm taking her home.'

'I don't think she wants to go with you.'

'I said, fuck off.'

Niall swallowed. 'And I said she doesn't want to go with you.'

'Look, are you deaf or what? Or do you just fancy getting the shit kicked out of you today? Because that's what's going to happen if you don't get out of my face right now.'

'I saw you hit her.'

The man shrugged. 'So what?'

'It's illegal.'

'She deserved it, the way she plays me up.'

'Let's ask her what she thinks, shall we?'

'Go fuck yourself.'

Niall didn't budge. 'Whether you think she deserved it or not isn't the issue here. It's against the law for you to hit her.'

'Look, no school teacher is going to tell me how to behave with my own stepdaughter.' The man's voice had risen to an insane bellow and curious heads were turning all over the car park. His shoulders had hunched dangerously forward. There was spittle on his lips as he watched Niall for a reaction, every muscle in his body tensed for a fight. 'Do you understand what I'm saying?'

Keely screamed suddenly, covering her face with her hands. 'Shut up, both of you. Shut up. Shut up.'

Out of the corner of his eye, Niall caught a flurry of activity and cautiously risked a glance in that direction, unwilling to take his eyes off Keely's stepfather for long in case the bastard lunged for him. But he felt a sense of profound relief when he saw what was happening.

There were two security guards approaching them at a trot from the lifts. One of them was speaking into the crackle of a walkie-talkie as he ran, the other man in uniform was holding up his hand to wave back a worried-looking pensioner. It was obvious that their argument must have been reported by one of the other shoppers, or spotted on the CCTV monitors by the car park security officers.

It was over.

'Get in the car, Kee.' It was her stepfather's harsh voice. Niall looked back too late to stop her. Helped along by one ruthless hand, Keely was climbing hurriedly into the passenger seat, her expression hidden by the dishevelled blonde hair.

Her stepfather strolled forward as the guards approached, shaking his head at them and laughing, his face suddenly relaxed and friendly. 'Excitement's over, lads. Sorry you had to be called out for nothing. We had a bit of a blow-out, it's true, but there's no hard feelings now. It was just a misunderstanding between friends.'

'What happened?' the taller guard demanded.

Niall tried to contain his anger. 'Look, this man hit his stepdaughter because she didn't want to go home with him. I was just pointing out that what he was doing was illegal.'

The two guards exchanged wary glances. It was obvious that they didn't fancy getting embroiled in some sort of domestic dispute.

'Is that right?' one of the guards asked Keely's stepfather, giving him a hard stare.

'Absolutely not. I don't know what this bloke thinks he saw, but I never laid a finger on my little girl. I might have raised my voice, yeah, but that's all. And you can hardly blame me for that. You know what kids are like, a right bloody handful. Enough to drive a saint up the wall.'

Guessing from the guards' expressions that they were reluctant to pursue the matter anymore, Niall tried desperately to decide what was for the best. Head bent and hands in her lap, Keely's face was obscured by the smoky glass windows of the BMW. Should he let the bastard take Keely away unchallenged, to suffer God knows what punishment once he got her home, or would it only antagonise the situation further if he continued to argue? He wasn't going to win today, that was obvious enough. Everything was against him here.

'All right, all right,' Niall muttered, backing off as the guards closed in. 'Don't worry, I'm going.'

Slamming the door on Keely and moving round to the driver's door, her stepfather glanced back at him across the bonnet of the old BMW. There was a mixture of triumph and hatred in his face, but the larger man didn't say another word. As the security guards headed back towards the lifts, he lifted one finger and pointed it deliberately at Niall's chest.

When her stepfather lifted that finger to his lips a second later and blew softly, Niall suddenly understood what the gesture was meant to represent.

CHAPTER ELEVEN

'Where did you swipe that lot from?'

'Jesus!' Keely nearly dropped her paint brush, she was so surprised to see her cousin standing in the dark doorway to the living room. 'Don't sneak up on us like that, Jess. I nearly had a heart attack.'

'It's not my fault you didn't hear us come in. You were in a world of your own as usual.'

Keely stepped back from the wall and stared up at her work in the dim candlelight, wiping sticky fingers on the backside of her oldest jeans. The smell of the different paints was so strong in the squat now, they could almost get high every time they inhaled. She felt a bit pukey, but these days anything made her feel sick. It wasn't perfect, what she'd managed to do so far across the walls, but it was miles better than the faded wallpaper she'd seen on her first visit to the squat. 'What do you think, Jess?'

'Bloody hell.'

Keely looked at her anxiously. 'You don't like it?'

'What exactly is it meant to be?'

'Nothing special. Colours and patterns. Whatever I felt like doing at the time. It's not brilliant, but it's better than what was there before.'

'What's that?' Jess stepped further in through the candlelight and pointed at the darkest swirls of paint, up in the left-hand corner. 'It's horrible. It looks like someone being sick.'

'Dunno.'

'But you painted it.'

'I told you, none of it means anything special.'

'Bollocks.' Jess came nearer and stared up at the patterns nearest the window frame and ceiling, where huge red and orange clouds of paint drifted into each other and turned to flame. 'That's got to be a fucking dragon. Look, there's its tail and its head, and that's definitely fire coming out of its mouth. Don't tell me you didn't draw that deliberately like a dragon.'

'Did you bring us a drink?'

'Yeah, but don't open it yet in case it sprays you. It got a bit shook up on the way home. I had to run for the bus again.' Her cousin handed Keely a can of Diet Coke and sat down cross-legged on the floor behind her, dragging her short sequinned skirt forward to hide the flash of knickers underneath. Jess must have been out on the town again. Her face was still shiny with make-up, mascara caught in those tiny creases under her eyes. 'Do you really enjoy doing stuff like this?'

'Being here with you?'

'Like painting the bloody walls, stupid!'

'Yeah, I guess so.'

'Perhaps you ought to take it more serious, like.'

Keely opened the drink can away from her body, letting the soft foam fizz out and over the lip before taking a sip. 'What do you mean?'

'You could become, I don't know, a proper artist or something. Be famous for doing strange things to peoples' walls. Paintings that aren't dragons. Shit, I don't know what I'm talking about. But if you can keep on doing stuff like that, you might be able to get out of this place before it fucks you up.'

She laughed. 'I'm only messing about.'

'It looks good to me.'

Keely turned and stared slowly up at the living room wall again. It was hard to see by the light of only one candle, but the dimness suited what she'd done. Her cousin was right. The dark little room of the squat seemed stranger than ever now, covered in swirling patterns of colour that crawled and leapt over the walls. Sometimes the brush seemed to move in its own strong circles and lines, she had so little control over it. Other times, she knew exactly what she wanted but the painting wouldn't come right, or it ended up looking completely different from the original idea in her head.

But that didn't seem to matter. As long as the whole thing came alive and danced on the wall. That was what she wanted.

'You said you might come and live with us soon,' Jess said in a small persuasive voice. 'Have you thought anymore about that? It gets so dark and spooky here some nights, all on my own. I miss you.'

'What about Eddy?'

'He's always working.' Jess made a face. 'Zal's got him doing all sorts of shit down at the club these days.'

'I can't leave my mam.'

'She doesn't need you. She's got him now.'

Keely looked away. 'He hits her sometimes when he's pissed.'

'That sort always do.'

'She doesn't think I know.'

'But we could share the bedroom here, babes. It'd be fun, just like when we were kids growing up together. Remember Skegness?'

'No,' Keely lied.

'Come on, that filthy old caravan by the sea? We had a right laugh that summer. I remember your mam threw a fit on the dance floor once and we had to go back to the caravan early. You were dead upset. It was so hot that night we slept with nothing on.'

There was a sudden memory of thick salt air and heat and somebody pressing against her in the darkness. Keely didn't want to listen to her cousin anymore. She was feeling sick again, only this time it was stronger than ever before. There was something hurting low down in her belly, a dragging sensation like she might be going to bleed soon. But she hadn't bled for weeks now. The candle flame dipped and danced crazily as she took a step back from the wall. Above her head, black and purple swirls shuddered and crawled over the walls like giant lizards with their tongues leering out.

'I can't move in with you yet.' Keely tried not to look at that part of the wall again. There was one dark threatening eye at the centre and it seemed to be watching her. 'Not yet, Jess.'

'All right, settle down everyone,' Mr Swainson was saying, clapping his hands. But the art room was buzzing as everyone walked round the long table, looking at the materials for their collage project. Bronze foil, velvet squares, dried grasses, seashells, swatches of soft fabric, flower heads, gold paint. He raised his voice irritably. 'I said, settle down.'

Tracey had come into class late as usual. She was tying her hair back, chatting to her cronies on the other side of the room. Keely knew they must be talking about her, because Tracey kept looking in her direction and smirking. It was obvious why. Tracey hadn't forgotten about their argument outside the science labs. But Keely didn't really care what she was planning in revenge. None of that shit was important.

'Choose your materials from the table and remember that whatever you use should reflect your theme. That means thinking about texture and shape as well as colour. So don't just go for what looks prettiest. Think carefully about the theme of your collage before choosing. This will count towards your final mark.'

Her eye caught by its pearly surface, Keely picked up one of the larger shells and held it to her ear. There was a distant rushing noise like the sea dragging itself up the beach at Skegness. She wanted to take it for her collage but she'd chosen to make a kingfisher so she put the shell down, fingering the multi-coloured velvet squares instead. She could cut them into strips for the feathers, shimmering reds and greens and blues. They'd look great across its wings and you could stroke them too as if it was a real kingfisher. Mr Swainson had said they ought to think about things like that. How to make their collage interactive.

It was raining hard that afternoon, a constant drumming on the roof and windows. Keely liked rain. She didn't mind getting wet, like other people seemed to do. Always running everywhere, holding umbrellas up in case it touched them. They said it was acid from the pollution, though it didn't taste like anything but rain when she put her head back on the streets and let it fall experimentally onto her tongue. She tried to imagine it eating away at her, like it was eating away at the streets and cars and buildings. But she didn't believe it could be acid. Rain was too clean for that.

The white walls of the art room were flushed now with that soft orange light, patches of shadow thrown up and flickering as it poured down. If she'd been alone in the art room, she would have been deep inside one of those shells, listening to the sea outside. But everyone was talking at once, shoving her aside and grabbing pieces from the table. They didn't care about things like that. The bag of mirrored mosaic tiles split and the pieces poured out glittering into the collection of dried grass heads.

Tracey slid past her, hissing. 'You think you got away with it, don't you? But I'm going to make you sorry.'

'You're full of shit, Tracey.'

'Well, you're nothing. Do you know that? Fucking nothing.'

Keely clenched her fist on the square of velvet. Mr Swainson was looking the other way, he hadn't even seen Tracey come up to her. She wanted to shout out, push her away, but that was what Tracey was after. Anything so she could point the finger and say Keely was in the wrong this time. She tried to calm herself down instead, slowly relaxing her fingers and watching the bruised velvet spring back into shape. 'I'm not interested, Trace. I'm not listening to you.'

'That's because you know I'm right.' Tracey was right behind her now, pressing Keely against the table. She could feel the wooden frame bite painfully into her thighs. 'You're less than nothing.'

'Go away.'

Mr Swainson had still not turned round. He was wearing his old blue shirt today, the one with the frayed cuffs. His hips were so skinny, the faded jeans were nearly dropping off his backside. But Keely loved the way he moved. He was like a dancer. Every movement he made seemed graceful and precise. Yet he was clumsy too, sometimes even knocking his coffee over while he was working at his desk, though he usually caught the mug just before it broke. It was strange how anyone could be both graceful and clumsy at the same time.

'Look at him, he isn't interested. Why would he want an ugly little bitch like you? I bet you're still a virgin, aren't you?'

'Shut it.'

Kicker was standing beside Tracey now, grinning at their conversation. He didn't say anything, but he made a hole with one fist and rammed his finger brutally in and out of it, watching for Keely's reaction. She looked away again, her face reddening.

Tracey laughed, nudging Kicker. 'See, I knew she was a virgin! And your mam's a right slut too, you ought to have lost it by now, what with all the punters she must bring home.'

Keely said nothing this time.

'Of course, you know why you're still a virgin, don't you?' Wrinkling her nose up, Tracey sniffed the air maliciously. 'Coz you ming like dog shit, that's why.'

Everyone around them was laughing now, watching Keely's face as she stood with her thighs and stomach pressed up against the table. One of the dried flower heads snapped under her fingers. She stared down at it blindly. The pots of glue, pencils, scissors, oil pastels, coloured chalks were all glistening now. She could tiny crooked fragments of herself reflected in the mirrored mosaic tiles spilling out of their plastic bag. They were like hundreds of frozen eyes scattered across the table.

She felt dizzy suddenly and her head was aching. The room had darkened to a thick cloud inside. The rain was almost deafening on the windows. It was a deep rumble like thunder coming nearer.

Keely stared helplessly across the room, but Mr Swainson was still looking in the opposite direction, helping some of the other kids shift their desks to make room for floor work. Shelly was asking him something. He was listening to her while carrying a pair of chairs across to the window, shirt sleeves rolled up to his elbows. Keely desperately wanted him to turn around.

Kicker was laughing stupidly right behind her. She hated his high-pitched laughter, he sounded like a girl. 'Dog shit, dog shit!' he started repeating. 'Dog shit, dog shit, dog shit!'

'Isn't lover-boy looking at you? What a fucking shame.' Tracey thought she'd won. It was in her voice, low and gloating. 'He'd probably rather step in you than shag you. Take a look in the mirror some day, Kee. You're a right troll.'

There was a sudden flash, almost like a bolt of lightning. It seemed to blaze across the whole art room.

Keely turned, raising her arm against her eyes. Tracey was screaming and everyone was clutching at Keely. One lad bent her arm painfully behind her back, and for a moment she thought it was going to break. It was Kicker holding her. They struggled together in the shouting. There was a terrible clatter as seashells and bronze foil and piles of spray cans fell to the floor. Then she managed to pull free of him at last, heaving herself away with a huge effort.

Everything was blurred and on edge. Her body felt strange and disconnected, like it belonged to somebody else. Keely walked slowly towards the door through a narrowing tunnel of desks.

'Keely?' Mr Swainson's voice was somewhere behind her, but she wasn't going to look back. Not even for him. 'Keely?'

'What do you mean, she's vanished?'

'I'm sorry, Jim. I wasn't on the ball quick enough.' Niall bent over coughing, hands on knees, still trying to catch his breath. 'She can't be on the school premises, we've looked everywhere. Even checked all the toilet cubicles and the girls' changing rooms.'

'Not you, I hope?'

Niall shook his head. 'Jane Southwell gave me a hand.'

'Well, to be honest, I don't understand how you could let a pupil do something like that right under your nose, and then just disappear into thin air. If you ask me, the girl's a bloody psychopath and ought to be locked up.'

It was typical of MacFerson to take that attitude. He seemed to expect Niall to be superhuman. What should he have done then? Left Tracey bleeding on the floor of the art room while he raced after Keely and caught her single-handed?

He'd done quite well to keep things under control as it was. Kids screaming all over the place, Tracey making as much fuss as possible about the blood on her shoulder, and Kicker standing on one of the desks, yelling threats at the top of his lungs and brandishing the scissors he'd taken from Keely.

It had taken a good fifteen minutes to restore order, take the scissors away from Kicker, and get Tracey taken down to the school nurse. Not an experience he ever wanted to repeat.

Niall straightened, looking MacFerson in the eye. 'She must have got out the main gate while I was looking after Tracey and basically trying to calm things down. She left that room in complete chaos, Jim. The kids are calling her a psycho.'

'Is the other girl hurt?'

'Only a scratch on her shoulder, it looks worse than it really is. But the nurse is checking her over, just in case.' They were in the head's office and the door was closed. There was nothing more to do for the moment but wait. Niall allowed himself to slump into the chair opposite MacFerson's desk. His hands were shaking and he felt bloody awful. What he needed was a large glass of whisky, but that would probably be many hours away. 'One of the lads managed to get the scissors off her before anything worse could happen, thank God.'

'I've called the police. They're on their way.'

Niall closed his eyes. Keely would be utterly terrified to be facing a police interrogation. This was probably his fault, at the end of the day. He'd known there was trouble brewing between her and Tracey, but it had never occurred to him that she would do something this crazy. The only good thing was that no one had been badly hurt. 'I suppose police involvement is absolutely unavoidable?'

'One of our students has been attacked with a pair of scissors. And in your classroom, I might remind you. Yes, in my professional opinion, I would suggest that police involvement is bloody unavoidable.' MacFerson was staring at him aggressively. 'If you'd kept a closer eye on this 'psycho', it might not have turned out quite so badly for the school.'

Niall held his breath for a moment. 'She's not a psycho, Jim.'

'But you just said – '

'That's what the other kids are calling her. I didn't describe her as a psycho.' Niall leant forward, touching the tips of his fingers together to try and stop them trembling. 'I think Keely needs psychiatric help, yes. But I also consider it our duty to give her the benefit of the doubt here.'

'Meaning what?'

'That attack didn't come out of nowhere.'

'Problems at home?'

'I think it's more complex than that.'

'I'm not so sure.' MacFerson shook his head, leaning back in his chair. 'I've had a lot of experience with kids like this, and I'm afraid it sounds to me like she's just a born trouble-maker. We should have done something more decisive after that incident outside the science labs.'

'Tracey's no innocent. She's a fairly nasty piece of work herself.'

'But has she ever physically attacked anyone?'

'With respect, Jim, that's not the issue here.' But Niall knew it probably was. He was wasting his time, trying to defend Keely after this latest trouble. As far as MacFerson was concerned, the poor kid was going to be drummed out of his school for good and that would be an end to the problem. He'd always taken a tough line with repeat offenders. There was no reason to imagine he could be persuaded into leniency now, but Niall pressed on stubbornly. 'Tracey's a verbal bully, not a physical one. And she's been at Keely for weeks. I did speak to you about this, but it was dropped.'

'I can't follow up every complaint. That's what Heads of Department and Year are for. You should have liaised with Frances and Tony about this if you still had suspicions, kept the ball rolling on your own.'

'Okay, fair enough.' Niall bit back his anger. 'Have the parents been informed?'

'Angela spoke to Keely's mother about ten minutes ago. She's coming straight in. No word yet about her stepfather.'

'And Tracey's parents?'

MacFerson looked grim. 'On their way in. Her father was absolutely raving on the phone, I shudder to think what would have happened if the girl had been seriously hurt. They may yet press charges for assault.'

'Christ, what a day.' Niall put his head in his hands, suddenly exhausted. 'Keely seemed to be really improving, you know? Working hard on her art projects, keeping out of trouble. It's so hard, when you've got no idea what they're facing outside school hours and no way of finding out. I know this probably sounds stupid, but I feel like I've failed the kid.'

'That's a natural reaction. But it's not your fault.'

'I should have noticed.'

'You're not a psychologist, Niall. None of us are. That's not our job. We're not here to look after social misfits, whatever problems they may be having outside school. We're here to teach. End of story. And Keely's not coming back here, not after this latest escapade. You were bloody lucky today, Niall. Don't forget that in your heroic rush to champion this girl.'

With obvious impatience, MacFerson picked up the telephone and began dialling.

'Permanent exclusion. That's the only possible response to this attack. If you expect me to go down a different path, Niall, you'll be disappointed.'

In the staff car park, Niall leant against the bonnet of his car and lit up a cigarette. His hands were still shaking.

Five seconds and his whole world had turned to shite.

If Kicker hadn't got those scissors away from Keely so quickly, Tracey might have been dead or seriously wounded. Whatever MacFerson said, it was still going to be him at the epicentre once the investigation got underway. He'd been in charge of that class. If there was any finger-pointing to be done, and he had seen it happen before with other teachers, it was going to be in his direction. Not without reason, either.

He'd been too slow to react, still staring open-mouthed like the others while Keely was doing her Norman Bates impersonation with the scissors. Nothing short of professional incompetence.

It had only recently stopped raining. His jacket and trousers were damp from leaning on the car bonnet.

Niall straightened up, taking another drag on his cigarette. He never used to hit the nicotine this heavily. It was the job. It must be getting to him. Not for the first time, he thought about getting out of teaching. Starting a new life somewhere as a used car salesman or a supermarket shelf-stacker. Anything rather than face that lot again. The daily hell that only led to scenes like that with the scissors.

'Fuck it.'

He wasn't proud of himself. He'd known there was something wrong with Keely months ago, but he hadn't pursued it properly, hadn't asked the right questions. Too busy thinking about his own problems as usual.

A taxi pulled up just outside the school gates and a woman hurriedly climbed out. This was probably Keely's mother. The short red leather skirt and high heels matched what he knew of the woman. At that distance, she looked to be in her early thirties, maybe younger. Straight blonde hair to her shoulders, almost an exact colour match with Keely's. Firm tanned legs, though her ankles were a little thick for his tastes.

Then the woman turned, hurrying through the school gates, and he saw her large tits bouncing under the white blouse. The jacket disguised the outline slightly, but he was fairly certain she wasn't wearing a bra.

He stepped forward nervously, grinding out his cigarette underfoot. 'Mrs Down?'

'You one of the teachers?' she asked sharply. There was a flustered note to her voice as she looked him up and down, assessingly, as a woman looks at a man when she's deciding which of her services he can afford. He noticed that she didn't look impressed. His faded shirt and creased trousers wouldn't hold out much promise.

'I'm Niall Swainson, the art teacher.' He held out his hand in welcome. 'We haven't met before, but I was in charge of the class when Keely – '

'Fucking hell,' she gasped, putting a hand to her mouth.

Niall stared at her. 'Are you okay?'

'Fuck me. Oh Jesus.'

He could see she was shocked by something, but he was at a complete loss to understand why. Perhaps the woman hadn't properly understood the seriousness of her daughter's situation until now.

'Do you need to sit down for a minute? There's a bench over there.'

She laughed wildly. 'You don't remember me, do you?'

'Mrs Down?'

'It's Anne.' Keely's mother stared up at him, leaning forward now, and with a shock to his stomach Niall suddenly realised who she was. 'Come on, you can't have forgotten when we met. It was my hen night. We were both very drunk.' She giggled, suddenly like a teenager herself. 'There was a bit of a misunderstanding and you came off worst.'

Anne?

For a moment, Niall couldn't say a word. He just stared at her like an idiot, slowly recognising the girl he had known behind the heavy make-up, the crow's feet around her eyes, and the perfume of dyed hair. She hadn't actually changed that much. There was still that air of cheapness about her, the way she deliberately tottered on heels that were too high for her. It was done for effect. The automatic smile when a man looked in her direction, turned on like a sensor. She knew how to get what she wanted.

She was laughing now, covering her mouth with her hand. 'I don't believe this. She kept saying her art teacher was called Mr Swainson, and I thought it was dead funny. But I never realised. Honest to God, I never clicked it was you.'

Getting her breath back, Keely waited on the corner opposite her mam's house for ten minutes before deciding it was safe to go inside. There seemed to be no sign of movement behind the net curtains and Zal's car had gone from its usual place. She hurried across the road, hoping none of the nosy neighbours had spotted her, then gingerly turned her key in the lock and stopped to listen.

Inside the house, she could hear nothing but silence. They must both be out, Keely realised, slipping quietly into the hall and closing the front door with a click. Now that she was out of sight of the street, her whole body sagged with relief.

Her heart thudding slightly from the exertion of running all the way home from school, Keely crept upstairs and paused outside her bedroom. To her surprise, the door was ajar. Warily, her nerves jumping, she pushed the door slowly open as if expecting to see someone in there, waiting for her to return. But her bedroom was empty. Maybe she'd left it open by mistake when she went out that morning. Or maybe her mam had been in to check for dirty clothes or something before going out. Her mam still did that sometimes, when she was in a good mood. Which wasn't often.

She dragged her old sports bag out from under the bed and unzipped it. It had plenty of room for what she needed to take: a couple of pairs of jeans, some tee-shirts and jumpers, knickers, socks, tights, and a few of her best clubbing outfits. Rolled up into balls and squeezed into the corners of the sports bag, her smallest skirts and tops wouldn't take up a lot of room. Anyhow, she couldn't carry much more than that. Earrings, her usual make-up, favourite necklace and rings. A handful of CDs, though there wasn't much point as Jess didn't have a CD player and she couldn't really take her mam's. Her bunny rabbit, who always lived under her pillow. Keely wasn't giving him up for the world.

The gold-coloured carriage clock her real dad had given her a few Christmases ago, before he stopped seeing her for good, went into the bag last. That was it then. No more room in the sports bag, except for a bottle of shampoo and some soap in the side pocket.

Keely was just slipping into her warmest jacket when she heard a key in the front door. But was it him or her mam?

Her blood seemed to have frozen in her body as Keely stood there in silence, hardly daring to breathe, and waited for footsteps in the hall so she could identify which of them had come home.

While she waited, her mind clicked desperately through the possible ways of escape. There was the window in her bedroom, but it was a sheer drop to the front garden and she'd probably break her leg. Then there was the bathroom window, dropping onto a flat roof and away across the back gardens until she hit the main road again. Or she might have to try running straight down the stairs and out of the front door before they had even realised she was in the house. But if they weren't going to be long, she might be able to just hide in her room until they had gone out again. That was the easiest option by far.

It was him. She could have recognised those footsteps anyway. Heavy and irritable, they went down the hall without bothering to close the front door. Then they stopped for a minute in the kitchen, where she heard a few cupboards opening and closing. Then the footsteps came back out into the hallway, paused at the bottom of the stairs as if listening, and then slowly began to climb the stairs to the landing.

Keely didn't know what to do. She stood motionless as the footsteps came closer and closer. It was the end of the world. She'd crammed all her clothes into this old sports bag so that it was bloody obvious she was running away from home, and he was coming upstairs.

'Why the hell aren't you at school?'

Zal stood there on the landing and stared at her, completely filling the doorway so that she had no hope of escape. He was wearing his big leather jacket that creaked as he walked and always smelt of smoke. She couldn't look at his face, because she hated his eyes. Instead, Keely lowered her head to look down at his shoes, the dark shiny leather which meant he'd been out doing business that morning. His shoes were both slightly damp around the toes from the wet weather outside.

He came straight into the bedroom without waiting for an answer. Her sports bag still lay open on the bed, bulging with clothes and make-up and jewellery. Watching her face, he deliberately dragged out a couple of her tee-shirts and chucked them on the floor. 'What's this about, Kee? You unhappy here? You planning on leaving us?'

She was scared but she didn't like him laughing at her. 'You know what this is about.'

'What, your little secret?'

Zal reached into the inside pocket of his leather jacket and pulled out a used pregnancy testing dipstick. He held it up for a second to make sure she recognised what it was, then threw it onto the bed in front of her. The little blue line across the results window stared back at her.

'Now come on, doll. You can tell your stepdad. Have you gone and got yourself up the duff?'

For a few seconds, Keely didn't understand how he

had found it. She took a step backwards, feeling suddenly sick and off-balance. Then it clicked. He must have stolen it out of her wastepaper bin. That was why her bedroom door had been open when she got into the house. He had gone into her room that morning after she'd left for school, and looked through her things, even stole stuff out of her bin like the dirty pervert he was. Perhaps he did that every day. It made her skin creep just thinking about it.

'You bastard,' she whispered.

'You don't have to worry, love.' He was smiling now, almost as if he was proud of himself. 'These things happen. It can be sorted.'

'I hate you.'

'Don't be soft, Kee. No one else is going to help you.'

He had put out a hand and she slapped it away. 'Don't touch me, you freak. I'm never going to let you touch me again.'

'You're not thinking straight.'

'I'm leaving.'

'Put those clothes back in the drawers,' he said sharply.

'You can't make me!'

He was suddenly angry. 'Now don't piss me about, Keely. You're not going anywhere, so you can do what you're told and empty that bag before I smack you one.' He took a step closer. 'You belong here, Kee. I know you're a big girl now, all turned eighteen and itching to leave home. But I'm still your dad and this is still your home.'

'You'll never be my dad!'

He smacked her round the face. Keely fell sideways like a doll, hitting her head on the bedside cabinet. Her ears were ringing with the blow. The open sports bag tipped onto the floor at his feet, make-up and jewellery scattering across the carpet.

Before Keely could even get her breath back, Zal was kneeling beside her. The brutal hands pushed her school skirt up to her waist and dragged her knickers down to her ankles. The cold air was a shock on her skin. She realised what he was planning to do and began to struggle instinctively against him, crying out for help as if someone in the street might hear her. But he was too strong to be stopped. He was already pinning her arms down with his knees as he unzipped his jeans.

'Shut your mouth.' His face was dark red. 'You're an ungrateful little bitch, Keely, do you know that? When I think of all the things I've done for you and your mam over the years. I've even said I'll help you get rid of it. Most girls would be pleased. But you're getting what you deserve now.'

Suddenly, he was crushing her chest. She couldn't breathe properly anymore, let alone cry out. He had shifted position, and she could feel his fingers scrabbling painfully between her thighs for the right place. She kept them closed for as long as possible, but he was so clever at getting round that sort of problem. She felt his legs squeeze in between hers and slowly force them apart. Her hands had been pinned together above her head. She tried pushing upwards, but his body was too heavy to lift.

She bit viciously into his shoulder as he lay above her. His gasp of pain was satisfying, then there was another dull crack across her cheekbone and blackness spun in front of her eyes.

'Keep still or you'll get the belt.'

Dizzy and sick, the side of her face stinging badly, Keely tried to focus on the bedroom ceiling beyond his shoulder. He was deliberately making it hurt worse than usual. There were little whimpering noises coming from her throat, but she decided to ignore them. It was too late. There was no point crying now. She shouldn't have argued with him. She should have run as soon as she heard his key in the lock. It was her fault again.

He had sunk his face right down into the side of her neck and was fumbling with his clothes. Keely lay very still beneath him, her body aching with the strain of trying to stop him. His breath was hot against her skin. She knew what was coming next and relaxed. He must have felt the change in her body because he suddenly stopped gripping her wrists.

'Good girl,' Zal muttered, kissing her neck. 'That's much better.'

From the corner of her eye, Keely could see the glinting edge of the carriage clock peeping out of her sports bag. She let her arm flop sideways towards it but he wasn't interested in what she was doing. He had his eyes closed now and was breathing hard. With her fingers stretched right out, she could almost touch the hard goldish surround of the clock face.

Keely's fingers closed around the carriage clock at last and lifted it out of the sports bag like a trophy.

CHAPTER TWELVE

It was close to dusk. Niall drove Anne back to her house through the grey, miserable streets, eyes fixed straight ahead while she chattered beside him. She seemed to have no idea of the impact she was having on him. His knuckles showed white against the steering wheel. He nearly went through a red light twice, having to brake at the last minute, throwing them both hard against their seatbelts.

'Sorry,' he muttered on the second occasion. She must think him a complete fool. 'I didn't notice the lights had changed.'

'That's all right. I can't drive anyway.'

He risked a glance at her. 'I've seen Keely out in a car once or twice. A black BMW, I think.'

'Oh that belongs to Zal. He's her stepdad now. Malcolm and me didn't last too long.' Anne laughed, nudging him. Niall could see her teeth shining in the dark car interior. 'No surprise there, though. I wasn't a very good girl in those days, was I? I don't do that sort of stuff anymore. Well, not unless it's a special favour for someone. You know how it is. There's always someone who thinks you owe them.'

'You happy with Zal?'

'Oh, he's not perfect. But he looks after us both. You

know, pays the mortgage and buys Keely all them nice new clothes she has. Not that she's grateful for it, silly little cow. I've had some run-ins with her over the years, I can tell you. Keely and that cousin of hers, they're a right pair for trouble. Kids these days, they don't want to work and they don't respect people who do. Zal may not be the world's best dad, but he puts food on the bloody table, day in, day out. But she's not interested in any of that, no. Plays us up all the time, telling lies or pulling some stunt or other.'

Niall stared ahead grimly through the dusk. Ask the question, he kept repeating to himself. Ask the fucking question.

But whenever he drew breath to ask her, his lips wouldn't move properly. For years he had wondered. He had lost that night in the painful aftermath, and he had always wondered. But now here she was sitting next to him, chattering blithely on about her daughter and the evil bastard of a stepfather that she had given the poor child, and he couldn't make his mouth form the correct words. But how could he put it?

He listened to her high-pitched voice rambling beside him, the endless stream of her inanity, and he just wanted to scream at the woman to shut up.

Oblivious to his thoughts, Anne directed him to a small mid-terrace house down one of the endless gloomy side streets that seemed to warren their way through West Newcastle.

'Here we are,' she said cheerfully, picking up her handbag. 'Looks like somebody's home. The lights are on in the hall.'

Niall didn't move, gripping the wheel hard in an attempt to keep control of his feelings. He couldn't let her get out without at least trying to find out the truth. It would be agony to watch her disappear back into her world again and still be none the wiser. 'Hang on a minute. I'm sorry, but there's something I really need to ask you.'

'About Keely?'

That was more straightforward than he had expected. Niall turned his head and looked at her properly for the first time. But in the shadowy interior of the car, it was almost impossible to make out whether or not she was smiling.

'Is she mine?'

She shot him a shrewd glance. 'Is that what you think?'

'I'd like to know the truth.'

'What difference would it make after all these years?'

'Is she my bloody daughter or not?'

The front door to her house jerked open and a large olive-skinned man came staggering out like a drunk, clutching the side of his head. Niall recognised him instantly from the incident at the shopping centre car park.

It was Keely's stepfather.

There was blood pouring in a sticky stream down the man's face and neck as he lurched blindly over the front step and fell sideways onto the pavement. His hand reached out and slammed against Niall's window for a second, leaving behind a thickly smeared blood stain in the shape of the man's five spread fingers.

The voice was muffled but clear enough for them to understand what he was saying. 'Get out the car, Anne. Look what your kid's done to me!'

'Jesus Christ.' Anne fumbled for the door handle, screaming as she ran round to help him back to his feet. 'Who did it? Who hit you? Oh my god, what's happened to your face?'

Niall got out of the car as well, closing his door with a deceptively calm expression. He glanced up and down the street, sensing the neighbours' eyes on his back. His heart was thudding erratically, which wasn't exactly surprising. Things were steadily getting beyond him. He was beginning to lose the plot and he didn't know how to get it back. Keely had flipped out for no reason and gone at

Tracey with the scissors. Then Anne had turned up in his life again out of nowhere and left him reeling.

Now Keely's stepdad was swaying and slamming against his car, half blinded by the blood running down his face which presumably had something to do with Keely. His grip on reality was slipping. Niall wasn't sure where he was anymore, or what was going to happen next. Most urgent of all, he was burningly aware that Anne hadn't even had time to reply to his question yet. It was still out there, waiting to be answered, hanging above them in the cold November air like an invisible sword.

'It was Keely,' the man managed to say, collapsing into a sitting position on the front step and clutching an open wound running across his forehead. 'Christ's sake, she could have killed us. Look at me, I'm covered in blood. The kid must be out of her fucking mind.'

'Sit still. Don't try to talk.'

'The vicious little bitch has run off somewhere. I've got to catch her, don't you understand?'

Anne had snatched a tissue out of her handbag and was ineffectively dabbing at his wound with it. The tissue was soon sodden with blood. She stared up at Niall desperately. 'We've got to get him in the car. Look, he's losing loads of blood. You'll have to drive him to the hospital.'

'Of course.'

'I'm fine, stop fussing over me. I'm not bloody going to hospital, so you can forget that for a start. She's not killed me. It's nothing a couple of stiff whiskies won't cure.' The man shook her away like a dog, frowning over her shoulder at Niall. His voice grew suddenly aggressive. 'And who's this bloke you're with? I've seen him somewhere before.'

'It's one of Keely's teachers, pet.'

But the man had got lumberingly to his feet, pushing past his wife and swinging out at Niall. 'I know your face. You're that fucking know-it-all bastard from the car park. I should have decked you there and then, but since you're here now...'

Swinging to one side, Niall dodged the blow easily. The man was almost blind from the blood running down past his eyes and he seemed to have lost normal co-ordination. He was swaying all over the place like a drunkard and didn't have a hope of making contact with these punches.

Niall stepped back, loathing the man for what he was obviously doing to Keely with this behaviour, but unable to retaliate in the way he would have liked. For as far as the police would be concerned, this school girl was none of his business. Niall had no place in this situation and was merely getting in the way. For all he knew, he was probably making it worse for Keely by provoking her stepfather.

'I think you'd better call an ambulance instead,' Niall murmured to Anne.

'I told you, I'm not going to no fucking hospital.' The man swore under his breath, wiping fresh blood out of his eyes. 'It's only a scratch. I can deal with this myself, so why don't you just fuck off back where you came from, teacher, and leave us alone?'

'Christ, let go!' Anne screamed as the man yanked hard on her hair, dragging her back up the front step into the house.

The door slammed in Niall's face as he tried in vain to follow her, and he heard the bolt shoot across inside to lock the door. Breathless, he shouted and hammered on their door for several minutes but there was no reply. He couldn't even hear shouting from inside the house.

Reeling back onto the pavement in defeat, Niall realised that some of the neighbours had come out on their front steps to watch. But he noticed that none of them were offering to help, and they were probably right to keep out of it. Much as Niall would have liked to call the police, there was nothing more he could do here. He had already over-stepped his responsibilities as a teacher and he didn't want to draw any more attention to himself. It wouldn't do the girl any good.

Net curtains were twitching across the street, and more than one curious face peered out as he silently got back into his car and turned his key in the ignition with trembling hands. He had no idea what he was going to do with this information. All he wanted to do at the moment was escape from the impossible chaos in his own mind. But at least he didn't need to wonder anymore how the girl could have grown up so violent, he thought grimly. Keely might be his natural daughter, but that evil bastard in there was probably more her father than Niall could ever hope to be.

As he drove slowly back to his flat, Niall realised with a sinking feeling that there was ice on the roads. The temperature on the streets of Newcastle must have dropped past zero.

Where had Keely gone to ground? Where could she be hiding?

The narrow red brick yard to the squat was dull as ever, concrete slippery underfoot with invisible ice. The wooden back gate squeaked and sagged off its hinges as she pushed it open. Kids must have been messing around with it again. The ancient-looking mattress leaning against the inside wall had only just arrived, a busted spring corkscrewing out of its middle like some sort of bizarre metal intestine.

The other day she'd seen council workmen in their orange coats with their yellow spray cans, moving up and down like bees along the two rows of houses. They were writing GAS OFF next to each front door. Keely had stood there for a moment, watching them, chronic with laughter. Then she had slunk out of sight down the alleyway and let herself into the house through the loose board at the back. Jess hadn't seen the funny side, but Keely thought it was bloody hilarious. Council graffiti aimed at the invisible army of squatters, and not a single one of them paying any attention.

Keely slipped silently into the squat. The empty rooms were ice-cold and dark, all the windows being boarded up except for the kitchen. So she decided to stay in that room for a bit, while it was still light outside and she could save on candles. She poured herself a small cup of metallic-tasting water, crunching quietly around the dirty kitchen lino in her trainers. Her head was still spinning from what had happened, but she didn't want to think about that. There was nothing she could do to change it, so it was best just to try and blot it out.

There was a taste of sick in her mouth and throat and Keely wanted to get rid of it. She took the bag of skunk and the Rizla papers out of her jeans pocket and laid them together on the kitchen table. Inside the bag, the skunk looked like little green rubbery bits of carpet underlay but when she opened it, there was that familiar strong sweet smell.

Fishing around in the kitchen drawers for a packet of ciggies, Keely eventually found an old packet of Regal King Size with two left inside. She sat down at the table and opened the packet, not entirely certain what to do but needing to stay occupied and busy so as her mind wouldn't keep returning to that bad thing.

It didn't look like there was going to be enough gear in there for a proper spliff, so Keely put more skunk in, sprinkling it on top of the tobacco like little green droppings, then picked the whole thing up in both hands like a corn on the cob.

She wasn't used to rolling and her fingers stung with the cold. The first thin Rizla paper split and she had to use another one, tipping the narrow little cylinder of gear and tobacco out onto the new paper and starting again. This time it rolled okay because Keely nearly had the hang of it now.

She licked the gum and sealed it all the way along, then did that twist thing at the top between thumb and finger. Remembering at the last minute, she tore a little strip off the Rizla packet and made a roach. It wouldn't fit in for ages and she thought maybe she should have put it in first and then rolled around it, but it was too late for that.

Then suddenly it went in, sweet as a nut. After admiring the spliff for a bit, she lit up the twist with one of the gas matches and took a few shallow drags until she was down to tobacco. Then she blew a big mouthful of smoke right up to the kitchen ceiling and watched it cluster.

Keely sat back and hooked her feet under the bar at the bottom of the chair to smoke it. It tasted just like she thought it would, thick and creamy in the mouth like real butter. She wasn't so cold now. Her head wasn't spinning but there was a tingling in her legs after a few minutes and it felt good and relaxed, like nothing really mattered.

Bent over the sink, Keely swore and straightened her aching back. She couldn't get the blood out from under her nails. There was no electricity in the squat and the bare trickle of water left in the system was freezing. There was old black and white lino in the bathroom, peeling at the edges. She didn't like looking at the pattern, even ghostly in the candlelight. It was too much like hospital floors, it made her head hurt.

She couldn't hang on any longer. Hitching up her school skirt, Keely crouched over the seat and had a long wee. She glanced round but there was no loo roll left. Keely hesitated, then shook herself a little, like a dog coming out of water. She had to use the hem of her skirt to dry herself because she wasn't wearing any knickers. She must have forgot them back at her mam's house. The material was rough against her skin. Keely examined herself silently for a moment, then pulled a face at the smell down there and let the skirt drop.

Beside the mattress in Jess's room were piles of dirty clothes. She sat down on the cold wooden floor and started to root through them until, at the very bottom, she found an old wire coat hanger. Dragging the candle closer beside her so she could see properly, Keely stared at the wire hanger for a few minutes, turning it over and over in her hands. It wouldn't be that difficult. She'd seen it done in a film once. You had to untwist the wire neck and bend the whole thing back until you could use it like a crochet hook. The pregnant woman in the film had crawled into the bath to keep the place clean. Keely remembered her face, a close-up of the lips drawn back and her teeth showing, then the scream. The sloping white sides of the bath were sprayed with blood. The baby had died inside her, but Keely couldn't remember if the woman had died as well. Probably.

Trembling slightly, Keely began to untwist the coiled neck of the hanger. It wasn't as easy to do as she had imagined, straightening it out into a sharp finger of wire. She made her fingers sore, jerking the clumsy wire backwards and forwards until it was the right shape for the job.

But it wasn't a cruel thing to do, she was pretty sure of that. It would only take a minute or two if she did it properly. Anyway, it was probably still too small to fit inside the palm of her hand. Smaller even than an eyelash. Maybe no bigger than a grain of rice. And something as small as a grain of rice couldn't feel pain. How could it?

This long wire finger would come sneaking in and burst its bag of waters, and it would trickle out gently like a late period. No pain, no memory.

Had her mam ever wanted her dead too? Had she ever sat like this when she was pregnant and wondered what would happen if she stuck something sharp up inside herself and ended her baby? Then Keely would have trickled out and never been born. It could have happened secretly to thousands and thousands of babies all over the world. Millions, even. Millions of ghost babies trickling out and not knowing what happened to them. Never given the chance to be born and breathe the air and find out who they were.

Slowly and carefully, Keely nudged the wire finger against herself and starting pushing inside.

'Christ,' she hissed aloud, suddenly jerking her hand away. It bloody hurt.

She would probably give herself an infection if the wire was dirty. Hesitantly, not really sure if this would help or not, Keely held the end of the coat hanger above her candle for a few minutes. The slim grey wire started to blacken almost immediately in the dipping flame. It must be like sterilising the wire, burning away the bacteria so she couldn't get infected.

Then she blew on the hanger until it cooled. 'I don't want to scald myself now, do I?' she muttered to herself, and pulled her skirt up to her waist again.

This time, she decided to crouch instead of sitting. It felt easier to control the wire in that position.

She eased it in part way, ignoring the horrible pain from her body, then closed her eyes and began gradually forcing it further up. Keely wasn't sure how she would know when to stop pushing the hanger inside, but she guessed it would probably hurt a lot more once it reached the womb. Then she would give it a few sharp jabs until the trickling started.

Her legs were shaking. There was sweat on her forehead at the pain that seemed to start between her legs and drive up her spine like electricity.

She didn't want to hurt her own baby but she didn't have any choice. It was his, wasn't it? It belonged to that evil bastard, and she would curl up and die if she had to tell anyone who put it inside her. If she had to admit what he had done to her.

CHAPTER THIRTEEN

The bell rang. Term was over at last. Niall pulled open the top drawer of his desk and dragged out the unwieldy mass of his Teacher's Planner, plus several other equally uninspiring files he might need over the next fortnight's holiday. From his gloomy window, he could see kids streaming endlessly out of the school buildings towards the main gate.

To be honest, he felt the same sense of relief as they did. The kids had been agitated and disruptive all day, knowing it was the end of term now and Christmas was only a matter of days away. They'd been pissing about, shoving each other in the corridors and refusing to listen to instructions in class, the usual pre-holiday behaviour that got on everyone's nerves.

Now the final bell had released them, the kids were tumbling out into the world like a swarm of crazy disorientated wasps.

The school corridors had fallen silent at last. Niall gathered his clutter together and wandered down to his car through the rapidly emptying school grounds, carefully avoiding the icy patches beside buildings. The temperature seemed to be dropping faster than ever. It had even looked seriously like snow a few times over the past week. People were already hoping for a white Christmas, though at the moment there was nothing but a thick frost on the car windows every morning, and black ice on the roads.

'Niall? Could I have a word?'

He turned at MacFerson's voice and nodded briefly, not altogether happy to see the head coming towards him in his tweed flat cap and anorak. The man had not been particularly supportive over the Keely situation. In fact, Niall had the strong impression MacFerson blamed him for what happened. 'I was just on my way home, actually. Was there something you wanted?'

'I was wondering how Tracey's doing.'

'Fine. There was no real physical harm done, I believe. She seems happy enough to be back in school.'

'Good, good.' MacFerson turned away but still hesitated by his own car door, fiddling with his keys. There was obviously something else on his mind. 'You've heard nothing on the grapevine about Keely? I was in touch with the police again this morning. The girl's still missing.'

'I haven't heard a thing, I'm afraid.'

'None of the kids have spoken up?'

'She never really mixed with the others,' Niall said briefly. 'Keely's a loner, she wouldn't have confided in any of her year group. I've already told the police what I think.'

'Which is?'

'That she's probably gone to ground with that cousin of hers. They were always hanging round together before Jess was excluded.'

'Ah yes. The appalling Jess.'

The wind blew suddenly through the school car park, sharp as ever, and Niall drew his jacket collar more tightly around his neck. He tried to sound apologetic although he wasn't particularly.

'I'd better go, Jim. Haven't done any Christmas shopping yet. I've left it a bit late as always, you know how it is.'

'Absolutely. I'm the same. Don't let me hold you up.'

'Give my regards to your wife.'

'Of course.'

'Hope you both have a happy Christmas.'

'You too, Niall.' MacFerson inclined his head in the tweed cap and climbed briskly into his Volvo. 'And I wouldn't worry too much. This Keely business is a storm in a teacup. She'll probably turn up at home in the next few days, ready for turkey and presents. No teenage girl in her right mind wants to miss Christmas, trust me.'

Driving back through traffic to his cold flat, Niall kept returning to that last remark. To the head, Keely was just another statistic, another faceless trouble-maker he had to deal with in the usual manner. One more child to face exclusion from the school for anti-social behaviour. Though that's probably what she would have represented to Niall if he hadn't met Anne again and seen the possible connections with himself. Now it was always at the back of his mind that this particular kid might be his own daughter.

Though that was no excuse for the head's disinterest. It had obviously never occurred to MacFerson that Keely's outburst might have been prevented with better care, that the warning signs were visible long in advance of her attack on Tracey. Niall had spoken to him about the girl on several occasions, and had always come away from his office with nothing but false reassurances and the vague suspicion that his fears were being dismissed out of hand. Faced with that apathy, Keely's sudden grabbing of the scissors had been almost inevitable. MacFerson had managed to miss the truth of the situation entirely, and his parting remark proved it.

Niall was pulling out from a busy junction when he saw the girl out of the corner of his eye. Concentrating hard on the cars moving hectically on either side, he might well have missed the flash of her red mini-skirt and pale exposed cleavage if he hadn't glanced in his mirror at that exact moment and instinctively slammed his foot on the brake.

A taxi cab behind him hooted at the sudden manoeuvre but Niall ignored the driver's angry gestures, pulling abruptly into a bus stop just ahead and parking the car.

He adjusted his rear mirror, staring back with disbelief at the girl who was now heading towards him through the crowd of Christmas shoppers.

She hadn't seen him yet, but Niall knew her instantly. The arrogant sway of those hips was unmistakable. It was the blonde with the clever mouth from the night of his birthday, the girl who had given him so much trouble when she was at school: Keely's older cousin, Jess.

It was getting dark when the girl finally got off the bus and turned down a narrow alleyway between rows of council houses. There were bollards at the end of the alley, blocking it off from traffic.

Niall pulled into the side of the road and parked his car behind a white transit van, hurrying after her on foot as quickly as he could. He had followed her for nearly an hour, first through the shopping streets and then for several miles on the bus, and he wasn't planning to lose her at this stage. The cloak-and-dagger approach felt a little bit ludicrous, especially since he had been on his way home when he spotted her, but this might be his only opportunity to find Keely and persuade her to go home and talk to the police.

Jess had been shopping for nearly an hour and must surely be on her way home. If his hunch was correct, and the two cousins were now living together, the girl should lead him straight to Keely's hiding place.

Niall wasn't enjoying himself much. The housing estate she had turned into was badly lit and his jacket was too thin for walking about in such cold weather.

Nevertheless, he carried on through the streets, keeping his distance from Jess. He didn't want to alert the girl that she was being followed. It was easy enough to keep track of her through the maze of little roads and alleyways; he could hardly lose sight of that distinctive red mini-skirt, which turned heads everywhere she went.

Wearing something so skimpy in sub-zero temperatures, he guessed she must be utterly frozen. But that probably wouldn't matter to her. All the young girls dressed the same way once they were out of school uniform, regardless of the time of year. He had often seen teenagers from school out on the streets after dark, wearing nothing but bra tops and tiny skirts above their bare legs even in the coldest of winters. They didn't seem to feel the cold.

After a few more minutes, Jess turned down a darker side road, where some of the street lights were no longer working and most of the houses appeared to be waiting for demolition.

A gang of lads on the corner, the oldest of them only about thirteen, laughed and yelled abuse at her as she passed. 'Come on, you whore. Drop your knickers for us.'

Not even changing her pace, Jess crossed the road without so much as glancing in their direction and moved into the shadows beyond one of the smashed street lights.

One minute she was there, the next she had vanished. It was only because he had been watching her so closely that Niall realised she had slipped down an alley behind the houses.

He watched silently as she pushed through a broken gate in the darkness, carefully negotiated a yard full of rubbish, and entered the back of a derelict house on the end of the terraced row. This must be where she was living now, presumably with Keely. Yet Jess couldn't possibly be renting a complete dump like that, she must be squatting there. Even the house beside theirs looked unsafe, its disused chimney stack leaning as if about to fall. Niall could almost smell the damp and decay of these places from where he was standing and it made him feel physically sick.

An unexpected anger flickered inside him. It wasn't the sort of place he would like to see any kid living in, let alone a teenage girl who might turn out be his own daughter. This was what happened when kids slipped through the net and onto the streets.

But she was going to make it back safely, he was determined to make sure of that now.

Keely remembered the hand on her mouth, stopping her from screaming in case one of their neighbours heard and knocked at the front door. She had felt her mouth start to bleed. Nothing much after that but the heaviness and salt of his palm forced against her lips and the creak of the bedsprings.

The sight of the white ceiling above and then his broad shoulders. White ceiling. Broad shoulders. White ceiling. Broad shoulders.

Then his gasped breath loud in her ear. Rolling away afterwards as if it had been nothing but a game. Fumbling with the zip on his jeans as he stood up and looked down at her.

'Not a single fucking word to anyone. Understood?'

She had nodded without speaking. His heavy tread going down the stairs then. His careless whistling in the kitchen as he put the kettle on. Water hissing through the pipes from the tank in the airing cupboard. Above her bed, the silent white ceiling stared back without moving.

She was aching and sore between her legs. Slow oozing dampness when she dropped her hand down there. A slight reddish tinge to the wet fingers brought back to her face.

Clamping her thighs together at last, Keely turned into the coolness of the pillow.

After a few minutes, she had heard his voice raised at

the foot of the stairs. 'Get up and put those sheets in the wash, Keely. We don't want your mam asking awkward questions, do we?'

'Christ.' Keely caught her breath again. The wire coat hanger had bitten violently into her. Crouched cold and alone in the bedroom at the squat, she dragged the hanger out from between her legs and saw the blunt metal tip slimed with her own blood.

It was so hard to focus on what was real these days. Even this pain now felt as if it was coming from a long distance. Everything that had happened to her in the past ten years seemed to have come apart, bit by bit, until it was like a jigsaw puzzle scattered randomly around her mind. But whenever Keely tried to put the pieces back together in the right order, the way it had been when she was younger, she ended up with what felt like someone else's memories. It was as if all she had left were the wrong moments. The odds and ends. Things she couldn't believe she had really done. Words she couldn't imagine hearing.

'I'm not having it,' she whispered to herself, then froze. She let the coat hanger drop silently from her fingers, hearing a sudden creaking noise coming from the kitchen. Rustling and creaking, like clothes and floorboards. Every part of her body tensed, ready to leap up and run if necessary.

Blotting out the hot aching pain between her legs, Keely made herself pull away from it like a coiled spring ready for the rebound. She didn't have time to feel the pain now. She had to concentrate on whatever was outside the door. That was the important thing.

The noise came again, louder this time. Too loud for one of the rats which sometimes wandered through from under the skirting boards. No doubt about it now. There was someone else in the squat.

Keely shrank back into herself, waiting for the inevitable shape in the doorway. Yet her heart-beat was surprisingly steady. She had almost expected panic to set in once they discovered where she was. But her hands were not trembling at all and her breathing was only slightly faster than before. In fact, in spite of having drawn her bare legs up beneath her, she felt quite calm and focused. If they had found her already, at least it meant the running and hiding was over before it had really begun. There was a sort of relief in that possibility, even though Keely knew that terror was mixed up in it too. But she didn't want to think about that, it made her head hurt just keeping those thoughts out of her mind.

The door was half open. It was one person on their own. Then she heard the clack of high heels and suddenly realised who it was. Laughter started bubbling up inside her. 'Jess?'

The heels stopped outside in the hallway. 'Kee?'

'Christ Almighty,' Keely gasped. 'I nearly had a heart attack. I thought you were the police.'

'What would they be doing round here, you daft thing?' Jess pushed the door open and then stood looking in at Keely, her mouth gaping. She was wearing clattering black shoes, delicate cross-straps with stiletto heels. Bare legs, short red skirt and tie-up white midriff top in spite of the freezing temperatures outside. She'd obviously been walking fast up the road and her breath steamed on the cold air of the squat. 'Why on earth have you taken your skirt off?'

Keely looked at her blankly.

'Bloody hell, kid. It's freezing in here and there's you with barely a stitch on your back. And what the fuck's that?'

Keely glanced down at the twisted wire hanger on the floor. There was still a trace of blood and fluids smeared across the blunt metal hook. She shrugged and looked away. 'Nothing.'

'Nothing?' Jess stooped to pick up the hanger. 'That don't look like nothing to me. What the hell you been up to, Kee? Trying to top yourself now, is that it?'

'Don't shout at us, Jess. It wasn't my fault.'

'What wasn't your fault?'

Keely put a hand up to her face. Her nose was beginning to run and she wiped it. Her legs were turning numb with the cold, though she hadn't noticed it before. Thinking too much about the pain, probably, and what that wire finger was doing to her insides. But now that Jess was here, Keely couldn't remember properly why she'd wanted to do it. She wasn't even sure why she had come to the squat at all. Everything had seemed so clear in her head before. Now it was all confused.

'Speak to us, Keely. Or I swear I'll fetch you one across the head.' Jess crouched down beside her. 'What have you done, you silly kid?'

Her voice was only a whisper. 'I got into trouble at school. I had to go home. And I might have hurt Zal.'

'You what?'

'I think I might have ...'

Jess gasped and rocked back on her heels in shock as the disjointed whisper started to sink in. 'Oh Jesus Christ.'

'He wouldn't stop, Jess. I begged him not to, but he wouldn't listen. He just kept on and on.'

'Kept on what?'

'It was there in the bag right beside me.' Keely's voice was high but she couldn't control it. 'I didn't mean to hurt him, honest I didn't. But he wouldn't stop, Jess, and I didn't know what else to do. I just wanted him to stop. It was right there next to my hand, like it was meant to be. So I picked it up and he stopped.'

'You're not making any sense.'

'My gold clock. I hit him with it.'

Jess covered her mouth, shaking her head. 'Please tell me you're joking. Otherwise we're both screwed.'

'It wasn't my fault.'

'Shit.'

'But it wasn't my fault,' Keely repeated automatically.

She could hear a high-pitched hissing and squealing noise coming from somewhere behind her. It sounded like there was a dying animal in the room. She wiped her face again and realised her hand was wet. Keely looked round for a tissue, but there wasn't one so she dried it on her tee-shirt. She couldn't breathe properly anymore. 'It wasn't my fault.'

'That bastard.'

Suddenly exhausted, Keely rested her head on Jess's shoulder, enjoying the familiar warmth and perfume of her cousin's hair. She didn't have to think anymore about what might be growing inside her. If she had killed Zal when she hit him, all that would be finished and done with. She'd be okay to go home again, just like when she was a kid before Zal ever came along and it was just the three of them. Just Keely, with her mam and dad. Kneeling up on her bed like she used to when she was little, one finger tracing the eyes of those huge scarlet poppies on the wallpaper.

'At least he's dead now,' she whispered under her breath. 'He's got to be dead, don't you think?'

The stained and splintered chipboard which had once covered the back door appeared to have been forced aside at some point, probably with a crow-bar. It hung down limply across the doorway like a broken arm.

Climbing through that barrier as carefully as he could, Niall pushed open the back door of the house and listened.

He could hear voices further inside. Unmistakably two girls, talking somewhere in one of the inner rooms.

Niall felt a burst of satisfaction that his theory had been correct. But he still hesitated in the doorway, cautiously taking in his surroundings before deciding to go any further. The kitchen in front of him was almost pitch-black, but he could just see the glimmer of what was probably candlelight coming from the hallway beyond. Its light danced faintly off the rusty taps in the sink and the cracked glass panelling in one of the old wall units. He caught a sudden movement out of the corner of his eye and realised with a shock that it was a rat, scuttling along the filthy black and white floor tiles until it disappeared behind a fixed cupboard.

Niall took a shuddering breath, hung on that threshold for another few seconds, then plunged into the darkness like a swimmer into a black tide.

'What was that?' Keely whispered, lifting her head.

They had been lying together on the bed for warmth, but her cousin moved away now to listen, freezing almost immediately as they both heard the gentle creaking noise again. For once, Jess looked frightened. 'There must be someone in the kitchen. I forgot to bolt the back door.'

'Shit.'

Jess reached forward and pinched out the candle with her fingers. It smoked and stank horribly but they were safer in darkness. Her voice sank almost to nothing. 'It can't be Eddy. He's gone to a party tonight on the other side of town. Nobody else knows we're here. It must be another of those crackheads off the estate, looking for something to steal. Eddy warned us about them only last week.'

'What are we going to do?'

'We need something heavy. Where's that big glass ashtray you nicked from your mam's?'

'On top of the box near the door.'

Jess nudged her in the ribs and started to fumble her way towards the door. They crawled side by side, searching as silently as they could, but whoever was outside the door must have been able to hear them by now.

Her cousin's whisper was so low she could barely catch it. 'I can't find anything in this sodding dark.'

Keely's hand closed on something large and round and cold. It was her mam's best ashtray. 'Got it.'

Suddenly, the door to the bedroom was pushed open. Someone came into the room on tiptoe. Keely could smell it was a man and she knew what that meant. She waited there behind the door next to Jess without making a single noise. He mustn't realise where they were hiding. Then, as soon as the man was far enough forward and she could almost see his outline by the light creeping round the edges of the boarded-up windows, Keely ran forward and smashed at the back of his head with her mam's ashtray.

The man grunted and fell face-down onto the floorboards so that the whole room shook with it.

'Get those handcuffs you showed us.' She turned shakily to Jess. 'That bastard's not going to touch me again.'

'Is it Zal then?'

'It must be.' Her legs trembling with reaction now it was all over, Keely scrabbled about in the darkness for the candle and lighter. She'd hit him pretty hard and he was probably dead, but it was always best to be sure. 'He must have asked Eddy where I was hiding. I knew we couldn't trust him. Get those handcuffs quick. He might come round again any minute.'

'But I never told Eddy you were living with me.'

'What?'

'I'll get the handcuffs. You check who it is.'

Keely finally managed to get the candle lit, burning her fingers on the lighter because her hand was shaking that much. She knelt down bare-legged beside the man's body and held up the candle for a proper look. She immediately knew there was something familiar about him but she still couldn't place him. For a start, he wasn't as broad-shouldered as Zal. His hair was short and dark though, almost like Zal's, but not quite.

As she raised the candle higher, Keely saw a little stream of blood already puddling on the floorboards from his forehead. The sight of it made her feel a bit sick because she realised now that she'd made a mistake. But that didn't mean they wouldn't need the handcuffs. He could turn out to be anyone, after all. He could be some drug addict looking for something easy to steal. He could be some dosser off the streets who would have raped or murdered them.

Then she tilted the man's head and saw his face. 'Oh shit.'

'What's the matter? Who is it?' Jess whispered, leaning forward to hand Keely the handcuffs.

'You're not going to believe this. It's the fucking art teacher.'

CHAPTER FOURTEEN

'How did you ever think you'd get away with it?'
Then the boot had smashed into him.

Even now, more than a decade later, Niall could still remember that incredible explosion of pain in his right side. He had yelped like a surprised puppy, returning to consciousness in an instant. Lying foetus-like on an unfamiliar carpet, the left side of his face damp from some puddle of wine, he realised that he must have either passed out or fallen asleep there at some point.

'Jesus Christ,' Niall gasped and jerked back instinctively to protect himself. There was another more haunting smell on the air, catching thickly at the back of his throat as he rolled over on the carpet, and it was with a shock that he recognised her perfume. In spite of the pain, his body was still heavy with some sweet unfamiliar pleasure.

There was an unshaded bulb directly overhead, burning straight into his eyes. For a moment of complete mental chaos, Niall couldn't remember whose house he was in, or why. He must have been drinking particularly hard that night. Everything about the place seemed hazy and unfamiliar. But he knew there was a strange man straddling his head with spread legs, and this man was seriously hacked off about something.

'It's just as well I called round tonight, otherwise I might never have caught you. But you're going to get what you deserve now.'

Sensing another attack was on its way, Niall tried to sit up and curl away from the approaching boot, but he was too slow. It crashed into his ribs in a blur of sickening agony.

'Who are you? What the hell are you doing?' Niall managed to gasp as he clasped his hands protectively against his rib cage.

'Don't play games with me, man. You know what you've been up to tonight.'

'I don't know, honest.'

'Jesus Christ. You've got some neck. You rape my fiancée and then pretend you don't know what's going on?' The man bent right down into his face, so close Niall could actually see the tiny black hairs quivering in his nose. His breath was an alcoholic blast of hatred.

Dragging him up by the front of his tee-shirt, the man pointed wildly at the half-open bedroom door behind them. 'Let me make this perfectly clear to you. My name's Malcolm and I'm engaged to that woman over there. You see her, do you? The one crying her fucking eyes out? She's told me everything. How you followed her back here from the pub. How you raped her.'

'But that's not true.' Only belatedly realising the danger he was in, Niall tried to scrabble sideways as the grip on his tee-shirt relaxed for a second. 'Oh shit!'

Malcolm had straightened too quickly and the vast boot exploded again without warning, this time straight into his face.

There was a loud, excruciating crack as his nose broke under the force of the impact. Niall felt blackness descending and fought it desperately, raising his hands to cover his head. This man was out of control. Which wasn't exactly surprising if he thought Niall had raped his fiancée. But in this mood, he could do anything and not care about the consequences.

'Call the police. Please call them. They'll sort this out.'

Niall was babbling, his drunken brain stumbling through whatever it was that had happened after he climbed into the taxi with Anne earlier that evening, trying to locate some memory which might save him, any scrap of information that might possibly stop this madman from killing him. He remembered stumbling across her room in the dark, falling over an opened bottle of wine and picking himself up with a laugh. There was a satin flash of a wedding dress against his skin, and her hands intimately gripping his body. But he didn't remember very much else after that, except waking up to this man's boot exploding into his rib cage.

'Police?' Malcolm's laughter was almost manic. 'Oh, you'd like that, wouldn't you? Some pervert doctor sticking his fingers up her and taking pictures for his mates to laugh over. This woman is going to be my wife in a week's time. It's up to me to sort it, and I'm going to do that my way. I don't need no police here.'

'I didn't rape her, you've got to believe me.'

'What did you say?' Malcolm kicked him again with even greater force, catching him excruciatingly in the groin. 'Did you think she was enjoying it, you bastard?'

'I thought she liked me.' Niall's face was slippery under his protective hands. His own blood, he guessed hazily. Everything in his body hurt like fuck. He was still struggling to remember what had happened earlier, why he was suddenly getting the shit kicked out of him.

'That's a lie. I told him to piss off when we were at the pub. The other girls will say the same. He must have followed us home, like I told you. Then he got into the flat and raped me.' It was Anne's voice above him now, high-pitched and trembling as if she was terrified. 'I'm telling you, the bastard raped me. Like he didn't give a shit.'

Malcolm took a quick step backwards, his mouth clamped white with the pressure. He was breathing through his nose, deep shuddering breaths as if he was trying to regain control of himself. His fists were clenched by his sides, shoulders hunched right forward. But Niall knew he hadn't finished. He was just winding himself up for another burst of violence.

'I'm going to kill you. Do you hear me?'

'I never raped her.'

Niall rolled and squirmed across the landing. He didn't deserve this. Each kick felt like there was a steel-tipped freight train behind it. His fingers were going numb and it was all he could do to keep them covering his face. One blow detonated right next to his ear. The dull echoing roar was deafening, followed by a thousand tiny firecrackers going off simultaneously inside his head.

Blood was trickling thickly from his temples into his eyes, leaving him blind and incoherent. 'Please. You've got to believe me. I didn't realise ...'

'You liar, you liar.' It was Anne's voice again, so distant he could barely hear what she was saying. 'I begged you to stop. I told you I was getting married. But you just kept going, you shit.'

Her voice faded away from him under the renewed kicking. Her face spun like a pale lantern in front of his eyes. She was telling Malcolm what had happened that night, hanging onto his arm as he plunged his boot repeatedly into Jack's body. She was making it sound as though Niall had deliberately broken into the flat and raped her, as though she hadn't asked him up there herself, hadn't wanted him at all. His head was buzzing with denials. He wanted to stop her from lying, shout something in his own defence, but he couldn't move his lips properly, could only just make the whistling sound of a word. His mouth was nothing but a thick rubber band, it gaped heavy and useless in front of broken teeth.

He never raped her, never did anything she didn't

enjoy. None of this was fair. Why couldn't she keep her mouth shut, couldn't she see the blood pouring into his eyes and mouth?

Niall was choking on his own sour dark liquid. The boot drove into his head again and again, smashing pitilessly into bone and pulverising nerve-endings, blotting out those disconnected whimperings that were him trying to hang onto consciousness, the voices growing fainter and fainter above him until Malcolm's boot was a sort of mechanical battering ram that advanced and retreated in complete silence.

Finally reaching its limit of physical agony, Niall blacked out into an oasis of nothingness.

'Mr Swainson?'

Slumped below her in the darkness, handcuffed to the radiator and with his mouth taped shut, was Mr Swainson. He looked much smaller and less important than she expected. But that was probably because Keely was used to seeing him in the art room with its huge bright windows. After all, the art room was where Mr Swainson belonged, where he was in control. And it would have been funny, looking down at one of her teachers handcuffed to an old radiator, if Keely hadn't been the one who had done it to him.

Instead it was sort of scary. Though she didn't feel scared. Not proper scared.

'Stupid beggar,' she whispered, bending close.

In the candlelight, she could see a trail of dried blood down his left cheek and the side of his throat. She had hit him quite hard, she knew that. But at least it had stopped bleeding, which probably meant that he wasn't going to die.

If only Mr Swainson had stayed away, minded his own bloody business, none of this would have happened.

But he was here now, and what the hell was she meant to do with him?

'Mr Swainson?' she repeated, close to his ear. At the sound of her voice, he groaned and shifted against the wall, beginning to open his eyes. 'Feeling better now, Mr Swainson?'

Mr Swainson stared up at her for a moment. His eyes were slightly unfocussed. Then there was an amazed grunt from behind the gag as he recognised her face. It sounded like her name he was trying to say.

Suddenly not sure what she wanted to say, Keely left him without another word and retreated into the kitchen.

Eddy had torn down the last shreds of chipboard covering the window above the sink and it was brighter in there. Her stomach was rumbling. She hadn't eaten in days. The sickness meant she only threw food up again soon as it was in her stomach. But now she was starving. She scrabbled about for jam and two slices of stale bread in the kitchen cupboards, making herself a tough little sandwich and not caring how much her teeth hurt on the crusts.

Keely shook the kettle and filled it from the blue plastic bin. The little camper stove was always tricky to light, and Keely used four matches before the gas caught. When it had been going a while, she watched steam gently collecting in clouds on the underside of the shelf above. It didn't matter that there was no milk. She could have a mug of black tea.

Scraping the last few leaves out of the tea caddy, she heard a rattling noise coming from the living room.

'Do you need the loo, Mr Swainson?'

But the rattling noise didn't stop. Keely realised that her hands were trembling. She wished he hadn't come round here, interfering in her life. She didn't want any trouble but he was begging for it. Breathing hard, Keely put down the caddy and tiptoed to the living room doorway.

Peeping through the gap, she felt her heart leap with alarm as she saw what he was up to.

'What do you think you're doing?'

Mr Swainson stiffened and stared up at her, obviously startled by her sudden appearance. He made another muffled sound through the gag. At full stretch away from the radiator, he was trying desperately to reach the armchair with his one free arm. The little nick on his temple had started bleeding again; he must have caught it against something. She thought he looked pathetic and helpless and angry. Christ, she thought. If only he could see himself.

Keely slipped past him, carefully keeping just out of reach of his foot in case he kicked her, and dragged the armchair a little further towards the boarded-up windows.

'Please don't do that, Mr Swainson. You can't get away, so there's no point trying.'

His groan seemed to be one of angry frustration.

'Now, do you want the loo or what? The bucket's right there for you if you need it.'

Mr Swainson shuffled back towards the wall, leaning his forehead against it in a dramatic gesture of defeat. That was obviously a "No".

But when she turned to leave the room, Mr Swainson knocked over the empty bucket so that it rolled noisily across the floorboards. Then he kicked out at the radiator. The whole thing shook, and plaster fell like confetti from the wall behind it, but there was no way he was going to shift it. The radiator was old and massive and built to last. That was exactly why she had chosen to handcuff him to it. Because he wasn't going anywhere until she was ready.

Staring down at the litter of little white flakes covering his jeans and the floor, Mr Swainson seemed almost pleased by what he had achieved.

He looked up at her, making a strange noise behind the gag that was probably meant to be laughter.

'Did that make you feel better?' she demanded, only then realising, with a stab of regret, that it wasn't laughter. His eyes were too shiny for that. Mr Swainson was trying not to cry.

She didn't like that. There was something horrible about seeing one of her teachers crying. It wasn't right. She brought the bucket back and placed it just within his reach, avoiding his eyes.

'Please don't do that again. It's either the bucket or you wet yourself.'

Keely stooped down, deciding to catch him off guard before he had a chance to react. She yanked off the silver tape as quickly as she could, feeling the skin tear painfully as the gag was ripped away from his mouth. Mr Swainson let out a shriek, jerking his whole body back against the wall so the radiator shook again.

'Sorry.' She backed away, glancing down at the curling piece of silver tape in her hand. The sticky side was covered with a strip of tiny bristling hairs. 'It's not meant to hurt as much if you do it quickly.'

Now that the gag was off, Keely thought Mr Swainson would have wanted to say something immediately, but he didn't. He just sat there making a funny face at the other side of the room, screwing his mouth up as if testing that the muscles still worked.

Keely found herself backing further away, waiting for the inevitable insults. Her heart was beating violently. But it was his fault this was happening, not hers.

'Why couldn't you have stayed away from me?' she asked him. 'I've finished with that school. This is my life now. Why couldn't you keep your nose out of my business?'

'Because I care about you, Keely. I was trying to help you.'

'You don't care. None of you teachers care.'

'OK, calm down. I wasn't trying to wind you up again. I was just answering your question.' Mr Swainson watched her for a moment. 'What are you planning to do with me?'

Keely wasn't sure how to answer him. She wanted to

seem in control, she couldn't let him think she wasn't. But she didn't have a clue what she was going to do. She hadn't thought that far ahead. All she knew for certain was that she couldn't let him go.

'You'll find out,' she said quickly.

His eyes flickered, but he lowered his gaze to the floor as if he didn't want to make her angry. He didn't seem angry, and that surprised her. Even though it was what she wanted, Keely was annoyed by his silence. It was as though he had wrong-footed her somehow by not responding, and now she felt confused, almost ridiculous. She had tried to sound confident and threatening, the way Eddy did when he was talking to Jess, but Mr Swainson had seen through the act. He had probably guessed that she had nothing to fall back on.

Keely knelt down in the middle of the room, deliberately keeping her back to him in order to hide her anxiety, and lit a fresh candle. The last one was already guttering in its saucer, nothing better than a charred wick in a pool of hot wax. Through the gaps where the chipboards across the window overlapped, she could see pale daylight in the streets and even hear the odd car going past occasionally.

But at least no one out there could see what was going on inside.

Later, she made tea and carried it through to the living room, but Mr Swainson seemed to have fallen asleep again. Cautiously, she knelt and slid his mug towards him, watching for any sudden movements. It wouldn't do to relax and trust him before she'd worked out how he had found her. 'Here, it's not too hot. You should be able to pick it up.' His eyes opened, focusing on the greasy black liquid in front of him with obvious disgust. 'Sorry. There wasn't any milk.'

Mr Swainson hesitated, then shuffled slowly forward to reach the mug. As if worried that Keely might be trying to poison him, he took a sip and shuddered at the taste, but took another sip almost immediately.

After a few minutes, he leant back again, watching her pick old pieces of wax out of the saucer. 'How long are you planning to keep me here?'

She said nothing, but laughed.

'You can let me go, Keely. I won't say a word to the police.'

'Yeah right.'

Keely glanced at her watch. She was nervous that Jess hadn't come back yet. Maybe she'd spent the night at Eddy's. She did that sometimes, if he had a lot of gear in and Jess was in the mood for making a long night of it. Which she often was recently. But Keely couldn't be sure and her stomach was beginning to ache sickly.

'You can't keep me here forever.'

'Who says I'm going to?'

It was crap but he looked scared. 'What does that mean?'

'Have some more tea. It's cold in here, but the tea should warm you up.' Trying to avoid his intent stare, Keely went over to the two bar electric fire and switched it on for him as a demonstration. Nothing happened. 'See? No electric. It's all been cut off. Jess may have a spare blanket. I'll ask her when she gets back.'

'How long until she gets back?'

'Fancy another blow job off her, do you?' Keely couldn't help herself. She almost laughed at his shocked expression. 'Yeah. Jess told me all about that.'

Without any warning at all, Mr Swainson suddenly threw the steaming remains of his tea right at her head. She ducked instinctively. But with the handcuffs locked onto his right wrist, he couldn't get the aim right. His arm jerked awkwardly and the mug just slammed up into the air and came straight down again immediately, splashing him with hot black tea.

He swore. The mug must have caught his ankle

because he clutched at it, wincing as if in pain. There was a damp spreading stain on his jeans. The mug had smashed and fallen under the radiator, leaving little chips of white over the rug and floorboards.

She stared at him angrily. 'What was that in aid of?'

'For God's sake, Keely. The police are going to find me in the end, you know, and you'll end up in prison.'

'No one's going to find you here.'

'What?' He was staring at her as if he didn't understand what she was saying. The veins were standing out on his forehead like thick blue worms. His voice became almost hysterical. 'You're insane. You're completely fucking insane.'

'There's no need to shout.'

'Fuck you.'

'Fine,' she said, walking quickly out of his reach as he lurched forward to grab at her ankle. She had to pretend that she wasn't bothered. 'You crack on, Mr Swainson. No one can hear you.'

She sat down in the kitchen and looked at her hands. They were shaking. The sickness was back and she felt dizzy again. Through the grimy window, she could see the faded redbrick backs of other houses facing her. There were children playing somewhere along the alley, just out of sight. She could hear their shouts of laughter and the sound of a football being kicked rhythmically against a wall.

He was still ranting in the other room. Then he started banging against the radiator. The endless metallic clunking grated on her nerves until she thought she could hardly bear it another second.

She wondered whether there was anyone next door. It was an end terrace house, that was why she had thought of coming here to hide in the first place, and Jess had said there was no one on the other side. The whole row was derelict and up for demolishing. But she knew there might be squatters in one of the other houses, and even they might draw the line at one of their next-door neighbours chaining someone to a radiator.

She tried to stay calm and keep the sickness from rising. But Mr Swainson wouldn't stop. He just went on shouting and banging against the radiator. The noise must be carrying right through the house. Passers-by might be able to hear it in the street. Any minute now, those boys playing football in the back alley might hear him and tell their parents. The police would be called. It would all be over.

She ran back into the living room. 'Stop that,' she screamed. 'Stop that noise right now.'

But Mr Swainson didn't stop. He was laughing. There were little bits of white plaster pebble-dashed all over his jeans from the wall. A faint sunlight was streaming through the gaps in the window boards now. She could see dust specks in the dark, spiralling and dancing.

Keely picked up one of the empty bottles from behind the door. She couldn't bear it any longer. Her heart was going crazy. She thought her ears might explode with the pressure of blood.

But when he saw her raise the bottle above his head, he jerked away immediately, scrabbling backwards, his free hand held up against his face.

'Please, no. I'll stop. Don't hurt me!'

Jess got back late afternoon. It was already dark. Keely had put lit candles on the kitchen table because she kept falling over the chairs as she tried to tidy up. When she heard Jess banging through the loose chipboard over the back door, she jolted up from the table immediately, aware that she had been on the verge of falling asleep.

'You've been ages.'

'I was at Eddy's place for a bit, then I went shopping with that money from your teacher's wallet. Now don't look at me like that. We have to eat, don't we?'

Jess thumped the supermarket bag down on the table

and started to unpack it. She looked tired and irritable. Keely helped her put the shopping away in the wall cupboards that still had doors, suddenly feeling hungry again. There wasn't much. Jess had only bought bread, chicken soup, tinned ham, loo roll, and another small packet of tea.

'Is this all you got?'

'There was only a few quid in the wallet.'

'I wish you'd been here. I had to give him the last of the tea because he looked half dead. Then the bastard broke one of your mugs.'

'Which?'

'The little whitish one.'

'Oh.' Jess didn't look really bothered. 'Cheeky fucker.'

There was a loud rap on the chipboard over the back door. Keely froze by the kitchen table and stared across at Jess. There was a long silence and neither of them moved. Her heart felt like a bird trapped in the house, beating its wings against the boards as it looked for an open door or window. She put a hand to her throat as Jess spoke.

'It's okay. That's probably just Eddy.'

'You sure?'

'He said he was coming round tonight.'

'But he might see Mr Swainson.'

'Who gives a toss?' Jess shrugged, closing the tea caddy with a snap. 'This is Eddy we're talking about. I know you don't like him much, but you're going to have to try. He's my boyfriend and he's not going to grass us up.'

'Well, give us a minute before you let him in.'

'Why?'

'Because I'm going to shut the door to the living room. I know you think it doesn't matter, but Eddy might blow up if he sees Mr Swainson. There's no point getting him upset for no reason.'

The knocking came again, even louder this time, and they heard Eddy shouting something angrily through the chipboard over the back door. The old frame rattled noisily against the bolt as he shook it.

'Thirty seconds, that's all. Or he'll break that bloody door down.'

Her heart seesawing at the sudden fear of discovery, Keely peered into the darkness of the front room. Mr Swainson seemed to be sleeping at last. He was curled up against the cold radiator, the rug pulled up around his body for extra warmth. Keely had put his gag back on after the little shouting incident earlier, but there was no harm in being careful. She wasn't sure if she could trust Eddy to keep his mouth shut if he caught sight of Mr Swainson. Besides, the fewer people who saw him the better.

Eddy looked up at her as she came back in and nodded. He was already sitting at the kitchen table, smoking a cigarette and talking to Jess. Luckily, he didn't seem too bothered that she'd kept him waiting outside. 'You okay, pet?'

'Couldn't be better.'

Eddy unrolled the newspaper under his arm and started flicking through the sports pages. 'Found yourself a job yet?'

'Have you?'

'I've already got a job.'

'Peddling drugs?'

He shrugged. 'It pays well enough. If you know what you're doing.'

'And you do?'

'No complaints so far.' Eddy looked up at her sharply as she placed the teapot on the table. 'You could do a lot worse, Keely. They're always looking for pretty faces to bring the stuff in and out of the country.'

'I'm not thick.'

'You can't look after yourself properly sitting around all day, kid. I can give you a job anytime.'

Jess shook her head at Keely. 'Don't listen to him.'

'Hey, whose side are you on?'

'She's too young for that, Eddy. She'll only end up

inside.'

'She's not a kid anymore,' Eddy said sharply. But he obviously wasn't up for a fight this time. He took another drag on his cigarette and looked across at Jess. 'Fine, how much do you need for these punters tonight?'

'An eighth and six tabs.'

'And how will you be paying for that, madam?'

Jess placed the notes in front of him. Eddy counted them out silently as if he expected it to be short, then put them away in his wallet and fished a couple of small plastic bags out of his jacket pocket.

'I like your regulars. There's nothing better than cash in advance.'

'I'm never sure which they prefer, the sex or the drugs.'

'Oh, the drugs, sweetheart. Don't flatter yourself.' Eddy smiled unpleasantly as he plumped up the bag of skunk with his fingers. He watched Keely across the table, his scarred mouth all crooked. 'Seriously, you could do worse than take a leaf out of your cousin's book. It's good work.'

'I'm not interested.'

He looked her over assessingly. 'Your tits are a bit on the small side, but some blokes like that. Especially the older ones. Come on, just one night.'

'I wouldn't know what to do.'

Eddy leant back in his chair. He glanced sideways at Jess as he tossed the bags into the centre of the table, then grinned. 'Now that's not what I've heard.'

Jess saw Keely's face, and hurriedly shook her head. 'Honestly, love, I didn't tell him deliberately. It just slipped out.'

Keely got up and walked out of the kitchen. She tried to close the door behind her, but it wouldn't shut properly. All the doors were hung slightly off, and the hinges were knackered from heaving on the bloody things, so you could only nudge them to in the end. But at least she couldn't make out what they were saying anymore.

She stood outside the door to the living room, listening hard to hear if he was awake. There was total silence inside. After waiting a bit longer to make sure no one was going to follow her, Keely pushed at the door and tiptoed inside.

Mr Swainson was still asleep on the floor but the rug had fallen away that he'd been using to cover himself. He looked sort of odd, lying half on his side, half against the wall. Keely realised she should have thought of getting him a pillow, but they didn't have a spare one anyway.

He woke up in the sudden draught from the open door. The candle near the window had nearly burnt down to nothing and she could barely see his face in the darkness. His breathing sounded strange, so she knelt to remove the gag, nervous that he might cry out but more worried in case he actually stopped breathing.

This time she tried to be gentler, but he still winced as the tape peeled off. Kneeling by his side, Keely offered him some water from the cup which he swallowed it with difficulty. 'Is that better?'

'I'm hungry.'

'There's some tinned ham.'

'I'm a vegetarian.'

'How about some chicken soup then?'

There was a long pause. His eyes flickered in the dying candlelight. 'Is that meant to be a wind-up, Keely, or are you just stupid?'

There was an explosion of rage inside her. Why was nobody on her side in this life? Without any attempt at being gentle this time, she fixed the tape back onto his mouth, snuffed out the remains of the dying candle, and left the room in darkness. He could lie there on his own and starve to death for all she cared.

After she had pulled the door almost shut, struggling like crazy with the dead hinges, she realised her right hand was wet and stinging. When she touched it experimentally to her lips, she could taste blood. Somehow, a cut had appeared across her knuckles. The skin was already puffing up and she would probably have a bruise there in the morning. But she couldn't remember how she had hurt herself.

She traced a hand over the wood panel in front of her. Maybe there was a loose nail sticking out of the door. She must have grazed her hand as she closed it. Too distracted to care, she wiped the blood off on her jeans and felt her way back towards the crack of light from the kitchen door.

Eddy and Jess sprang apart as she came in. Even by candlelight, Keely could see her cousin's red lipstick smeared over his mouth and shirt collar. The air above them was thick with smoke and the heavy stench of skunk hit Keely like a punch in the throat. Jess looked at her face anxiously, then whispered something to Eddy. He swung his leather jacket off the chair and banged out of the back door without another word.

Jess picked up her spliff and relit it, blowing the smoke up into the air without meeting Keely's eyes. The cannabis smelt sweet and rotten at the same time. 'Your bloke asleep?'

Keely shrugged.

'Did you not check? Fuck's sake, we've got to keep an eye on him. Is there a candle in there?'

When Keely shook her head, Jess picked up one of the candles on the kitchen table and left the room, spliff still burning away in the ashtray. Keely couldn't think straight anymore. The thick drifting smoke from the spliff was choking her head up.

Jess came back after a few minutes and stared at her from the doorway. 'What's the matter with his face?'

'I don't know what you mean.'

She got up and tried to light the gas for another pot of tea, but she couldn't get the match to strike. It kept slipping on the sandpaper strip. Her fingers were all over the place. The smell of gas was getting stronger and she could feel Jess staring at her from the doorway. No one seemed to be moving anymore and the room was completely silent. Shadows cast by the candles on the table were heaving up and down the blackened kitchen walls in the draught. It was like being on a ship.

Suddenly Keely felt like she was going to be sick. Her knuckles were stinging badly.

She turned to Jess, holding out the matchbox. 'Help us, would you? I can't get it to strike.'

CHAPTER FIFTEEN

Jess was in her little downstairs bedroom, doing her make-up in front of the dressing-table mirror. Standing hesitantly in the doorway, Keely stared across at her. Her cousin was wearing nothing but bra and knickers. There was a short black skirt and a glittery top laid out on the bed. The room stank of perfume. It was like watching her transformation into a bird of paradise, something amazing and exotic. Whatever drew the punters to her side of the street or bar.

'I thought you weren't working tonight?'

'I'm clubbing.' Jess took a drag on her ciggy, then balanced it on the edge of the dressing-table. She stretched her eyes wide into the mirror, expertly stroking the underside of her lashes with mascara. 'Why don't you put your glad rags on and come with us?'

'I've nothing good enough to wear.'

'God's sake. Borrow some of my stuff.' Taking another drag on her cigarette, Jess blew a perfect smoke ring into the air. It coiled thickly above her and she watched it with satisfaction. 'It's all under the bed. You can take anything except the red velvet. Eddy gave me that for my birthday. I'm saving it for New Year.'

'Is Eddy coming tonight?'

As if she hadn't heard, Jess reached up and tore a hole through the smoke ring. It trembled and dissolved into eddies.

'Nobody should die a virgin,' she murmured, not meeting Keely's eyes in the mirror. Tapping the mascara against the dressing-table to stop it from clumping, she started to apply a second coat. Her mouth fell open automatically, as if looking astonished was a natural part of the process. 'You going to choose something to wear or what?'

'I don't like him.'

'You don't have to shag him, Kee. You just have to sit next to him for a few hours.'

'What about his mates?'

'Look, you get free drinks all night and they get to squeeze your bum. Where's your problem?' Jess sniffed the air, frowning. Then she screamed, grabbing at her cigarette too late. There was a charred black channel in the dressing-table where she had left it to burn away. Holding it up to Keely with a look of accusation, she threw the dog-end onto the floor in disgust. 'That's your fault, mithering on at me over nothing. Waste of a good ciggy, that.'

Niall woke suddenly. Something icy was trickling down his chin. His body jerked away instinctively, then relaxed when he realised what it was. He was slumped against the radiator in the living room, lips dry and cracked as Keely fed him a few drops of water from a saucer. His wrist ached from being suspended continually above his head by the handcuffs and there was a dull pain in his bladder now because he hadn't used the bucket for several hours. But he hated the smell of it.

It was unpleasant, having to return to full consciousness. The first thing he always saw on waking were Keely's strange wall paintings opposite his position, swirls of dark colours and violent patterns stretching from ceiling to skirting-board right across the living room.

If anything could persuade him that the girl needed psychiatric help, it was the way she had painted these walls.

Slowly becoming aware of his surroundings, his eyes widened on her high heels and strappy top. 'Are you going out somewhere?'

'Aw, what's the matter?' At that moment, Jess tottered into the room on even higher heels, obviously catching what he'd said and taunting him. 'Is our teacher scared of the dark?'

'Bitch,' he said deliberately, unable to help himself.

Furious, Jess lashed out and kicked him in the stomach. He doubled up, groaning in agony. Her stilettos were lethal. It felt as if someone had put a knife in his belly. Jess turned away as if she'd finished with him, then whipped quickly back round, catching him full in the mouth this time. The room exploded into blackness.

Her voice rang like a gunshot somewhere above him. 'Don't ever speak to me like that again. D'you hear me?'

When he eventually opened his eyes again, Keely was kneeling beside him on the floorboards. She smelt of perfume. Niall put a hand up to his lip and realised it was still bleeding. He should have kept his mouth shut. He wouldn't make that mistake again with Jess.

Leaning forward, Keely placed one hand on his stomach. Even though she was gentle, he couldn't help wincing. Ignoring his protest, she yanked up the tee-shirt and looked at the skin underneath. 'It's not serious. Just some bruising. She didn't hit you that hard.'

Jess came back into the room, swinging her handbag aggressively and watching them. It was obvious she was impatient to be out of the house. 'But I will next time, teacher.'

'Shut up, will you?' Keely snapped over her shoulder.

To his surprise, Jess said nothing in reply but simply lit up another cigarette, tapping her metallic heels on the floorboards as she paced to the boarded-up window and back. The sound bounced eerily off the walls of the empty house. Wary of the older girl now, Mr Swainson watched those feet as they stopped in front of him. He drew himself up into a ball as if expecting her to lash out again and heard her laughter.

Keely glanced back down at his stomach. There was a faint flush on her cheeks. She met his eyes, dropping the tee-shirt and getting up. She had to dust her bare knees in the short skirt. The skin was shiny and pink from where she had shaved her legs.

'I'll have to put this back on you,' Keely said apologetically, tearing a fresh strip of silver tape from the roll. 'Head up.'

'I won't shout.'

But she ignored him, pressing it swiftly down over his mouth in spite of his struggles and checking it was secure. 'Sorry, Mr Swainson. I can't take the chance.'

He looked up at her, experiencing a tremendous inner wave of rage and hatred. For the first few minutes, the tape across his mouth always made him feel as though he were going to suffocate. Remembering the other times, he took several long shuddering breaths through his nose, trying to keep control. If he panicked, snatching repeatedly at the air like a drowning man, he would only become dizzy and faint again.

Keely glanced at Jess. 'Come on, let's get out of here.'

'About bloody time.' Jess stumbled out of the room in those lethal stilettos, clutching at the door frame for balance. She looked ridiculous, like a school kid dressed up in her mother's clothes. Glancing back at Niall, her voice was almost a hiss, as if she knew what he was thinking. 'Look at me, I'm all nerves now. I need a hit.'

The door was pulled shut after them, leaving him in semi-darkness with the flickering stump of a candle. He heard the bang of chipboard over the back door. Their heels and voices faded away into the evening.

There was a strange buzzing silence for a few minutes

afterwards, as though some unbearably loud music had just stopped and his ears were adjusting. Then he gradually became aware of other sounds. The painfully slow drag and whistle of air through his nostrils. Floorboards ticking abruptly as they settled. Birdsong somewhere outside, faint but somehow encouraging. Hot candle wax pooling and almost imperceptibly dripping over the edge of the saucer. The rattle of a passing car with serious exhaust problems. His own heart, thudding erratically under his ribs.

It was cold enough outside to freeze the balls off a brass monkey, so they linked arms for warmth on the way uphill to the bus stop. A thin white layer of frost had already formed over tarmac and windscreens. Their heels clacked against the pavement like pit ponies' hooves, little puffs of breath steaming out onto the air as they climbed.

There were some lads up on the corner, hanging round the last house with the old couple still in it. Someone must have thrown a brick through the window or something, because the curtain was hanging out of a great hole in the glass. The old man was in the doorway, holding it warily on the latch and shouting at them through the gap, though he wasn't stupid enough to go out into the street. The lads were calling back and laughing at him. One of the youngest had a baseball bat in his hand, he kept swinging it against the outside wall, but they were only messing. The older ones were lounging under the lamp post, smoking and not paying much attention to the shouts.

Up the top, all the shops were grilled-up for the night except for the burger place and the fish and chips and the late night shopper. Keely was starving as usual, but there was no point eating when she would just puke it up again within a few minutes. So she glanced at the battered fish and the meat pies through the chip shop window and carried on walking.

The frying smell followed her along the road. It made

her feel horrible sick again so she gripped Jess's arm even harder and smiled at herself in the estate agent's window. The houses up for sale notices were a joke. They couldn't have shifted those ugly piles of rubble even if they were giving them away.

In the bus queue, Jess unslung her big handbag from her shoulder, rummaging through it for change. She kept coming out with coppers and chucking them back in.

'Why don't you get shot of that fucking teacher, Keely? It's worse than having my mam in the house.'

'You know I can't. He'd be straight down the nick.'

'Fuck's sake.'

'I'm going to sort it.'

'You better had, and soon.' Jess pulled out a tenner. 'Because if you don't, I'm going to tell Eddy and he will.'

The club was packed as usual but Eddy found them soon enough. He seemed to have built-in radar when it came to Jess. Leaning against the bar at the far end, he already had some of his mates with him. Keely had seen a few of them down the park. Except for one, who was older than the rest and was smoking a cigarette. Keely didn't much like the look of him, but Jess dragged her through the crowd with an iron hand.

Eddy beckoned them over, putting his arm along the older bloke's shoulder as if they were old friends. The music changed from hip-hop to jungle. Eddy raised his voice, shooting Jess a meaningful glance as she reached the bar. 'I'd like you to meet Rab. He's the sort of lad you want to be very nice to. Very nice indeed.'

Jess took one look at Eddy's face and pushed Keely forward. 'This is my little cousin. She's a bit shy.'

Caught off guard, Keely found herself thrust face to face with Rab. He was a tall thin bloke wearing a brown leather jacket with rubbed elbows, faded blue jeans and trainers. The jungle beat was thumping through her, right from her feet to the back of her neck.

There was a thin smoke haze clinging to him. He

watched her through it, stubbing out his cigarette. 'What's your name, gorgeous?'

'None of your business.'

'It's Keely. Her name's Keely.' Eddy laughed, giving her cheek a playful slap that stung. 'You can ignore the wisecracks. She's only a kid.'

Rab was looking her over. 'But legal?'

'She got in here, didn't she?'

'That's no guarantee these days.'

Eddy smiled and shook his head, yelling to make himself heard above the music. 'Don't fret yourself about it. You're sorted, okay?'

The dance floor was heaving, everyone jerking awkwardly under the strobe lights. Keely thought it was like something off an old black and white horror film. Jess had thrown her bag down in the middle and they did the wolf dance, circling it. Keely looked across at her cousin. Jess was laughing: head was thrown back, eyes shut.

After a bit Keely shut her eyes too and just listened to the music. There was a hot red darkness behind her lids, except for the odd flash of strobe whenever she whirled to face the DJ. She could feel bodies all around her, pressing relentlessly into her, elbows in her ribs and knees against her legs. There was a reek of sweat and Keely suddenly remembered him back at the house, slumped against the wall, lips cracked and dry.

One of the lads nearby drew her into a corner with him but Keely wasn't interested. She let him put his arm around her waist for a minute or two, then squeezed back into the middle of the dance floor. He had pockmarks all over his face anyway.

Then everyone was doing jungle. It was almost like running on the spot, only kicking her feet at the same time, and soon she was sweating buckets too. She was right in the thick of it, shoved and elbowed, but with the drums so deep inside her that her whole body seemed to be connected to the floors and walls by the music.

Jess reappeared at her side with a bottle of water. She yelled right up against her ear. 'Fancy an E?'

'Toilets,' Keely shouted, pointing.

'Stand in front of me.'

Keeping an eye out for anyone watching them, Keely shielded her from the bouncer hovering by the dance floor while Jess quickly took an E from her bag. She snapped it in two with her teeth, handed one half to Keely and swallowed the rest.

As the music changed tempo, they managed to push their way through the crowd of dancers to one of the poles with a high table round it. Jess pulled herself up onto a stool and took a large gulp of water from the bottle. She took so much it started to trickle out of her mouth and down her chin. Grinning, she offered Keely the bottle. 'That should do the trick. You having a good time?'

Keely shrugged, taking a swig and knocking the half tablet back. She glanced around the club. 'Don't know. It's all right.'

'What do you think of Rab?'

'Don't like him.'

Jess looked at her. 'Bit old for you?'

'It's not that.'

'I thought you were trying to look out for yourself? He's all over you. You'd be stupid not to let him buy you a few drinks.'

But Jess had spotted Eddy again across the crowded bar. The lads had found a small table near the men's loos. She waved madly and Eddy raised a hand, continuing to talk to Rab.

'Boys' talk. I'm not going over there yet. Come on, let's dance.' Jess carefully held down her skirt as she slid from the high stool. She grabbed Keely's wrist and started to drag her back to the dance floor. Her hand was hot and clammy. It made Keely feel sick again.

'There's no room.'

'There's a space near the speakers.'

"Yeah, because they're too loud,' Keely protested.

But she gave in and let Jess pull her through the suffocating crush towards the emptier spaces at the back of the floor. It was going to be deafening under the speakers, but anything was better than standing about like a lemon. Besides, Keely liked dancing. She'd been cooped up in the squat for so long, she had almost forgotten what it felt like to be out on the town.

Then the strobe light started again and everything got confused. They had to squeeze past a pack of lads, all completely bolloxed out of their heads, staggering about the dance floor and leering at every girl within vomiting distance.

One of the lads pushed hard against Keely and tried to fumble his hand up her skirt. She knocked him away with a filthy look that sent all the rest howling and whooping hysterically behind her back. Jess didn't pay them any attention, but Keely hugged her arms to her chest, suddenly wishing she hadn't chosen such a revealing top.

'I hate clubbing.'

'WHAT?' Jess yelled.

The speakers were booming above their heads. 'I ... HATE ... CLUBBING.'

'WHAT?'

Keely shook her head and danced.

Rab kept bringing back double whiskeys with ice for her from the bar. He was always putting his hand on her thigh too. Her head must have been spinning from the alcohol and the sickness because eventually she stopped pushing him away.

'Was your mam a Neighbours fan, Keely?'

'That's Kylie, not Keely.'

'Oh aye. Where does your mam live then?'

'She's dead,' Keely lied automatically.

'That's shite luck for you.' Rab leant further forward and she could smell his breath. His hand tightened on her thigh. 'And what about your dad? Is he dead too?'

Her throat was like sawdust. It was really hot in the club. Keely drank some of her whisky but it didn't seem to help. 'I don't know where he is. I've only got a stepdad now.'

'Do you love him?'

'My stepdad's a bastard pervert. I want to kill him.'

'Aw, it's all shite. That's life all over. Pure fucking shite. But at the end of the day, he's still family and you've got to love him.'

Rab kissed her throat and cheek for a few minutes. The room was spinning black and red behind her tight-shut eyes. Then he shifted slightly and put his tongue in her mouth.

Keely didn't like the taste so she pushed Rab away before he suffocated her. She felt dizzy now and the sickness was back in her stomach.

He looked at her, angry now. 'What did you do that for, pet?'

Keely shrugged, silent.

'I'm good enough to buy you a drink but not good enough to kiss you, is that it?' He gripped her head, staring straight at her, and his hands were like a vice on her jawbone. She stared back without speaking, only just able to breathe. His pupils were strangely dilated and Keely wondered what else he'd been taking besides the whiskey. 'Listen, sweetheart, my tongue's as good as any man's. Why don't you like it?'

'Hey, don't hurt my cousin.' Jess leant forward unsteadily. 'Eddy, he's your mate. Tell Rab to leave her alone.'

'Leave the kid alone, man.'

'Mind your own fucking business.' Rab wasn't amused and he wasn't letting go of her face either, though his fingers had loosened a bit. 'I was talking to the lady here, not to you two jokers.'

Keely struggled under his hand, changing her tone. There was no point making the stupid bastard angry. The last thing she wanted was for a fight to start in a public place like this, in case somebody recognised her and it got back to Zal.

'I just didn't like being kissed, that's all,' she told him.

'And when will you like it?'

'Maybe later,' she murmured.

'You better had. I don't like being pissed about.'

'I'm not pissing you about.'

'Four fucking doubles? And I can't even put my tongue in your mouth? That's what I call pissing me about.'

Eddy was still grinning at his mate over the top of his pint. He shook his head knowingly. 'You picked the wrong lass there, Rab. It's the tightest cunt in the whole of Newcastle.'

Rab looked Keely over with a dirty light in his eyes. He put his hand back on her thigh, only higher this time. Then he fixed his gaze on the small breasts under her gold tee-shirt and laughed. 'Not for much longer it's not.'

Jess seemed to have given up the ghost. She was lying back against Eddy's shoulder now like one of the undead. Her face was dead white but her eyes were unnaturally bright and shiny. She kept jumping up to dance and then collapsing again, sometimes laughing, and sometimes lapsing into an almost comatose silence. They were all squeezed together in an alcove. Eddy's mates were playing some drinking game and a couple of long-haired girls Keely didn't know were sitting on their laps and wriggling.

The music was almost deafening but she didn't care. She had sort of gotten used to it and her voice was hoarse from shouting.

'You all right?' Eddy asked her once.

She nodded automatically. All she could really focus on was the half finger of whisky left in her glass and Rab's hand on her thigh. He was moving his fingers under her skirt now, right in front of everyone, like hot little worms burrowing into her skin, but Keely couldn't concentrate on what he was doing. Every time she tried to think about it, the idea slipped away into the music and the hot squeeze of bodies.

Then Eddy put his arm round Jess's waist and hoisted her into a sitting position. 'We going back to your place then, doll?'

Half a life away, lying alone in freezing darkness, Niall remembered his first and only night with a woman. It had been down to Jack, not surprisingly. Most of the shit in his life dated back to his friendship with Jack.

'Go on, I dare you,' Jack had muttered hoarsely in his ear, pushing him forward. 'This is it, lad. You've been staring at her all evening. Last Chance Saloon.'

Niall shook his head, embarrassed. 'I only met her once, years ago. She'll think I'm mad.'

'She's begging for it. Look at her. Right little goer.'

'I'm not in the mood.'

'Jesus Christ, man.' Jack snorted, taking Niall's pint away from him and prodding him in the right direction. 'It's your birthday. Quit stalling. You want to stay a virgin for the rest of your life? Get over there and introduce yourself to the lass. Go on with you, you soft bastard. I'll be fine on my own.'

'She's pissed.'

'So much the better. That means she won't realise how crap you are in bed. I'm telling you straight, man. If you don't dip your wick tonight, I swear it'll be all round Newcastle this time tomorrow that Niall Swainson's a virgin. Now what are you going to do about that?'

Niall stared through smog across the pool table, watching the drunken crowd of girls stumble across the pub for last orders. Jack might be a wanker, but tonight he was right for once. Niall owed this one to himself. He was sick of being the only virgin of his acquaintance. There was the gorgeous lass right in front of him, and he even knew her name already. Now all he had to do was not screw this up, like he'd screwed up all the other times.

Hurriedly, Niall blew on his hands to check his breath but couldn't smell anything except lager. Which seemed okay.

She was a flushed blonde in a tight tee-shirt, almost held upright by the other girls, who was trying to get money out of her purse, but no one would let her. 'Put that away, you silly cow, it's our shout.'

She kept pushing the ten pound note in their faces, stumbling about on her high heels. 'No, you've got to take it. It's not right.'

Trying to look casual about it, Niall wandered over to the bar and stood next to the girls for a moment, still a little embarrassed and undecided. But this was his best chance yet and he leant forward into the group as soon as one of the other girls had moved slightly. 'Anne?'

When the blonde's head turned at the sound of her name, Niall met her eyes with a shock. It was definitely the same girl.

'Who are you?'

He hesitated. All heads had now turned in his direction. 'It's Niall. Don't say you've forgotten me?'

'I've never seen you before in my life.'

'Oh come on,' Niall laughed, but felt a sudden heat come into his face. The ring of female eyes scared him, examining every detail of his appearance from his trainers to his spiked hair as they closed ranks around him, cutting off his escape route. 'Niall Swainson. I met you years ago when we were kids at somebody's party. You must remember. You're breaking my heart here.'

One of the other girls giggled, and Anne laughed too, holding a hand against her face. Her voice was slurred. 'You're full of shit.'

'No honest. We had a chat, like. You told me stuff

about yourself.'

'Like what?'

Desperately, Niall dug into his memory. 'Horses. You told me you liked horses. That you wanted to be a vet.'

'That was years ago. I haven't wanted to be a vet since I was about ten.' Anne stared at him unsteadily, as if she was beginning to recognise his face. Her brown-flecked pupils were hugely dilated. 'But he's right about the other. No, don't laugh. I really do like horses.'

'Yeah.' One of her friends grinned, making an obscene pumping gesture with her fist. 'Between your legs, you tart!'

There was a scream of delighted outrage from the tight-packed group of women. One of the younger ones immediately started chanting 'BIG DICK! BIG DICK! BIG DICK!' and waving her arms drunkenly in the air as if conducting an invisible orchestra. The other girls joined in with the chanting, even Anne herself, their voices growing louder and louder until heads were turning all over the pub.

'Stop it.' Anne collapsed with laughter on another girl's shoulder, mascara running down her face. She was wiping it away with the back of her hand and grinning up at the lipsticked mouths stretched wide for the chant. 'Oh Christ, I think I'm going to piss myself.'

Niall could hardly bear to stand there with them any longer. The blonde was bad enough, but the rest of them didn't even seem to be human. Instead, they were terrible roaring animals on the loose in Newcastle city centre. Drumming their heels chaotically on the wooden floorboards like a herd of deranged Flamenco dancers, the girls yelled and screamed repeatedly at each other across the crowded bar. Niall was almost choking on their overpowering smell of cosmetics and perfume and sweat.

But if he gave up now, if he walked away defeated, nothing but a useless pathetic virgin, he would never be able to face himself in the mirror again. After all, he reminded himself, it really didn't matter how appalling the experience was or whether he had to be sick afterwards. He only needed to do it once, and the terrible years of uncertainty would be over.

He needed to get Anne on her own, but how? They all seemed to be high on one kind of shit or another. One of the black girls beside him lifted her arms above her head to clap her hands loudly at some joke somebody had been telling, and Niall caught sight of slick stubble under her armpits as her sleeve was tugged away. Her eyes were glazed and there were beads of sweat along her upper lip.

He grabbed Anne by the arm, speaking low into her ear. 'Come and have a drink with us over here. Forget this lot, I'll buy you a whisky and coke.'

'I can't leave them. They're my mates.'

'She called you a whore.'

Anne laughed again, shaking his hand away. Slightly unfocused, her eyes wandered over his face. 'It was only a joke. She's taking the piss.'

'I like you,' he said sullenly. 'I want to buy you a drink.'

'I can't let you. I'm getting married next weekend,' she said, showing him her engagement ring. 'This is my hen night.'

Knocked back by that information but only too aware of Jack's eyes on his back, Niall persisted doggedly. 'I don't care.'

'Don't care was made to care! Don't care was hung!' Anne began to chant loudly, dancing sideways on her high heels and giggling at his expression. 'Oh shit. What's the rest of it? Don't care was put in a pot and boiled till he was done!'

The other girls whooped with laughter, one of them nudging Anne so violently that she nearly fell over, but Niall caught her in time. 'Easy does it, love,' he murmured in her ear.

The woman standing behind Anne's shoulder was a

vast bleach-blonde with heavy blue eyeshadow and gold hoop earrings. The shiny straining material of her top heaved as she leant protectively over the younger girl, wagging a pudgy nicotine-stained finger in his direction. 'Don't listen to that little twat, sweetheart. He just wants to get in your knickers!'

'In your KNICKERS!' they all screamed together, obviously enjoying his discomfort.

'I do not.' Abruptly, Niall let go of the girl and stuck his hands deep in his pockets, glaring round at them all. Stupid drunken tarts. The noise was almost deafening. He had to shout just to be heard above their high-pitched screams. 'I bloody don't.'

'Go on,' Anne whispered in his ear, her nails agonising little pincers on his back. 'Just stick it up me, for fuck's sake. It's my hen night. I've got to get shagged.'

For the third time, Niall closed his eyes and pushed himself against the warm moist opening, but it was no use. It wasn't going to happen. He wanted it badly, but his body simply wasn't interested. It was wonderfully ironic, considering all the thousands of hours Niall had spent playing with himself, imagining how it would feel to be with a woman, the intense excitement involved. Now here he was with a real flesh-and-blood woman, and she was begging for it, like they always did in his fantasies. Yet he couldn't even manage a respectable hard-on.

'What's wrong?'

He buried his head between her tits. 'Nothing.'

'Is it me?'

'Don't be soft.'

'Well, what is it then? You were keen enough before.' Anne pushed him away, struggling to sit up on the sofa.

They were lying in her flat with the lights out, just a few candles flickering on top of the telly. The sitting room smelt damp and the coarse wallpaper was sagging and peeling off in thin mouldy strips along the street-facing wall. Staring at her body close-up, Niall watched the full tits wobbling in the candlelight as Anne heaved herself up from the cushions. He could see thin silvery stretch marks running streakily towards the nipples and down under her armpits.

He asked, 'Don't you love him? This man you're going to marry.'

'He's all right. Painter and decorator,' she told him, almost proudly. 'Got his own van, and all. Not a bad catch, is Malcolm.'

He wasn't really sure how he'd got to her flat. They'd opened a bottle of Chianti after coming in from the pub and Niall knocked his glass over on the carpet, but nobody seemed to care about the dark red stain. Her flat-mate, the loud bleach-blonde with the blue eyeshadow, had staggered off to bed an hour before and left them to it. They'd carried on chatting for a few minutes, then she'd got up to change the music and he'd looked under her short skirt, lying on his back on the carpet. She'd slapped him, calling him a dirty buggar, but it was laughter not anger. Niall had pulled her down beside him, finding it surprisingly easy to remove her top and unclasp her bra. She had started moaning with excitement when he groped her tits, then stuck his fingers inside her.

'So why do this?'

She shrugged. 'Why not? Last time for a shag with a stranger before I get hitched, I suppose. Now come on, let's do it.'

He pulled off his jeans and underpants, falling over on the carpet like an idiot, desperate to get inside her. Anne climbed onto the sofa without any hesitation, hauled her skirt up to her waist and stretched her legs wide. As her thighs opened, the lips sprang apart like a gaping mouth with a thick ginger beard.

Niall dragged himself up on top of her, trying hard not to put his full weight on her chest, but his hands kept slipping on the dirty cotton sofa cover. He'd somehow forgotten to take his shirt off. Laughing again, she started to unbutton it while Niall stared blindly into the cushions, fumbling with his right hand as he tried to manoeuvre himself between her legs.

'No rubber?' she asked.

'Shit.'

He hadn't thought of that.

'It don't matter. Stop looking so bloody worried.' She reached down to help him, smiling. 'Just remember to pull out, okay?'

He tried to remember, but it was impossible. All he kept thinking as they had sex was, I'm not a virgin anymore, I'm not a virgin anymore.

CHAPTER SIXTEEN

Eddy tore another strip of the Rizla packet and made a roach for his spliff, fingers clumsy and shaking as he tried to skin up at what felt like sub-arctic temperatures. 'It's ridiculous cold in here, Jess. Why can't we sit in the other room?'

'Shut up. I feel sick.'

Eddy pulled a face, grinning at Rab. 'Narky bitch.'

Their breath made little white clouds on the air even though they were indoors. Keely had pulled the curtain across the kitchen window as soon as they came in, but it was still freezing. Her feet were gradually turning to ice in the high strappy sandals. It must have been easily below zero outside and not much higher in the flat.

They had been home half an hour now and the whiskey Keely had drunk was beginning to wear off. Slumped forward over the kitchen table, she felt dull and lethargic, except for a tremendous thirst. Her tongue was like old shoe leather. But she couldn't be bothered getting up for some water. Her whole body was hanging.

Rab sat beside her, dragging mechanically on his ciggy and bursting occasionally into some drunken tirade against the taxi driver who'd brought us back. 'Bastard,' he kept muttering. 'There was no way it should have cost that much. Taxi drivers are greedy sods. Fuck the lot of them, that's what I say.'

'This is too bloody cold,' Eddy suddenly said, getting up. 'C'mon, let's go in the other room.'

Jess woke up from her stupor, looking frightened. 'No, sit down Eddy, we can't.'

'Why not?'

'We just can't. It's okay in here, honest.' She whined, putting on the agony. 'Get us another drink, will you? I'm dying here. Keely, sweetheart, is there anything left in that wine?'

'Not much. There's vodka in the cupboard.'

Eddy staggered up, found the vodka and poured a couple of capfuls into a mug. He handed it to Jess with a fatherly look, almost missing her hand because he was so drunk himself. 'That's all you're having, love. I don't want you puking on us in the night.'

'Who asked you to stay the night?' Jess asked, giving him a sly smile. 'You're a bit of a chancer, aren't you?'

'And you're a tart.'

'You won't get anywhere speaking to us like that.'

'You enjoy it.'

'Maybe I do,' Jess grinned. 'And then again, maybe I don't.'

'Which is it?'

'You'll have to wait and see.'

Without any warning, Rab leapt to his feet, grabbing the vodka bottle with one hand and snaking the other around Keely's throat, yanking her to her feet with one strong jerk of his arm. 'I'm going crazy, Keely love. It's freezing in here. My balls are turning to stone.'

He stared at the other two, his eyes bulging wild. Keely's chair fell over backwards with a clatter and she could feel his fingers flatten against her windpipe as he dragged her round the table towards the door. He kept talking the whole time, almost compulsively, like a tap that someone had left running.

'C'mon you two, let's get in the other room, warm us selves up. I've been on warmer ice-floes. This place would make the Antarctic feel like the Caribbean. Are you two lasses Eskimos or what?'

Keely couldn't reply because she couldn't even breathe. He yanked her out into the hall and kicked the door open to the other room. The other two followed without saying anything, though Eddy was watching her face carefully.

Rab stopped dead in the doorway, still gripping her throat. 'Who the fuck is that?'

Sir struggled up on his elbow, stubbly face lit by candlelight, hair limp and greasy. 'For God's sake, get me out of here,' he managed to say, though his tongue seemed to be getting in the way when he spoke. Thirst, probably. His eyes were dull as well, but his movements were swift and overexcited. 'She's insane, she won't let me go. I've been here for days. Please help me. Call the police, please call the police.'

Rab looked down at Keely. 'You did this?'

She nodded silently.

The fingers loosened on her throat. Rab stepped back and stared at Keely with his mouth open. He seemed sort of impressed. 'You mad bitch, what did the poor bastard do to you? It's not your dad, is it?'

'One of my teachers.'

'I thought you were eighteen? You're still at school?'

'I'm in the sixth form.' She shrugged. 'But not for long. I've had it with school.'

Rab laughed. 'I'm not surprised.'

'Call the police and let them know where I am, for god's sake,' Mr Swainson groaned, trying to pull himself up and away from the radiator. The handcuffs rattled noisily against the metal. 'Didn't you hear what I said?'

'Shut up,' Rab snapped, kicking out at him. Mr Swainson yelped at the pain and rolled into a ball for his own safety, cuffed hands tight over his bent head, legs drawn up to his stomach. Even in the candlelight Keely could see how pale his skin was and how his whole body was trembling now like a beaten dog's. 'If she's keeping you here like this, you probably deserve it.'

Eddy was astonished. The spliff hung down from his lips, still unlit. He just kept staring across at the ball of human flesh, shaking his head and saying 'I had no idea he was here. I had no bloody idea.'

'So nobody fucks with you, Keely? Are you a real hard bitch?' Rab held her at arms' length and shook her. But his fingers were no longer iron pegs in her skin and he was smiling, glancing over at Eddy and Jess as he spoke. There was a strange light in his eyes that she didn't like. 'What did the bastard do to you? Did he give you a detention, like? Did he make you stand in the corner?'

Jess started laughing wildly, as if she couldn't control herself.

Rab threw himself down into the only armchair in the room. It smelt of mould but he didn't seem to care, throwing one leg casually over the arm as he settled back into it. 'Will you get some more candles for us, Jess? And close that door, it's still freezing.' He took a long swig from the vodka. The red heart tattooed on his forearm gleamed in the candlelight as he lowered the bottle. 'Do you fancy a fuck, Keely love?'

'No.'

'Well, thank you very much.'

Rab stared at her for a moment without speaking, his face hardening. Keely wondered whether she'd gone too far, but couldn't seem to get her mind to focus on the situation.

He took another swig and passed the bottle to Eddy. 'Nothing like letting a man down gently, is there? These lasses are all the same. Expect us lads to pay for the drinks, then they won't open their legs for us.'

Jess came back in with candles and matches. 'I found

some crisps too, at the back of the cupboard. They're out of date, but I'm dead starving. My stomach thinks my throat's been cut. It's a pity we can't eat candles. We've got a whole sodding packet of them.'

Eddy leant back against the wall, lazily handing the spliff to Jess so that she could hand it to Rab. 'That's some grade A shit there, Rab. Do you want to take some home with you? I can let you have an eighth right now if you've got the cash on you.'

'It's not bad,' Rab said, shrugging. He exhaled slowly, watching the smoke drift and coil upwards in the candlelight.

'You want something else?'

'Mebbe.'

'With a bit more kick?'

'Aye, mebbe.'

'I've a few rocks on me.'

'Good crack?'

'Best this side of the Tyne, man.'

'Sounds right enough. Have you anything to smoke it with? An empty bottle of pop, like?'

Eddy riffled through his coat pockets for the bag of rocks. Jess got up and staggered into the kitchen again, stepping over Sir in her tiny skirt without glancing down at him. Even from a distance, Keely could see the goosebumps standing out on her legs. Her calves and thighs looked like they belonged to a skinned chicken. It was still very cold. Keely curled up against the side of the armchair to keep warm, resting her head on Rab's leg. She was too tired to care what he might think. Instead, she watched Mr Swainson through sleepy half-closed eyes.

But Rab didn't seem that interested in what Keely was doing. He was watching Mr Swainson too. Then he laid one hand on Keely's throat and stroked gently at the skin he had bruised. 'Hey, teacher. Don't you go looking up her skirt, do you hear me? I'll have your balls on a rope if you so much as take a peep up there.'

'I didn't look, I swear,' Mr Swainson said.

Rab looked at Keely. 'What are you planning to do with him? You can't keep him here forever, like.'

'Dunno.'

'Would you like me to get shot of him for you?'

'No thanks.'

'He'd be happy enough in the river.' Rab took another drag on the spliff, and offered it to her.

'I don't smoke.'

'I can see you're a clean lass, Keely love.' The red heart on his forearm looked shiny with sweat. 'You must be getting cold down there. Come and sit on my knee.'

'No thanks.'

His voice hardened. 'I said, come and sit on my knee.'

'I don't want to. Why don't you leave us alone?' Trembling suddenly, Keely left the room, wiping her face and nearly knocking into Jess, who was weaving her way back in with an empty plastic pop bottle and a small kitchen knife. 'Just leave us alone.'

Keely sat on the edge of the bed for a while, staring at nothing in the darkness. She felt so sick, it was awful. Her belly wanted to chuck. The wind was whistling in through a gap behind the chipboard. One of the window panes must have been cracked. She slipped off her strappy sandals, threw them into a corner of the bedroom, and slowly rubbed her feet. Her calves ached too from the dancing.

After a bit she went back in to the other room, because it was warmer where the others were. Mr Swainson was curled up under the radiator like a dog, his face to the wall. He smelt awful as usual. Eddy and Jess were huddled together under a blanket on the floor, giggling sometimes and then lapsing into long moments of silence while their bodies moved like eels under the thin material.

Rab was holding the crack bottle between his knees.

He was hunched over it, about to take a deep drag. When he heard her come in, he raised his head and grinned at her as if nothing had happened. 'Just in time. Come over here and keep me company.' He held out the plastic bottle. 'It's excellent. You've never felt anything like this, Keely.'

Keely took the bottle mechanically and stood there, doing nothing. Out of the corner of her eye, she noticed Mr Swainson shifting his position slightly. Like some kind of secret signal, his handcuffs clinked against the metal radiator and caught her attention. When Keely glanced across to see what he was doing, she realised he had lifted his head at last and was watching her.

Rab looked at him too. 'Face the wall.' Mr Swainson hesitated, then slowly faced the wall again. Rab laughed under his breath. The contempt in his voice was only too obvious. 'Good dog.'

Then he leant back and nodded encouragingly at Keely. 'Go on, love. Fill your boots.'

She put the biro tube to her mouth and inhaled.

Once she was able to stop coughing helplessly, Keely wiped the tears from her cheeks and looked around herself. At first, all she could see were Rab's eyes glittering icily in the candlelight. The bottle felt cold in her hands and there were enormous shadows on the wall of the room. They looked like huge spidery men coming towards her.

Everything was incredibly clear now, as if the whole room had been captured in crystal and she was staring down into it. She could even hear Mr Swainson's heart beating as he lay facing the wall. The tiny valves were struggling to open and close. His blood was running out onto the floorboards in long pulsating waves of red. She was standing in his blood, it was creeping stickily towards the very edges of the room. It was going to pour out into the street where everyone could see it.

Keely dropped the bottle as if it had stung her.

She stared across at Rab. He had a tongue like a

wolf's and it dropped out, lolling from his mouth as he came towards her, stepping over the writhing bodies of Eddy and Jess. He had incredibly light feet, he could have been a dancer, but the candles still flickered and grew tall again as Rab passed, sending his amazingly long shadow shivering across the room. Her paintings on the wall and ceiling swirled and leapt in a strange warning, almost as if they could sense he was coming for her.

His hand was stroking her face. She could feel every tiny pattern on his fingertips. 'C'mon , Keely love. Let's go somewhere more private.'

The scream was unearthly.

Keely felt it in every pore of her skin and shuddered, tearing away from him. It was dark in the bedroom and she was naked. She couldn't remember how she got naked, but she grabbed at the bed sheet and jerked it up over her body, instinctively trying to cover herself even though she knew he couldn't see her.

Something clattered noisily to the floor beside the mattress. Keely couldn't see exactly what it was, but it might turn out to be important.

She bent to find it, scrabbling about with her fingers in the dark.

'What the fuck?' Rab lunged after her. 'Come back here. You nearly burst my eardrums.'

He fell over something as he came round the bed. Probably the pile of old magazines Jess had left there for her to look at, and he staggered into the wall with a crash. There was a murderous edge to his voice when he reared up again.

'I've cut my head open. You stupid bitch. You've made me cut my fucking head open.'

She found what she had been looking for. It was her mam's heavy glass ashtray, the one they'd used to hit Mr Swainson. Mam said they always come in handy, those big glass ashtrays. Now it curved perfectly under her fingers, smooth and round. She considered throwing it, but it was too dark for her to make sure of hitting him.

'Don't come any closer,' she warned him.

Eddy was outside the door now, hammering on it. 'What the hell was that? Keely, are you okay in there?'

Rab growled with frustration. He was at the bedroom door instantly, pushing his back against the wood to keep it shut. Keely could see edges of light straining to get in around the frame as the two men struggled with the door. The older man's voice was ragged as he tried to keep Eddy out of the room. 'Back off, man. It's all under control in here.'

'It doesn't sound under control to me.'

'Keely? Keely?' Jess was hysterical. Her voice rose higher. 'She's not answering. What have you done to her, you bastard? If you've touched a hair on her head I'll kill you.'

Then the door gave way. Eddy fell into the room, wearing nothing but his shirt, creased and completely unbuttoned where he must have grabbed it when she screamed. He staggered in like a drunk as the door crashed open then straightened up as if ready to fight, assessing the situation with one brief scan of the room.

Rab scrambled back from the doorway, blinking at the sudden light, and Keely realised for the first time that he too was naked. She had no memory of either of them undressing. His balls hung down between his legs like a dog's, heavy and dark-veined. There was a small red scorpion tattooed across the small of his back. His buttocks were covered in thick black hairs like a gorilla.

Keely wanted to look away from Rab's body, but somehow she couldn't. It was like she'd been hypnotised.

'Did he hit you? What did he do to you?' Jess stood in the doorway behind him, holding a candle shakily in her hand, stark naked herself, pupils massively dilated as she stared across at Keely. Her face was flushed and sweaty. Her small breasts swayed as she came into the room. She did not seem to give a toss that Rab could see everything. 'Say something, for Christ's sake. What did he do?'

Crouched for the attack, Rab took a swing at Eddy.

Eddy ducked the punch, slipping on the glossy magazines littering the floor. He went down heavily, catching at Rab's leg as he fell.

The two men lay tangled together on the floor, panting as they wrestled with each other, swearing and flailing about in the flickering light. There must have been a bottle of perfume lying on the floor somewhere, because one of them threw it at the other. It smashed against the wall behind them, a sweet unexpected smell filling the room immediately.

Then suddenly Rab was free. His eyes were wild and there was blood running down his cheek from a small cut on his forehead. He saw his jacket on the floor, grabbed it up, and there was a knife in his hand. It was one of those old switch-blades. The candlelight glinted off it as he moved it quickly from one hand to the other.

Rab straightened up as if he already knew that he'd won, running a sweaty hand down his flat chest and stomach. The glittering eyes were wild now.

He waved the knife provocatively in Eddy's face. 'Is this what you want, man? Come on, I'll have you.'

'Put the knife down.'

'Not so ready for a fight now, are you?'

'Put it down, Rab.'

'Fuck off.'

'What did you do to her, you bastard?' Jess interrupted, screaming now as if she couldn't hold back any longer. The candle was shaking between her cousin's fingers. Hot wax dripped onto her skin and she hissed. 'The poor little cow's terrified. She can't even speak. Look at her, Eddy.'

Eddy's eyes flickered briefly in her direction, and Rab immediately lunged forward with the knife.

Keely closed her eyes.

'Someone's got to call the police,' Jess kept moaning.

'Don't be so fucking stupid.'

'But there's a dead man in my bedroom, Eddy. What am I meant to do? Step over him every time I want to go to bed? What about when he starts rotting?' Jess demanded, rocking herself to and fro on the living room floor. 'Oh Christ. Oh Christ. Oh Christ. I need something for my nerves, Eddy. I need something right now.'

'Shut up. I can't hear myself think.'

'Why did you do it?'

'Because he had a knife in his hand.'

'You didn't have to kill him.'

Eddy wiped his face shakily. 'I didn't mean to. When he slipped, Keely gave me that ashtray and I used it. I didn't know it was going to come down so hard. Bloody thing must weigh a ton.'

'What are we going to do now?'

'Simple,' Keely said. 'We have to get rid of the body.'

They both turned their heads and looked at her. She was standing in the doorway, barefoot and only a little paler than before, listening to the conversation. She had washed her face and hands in a saucer of cold water, crouched down in the pitch-black bathroom, but now she could see there was still blood under her nails where she had touched the blood-soaked dent in Rab's head. Jess had tried to stop her, but Keely just wanted to know what it would feel like, a hole that size in somebody's skull.

'It's not that easy, Kee. You can't just take a dead body out and stick it in a dustbin for collection,' Jess moaned.

'Why not?'

'Shut up, both of you.' Eddy thought hard for a moment. 'Okay, how about the river? We could wrap him up in some sheets, get hold of a van that nobody can trace, take him down after dark and throw him in. No one knows he left with us last night. No one even knows you're living here. That's the beauty of it. We chuck him in the river and no one ever has the faintest idea what happened to the bastard.'

'Fine. Dump him in the river. But don't leave without giving us one last hit, okay?' Jess hung onto his arm, clawing at the sleeve of his shirt like a small scared animal. 'Please Eddy, just something to take the edge off. I can't bear it. You must have something left.'

'It's in my jacket pocket.'

His leather jacket was lying on the floor near the boarded-up window. Jess crawled over to it as if he couldn't even get to her feet anymore, tearing at the pockets with desperate hands. 'Where is it?'

'Take it easy, Jess. You're all over the place.' He helped her find the package, looking down into her face like he'd never seen her before. 'Here, use this one. It's clean.'

Her hands were shaking so much that she fumbled the strap and he had to push her fingers aside, tightening it for her. It was quite dark in the room but Keely could still see her face by candlelight. Jess looked like one of the undead. She kept slapping uselessly at her arm, muttering under her breath. The skin beneath the syringe was whitish-grey and flaking, like the scales on a long-dead fish. 'Give me a vein, for Christ's sake.'

They sat in silence for a while after that, watching Jess as she fixed herself. The terrible whimpering noise soon died away and she lay down on the floor of the living room, strap relaxed on her arm, her face good and peaceful now. She wasn't asleep, but Keely could see that she was dreaming. Somewhere high above all the shit so it couldn't touch her. Lying on her side like a dog, eyelids and fingers jerking.

Eddy rolled himself a joint and burnt the end twist from the spliff, taking a deeper drag as the heat scorched down to the tobacco. Flicking the first hot ashes onto the floor beside him, he squatted down against the wall to smoke it. The relief on his face was immediate, though Keely couldn't help noticing that his hands were still shaking slightly.

The sweet stench of gear filled the living room and Mr Swainson started to cough helplessly, holding his side with one hand as if it hurt. He'd been doing that a lot lately. She wondered if he was getting ill.

Eddy paid no attention to him. 'I'll need your help tonight, Kee. The fewer people know about this the better.'

'Okay.'

He raised his eyes and stared at her thoughtfully through the smoke. 'You're definitely up for this, then?'

'Uh huh.'

'You're a strange one, Keely.'

She said nothing.

'Why don't you get some rest before we have to do this?'

'I'm not tired.'

'Well, I am.' Eddy finished the joint a few minutes later and stood up. 'I'm off to find us a van and maybe grab some shut-eye. We'll take him down to the river after dark. Be ready, okay?'

Once the house had fallen quiet again, Keely went through into the bedroom to find her mother's ashtray.

It took a few minutes to see it in the glimmering half-light. Then she spotted it with relief. It must have rolled into the corner after Eddy used it. She could see blood and traces of dark hair on the rounded glass edge, but it didn't seem to be chipped or cracked. Stepping over the motionless naked body just inside the door, Keely picked up the ashtray and took it through to the kitchen. She wanted to wash it but there wasn't much water left in the container so she just wiped the ashtray with some old newspaper and placed it carefully in the middle of the kitchen table.

Then she stood there in silence for a bit, leaning her

hands on the sink, feet growing cold on the lino.

It always felt like night in the living room, with the candles flickering and the boarded-up windows, but it was daylight in the kitchen. No sunshine though. It was a dull enough morning and still quite early. There were kids playing outside again. Keely could hear one of them kicking a football, sometimes along the pavement and sometimes up against the house walls with an irritating thud, thud, thud. Boys were shouting at each other in hoarse voices but she couldn't make out what they were saying. Her pink toes wriggled, trying to get warm.

She shivered then and thought about getting dressed properly. She was wearing nothing but a loose black tee-shirt. It wasn't hers. It had been the first thing to hand after the screaming stopped.

Keely glanced down at the tee-shirt, but she still didn't recognise it for a moment. Then she realised it was Rab's.

Left alone with the flickering remains of a candle and the soft heap in the corner that was Jess, jerking and muttering in her sleep, the damp squalor of the living room seemed more bitter than ever to Niall. For a while, he squatted there dumbly, trying not to think about what he had just witnessed. Just rubbed vaguely at his arms and shoulders, attempting to warm himself up after the cold of the night. But it was useless. His hands felt over-large and ridiculously clumsy, unable to make any difference to his failing circulation.

There was a half-smoked spliff abandoned in the ashtray and Niall focussed longingly on it. He could really do with the some nicotine in his system. It had been such a long time since any of them had so much as offered him a cigarette. But this handcuff fixed his wrist tight to the frozen metal of the radiator and there was no chance of stretching for the ashtray. Even though it was only a few feet out of his reach across the floorboards, it might as well have been a mile away.

Would they murder him too?

Niall froze at the sound of footsteps. It was Eddy. The man pushed the door open and stood there, blocking out pale light from the hallway. It must be nearly morning.

Eddy looked at him for a moment without speaking, then came forward to retrieve the spliff from the ashtray. He crouched silently in front of Niall, lighting it with his head tilted away from the candle flame. His eyes glittered as though he were immensely tired, or perhaps drugged up. 'Enjoy the floor show last night? It makes life a bit difficult for us now though, doesn't it? You being a witness and all.'

Niall licked his dry lips, watching Eddy's face. He knew what was being said. 'There's no need for that.'

'Isn't there?'

'I can keep my mouth shut. Anyway, there's nothing to tell. The whole thing was an accident.'

'Yeah, that's right.' Eddy smiled slightly, taking a drag on the spliff and blowing the thin coiled smoke towards him. 'It was an accident. But I don't think the filth would see it quite like that. They tend to make a bit more of a fuss about dead bodies, like.'

'I won't say a word.'

Eddy looked at him silently, then bent down to put the last inch of the roach between Niall's lips. 'Here, take a drag on this.'

'But you believe me, don't you?'

'I'm just telling you, we're in a bit of a fix because of that dead bastard out there.' Eddy pulled the spliff back for a second as Niall choked helplessly on the smoke. 'Keely should never have done this to you. Kept you here, like. She's really fucked up this time.'

'So let me go.'

Eddy held out the spliff again. 'More?'

'Yes.'

'You don't understand the full situation, man. This bloke I work for, he doesn't like to draw attention to himself. Especially any attention that might involve the police. In other words, he won't be happy if he ever finds out about that dead bastard. And you're the weakest link.'

Niall dragged on the dying spliff once more and took the last dregs of smoke deep into his lungs. There was a slow sweet melting sensation in his blood and bones as the drug took effect. The room felt a little less cold. It gave him a moment of false courage. 'So I'm next for the chop?'

'It's not looking good.'

'Why bother telling me? Why not just kill me?'

'Calm down. I'm not going to off you right here and now, am I? That's not my style.' Clumsily, Eddy stubbed out the roach on the floor and straightened. His face was unreadable in the semi-darkness, but his voice sounded strained. 'I don't know why I'm bothering. Maybe I'm just giving you a chance to get out of this alive.'

'I've told you, I won't say a word to the police.'

'I heard you.'

'What else can I say to convince you?'

'Not a lot. That's your problem.'

'So that's it?'

Eddy shrugged. 'That's it.'

Keely couldn't believe how easy it was to get rid of a dead body. First, they managed to wrap him up in the bed sheets that had got all spoiled with blood, then Eddy found some tape in the back of the van and made sure he wouldn't come unrolled. But it wasn't like in films where the body gets wrapped in a carpet and it's just a sausage shape. The sheets were thin and Keely could see bumps of arms and legs, and blood at the head end starting to seep through the white material.

Jess was only just coming out of it when they finished, sitting up after her trip and complaining she was thirsty. She gagged when she saw the blood and refused to give them a hand, so Keely and Eddy carried the heavy rolled shape between them to the van. Eddy had parked it right at the back of the house, down the alley running behind the rows.

Eddy stumbled as he came out and hit his elbow on the back gate. Caught off balance by the sudden jolt, Keely dropped the bundle.

The head dumped against concrete with a thick softish thud.

'Fuck's sake,,' Eddy said.

'Sorry.'

It was starting to rain again, so they gathered him quickly back up before he got too wet, the package slipping around in their arms now like a gigantic fish wrapped in newspaper.

Keely didn't want to think about anything in particular. She tried to keep her eyes fixed on the van doors, standing wide open, then stared at the scratched corrugated floor as they forced the bundle in and up to the seat backs. A loose piece of tape had caught on her sleeve when they were shifting the package and she stood there for a moment, fumbling to detach it, while Eddy slammed the double doors shut.

The van pulled slowly out of the alley and along the road, chugging with each surge of the choke.

Keely rubbed a clumsy little porthole on the steamed-up window, staring out at the CCTV camera positioned at the far end of the street. It was an alien with enormously long legs. Its oblong tilting eye glinted strangely as it watched the streets. She had seen them sometimes on telly, grainy black and white pictures that could spot movement even at night, using infra-red or something to monitor the dark streets and estates of the West End. What did everyone look like on those things? Black ants, scuttling from one parked car to the next or hanging round on the corners.

Or watching her and Eddy driving a small white transit van out of the Benwell maze towards the river.

To her surprise, a thin unexpected warmth started

drifting from the air vents in front of her a couple of minutes later. She hadn't expected the heating to work, the van was so old. Keely leant forward and pushed her hands up against the grill, one at a time. The weather had turned so cold she could barely feel her fingers anymore.

Suddenly there was a bright flare of light ahead of them. Eddy swore and braked sharply, probably thinking it might be the police, but it was only a bunch of kids messing about in front of one of the houses marked for demolition. One of the kids had a burning glass bottle in his hand. There was a shout. The lad with the bottle turned his head slightly, narrowed his eyes on the transit van, then yelled something and chucked his missile in through a gaping black door frame behind him.

The glass bottle hurtled through the air like Haley's comet. Its flickering tail scorched across her eyeballs and exploded into the roofless house in a loud whoosh of flame.

Eddy turned out onto the main road. 'Bloody kids.'

'Can I have one of your ciggies?'

He looked at her for a few seconds, then fumbled for them in his jacket pocket, keeping his eyes on the road. It was bright under the streetlights and there were quite a few cars. 'Light us one too, will you?'

The cigarette smoke made her cough and her eyes water. But Keely kept on dragging and dragging, gulping in down into her lungs, filling the whole van with the smoke until Eddy opened his window a fraction and it escaped like a flock of white birds high into the frozen night air. With that acrid taste in her mouth, she couldn't smell the blood anymore.

It was impossible to get down to the river itself without being seen. Every time they found a likely spot, someone would drive past with their headlights full on or there'd be the sound of sirens from up in the city and Eddy would freak out, starting the engine and driving off again at speed, wheels spinning and him crouched over the wheel, sweating and swearing like he thought he was in a film or something. He prowled along Scotswood Road dead slow, staring at the closed factory gates.

Eventually he found a lane which took them down off the main road towards the river. There was a high place just past the works that looked quiet and dark enough. Eddy backed the van up to the wall, then threw the double doors open, sending Keely to check for closed circuit cameras while he dragged the package right to the edge.

They both lifted together on a count of three and got the body out of the van, staggering forward to heave it up onto the wall.

'Hold it still a tick.'

'It's too heavy,' she said.

He ignored her, glancing down into the water. 'Okay, it's a clear enough drop. Let go when I say so.'

The sheet-wrapped body balanced there on the wall for a moment, wobbling hesitantly as they supported it, dark bulge of the head slippery with blood. Then Eddy muttered something and let go of his end.

Keely let go of her end a split second later, feeling the entire thing wrench itself out of her arms and drop heavily into the river.

There was a strange silence during the fall, followed by a clean-sounding splash. Echoes bounced off the stone walls briefly and died away.

She glanced around the dark street as though checking for witnesses, but actually trying to avoid remembering how the package had twisted clumsily in its descent. For a moment there, it had become a body again, sickeningly real in its sharp lumps of knees and elbows under the strapped-down sheets.

When Keely leant over the edge and stared down into the river afterwards, there was nothing to see but dark water and a shivered reflection of bridge lights, lapping more noisily than usual against tarred greeny-black walls.

'Good job.' Eddy nodded, slamming the back door of the van. He looked at her strangely. 'What was it Rab did to you, anyhow?'

She did not answer.

CHAPTER SEVENTEEN

They were all sitting in the kitchen of the squat, mid-afternoon. The light was soft and gloomy, easing towards dusk. Eddy had come round to collect his money, but Jess had blown it all on clubbing as usual. Most weeks, he'd let the matter slide until she was flush again, but today he seemed determined to get some sort of return on his merchandise.

'Sorry.' Jess shrugged. 'I'm broke.'

'Okay.' Eddy took a deep drag on his spliff, leaning against the wall to study Jess. His leather jacket creaked every time he moved like he was a piece of old furniture. 'But you'll have to do something for us if you can't come up with the cash.'

He switched his gaze towards Keely. No prizes for guessing what he wanted.

Jess shook her head, sitting up straight. 'No fucking way. She's my cousin.'

'I thought she needed the money. There's plenty of other girls who'd jump at the chance.' He pulled a tiny folded square of paper from his pocket and threw it down in front of Keely. 'Here you are, Kee. Just a little taster for you. You do what I tell you, you'll never have to worry about money again. And that's a promise.'

The coke wrap lay innocently next to the teapot. Keely tried not to look at it. But she knew she had to make a decision. It couldn't be delayed any longer. For days, she had been sailing closer and closer to that precipice she knew was waiting for her, and all she had to do now was let herself slide over the edge and hope she didn't drown in the white water.

Besides, it was logical. This was the next step towards growing up, wasn't it?

Eddy was watching her through narrowed eyes. It was a little game he was playing. She looked down at her hands.

'It's a freebie,' Eddy told her. 'There's plenty more where that came from. You keep me happy, I'll see what I can do for you.'

'Like what?'

'Cash,' he shrugged. 'More coke. Whatever.'

'How much cash?'

'That depends.'

'On what?'

'Jesus Christ.' Eddy stared at her, handing the spliff to Jess. He made a choking noise that might have been laughter. 'How many blokes you can blow in a night, what the fuck do you think?'

'She's my kid cousin,' Jess said angrily, pushing the spliff away. 'Keely's smart, she could get a proper job. She doesn't need to do this.'

'Leave it, Jess.' Keely laid a hand on her arm. 'I've got this.'

Eddy waited. 'So, are you interested?'

'When and where?'

'There's a private party in Denton Burn this Friday night. The bloke who owns the place needs girls for some special friends of his. I'll take you along.'

'What if someone sees me and tells Zal?'

'That's not a problem. Nobody there will recognise

you.'

'How can you be so sure?'

'Trust me for once, would you? These lads won't give a toss who you are. They'll only be interested in your tits and what's between your legs. And if you do your bit properly, I might even be able to find you a few regular punters after that.'

'Okay, I'll do it.'

'Good.'

Her cousin moaned. 'No.'

'Don't interfere, Jess. This is my life. I'm not a kid anymore and I need the cash, all right? I can't hide here forever, sponging off you and hoping Zal doesn't find me. I've got to get out of this place. Get my own flat, like.' Trying to hide the fact that she was trembling, Keely grabbed up the coke wrap. 'Is that so hard to understand?'

She unfolded the paper right down to the cocaine, licked one finger and rubbed some of the powder into her gums. The effect was immediate and energising. Within seconds she felt better, more focused, able to face what was coming.

'I'm only looking out for you, babes,' Jess said gently. 'Christ, you don't know the first thing about the streets.'

By way of a reply, Keely took the spliff out of Jess's fingers and drew on it heavily, almost choking as the acrid smoke hit her lungs. It seemed like the strongest spliff she had ever smoked. Her head spun sickeningly and she thought she might puke. But they were watching her and she couldn't make a prat of herself.

She took another drag and this time exhaled more slowly, forcing herself not to cough.

'Then you better teach us, hadn't you?'

Mr Swainson was slumped against the wall. His face was grey-looking and there were purplish black bags under his eyes.

'You okay?' Keely crouched down beside him but Mr

Swainson didn't react. Gently, she held the mug of water to his lips and tipped it so he could drink. The skin around his mouth was cracked and little trickles of water dribbled helplessly out of the sides and down his neck.

He gagged and she pulled the mug back at once. 'Just small sips. You'll make yourself sick otherwise.'

'Hungry,' he whispered.

'There's still that tinned ham in the kitchen.'

'I told you, I don't eat meat.'

Jess appeared in the doorway, wearing a skirt so short her knickers were practically showing. She'd put on her silver-tipped black stilettos and a silver midriff top, tight enough to pull the punters. Stubbing out her cigarette on the floor, she slipped a shiny black jacket over her bare shoulders and twirled eagerly for Keely. Gold eyeshadow, plum lipstick and new earrings. They were little silver teardrops.

'What do you think? I'm off to work, babes. Eddy wants us in town for six and the bus is due in a few minutes.' Jess frowned down at Mr Swainson's white face. 'Bloody hell, he doesn't look too clever. Do you want us to bring him back something to eat?'

'No, I'll sort it.'

Jess looked at her, nodded and left the room, but didn't get any further than the kitchen. It was obvious she wanted to say something else. Keely heard her lighting another cigarette in the hallway, then swearing softly under her breath. 'You know, if I worked every single night, you really wouldn't need to go out yourself.' Jess came back into the room. The tiny silver teardrops shivered in her ears as she walked. 'I'd never forgive myself if anything happened to you, babes. There are some cheap flats across the river. We could share until – '

'I'm not changing my mind.'

'Please, sweetheart.' Keely flashed her a look and Jess shut up, glancing nervously at Mr Swainson before retreating. 'Okay, fine. I'll talk to you about it later then.

See you.'

Once the sound of her heels had died away down the back alley, Mr Swainson raised his head and looked at Keely. His face was whiter than ever and he sounded exhausted.

'What day is it? How long have I been here?'

'You got something better to do?'

He closed his eyes. 'What was Jess talking about?'

'Nothing. Go back to sleep.'

There was silence between them after that. Keely stayed where she was, kneeling beside him without speaking even though it was uncomfortable. She forced herself to listen to his breathing until it slowed. He must have fallen asleep again. The living room became peaceful and still.

Gradually, Keely found her own eyelids beginning to close. It was strange but she always seemed so tired these days. Like her whole body was running down like a dead battery. After a few more moments of blinking and shivering, she gave up the struggle to stay awake, dropping into a strange dreamless sleep exactly where she knelt.

It must have been several hours later when a strange high-pitched noise woke her.

Keely was lying on the floor of the living room now, just out of his reach. She stirred and wiped her face with the back of her hand. She must have been crying in her sleep. Her face was damp. There was nothing to wrap herself in for warmth and it was so cold she had lost all feeling in her arms and legs. She was nothing but a bent spine packed in ice. There was sickness inside her again, churning in her stomach and making her want to retch. The candle flickered thinly beside her, almost ready to die.

Suddenly she heard a bird singing in the street. That was what had woken her. Keely had never heard a bird out there before. The streets always seemed so empty of life when she walked down them. It was all brick and cars and rubbish out there. There were no trees left for the birds to nest in and no grass left for the worms. Even the plants in the shopping arcades were made out of plastic. Everything natural seemed to have been built on or pulled up.

She listened to its beautiful song, and felt like crying again. It was probably the last bird in Newcastle still singing.

Keely didn't know how it happened. But it felt wonderful to be in his arms instead of alone on the cold floor. One minute she had been crying in her sleep and dreaming of being held, the next it was happening for real. The sickness inside seemed to have vanished. His left arm was stretched around her for warmth and they were lying close together at last.

'You fancy Tracey, don't you?' she whispered, but it was a bit muffled, on account of her face being stuck into his chest.

'*What?*'

'I've seen you looking at her.'

'Don't be ridiculous. That's pure fantasy. I've never thought about any of you girls in a sexual way.'

Keely smiled. 'No?' She moved slightly, wriggling her hand down the gap between their bodies.

'Stop that.'

She ignored the anger in his voice. They had to pretend to be angry, it was part of the game. Letting herself go heavy and limp in his arms, Keely dropped her head back to smile up at Mr Swainson. His breathing had quickened and his eyes were narrowed as he looked down at her. She couldn't quite read his expression, but there was a sharp little burst of triumph inside her. She knew the signs. He wanted her.

'You could have me right now, you know. I wouldn't stop you.'

'I don't rape school girls.'

His voice had been harsh and Keely hesitated, suddenly uncertain. 'I'm eighteen. And it wouldn't be rape.'

'I don't fuck my students,' he said then, and pushed her angrily away. There was dark colour in his face as Mr Swainson sat up, driving his back against the radiator with a metallic thud. She could see the bulge in his jeans, so she knew he was interested, but he wasn't looking at her anymore. He was staring at nothing instead, shoulders shaking as he drew breath. Keely didn't know what he was thinking, though she could guess. The look on his face was one of horrified disgust.

'But you want to,' she hissed at him.

Mr Swainson shook his head and said nothing. He didn't once look up at her. He had even pulled his body away slightly, leaning into the radiator as if he preferred it to her. Suddenly she hated him. Christ, he thought he was so much better than her. He thought she was nothing. Worse than nothing. Pure fucking shite under his feet. Something cold and hard and angry flared inside her.

Her hands went to her hips and she stood over him, longing to kick him in the mouth, smash the contempt off his face. Her voice was trembling. 'You didn't exactly push Jess away, did you? She said you were gagging for it on your birthday.'

'She's a prostitute. You're not.'

'What makes you so sure of that? I've got my first punter soon. Eddy's setting it up for us.'

'Christ's sake!'

'But isn't that what you wanted to hear? So you can be first in line for it?' Keely yanked the short skirt up so he could see her knickers underneath. 'Fancy a freebie, Mr Swainson?'

There was an ugly crash and she left the room, her ankle aching where she must have caught it against the metal radiator.

Her head hurt. She felt sick again and she didn't care what happened to Mr Swainson anymore. Let Jess give her the drugs to shoot him up. Let them dump his body into the river like they'd done with Rab. The stupid bastard deserved everything he got.

Jess came back soon after three in the morning, crying and stumbling through the back door.

When she saw the candles and Keely sitting wide awake in the kitchen, she dropped limply down onto one of the chairs, trying to hide her face by lighting a cigarette but failing completely. Even from the side, it looked like someone had been at her with a baseball bat.

Keely stared. 'What happened to your face, Jess?'

'Isn't it fucking obvious?'

Flicking her ash onto the floor, Jess deliberately leaned forward into the candlelight so that Keely could see her face properly. She was a right mess. Mouth swollen, right cheek puffing up, dried blood under her nose. She tried to laugh at Keely's horrified expression, but it obviously hurt too much because she ended up just sort of gasping and twitching her lips.

Keely could hardly breathe. 'Christ.'

'I got a bit mouthy so Eddy laid into me.'

'That bastard.'

'He did this, with his rings.' Gingerly, she touched her swollen face, then lifted her skirt and stared down at herself. There were red and purple bruises across the tops of her thighs. They looked like pressure marks from fingers, with a large ugly dark thumb at each side. 'And the rest.'

'He's such a prick.'

'I thought he loved me, Kee. I really did.'

'Eddy couldn't love anyone.'

'He took all the money too. Working all night and I'm still skint, the bastard.' Jess picked up her handbag off the floor, wiping streaks of smoky black mascara onto the sleeve of her PVC jacket. 'Look, I've never been much of a cousin to you, sweetheart, but this is the best advice anyone can ever give you. Stay off the game.'

'It's only for a bit, Jess.'

Her cousin smiled bitterly, rummaging through her handbag. 'Yeah, I know. You say 'one more time, and then it's over'. Only that's every time. Because you start but you can't stop. He won't let you stop and in the end you can't afford to stop. But I want to this time, I'm dead serious.'

'You've said that before.'

'Okay, but now I mean it. I want out.' Jess pulled a small cracked mirror out of her handbag. 'Come on, I need cheering up. Where's that coke he give you?'

'Not now Jess. Everything's upside-down. I really need you to stay straight.'

'What am I, your mam? Give us the coke.'

Keely shook her head silently.

'Fine. I'll use my own.'

'You haven't got any coke.'

'That's what you think, clever clogs.'

'Bollocks.'

'Listen up babes, I've got something to tell you. Hang on a min.'

Jess stripped off her spangly top and bent down to rummage for something warmer. She wasn't wearing a bra and even in the dim light Keely could see goosepimples on her arms and chest. Her nipples were sticking out because of the cold. The left one was pierced by a thin silver hoop. Shivering violently, Jess dragged a blue roll-neck jumper down over her head, then hurriedly stepped out of her skirt and knickers. Scrabbling through the tangle of black tights in her top drawer, she pulled out a clean white pair of knickers with Top Tottie written across them.

As Jess bent slightly to put them on, Keely could see a criss-cross of thin bluish-green lines across her buttocks. Surrounding them were less visible lines, older bruising from some earlier trip into town.

'Eddy says we can't let your man go,' Jess said at last, and there was a slight shake in her voice. She bent to rescue her jeans from a pile of dirty clothes in the corner.

'We have to get rid of him instead, shoot him up with heroin and dump him in the river same as we did with Rab. Make it look like another suicide.'

'You're taking the piss.'

'I'm not. Eddy's given me the stuff to do it.'

Jess fastened her jeans, nodding towards the handbag she'd dumped on the bed. Keely noticed suddenly that Jess had a nervous tic starting at one side of her face, just under her eye. The tiny muscle kept jerking and jerking as she was speaking. Her cousin stumbled out of the bedroom, laughing wildly over her shoulder at Keely's expression.

'Yeah, I know. It's a shame to waste that stuff on a teacher. There's enough there for a week of sheer fucking paradise.'

Keely didn't know what to say. She followed Jess slowly into the living room, feeling her stomach clench into a fist as she realised her cousin was serious. The sickness was coming back. This wasn't exactly how she had planned things to work out. Everything was turning into a disaster.

It had all seemed so simple in the beginning. All she had to do was hide out in the squat until the situation with Zal and Tracey had been forgotten, then maybe take a train down to London or up to Glasgow, get a job and start again there. But Mr Swainson had ruined everything by following Jess back here. And now what Keely was meant to do? Protect the stupid bastard of a teacher and run the risk of prison, or follow Eddy's plan and dump his body the same way they'd got rid of Rab?

Keely didn't know if she could do either of those things. She didn't think she could do anything, except carry on wondering when the police were going to find Rab's body. Someone was bound to know he had left with her that night. Whatever Eddy might think, the police wouldn't just let a murder drop like that. They'd find the squat in the end and blame her for what happened. She was trapped.

Mr Swainson had scrambled hurriedly into a sitting position as they came into the room, blinking and rubbing his face. There were grubby dust streaks on his cheeks as though he had been crying.

Hands slammed onto her hips, Jess towered over Mr Swainson in her high heels, staring down at him as if he was nothing more than a piece of meat on a butcher's slab. Her voice was cold and glittery. 'He's going to land us all in the shite when he talks to the police. There's no way you can let him go, Kee.'

He was dead white. 'I won't say anything to the police. You've got to believe me.'

'You would say that though, wouldn't you?'

'But you can't just kill me.'

'I can do whatever I like, sweetheart.' She kicked him once in the ribs, hard. 'You just ask Keely about that if you don't believe us. She knows what's got to be done.'

Once Jess had staggered back into the bedroom on her high heels and they were alone together, Mr Swainson stared up at Keely in disbelief. He put his hands on his knees to steady them, but she could see they were still shaking violently. She felt like lying to him, telling Mr Swainson that everything was going to be okay. But it was dangerous to feel sorry for him. If she started feeling sorry, she might make a mistake and fuck the whole thing up.

'Tell me she's joking. You're not in the playground now, Keely. This is real life. You can't just murder me. What on earth have I ever done to you, for Christ's sake?'

She ignored him, folding her arms across her chest. It was the easiest way to deal with his questions.

'None of this is my fault.' Mr Swainson paused and his voice softened. 'Please talk to me, Keely. What do you want from this situation? What do you need? I really want to help you.'

That voice was deadly to her. Keely stood there listening to it, hearing the voice but feeling it wash over her in a wave of sound. Then she turned away so that he wouldn't see her putting a hand up to wipe her face. But it was so cold she couldn't feel her fingers and toes properly, and her hand was clumsy.

Trying to seem uninterested by what he was saying, Keely moved to the boarded-up windows and leant against the cracked glass on the inside. It was icy on her cheek. She wondered what was going to happen to the little bird she had heard singing in the street. It was winter and there were no trees growing out there. No grass, no berries. Nothing for the bird to eat. There wasn't even anything she could do for it. Even if she put down some breadcrumbs, one of the stray cats would catch the bird. They knew every corner of the terrace, they would have it in ten seconds flat, even if the bird hopped down quick, even if it knew they were waiting there.

She didn't even know what the bird looked like, only how it sang. It was winter and there was nothing she could do for it.

'Keely?'

She ignored the husky pleading note in his voice. Her hands made useless fists on the glass and the cold knuckles stuck up like humps on a camel. She put one hand up against her mouth and bit at the flesh. There was a lingering smell of smoke on her fingers. It took her a good minute to remember that she'd had one of Eddy's Regal King Size.

Suddenly, her right hand felt strangely wet and Keely turned it over, staring at the red-stained skin. Her knuckles were bleeding. She felt drowsy and stupid all of a sudden. Frowning down at her hand, she couldn't work out what was wrong with it. Her voice was barely a whisper. 'Shit. I must have cut myself on something.'

'You just smashed the window,' he said urgently.

Keely raised her head. The candle flame was shivering and dancing. There was a cold draught in her face. The glass in the window right in front of her was broken. She could reach through with a couple of fingers and touch chipboard if she wanted. 'No I didn't.'

'Look down at your feet.'

Her right trainer was covered in tiny slivers of glass. Keely shook it automatically and the slivers fell to the floor with a tinkling sound. In the candlelight, she could see a thin powdery brightness still clinging to the laces and white plastic toe. As an experiment, she wiggled her foot from side to side, and the whole thing glittered as though she was wearing a glass slipper. Everything was unreal.

There was a larger piece of glass lying on the floor, just to her left. It was shaped a bit like a triangle. So was the hole in the window. There was a musty smell coming in from the broken window. The chipboard under her fingers was rough and flecked damp orangey-white.

'Keely, listen to me. You need help. Let me go. I'll make sure you get treated properly.'

'You mean I'm crazy?'

'I didn't say that. I said you needed help. It's nothing to be ashamed of. Lots of people get into situations they can't control.'

'I'm not a fucking nutter.'

'I know that. It's okay.' He paused, watching Keely warily as she came away from the window. 'You probably think of me as the enemy. But when you attacked Tracey with a pair of scissors, what was I meant to do? I couldn't just ignore that, pretend it hadn't happened. You're lucky it wasn't that serious and her parents didn't press charges.'

'I don't remember doing it. Any of it.'

Mr Swainson held her gaze. 'I realise that, Keely.'

'So why did you come looking for me?'

'Because I care about you.'

'That's crap,' she said angrily, and her voice rose suddenly to a shout. 'You don't care about me. You only care that we might kill you and no one would ever find out what happened to you. You only care about saving your own skin.'

'No, that's not true.'

'Shut up,' she screamed at him. 'You think you're so clever but you just make my head hurt. I hate you and I'm going to have to kill you now. Why did you have to come here? Why did you have to interfere? Why didn't you stay out there where you belong, you stupid bastard?'

'Just calm down, Keely. I can explain everything.'

'No,' she hissed, clamping her hands over her ears and stumbling out of the room. It felt like thousands of bees were swarming and buzzing and crawling in and out of the dark spaces of her head. 'You make me sick. I don't ever want to hear your voice again.'

Keely managed to make it safely to her cousin's bedroom, but the door was already slightly open. There was a candle guttering inside on the floor, throwing ugly shadows across the walls. The room stank of perfume and sweat and sickness. Somebody had tipped all the crap off the bed onto the floor in a hurry and the place was a complete mess. Strewn higgledy-piggledy across the floorboards like the wreckage of a plane crash, Keely could see clothes and shoes and make-up and towels.

And the half naked body of Jess.

CHAPTER EIGHTEEN

The body on the bed had that wax stillness about it, too unnatural for any living thing. For a few silent moments, Keely looked across at her cousin's body without moving, stood there in the doorway like an idiot, then she went into the bedroom and pushed the door almost shut behind her, so as to be private.

Stepping carefully over the clothes and other crap littering the floor, she reached the bed where Jess was lying on her back as if asleep. Close up in the candlelight, Keely could see that her cousin's head was cranked to one side and there was a pale frothy yellowish vomit already drying on the sheet and floorboards, left arm dangling to the floor.

'Jess?' Keely bent and touched the body. A cold-jerk flashed through her. Her fingers turned electric and pulled straight back into herself, tingling with shock.

Trying to breathe without gasping at the air, Keely knelt gently on the bed next to her cousin. She didn't bother wiping her own face, just let it get wet. Stroking Jess's long hair and her face and her bare arms, Keely gradually let herself start a little whimpering noise. She was rocking back and forth because it felt right and it eased a little the tightness and hardness in her stomach. She thought of him in the other room, not knowing, and then the whimpering was louder, but not so loud he might hear.

Jess must have taken her jumper off to inject because the sleeve was too bulky and tight for rolling up. There was a thin trail of blood spattered on the wall behind her where she must have missed first time. Her navel and chest were soft and white though. Keely bent down and put her head on Jess's naked chest. It was cool, but not icy yet. There was no beat there. She had known there wouldn't be a beat, she wasn't making sure, she just wanted to lie there and be right at the heart of Jess for a while. After a few minutes, it started to feel okay again. Like this was something she could manage. There was no need to move. There was no need to do anything. She could just lie there on the soft chest and stare sideways out of one eye at the white skin mound, the little pink pierced nipple close by her mouth.

The room shrank to a piece of skin only just in focus, the thin silver hoop lying above it, and everything else was a blurring that didn't matter. Her nose was running and her mouth was a bit open on the chest. It was dribbling because her face was wet, and her own chest was heaving but the one underneath her was still, the breastbone was right under her cheek, it was being on like a raft or something.

Keely clung to it with the side of her face. Her hand was down at Jess's side paddling in the frothy yellowish stain on the sheet while she made the little whimpering noises which made her feel okay.

After a while, Keely began to hear his voice from the other room. She lay still for a bit longer, then sat up. Her face was itchy with wet so she went to wipe it, but there was yellow froth on her hand and she had to use the edge of the sheet. That was dirty too.

Her head hurt. She didn't want to leave Jess.

Otherwise, she would come back into the room later, stumbling across the smell that always went with dead bodies, and find her gone. So Keely stood up off the bed and turned her head, but secretly kept watching out of the corner of one eye. It was the eye she had kept closed against the white chest. But Jess didn't move. Her body lay there cooling and stiffening.

He was shouting now. Keely knew she couldn't ignore him forever. She would have to go and tell him what had happened. But she didn't really want to leave in case of coming back and finding her gone. It was getting really nippy in the room now and she was shivering with just her tee-shirt. She had a quick skeet round and found Jess's jumper on the floor, then pulled her tee-shirt off and dragged the jumper down over her head just as Jess had done before. It smelt of her perfume and underneath that a faint hint of Jess herself, that warm smell when they cuddled sometimes.

The syringe was lying on the bed with the strap and other stuff. Keely picked it up and stood there a moment, not knowing what to do with it, then she put it back down again. She didn't like needles. They gave her a prickly feeling in her palms. The small plastic bag Jess had brought back from Eddy was nearly empty. It was all inside her.

She hadn't looked at Jess's face properly before now but she did at last, forcing herself to do it without feeling too much. It was all messed up. Eddy's bruises had swollen her right cheek and the rest of her skin was frighteningly white. It needed serious help to look decent again.

Keely wiped the yellowish froth from her cousin's lips and chin. She was still in old make-up from the night before. The eyelids were faded gold and glittering. The plum lipstick was mostly gone but for bits of it sticky in the creases. There was a smear of creamy foundation on the pillow where she must have lain down before the puking started.

Keely knelt again for a minute, trying to remember what you were meant to do in an emergency. She tilted Jess's head back the way you were meant to, near heaving with the smell when the limp mouth yawned. She peered inside but couldn't see anything on account of the poor light. So she picked up the candle and held it above her, moving the jaw back again, but it was just yellow froth on the tongue and tonsils and she didn't really know what else you were meant to do. Her cousin was so cold.

Keely let go of her head and the jaw flopped back to its resting position, but slowly, as if she still had life in her.

Suddenly realising what she had to do, Keely scrabbled about for Jess's big black handbag in the mess of shoes and clothes beside the dressing-table, and felt around inside for her make-up. She found gold eyeshadow, plum lipstick, mascara, and a kohl stick. She didn't think Jess needed the foundation or blusher, on account of her complexion looking so perfect white already and not wanting to spoil it with fake colour, but she took them out anyway and laid them alongside the others on the dressing-table. They would probably help hide the bruising on her right cheek.

Then she found her cousin's favourite nail varnish, Blue Ice. It was like Jess was at one of those professional salons, having a full make-over before hitting the clubs. She would have liked that.

Cradling the head in her hands, Keely moved it so that she could work from above. She balanced on the edge of the bed, unscrewed the plum lipstick and smoothed it onto the sticky purplish lips.

Her hand was trembling a bit and she slid outside the lip-line a few times, but it wasn't too bad and nothing a quick dab with a piece of loo paper wouldn't mend. Jess always kept a roll on the dressing-table. Then Keely moved up to her eyelids. They were terrible heavy and solid, almost like rubber. Underneath she could feel the hard-boiled egg of her eyeball squidging up and down whenever she pressed too hard.

It made the sick rise in her throat but Keely didn't stop, just tried not to press too hard. The gold eyeshadow was lovely and thick anyway. She did all the way from the little corner to the far edge of her eyebrow on each eye, then tapped the mascara on the back of her hand, because it was the nearest thing and she couldn't reach the wall. Then she tried to stroke it on without smudging. But she really needed the eyes open for that, it was tricky without.

Trying not to think too much about what she was doing, Keely dragged the right lid open with the index finger and thumb of one hand, touching the mascara against the lashes with the other hand. Before letting the lid drop again, she took the kohl and drew a black line as neat as possible under the lower lid. Once she'd done that side, the other was easier.

Both eyes smudged a bit when she let go of each lid, but she knew they'd look cracking from a distance.

With the nail varnish remover, she cleaned the chipped scarlet from Jess's fingernails and gave them a quick polish with another piece of loo roll. The varnish remover made her eyes sting and water. She pushed each cuticle back, then applied the Blue Ice in long firm strokes, like Jess had shown her once, from the half-moon right up to the tip, taking care not to run over the edges. Jess had taught Keely everything she knew about putting on make-up, though she didn't really like the stuff once it was on. It felt wrong somehow and besides her dad had never approved. Jess would have laughed to see her now. She was a proper little beautician.

After Jess was ready, she sat there a while longer, holding her hand and talking to her. Keely knew she couldn't hear her. But it felt like the right thing to do. And she'd done a good job of the make-up. Jess was really beautiful now. She looked like Cleopatra or some foreign movie star from the black and white films, exotic and mysterious and full of magic.

She went through into the other room in the end, holding the candle and closing the bedroom door behind her for no good reason except that Jess was half naked.

Keely knew that even in the candlelight he would see her face was wet from crying, so she didn't bother pretending that nothing had happened. 'Sir, she's dead.'

Mr Swainson stared at her blankly. 'What?'

Keely knelt down in front of him and retched. But she hadn't eaten for ages so there was nothing but frothy water to bring up. Her belly ached and the sickness was inside her again. The whimpering was going to start soon, she knew that, though she was still holding it back with her lips drawn up tight against her teeth like a dog. 'Jess is dead.'

He said nothing for a moment, then asked, 'Are you absolutely sure?'

'She's dead.'

'How?'

She shrugged. 'Shot herself up with something.'

'But did you check for a pulse?'

Keely hesitated, shivering violently now. 'I don't think so. But her body was so cold.'

'Jesus Christ. Quick, where's the key?' When Keely stared up at him, not understanding, he jerked his wrist on the radiator. The metal jangled angrily against the handcuffs. 'You've got to get me out of these before it's too late. If she's taken an overdose, we might still be able to help her.'

Of course, he should have realised nothing could be that simple. Weak as a new-born calf, Niall sank back to his knees and shook his head. The situation was hopeless. He couldn't walk. He could barely even stand. Humiliated by this renewed sensation of powerlessness, Niall rubbed at the chafed red skin of his wrist, still deeply indented where the metal cuff had been.

'Give me a minute, would you?'

'What?'

'I need to rest. My legs feel like rubber.'

'Rest?' Keely stared at him, eyes stretched wide as a young child's. 'But we haven't got time for that. You said Jess might still be alive. You said you could help her.'

'I know what I said. But you can't just expect me to just leap to my feet after weeks chained to this thing.'

She said nothing, but he could sense her sudden disappointment in the silence. It wasn't bloody fair. Niall slammed his fist violently against the radiator, infuriated by his own physical weakness. Kept in relative inactivity for over a month, his legs had stopped functioning properly. They trembled and hung limply beneath him, little better than useless. It was the ultimate irony. Niall had dreamt about this moment for weeks now, yet now that he was on the verge of regaining his freedom, his own body had betrayed him.

He could feel his temper soaring at the thought and fought to control it, hanging his head for a moment to get his breath back. He had only just gained a little trust from the girl. It would be crazy to jeopardise that by losing his temper, especially with escape so tantalisingly close.

'Help me up then, would you?' he muttered, meeting her eyes briefly. 'That's it. Put your arm round my shoulder.'

Step by step, his legs dragging painfully behind him, they eventually made it to the door of the living room. Niall could already feel the sensation returning to his legs as their circulation improved, each muscle throbbing and jerking as if it had been plunged into a hot bath after being packed in ice for months.

'Jesus Christ.' He yelped as Keely let go of his shoulder in the doorway and his left leg crumbled instantly, dissolving into jagged thrusts of pain at the knee and ankle. 'Don't let go. Keep me upright, for God's sake.'

'Sorry. Is that better?'

Unable to prevent himself wincing, Niall nodded slightly as her arm supported him again. Working together, they staggered a few more steps into the hallway and towards the door of the other room. Yet even that short distance felt like an eternity to him, wracked by almost intolerable shooting pains in his legs and spine. He should have waited for a few minutes before trying to walk, maybe even rubbing at his legs until the blood was flowing properly.

'No,' he gasped. 'Stop a minute. This isn't going to be as simple as I thought.'

Pausing to catch his breath as he hung there, helpless on her arm, Niall stared about himself. It was the first time he had seen the hallway properly since Keely had struck him on the back of the head, apart from glimpses of a pale expanse whenever the door was opened. The hallway seemed smaller than he remembered, unless that was because his world had gradually shrunk to the size of that tiny living room. The dirty floorboards were cluttered with debris: old newspapers, dusty heaps of curtains and ripped-up carpet, faded piles of ancient junk mail near the boarded-up front door. The remains of a bicycle leant uneasily against the door to the cupboard under the stairs, chain rusted, saddle slashed and most of its wheel spokes missing.

The whole place stank like something long dead, of stale urine and decay and the corpses of trapped insects. And its hollowness struck him for the first time, the way the sound of their breathing reverberated in these empty spaces. The cold was intense. The house was dead.

Suddenly, he wanted to push Keely away and run. Smash his way straight through the boards covering the front door. Get out of that evil black hole as quickly as possible. But Niall knew his legs were useless. All he could do was stagger forwards and sideways like a drunk. Escape was out of the question until he had his strength back. Besides, he had a reason not to run away now, if only because he had promised to help Jess if he possibly could.

It hadn't meant a thing at the time, that promise to Keely. It had been a godsend when she came back into the room crying like a little child, needing teacher's help for once, nothing more than a way to get himself out of those handcuffs. And it had worked. She had fetched the key and here he was on his feet, unsteady or not. A free man at last. There was no reason for him to keep his promise, he knew that. Not after what had happened to him in this house. But suddenly it seemed like the only thing that made any sense.

'Where is she, Keely?'

She pointed at the closed door opposite. 'In there. On the bed.'

'Help me then.'

As she pushed the door open and his eyes slowly adjusted to the flickering light, Niall found himself strangely afraid of what might be waiting for them inside that room. Instinctively, the skin on the back of his neck began to creep. He suddenly wished he had not decided to keep his meaningless promise to Keely.

Niall stopped dead on the threshold, feeling his breath catch in his throat. Even though he had been steeling himself to find a dead body in there, he still wasn't prepared for the girl he saw on the bed, the sheer whiteness of her skin shining in the candlelight like marble against the crumpled sheets. With her eyelids heavily made-up in shades of gold and purple, she would have looked more like a Pre-Raphaelite painting than a real woman if the tight jeans hadn't lent her body such a disconcerting air of reality.

Jess was naked from the waist up, and a tingling shock ran through him as he realised that her left nipple was pierced with a silver hoop. Reclining on the sheets, one arm languid above her head, the other dangling to the floor, golden eyelids closed as if asleep, the whole pose looked as staged as the theatrical make-up. Which it probably was.

That first glance had probably only taken him ten seconds, but it felt as though he had been staring at her forever. Leaning unsteadily on Keely, he felt his legs tremble beneath him like an old man's. His lips were almost too dry for speech.

'Is that how you found her?'

'More or less.'

Niall glanced down briefly at Keely's face, seeing her pale cheeks and fixed gaze, then moved towards the bed without her help.

He stumbled almost immediately and would have fallen, exactly as he'd done when she released him from the handcuffs and he had stood up for the first time in weeks, but he caught himself at the last second, clutching at the wall for support. Yet even his clumsy posture here, half-kneeling, half crouching at the girl's bedside, seemed to fit the unreality of this situation. It wasn't the first time Niall had seen a dead body, but this one seemed so young and alive, he half expected her eyes to fly open at any moment and the two girls to laugh at his gullibility, frozen beside the bed in sheer disbelief.

Gingerly, he took the wrist between his fingers. The shock of her skin hit him immediately. Keely was right. The body was cold.

'Is there a pulse?' she whispered.

'Hush!'

Keely drew her breath in sharply, taking a step back from him. There was silence again for a moment. And he had done this before as well. Holding a dead wrist in one hand, searching for that tiny thudding sound that would never come again. He had little hope. The stupid kid must have been gone for hours, she was too cold to bring back from the edge.

Then he caught it, pressing his fingers into the limp pale flesh, feeling somewhere deep beneath her skin, a pulse.

'She's alive.' He looked up at Keely urgently through the dark, catching the glitter of her eyes in the guttering candlelight. 'Only just, but she's still alive. Quick, don't stand there like an idiot. Fetch something warm to cover her with. She's absolutely frozen. Blankets, clothes, a thick coat. Whatever you can find lying around. She's so far gone though, I think she may be slipping into a coma. What exactly has she taken?'

'It's there, on the bed.'

Furious, Niall picked up the small plastic bag and sniffed carefully at the remains of its contents. 'What is this crap?'

'Heroin, I think.'

'How much did she have?'

'Dunno. Probably a ton of the stuff.' Keely came back to the bed. Her voice began to crack slightly as she laid a thick red jumper over Jess. He could see her hands trembling. 'It was meant for you. But she couldn't keep her hands off it, could she?'

'Meant for me?'

'Eddy gave it to her yesterday. He said we had to shoot you up with it, so you wouldn't tell the police anything. Then dump you in the river like we did with Rab.'

'Charming.'

'I told her I wouldn't do it. But Jess said we didn't have any choice. That you'd be straight down the police if we let you go. She said you're all the same, you all work for the government, so you have to stick together like. She said you wouldn't care if I got put inside for years. That you'd shop me for what happened to Rab soon as look at me.' Keely paused, looking at him suddenly. 'It's not true, is it?'

'You didn't kill him. Eddy did.'

'But it was my fault.'

'That's not true and you know it.'

She looked away, putting a hand to her wet face.

'None of it matters anymore. We've got to help Jess.'

Niall remained silent for another few seconds, then nodded. 'Okay. But you'll have to help me lift her. I'm still a bit too shaky to do it alone. We need to get Jess onto the floor and into the recovery position. Then one of us will have to go outside and find a phone.'

'Outside?'

'We've got to get her into hospital fast, Keely. There's nothing we can do for her like this. Jess has obviously taken a massive over-dose. She needs her stomach pumped out, maybe even to be put on a life-support machine.' Niall looked up at Keely when she stayed motionless, meeting her eyes. 'Look, you're going to have to trust me for once. This is your cousin's only chance. If we leave her like this, she's going to die.'

He must have finally got through that mute defensive mask to the real girl beneath. Keely nodded. 'Okay. I'll help you.'

'I need my keys and wallet back too.'

She hesitated. 'They're under the mattress. She took the cash for shopping though. We needed it.'

'Fair enough.'

Together they dragged Jess onto the floor, cradling her head to prevent further injury, and gradually manoeuvred her limbs into the recovery position. She seemed to be getting colder every minute, but there wasn't much they do about that except continue to keep Jess covered up. Her body looked so fragile and unreal in the candlelight, as if made of wax. But a faint pulse still beat at her throat and wrist, hanging on through the darkness, reminding him that there might be very little time left to get any help.

Niall tilted her head back carefully, clearing away some of the dried vomit from her lips and tongue, then somehow managed to get to his feet unaided. The circulation appeared to be returning to his legs more consistently now, so that the terrible pins and needles had subsided to a dull ache which left him able to walk on his own, if still in pain. But at least he was now able to walk. That would be useful now that one of them had to go and find a phone so they could call an ambulance. Niall wasn't entirely sure he trusted Keely to do that. She might leave but never come back.

The sound of someone thudding through the boards into the kitchen brought them both up short, staring at each other across the dying candle flame.

Urgently, Niall put a finger to his lips.

She nodded and stayed silent, crouched by Jess's side, watching the half-open door into the hallway with a look of sudden apprehension. His own heart was racing at the speed of light but he fought to stay calm.

Panicking wouldn't help either of them. He had to think clearly.

It was a man's heavy tread, creaking slowly across the kitchen and into the hallway outside their half-open door. He presumed it could only be Eddy. But what would be his reaction when he saw Jess in that state? He had never shown much affection for the girl, even though they were clearly sleeping together. So would he help them get the kid to hospital and risk getting the police involved? It was doubtful.

Niall quickly felt around under the mattress for his keys and wallet, slipped behind the door and motioned Keely to stay where she was. It might be better to keep his presence a secret until it was clear which way Eddy was going to swing. Keely herself seemed to understand the way he was thinking because she nodded briefly at his gesture, fixing her eyes on the doorway. They both realised it might be dangerous to assume Eddy was a better man than he had always appeared to be.

He flattened himself against the wall as silently as he could, wincing as his legs ached and shook with the effort of holding himself upright and still. But he had no choice if he wanted to get himself and the two girls out of this situation as safely as possible.

Keely's eyes widened in sudden shock as the man pushed open the bedroom door and stood in the doorway.

She began to back away until she hit the wall behind her, shaking her head. 'No,' she whispered hoarsely, and the fear in her voice was perfectly real.

'Thought I'd never catch up with you, didn't you?' It wasn't Eddy who had come into the bedroom, that was for certain. This was an older and larger man, rage trembling through his voice as he took another step forward. 'You stupid little bitch. I'm going to make you wish you'd never been born.'

Through the slowly narrowing crack between them, Niall could hear the creak of leather, smelling cigar smoke and aftershave. Then as the man came clear of the doorway and stood with his back towards him, large fists clenched at his side, Niall suddenly realised why Keely was so terrified of this newcomer.

It was Zal.

CHAPTER NINETEEN

Keely couldn't breathe for a moment and her chest was strangely tight. The sickness was back. She found herself staring at Zal without moving or making a single noise, just as if she was in a dream or remembering something that had happened to her before. But this was real, not pretend. He was here. In the last safe place. He had tracked her down and she had lost her chance to escape by not leaving Newcastle. It was the end of everything.

He smiled at her. 'Surprised to see me, pet?'

She wanted to run but there was nowhere to go. There was nothing she could do anymore. Zal was completely blocking the doorway and she knew Mr Swainson was too weak to help if she tried to fight him off. Avoiding the shock of that dying body beside her on the bed, her eyes searched the room for weapons. There were some aerosols on the floor and the heavy glass ashtray that had belonged to her mam. But they were out of reach.

'It wasn't that hard to find out where you two were hiding. Eddy's a soft enough bastard once you put a gun to his balls.'

There was an ugly reddish scar along his hairline

where she must have caught him with the gold clock. It was a pity she hadn't killed him. But at least she had marked him. Just like they used to mark criminals in the old days so that everyone would know what they had done. With an iron brand straight out of the fire. Though he was probably planning to grow his hair now to cover the scar. Try to hide what he had done to her.

'Oh dear. Is that useless slut dead?' Zal came further into the room, kicking the edge of the bed without taking his eyes off Keely. The body jerked once but didn't stir. 'Don't worry. You'll be seeing her again soon. It's your turn next, sweetheart.'

He was laughing now. There was a red mist in front of her eyes again. Jess was dying and he was laughing at them both. She must have run forward to hit the bastard because suddenly she was crumpled on her side with her ears ringing and her face hard against the wall.

The world turned black for an instant. She heard a strange rushing noise like angels' wings above, and then a deep muffled grunt. The floorboards shook and his dark head was lying next to hers. Zal's eyes were closed and he wasn't moving. She lay there without thinking or speaking. His face was right beside her. She could see the rough pores of his skin close up. It was just like the last time, only there was no reason to run. The cut on his temple had even started to bleed again, weeping gently into the silence as a hand reached down to drag her into a sitting position.

'You okay?'

'My head hurts.'

'Sit still.' Mr Swainson lifted her fringe with careful fingers. 'Nothing worse than a bruise, probably.

'What did you hit him with?'

'That bloody great thing.' He smiled slightly, squatting back on his heels and pointing at the heavy glass ashtray that had belonged to her mam. 'It was lying at the bottom of the bed. When he hit you, I just knocked him over the head with it and gravity did the rest.'

'What now?'

'Get out of here before he comes round again, I suppose. My legs aren't up to a fight.' He turned and began rummaging quickly through Zal's jacket pockets. 'Where are his bloody car keys?'

'He'll murder us if you take his car!'

Mr Swainson laughed. 'He'll murder us if I don't, Keely. This way it'll take him a while to catch up with us. We certainly don't have time to get round to my car, assuming it's still there after all these weeks.'

'Hurry up then,' she whispered, scrabbling to her feet and stepping over his body to get to the door. She put a hand to her mouth. The floor was moving and her stomach was heaving in waves. It was happening again. But she didn't have time to be ill. They had to get Jess to a hospital if there was still any hope of keeping her alive.

Her body had started to shiver violently. It was so cold in this house, it was like being stuck permanently in a freezer. She grabbed up another jumper from the floor and pulled it over her head. It didn't seem to make much difference to her trembles, she might as well not have put it on. There was even sick somewhere on the sleeve. She was sure she could smell it and tried scraping the damp wool against her jeans. But it was pointless. Everything seemed to smell of sick in this room. It was the candlelight in the icy chill that did it. The frozen glow of the walls was hurting her eyes.

Keely looked down at Jess, focusing hard on that pale blueish arm hanging limply over the edge of the bed. Staring at it seemed to take her mind off what was happening inside, stopped her actually being sick. The arm looked so cold and dead there, almost lost against the flickering whiteness of the room, it was hard to believe her cousin could still be alive. But there had to be a pulse there. She couldn't keep going alone.

'Here they are. Thank Christ for that.' Mr Swainson's voice startled her. She'd almost forgotten he was there.

'Now help me get Jess out of here. You take her other arm and we'll lift together. That's right, keep going. Don't worry about dragging her. It's more important to get her to the hospital while there's still time.'

'But she might be dead already.'

'We'll have to take her through the kitchen. That's the way he came in. He drives a BMW, is that right?'

The frozen night air hit her in the face, knocked her back for a second so that she had to stop. The sickness was back in her belly. Her arm and back muscles were aching horribly, she didn't think she could carry Jess much further. 'She can't be dead. She mustn't be dead.'

'She's not dead, calm down.'

'How can you be sure?'

'Just stay quiet and trust me for once.'

Mr Swainson lifted his head and stared up and down the dark street, panting hard and almost stumbling as they came clear of the alley. There was sweat above his eyebrows in spite of the freezing weather.

He looked much older and sicker than he ever had done in the art room. Now that they were out of the candlelight and she could see his face more clearly, Keely couldn't believe she had ever found him good-looking.

'There's his car,' he said at last.

The digital clock was showing nearly midnight. It was probably going to snow before morning. That's what the woman said on the car radio. Severe weather warning up towards Scotland. The heater in the BMW kept them warm through the icy streets, almost burning Keely's feet until she tucked them back under her seat and turned to check on Jess in the back. She still didn't look very alive. There was no colour in her face except a faint touch of blue around her mouth. More like a mannequin than a real person.

Mr Swainson was saying something to her, she could see his lips moving, but she wasn't really listening to him.

She had turned the radio up and was listening to the music instead. Nodding her head in time to the fast beat, she watched his face. Because of all the shit, it had been a few days now since she had bothered shaving him. He looked very pale above the heavy stubble on his chin, almost as pale as Jess. It was that sickly winter look, like the night frost before snow. Her own skin was pale too.

She turned her hands over to examine them as the car passed under a street-light. Rice pudding skin with tiny blue veins threading her wrists. Not getting enough sunlight, that was the problem.

'Have you ever been abroad?' she shouted above the music.

'I beg your pardon?'

'You'd look good with a tan.'

Mr Swainson turned the radio down and stared at her for a few seconds, then glanced down at the automatic gearbox as they came up to traffic lights. He seemed to be having some trouble remembering that he didn't have to change gear in order to slow down. It was ages before the lights changed to green. The trickling rain against the windscreen was beginning to drift into thousands of tiny snowflakes. They looked so beautiful under the street lights, icily brushing the glass and being flicked away by the wipers. Keely felt herself shivering and hugged herself deeper into the front seat, sometimes rubbing her arms in the sick-smelling jumper.

When he spoke again, he sounded slightly out of breath as if he was getting tired. 'How's Jess doing back there?'

'Same-ish.'

'Don't worry. We're nearly there now.'

'I'm not worried.'

'You're very close to your cousin, aren't you?'

She looked out of the window, tracing the delicate frost patterns with one finger without really seeing them. 'She's never been abroad either.'

'She'll be fine once we get her to a doctor.'

'Uh huh.'

The hospital was well-lit and busy with ambulances even though it was so late. It came out of the darkening snow like a great ship and Keely gripped the edges of her seat as they slowed outside the main doors. She felt light-headed and uncertain where she was.

Mr Swainson was talking to her again but she didn't even look at him this time. Then the driver's door was open to the freezing night air and he had disappeared for a few minutes. Her breath came shooting out in rapid white clouds and snow blew in through the open door. Her hands wouldn't ungrip the seat. When he came hurrying back outside there were suddenly men by the car with a trolley, lifting Jess carefully out of the back and taking her into the hospital.

'Why don't you go inside and keep warm for a while?' Mr Swainson said, opening her door. 'I've got to register her details with reception once I've moved the car somewhere safer. There's a coffee machine if you need a hot drink.'

He was helping her out of the car when she pushed his chest hard and broke away. She couldn't breathe properly. She didn't know which way to go. There were men in uniform inside, she could see them clearly through the large windows. They knew she was there, they were waiting for her.

'You shit. You told the police where I was.'

'What?'

'Get your hands off me.'

He came after her a few steps into the darkness. 'Keely, calm down.'

'You must think I'm stupid.'

No.' His voice was deliberately gentle. He wanted her to turn around and walk straight into his trap but she wouldn't give him the satisfaction. 'I think you're very tired and probably ill.'

Keely started to run across the grass away from him. It was dark in the grounds and within a few moments she'd lost all sense of direction, but if she steered away from the hospital buildings she should hit a main road in the end. She didn't look back to see if he was following her. He could waste his time out here in the cold if he wanted to. Jess was safe at the hospital now and there was no reason for her to wait around. There wasn't anything to do but find somewhere new to hide. Zal must know by now that they had stolen his car. Soon he would come looking and she couldn't let him find her. There was snow caught in her hair and chilling her face. It was thickening now, freezing underfoot and blinding her as the wind got up.

'Keely?'

She could hear his voice behind her, but ignored it. Almost slipping on the icy pavement, Keely managed to reach the main road and stood there for a moment, staring up and down. There were still plenty of cars about. She felt too visible in their headlights but she wasn't sure which way she ought to go in order to hide properly. There was nowhere for her to be safe now, not since Zal had found the squat.

Biting her lip, she tried to think without losing it. She had to find herself a warmer drier place to sleep than outside. Down at one of the city parks perhaps or beside the river, past the high fences, somewhere she could spend the night without being spotted. No coat on her back though, because she hadn't had time to grab it, only this jumper already dampening under the snow drift.

Glancing down the side alleys, it was darker than she had imagined away from the traffic and the street lights. There always seemed to be shadows moving just out of sight. Suddenly, she wished her cousin was there with her, just to hold her and tell her what to do. Jess would know what the next move was in this situation, where they could both find somewhere safe and warm to hide.

Keely had never slept outside before and she didn't know anyone who ever had. It wasn't fair that Jess had left her alone like this. Now she felt sick again and her stomach was absolutely killing her.

Everything seemed to be going wrong. Niall had to pull the BMW out of the path of an incoming ambulance and find somewhere to park it, then he began to follow Keely urgently on foot across the hospital grounds. Her cousin was in safe hands now and at least the doctors knew what she had taken. Registering her details, what he knew of them, could wait until later. Keely was more important at the moment.

When he reached the main street at last and bent over to catch his breath, thighs aching from the sudden exertion, Niall realised that he had probably lost her. Infuriated by the mess he had made of this escape, Niall shouted her name frantically up and down the street as if Keely, by some miracle, was going to hear him and respond.

A passing woman stared at his face before hurriedly crossing the road. There was a group of clubbing girls swaying arm-in-arm through the snow flurry, bare legs illuminated by the passing headlights, and a few homeless sheltering under old blankets in doorways, but absolutely no sign of Keely. Raucous laughter from the girls and an invitation he ignored were the only response to his shouts.

'Keely?'

She must have come this way from the hospital. Perhaps she had simply ducked straight down one of these back streets, trying to avoid the night crowds and traffic. But where on earth could the kid be heading? She couldn't go back to the squat now, he knew that. It was the very first place anyone would look for her. And Keely certainly couldn't go home.

Standing motionless and undecided on the street corner, Niall hugged himself against the cold. He had started shivering violently in the same shirt and jeans he'd been wearing for weeks. Suddenly aware that his body stank like a urinal, he realised with a shock how accustomed he must have grown to the smell. It must have been weeks since he last had a bath or changed his clothes. Shifting his toes uncomfortably, Niall grimaced at the unpleasant sensation. Even his socks felt as if they had rotted inside his trainers, damp and foul smelling. If it hadn't been snowing he would have gladly removed them and walked barefoot.

There was a large white van parked at the side of the road: glancing in its near side window, Niall caught sight of his own reflection and wiped snow clumsily from the glass, staring in sheer disbelief. But he no longer recognised the man peering so desperately back at him.

'Jesus Christ.'

The teacher had completely gone and in his place was this half-man, half-animal shuffling forward through the snow drift to examine himself more closely. He looked like an escaped convict from a Victorian prison, or perhaps some kind of drug-crazed addict. No wonder that woman had crossed the street so quickly to avoid him. His hair hung greasily around his temples. The prickle on his chin and around his mouth was the heavy stubble of a makeshift beard and moustache. His eyes looked strange and sunken in his face as if he was suffering from some terrible wasting disease.

Niall bent down over his knees suddenly, coughing and breathing hard. His heart rate was all over the place. It wasn't only the sudden exercise that was making it jump like a firecracker, but the realisation of what he had been through. He didn't know the date or even what day of the week it was. But he remembered Christmas Day coming and going: Keely on her knees beside him, washing his face. So he guessed it must be at least mid-January. He had spent nearly a full month tied to that radiator, by his estimate. He looked like shit. And he was starving.

Then he suddenly saw her, crossing the road up ahead, a slender child-like blonde dodging the lights of oncoming cars.

'Keely!'

Her head spun at his shout. She stopped dead in the middle of the road, staring in his direction. There was a violent blast on a horn and the sound of brakes squealing. His fatigue simply dropped away. He had started to run as soon as he saw her. Moved like a wolf through the teenage girls who screeched and scattered as he passed. Her pale face in the blinding snow lights, scanning that outer ring of darkness for him.

He caught her up, seizing her frozen arms and pushing her to the side of the road. 'For God's sake, Keely. You could have been killed.'

'So cold.'

She sounded plaintive, almost like a little girl. Which she was, he reminded himself angrily. Her eyes half-closed as she leant against him. He pulled the kid closer and felt her heart beating thinly against his chest. It was impossible for him to stay angry with her. She was lying limp in his arms now as if she had just been rescued from drowning.

'Why did you run away?'

Her voice was only a thread of sound, he had to bend to hear it. 'Doesn't matter anymore. There's nowhere to go.'

'Christ, you're freezing.'

'He's going to kill us both, you know.'

'It's okay, kid.'

'What are we going to do?'

'Take a joyride in his car and burn it out?' He brushed the snow away from her damp fringe and gave her what he hoped was a reassuring smile. There was no point mentioning the police at this stage. The kid was too exhausted, it would only frighten her off again. 'For a start, you can come home with me tonight. We both need a hot bath and something to eat before we make any decisions. I've got money and clean clothes back at the flat.'

'But he'll come looking. He'll find us in the end.'

Niall looked down at her white face for a moment without replying. She was so cold and still, it was like holding an ice sculpture.

'With any luck, yes.'

In the end, he managed to park the stolen BMW a few blocks away from his flat and they stumbled through the snow together. His legs were shaking quite severely now that the initial adrenaline rush of escape had faded. The first floor flat was in darkness, and for a few moments he was afraid that the landlady had given it to someone else in his absence, but his key still fitted the lock and once they got inside he found everything exactly as he had left it. The place was like a morgue though and he put the heating on immediately, clearing a musty pile of magazines off the sofa so she could sit down.

'The best I can offer you is some cheese and tomato pizza,' he told her, checking the freezer compartment briefly before heading into the bathroom for a long hot shower. 'But at least they haven't cut off my electricity. God knows what my landlady will think I've been doing all this time.'

'Just tell her the truth.'

He glanced over his shoulder and saw her already huddled up on the sofa, hands cradled tightly about her knees. It was as though he were seeing a different girl from the Keely he knew, the one with the cruel mouth who'd handcuffed him to a radiator and tormented him for the past few weeks. She looked so young without the lipstick or eyeshadow. Little better than a guilty confused kid.

'Things aren't that simple though, are they? You can't hide from the facts forever. The police have to know what Zal's been doing to you. And I'll have to admit I knocked him out and stole his car.'

'But what about Rab?' she whispered.

'One thing at a time.'

'But if we go to the police, Eddy's going to tell them I killed him. He already said it was my fault, what happened. Eddy won't go down for murder, not in a million years. He'll blame it on me. And now Jess is going to die and it'll be my word against his.'

Niall took a deep breath, watching the shake of her shoulders. This probably wasn't the perfect time to cover such dangerous territory. For a start, he didn't want the kid running out on him again, especially not in this weather and with him too bloody exhausted to do anything but stand here swaying, one hand on the wall to support himself.

Maybe it was better just to let things go for tonight. They were probably both starving and knackered beyond belief. It was fairly pointless trying to discuss ethics with a disturbed teenager at the best of times, let alone under such difficult circumstances.

'Okay, let's skip over this part,' he said. 'We're both tired. I'm going to grab a shower and sort out some clean clothes for myself.' He pulled at his jeans disgustedly. 'This lot ought to be burnt, they stink. When I come out of the shower, I'll put a pizza in the oven for us. Why don't you put those damp things on the radiator and get some sleep? You can have my bed, I'll kip on the sofa tonight.'

'Whatever.'

He looked at her for a moment. 'Give me your trainers.'

'What?'

'I'm not having you run out on me while I'm defrosting in the shower. So unlace your trainers and let me have them.' He snapped his fingers when she hesitated. 'Come on, take them off. None of my shoes are going to fit you and I can't see you heading off into the snow barefoot. And in case you were thinking about doing exactly that, let me remind you that it didn't work out for the Little Match Girl.'

She stopped unlacing her trainers and stared. 'The who?'

'Forget it. Just give me the shoes.'

He hadn't slept so soundly for weeks. It was strange, waking up in his own flat again. Even stranger to find himself scrunched up under a blanket on the sofa instead of comfortably in his bed. It was nearly midday and cold light was streaming in through the uncurtained windows of what passed for his living room. For a few seconds Niall lay there frowning at his watch, trying to work out where he was and why. Then he gradually remembered the events of the night before, and apprehension began to set in at last. Keely probably hadn't been exaggerating when she said Zal would come after them both.

There was no time left to hang around his flat, waiting for the man to catch up with them. Niall had washed weeks of grimy sweat from his body, shaved at last, changed his clothes, eaten something hot, and slept for several hours. Now he had to act before it was too late.

There was nothing for breakfast but black coffee. It was ridiculous. He felt like someone coming home from a lengthy holiday abroad. The place was in chaos. It was still freezing cold, in spite of leaving the three bar fire on all night in the living room. Everything felt damp and smelt musty. Even the kitchen surfaces were covered in dust. There were no eggs, no bread, no fresh milk. While boiling the kettle, he found a decaying carton of the stuff in his fridge and chucked it in the bin with the rest of the rotting food. The stench of that bin bag was almost more than he could stomach.

But at least he felt vaguely normal again, even if he was still experiencing the shakes from time to time. The worst had not happened. He hadn't been executed by lethal injection at the squat, handcuffed ignominiously to a radiator for his last sickening moments of life, then thrown into the river to be found probably weeks later: bloated, half frozen, unrecognisable. He didn't know exactly how, but he had somehow managed to survive the experience.

'I actually made it home,' he muttered, making his own coffee strong enough to blow his eyeballs out.

Half expecting to find Keely and his entire CD collection gone, Niall carried her coffee through to his bedroom. There was no answer to his tap at the door, so he opened it. The room was still in semi-darkness. His bed was empty, covers thrown back and the pillow on the floor, but she hadn't left the flat. Above the sound of running water, he could hear a strange muffled noise from inside the locked bathroom.

He put her coffee down and knocked tentatively at the bathroom door. 'It's gone midday, Keely. You okay in there?'

'Go away.'

He listened to her retching again. 'What's the matter?'

'Fuck off, would you?'

'I'm not moving until you open this bloody door.'

Less than two minutes later she flushed the toilet and unlocked the bathroom door, throwing it open aggressively to face him. She was wearing one of his old shirts, barely covering the tops of her thighs. Her face was pale and still dripping where she had splashed herself with cold water. 'What do you want?'

'I thought you might need help.'

'I was just being sick, okay? I didn't know I needed your fucking permission to chuck up.'

'Well, you must be ill. Are you running a temperature?'

She took a shaky breath. 'No.'

'But if you're not sick ... '

Realisation hit him and the words died on his lips. Niall took a step backwards and stared at her. There was only one possible explanation and he suddenly couldn't believe he hadn't realised it before.

Keely was pregnant. But whose baby was it?

He didn't actually want to know the answer to that, because he suspected that he already knew the truth. It was looking back at him through her eyes. But it was so appalling that he almost wanted to push past her and vomit himself. No wonder her head was screwed up. He should have seen it long ago. Blind and stupid, so completely wrapped up in his own problems that he hadn't noticed what she was going through. He had put it all down to drugs and mental illness when the reality had been walking past him every day, making itself known, literally shouting out for attention.

She had started to cry now, holding her head in her hands as she leant back against the swaying bathroom door. It was as if she could only be hard about the situation until someone else knew what was happening to her. The sobs were heart-wrenchingly genuine, but he didn't dare touch her. Not even for the sake of comfort. Not yet, anyway. She could easily read it wrong and then they would be back where they started, hitting out at each other's shadows in the dark.

'How far gone are you?'

'Nearly three months.'

He forced himself to ask the question he wanted to avoid. 'Whose?'

'Take a wild guess.'

Niall shook his head. He knew that game only too well and he didn't want to play it. 'Tell me straight, Keely.'

'Zal.'

'Your own stepfather? Jesus Christ. How long has he been ... I mean, when did he start ... ?'

'About a year ago. Maybe a bit longer.' Her voice dropped to a whisper and she suddenly looked like a little kid, her eyes huge as she watched his reaction. 'I can't be sure anymore. It's sort of hazy. He did other things before. Touched me when mam wasn't there.'

'You didn't tell anyone.'

She looked confused. 'Was I meant to?'

Niall didn't have an answer for that. His head was in pieces. But the kid was shivering now, standing there in nothing but his shirt. He picked up the coffee he'd left on the carpet and handed it over to her. 'It must have been hell. Why didn't you tell Jess what was going on? She's a couple of years older than you, she could have helped you.'

'I couldn't tell her, could I? Not until after I'd run away from home. He might have hurt her too.'

Her face was frighteningly pale as she stared down into the coffee without drinking it. She looked as if she was about to faint. Never taking his eyes off her face, Niall slipped his hands into the back pockets of his jeans. His clothes were so loose on him now, he felt slightly ludicrous. It had been that starvation diet at the squat. Yet none of that seemed important at the moment. Everything was focused on this tiny space between the wall and the bathroom door instead.

He took a sharp breath, thinking back and realising why she had behaved so strangely in the past. Poor bloody kid. So many things were explained by this, he could barely think straight anymore. 'Okay, but why on earth didn't you tell me?'

'I didn't think you'd believe us,' she muttered.

'Oh. We're the enemy, right?'

'Something like that.'

Niall felt a sudden urge to lean forward and shake some sense into her, but fought it back. There was no point losing his temper with her. She was the victim here. It was that total bastard of a stepfather that he really wanted to get to grips with. Of course Keely hadn't felt able to approach any of the teachers, even him. He was being naive again. That simple trust wasn't there anymore. The system had murdered it.

Perhaps he had almost expected this, maybe even known it for certain somewhere in the depths of his subconscious. She had given him enough clues over the past few weeks, after all. He would have to be completely deaf and blind not to have picked up on a parent-child relationship which just didn't seem normal.

But it was the pregnancy that really shocked him. It was as if sexual abuse was one thing, but a baby was quite another. That attitude made little sense on the face of things. But he felt it strongly and that was enough for him. His hands were shaking but he managed to clench them into fists.

'I'm going to kill the filthy bastard.'

CHAPTER TWENTY

He persuaded Keely to lie down for a few hours, then walked up to the main shopping area about half a mile from his flat and hailed a taxi. He asked the driver to drop him off a few blocks from Keely's house. There was no clear-cut plan in his mind. He just knew he had to sort some things out for himself before making any irrevocable decisions.

It was raining lightly now, but Niall turned the collar up on his jacket and trudged the rest of the way on foot. The pale snow which had been falling for several days appeared to have eased at last and was beginning to thaw. Sludge still lay in thick dirty heaps at street corners and lining the gutters, only half concealing the usual debris of sweet wrappers and cigarette butts. Even stark branched trees were patched with it, occasionally shaking trickling white lumps onto the people below. Melted snow gradually soaked through his cheap shoes and left his socks damp. It was bitterly cold out on the streets but there was something of childhood here, Niall thought, peering up at the grey sky: a barely acknowledged sense of astonishment inside at how a little snow could change the landscape so completely.

Considering where he was going, and why, that sense of childish delight was incongruous enough to make him uncomfortable. He tried to shrug it off, walking faster and keeping his eyes straight ahead. But it lingered tangibly at the back of his mind, cold to the touch and inexplicably sweet-smelling.

It took him a few minutes to remember which house was hers. He walked up and down the street a couple of times on the opposite side of the road, trying not to appear conspicuous by stopping at the corner newsagents for a paper and reading it slowly on his way back.

Eventually, he became pretty sure that he had located the right house. That was definitely where he had parked last time. The blue front door was shut. The curtains in the front room were drawn back as if someone was at home, but it was impossible to see inside from that distance.

Now that he was here, Niall couldn't be sure what he was going to do, how exactly he should play this. He wasn't a policeman. He wasn't even a social worker. On the face of it, he had no right to be interfering. He ought to be at the police station right now, describing the events of the past few weeks and letting the dice fall where they may. Yet what if Keely really was his daughter? He couldn't go on pretending it wasn't possible, not when his testimony about Rab's death might perhaps make the difference for her between going to prison and leading a normal life. Not that she knew any longer what 'normal' was meant to be.

But Keely wasn't the only one. His own head was fucked up too. Nothing was as clear as it had seemed in the beginning, when he would have done anything to escape from that squat and find the nearest policeman. All he knew now was that he couldn't move in either direction without nailing the truth about Keely first.

In the end, he didn't have to wait long. A radio cab arrived about ten minutes later, beeping its horn outside their front door.

The door opened and Zal came out, his face set in grim lines as he glanced up and down the street before climbing inside. Niall buried his head in the newspaper as the cab pulled rapidly away from the kerb and passed him at the corner, his stomach clenching at the thought that Zal might recognise him. It was ridiculously unlikely, his appearance had changed so much since they had met that day in the shopping centre car park. But he couldn't help that instinctive fear, however much he despised himself for it. The man was dangerous, Niall had no doubt about it, and there was no knowing what he might do to whomever was protecting his stepdaughter.

As soon as the cab had disappeared, Niall crossed the road and rang the doorbell. He didn't know what he would do if Anne wasn't at home, but he had to try. Nobody answered at first, but he could hear music somewhere inside, so he tightened his jaw and leant heavily on the bell. Keely was in serious trouble and she needed his help. There was no way he was going to just give up on her and walk away this time.

She threw the door open impatiently, tucking her hair under a damp towel and staring at him without recognition. 'Yes, what is it?'

'Remember me, Anne?' He could tell by her sudden intake of breath that she did. Taken by surprise, Anne stepped back for a second as if to look at him better, then tried to slam the door shut on him. Niall put out a hand and stopped her. He was filled with a sudden wild rage at her attitude. 'No, you don't. You know why I'm here.'

'Get lost.'

Niall shook his head, stepping past her into the house. 'I think it's about time we had a serious talk about Keely, don't you?'

It was dark when Keely finally woke again. She had been curled over sideways to avoid the pain in her stomach, but it had only left her muscles aching. She could still taste sick in her mouth, so she had a quick sip of water from the glass he had left beside her bed. Her tits hurt too and they were covered in tiny blue veins. She decided that must be because of the baby. The clock said six thirty, but for a moment Keely wasn't sure if that was morning or night. Then she looked out at the car headlights below, and guessed it must be evening.

The flat was cold and silent. She stumbled from the bedroom into the living room, calling his name in a low voice, but the whole place was in darkness. It was strange to be able to flick a switch and see the lights come on. The electric fire worked perfectly too. Keely clicked both bars and sat down cross-legged right in front of the orange glow, trying to get warm. The hairs on her naked legs got hot very quickly. The electricity was making that strange humming noise and she suddenly didn't like it.

Keely had got used to living by candlelight, everything was so bright it hurt her eyes. She wasn't really sure she wanted to be inside anymore. It might be cold out on the streets but at least there she wouldn't feel so trapped.

The bastard must have slipped out while she was asleep and left her there on her own. Jess used to do that at the squat when she didn't want Keely to ask where she was going. It seemed like she was always the one who woke up alone. She felt stupid for a moment, because Mr Swainson had obviously tricked her into going back to sleep, then suddenly she felt angry. He hadn't even touched her yet.

Why had he bothered running after her last night if he wasn't interested, if she wasn't worth anything to him? He had even knocked Zal out and stolen his car, as if he'd been showing Zal that he wanted Keely for himself. Her stepdad would be mad enough to kill them both because of that.

Keely would get the blame for that too. She always got the blame. It might have been better just to let her face Zal and get the punishment over with.

'I just want things back the way they were,' she whispered.

Everything was her own fault, right back to the beginning. She shouldn't have lost her temper at school so often, it had only drawn more attention to herself and made Zal angry. She shouldn't have fought him at home either, she should have kept her mouth shut and let Zal do what he wanted. Then he would have carried on buying her presents and everything would have turned out okay.

She should never have hit him with the gold clock. It was the stupidest thing she'd ever done. Zal wasn't going to let it rest. He'd keep following until he caught up with her, and then she'd suffer worse than ever before.

There was no one to stand in his way. Her mam didn't care what happened to her and Mr Swainson wouldn't protect her. She meant nothing to him. She'd hoped she was special to him. But he wasn't even interested enough to want sex with her, so why should he risk getting beaten up or worse just to stop Zal taking her away from him?

Keely drew her knees up to her chin in front of the two bar fire and let herself have a little cry, wiping her nose on the back of her hand. There was enough time for that. Mr Swainson probably wouldn't be back in any sort of hurry. Maybe that was why he had left her alone in the first place. So that she would get dressed and leave before he came back to his flat. Disappear back into the night like the whore he thought she was. It would only mean more trouble for him if she stayed, they both knew that. He must want to see the back of her as soon as possible.

After she had cried until she was empty, Keely got dressed in the cold bedroom. Her bare legs were shivery and goose-pimpled as she balanced on one leg and then the other to pull her knickers back on. Then she took the cash from his bedside drawer. There was enough for her bus fare and maybe some chips too. That was all she really needed.

The front door to the flat was locked and Keely couldn't work out how to open it, so she pushed up his window at the back and climbed down the fire escape instead. It was rusty and shook against the wall at every step, but she got to the pavement safe enough.

She put her head right down and walked as quick as she could in the slippery snow. She didn't look anyone in the face. Things would be easier if she had a hood on the jacket, she thought, keeping her eyes fixed on her feet. Maybe she should have stayed in the flat until later in the evening. It would be the end if anyone recognised her.

The hospital was just as brightly-lit and busy as it had been the night before, and it took Keely a few minutes to push herself out of the darkness and towards the reception desk. She hated the place, but she had to find out if Jess was alive.

'Are you a relative?'

Keely hesitated. 'She's my sister.'

'Oh good.' The blonde receptionist was looking at her computer screen. 'That could be useful. We haven't got her full details here. Perhaps you could give me her home address.'

'She hasn't got one. I mean, she's homeless.'

'What about a last known address? And her date of birth?'

Keely wanted to lie but her mind was blank. She should have prepared a false address in case they asked. But it probably wouldn't matter to let them have Aunty Jean's address. She'd never cared what happened to Jess anyway. Why would she start now just because of some stupid overdose? So Keely told her what she remembered, stumbling a little over the year of birth, but the woman didn't seem to notice. Her pinkish nails clacked against the computer keyboard as she typed in the details. Those irritating little noises went straight through Keely's head.

There was no air in this place. It was like being inside a huge shining coffin. Her stomach was starting to hurt again and the lights made her feel sick. If she hadn't been so desperate to see Jess again, Keely would have run back out of the double doors into the darkness. But she couldn't give up now, she was so close.

'How is she anyway? Can I see her?'

'Well, since you're her sister ...' The receptionist checked the computer again. 'She'll be on the second floor at the moment. Hold on while I check which room.'

The lift would probably have made her puke, so Keely took the stairs instead. It wasn't far to climb but she still felt exhausted before she got there. The corridor on the second floor was just as brightly-lit as the rest of the hospital, except now there was a strong smell of disinfectant that almost made her heave. She hated the smell of hospitals too. People shuffling along in slippers. A woman mopping the floor near the lifts who stared at her suspiciously. Half open doorways into more strong-smelling rooms with high white beds and whispering nurses. Even the corridor walls looked like they'd been scrubbed clean.

It was just like when she was a kid and her dad hurt his back falling off the ladder. He'd been in hospital for months and months. Someone in a wheelchair was sitting in one of the doorways as she passed, so Keely turned her face away. Everyone here was sick.

The door to her room was firmly shut. Keely stood there for a few seconds, half expecting someone to stop her before she could walk inside and see her cousin, but there was nobody about. Her palms were damp so she wiped them on her jacket, then opened the door. It was darker in there than in the other rooms, and for a moment Keely thought she must be in the wrong place, then she suddenly recognised her cousin under the tangle of wires and monitors around the bed.

'Jess?' She tiptoed forward, letting the door shut behind her. 'It's me, Kee. Can you hear me?'

But there was no answer. Jess looked pale and almost

dead against the clean white sheets. She didn't even stir when Keely put a hand on her arm and gently squeezed. Shutters were half-open over the windows, and through each narrow slit Keely could see buildings lit up for the evening. It wasn't so far up, but it reminded her a bit of when her and mam lived in that high-rise flat, when she could see thousands of car headlights streaming across the city for miles. The smell of that high-rise came back in an instant, the constant stink of wee down the stairs and along the corridors with their broken lights. She had felt really alone there some nights.

She could see her cousin's heartbeat on one of the monitors beside the bed, moving in a slow but steady ripple across the screen. There was a thin tube coming out of her arm and a thicker one out of her mouth, both of them taped to the skin. This wasn't what Keely had expected. She'd thought the doctors would be able to help Jess properly if there was still time, but she didn't even look alive anymore. It was more like she'd been in a bad car smash and wasn't going to make it through.

'Can I help you?'

Keely jumped violently and turned round. There was a nurse in the doorway, smiling as she propped the door open and pulled through a trolley. It stood there, blocking the doorway. She was trapped.

'No thanks. I'm her sister,' she said quickly, sticking to the story she'd given the receptionist. 'I was just going anyway.'

'Don't go yet, would you? The doctor needs to talk to one of the relatives. I'll fetch her if you wait here.'

'I'm in a bit of a hurry.'

'It won't take a minute. The doctor's only a few doors down.'

'How bad is it?'

'Your sister hasn't regained consciousness, if that's what you mean.' The nurse smiled sympathetically, slipping past the trolley to look up and down the corridor. 'It was quite a serious overdose. But the doctor will let you know what's happening in more detail. If you just wait, I'll ask her to come and talk to you.'

As soon as she'd disappeared, Keely leant forward and kissed Jess on the cheek. Her skin was strangely warm. It wasn't anything like the coldish marble she remembered from the squat. Her heart hurt but she couldn't stay in the hospital any longer. It was too dangerous.

'I've got to go now, babes,' Keely whispered in her cousin's ear, even though she knew Jess probably couldn't hear her. 'But don't worry. The doctors and nurses are going to take real good care of you. I'll come back to see you in a few days, okay?'

The heartbeat on the monitor above the bed didn't change.

'Look, we'll get straight out of Newcastle when you're well again,' she added hurriedly, checking over her shoulder that the nurse hadn't come back yet. 'We'll go somewhere warm and spend the summer getting pissed on the beach, you and me. So you get better soon, right?'

The silence from beneath the tubes was horrible. It wasn't Jess in there at all. She might as well be talking to a statue.

There were suddenly voices in the corridor outside, coming closer and closer.

Keely turned and ran, knocking painfully into the trolley. Her leg and hip hurt, but she didn't look back until she was safely down the stairs and out in the darkness and the snow again. No one seemed to be coming after her. Even the ambulance crew she had passed on her way out didn't do more than glance in her direction before carrying on.

Her face felt weirdly numb and Keely leant against a brick wall for a moment to catch her breath, touching her cheek. It was wet. That was the first time she realised she had been crying.

Niall knew she was gone as soon as he unlocked the door. There was a quality to the silence of the darkened flat which gave it away. It was as if she created a vibration in the air that was no longer there.

For a moment, he felt an enormous fury spiral up inside him at her ingratitude, but it subsided almost as quickly as it had arrived. He was too tired to give a toss about her absence yet. First he needed to sit down with a strong whisky and close his eyes until the world stopped spinning. It had been a difficult twenty-four hours.

Half an hour later, Niall realised he was slightly pleased the kid had done a runner. Her familiar girly scent still lingered in the living room, and there were traces of her blonde hair caught on his cushions, but the unexpected silence was more than pleasant. He was even finding it hard to keep his eyes open, it was so comforting to be alone in his own place again.

With his feet up and his head reclining on the sofa, a whisky in his hand and nothing but the sound of soft rain falling outside, Niall could almost imagine that the past few weeks had never happened. He was free of it, or at least that was how it felt for the time being. As if he were slowly coming round from some sort of living nightmare into which he had been plunged without warning or explanation. That frantic inner voice which had been keeping him awake for weeks, endlessly awaiting the pain of execution, had finally been silenced. Except of course for the vague awareness that he was still in danger. But Niall wasn't listening to that yet.

He found it incredible that he had come out intact on the other side. If there was such a thing as a guardian angel, it must have been at his side during those dark weeks at the squat. He had never felt so frightened and isolated in his life, yet somehow he had not been harmed.

Did he believe in God? It had never really been a question that he had bothered with. Now it seemed increasingly important to get it straight in his head.

At one point, roughly when Keely was talking about shooting him up with heroin and dumping him in the river, the odds had been stacked against him getting out of that place alive. So someone, or perhaps something, must surely have helped him through that appalling experience. If it all came down to luck and coincidence, Niall wasn't sure what he could learn from that. Unless it was simply that he was a jammy bastard.

He must have drifted off to sleep in the end, because he woke abruptly to the sound of knocking at the window. It was pitch black outside and his first instinct was to freeze in fear. The bastard had found him and was going to kill him. Then his brain slowly came back to life, and he realised that the white face against the window was Keely's.

'Where the hell have you been?' he found himself demanding as he helped her climb inside. It was almost ridiculous but he sounded like an over-protective parent. 'I've been worried sick about you. And what was wrong with the front door? You could have been killed climbing up there in this weather. That fire escape's a death-trap.'

'I didn't want to be seen.'

'Obviously.'

He poured her a small whisky and made her sit in front of the electric fire. She was pale and shivering with cold. Her trainers were sodden with icy sleet and he ordered her to unlace them. Her fingers barely worked so he had to do it for her, kneeling in the damp patch she had left on the carpet. He stripped off her useless jacket and threw it to one side. Underneath, all her clothes were utterly soaked. She looked as if she had been standing out in the rain for hours. Moving quickly, Niall fetched a blanket from the bedroom and covered her trembling shoulders with it.

'I don't understand why you left anyway. You're safest here, you must realise that.'

'I had to see Jess.'

He stared. 'You went to the hospital?'

'I needed to know if she was going to make it, didn't I?'

'And?'

'Dunno really.' Keely shrugged, huddling up under the blanket. 'She wasn't awake. They had tubes in her and everything.'

'I know you wanted to see your cousin, that's only natural. But it was incredibly stupid to go on your own, Keely, it's too dangerous. You should have waited for me and we could have gone together. Your stepdad's out there now, searching for you. How am I supposed to protect you when I don't even know where the bloody hell you are?'

'I never asked you to protect us, did I?'

'You're my responsibility.'

'I'm not a kid anymore. I can look after myself.'

Niall was so angry, he wanted to shake her. 'Is that why you came back here in this god-awful state? Because you can look after yourself?'

'It's raining if you hadn't noticed.'

'You look half dead.'

'Just piss off out of my face, would you?' Her voice rose and there was colour in her face at last. 'Where do you get off anyway, telling us what to do and that?'

'Because I worry about you, Keely.'

'Why should you? You're not my dad.'

'No,' he said heavily, and sat down on the sofa. His legs were suddenly trembling. 'I'm not your dad. But I thought there was a chance I might be, right up until this afternoon.'

'What?'

Niall could have laughed at her blank expression. 'I went to see your mother today. I shouldn't really have shouted at you for going out. It was hypocritical. Like you, I had something very important to sort out, and I took an equally stupid risk in order to do it.'

'You went to see my mam?'

'Don't look so worried, I didn't tell her where you were.'

'But how could you think you were my dad?'

He hesitated. 'There's no easy way to tell you this, so I won't bother trying to soften the blow. I'm not proud of what I did, but I slept with your mother once., just before she married your father.'

She stared.

'I didn't know who you were, honestly. The surname was different. You don't even look that much like her. In fact, I had absolutely no idea until I met your mother the day you ran away from school.' He laughed. 'I'd always been told I couldn't have kids. Thinking you might be mine. It felt like a miracle. But she put me straight today. She was already a few weeks pregnant when I slept with her, though she didn't realise until afterwards. You're not my child.'

Keely didn't say anything for a few minutes. She was staring into the electric fire, her face very pale. Her fingers plucked repeatedly at the edge of her blanket. 'She had sex with you just before she married my dad?'

'We were both drunk.'

'That's no excuse. She's always been a cheat.' She hesitated. 'How do you know she's not lying now?'

'Why would she bother lying about something like that? She hasn't seen your real dad in years. In fact, I even offered to look after you financially if you were my child. She could easily have said yes and taken the cash. But she told me it wasn't true. You're Malcolm's kid, not mine.'

'What about DNA tests?'

'Keely,' he said gently. 'I'm sorry, but I'm not your dad.'

She buried her face in the blanket and he could see her shoulders beginning to shake quietly again. Niall didn't know what to say, though he couldn't help feeling a secret pride and gratitude inside. He couldn't understand why, but it sounded as if she might have preferred him to be her dad rather than Malcolm.

Keely had hurt and humiliated him over the past few weeks, and even thought about killing him, yet there was something about the kid that made it impossible for Niall to hate her. Not for the first time, Niall wished he really could have been Keely's dad. But her mother had been straight with him about what happened that night and he was grateful for her honesty, at least. He had seen the sympathy in Anne's eyes after she told him and tried to hide his own reaction. It was simple enough. There was no way he could have made the woman pregnant, and that was an end to it.

She looked up at him after a while, wiping her damp face on one sleeve. 'You said you can't have kids now. why's that?'

'It's not a pretty story. Your real dad came round and found us together that night. Basically, he kicked the living shit out of me. I was in hospital for about six weeks afterwards. Once I was well enough to go home, they told me I'd never be able to have kids. That's why I kept on ...' He stared at his hands. 'As soon as I realised it might be possible, I hoped you were mine. It would have meant something worthwhile had come out of that whole mess.'

'What's worthwhile about me?' She had started crying again. 'I should have got rid of this kid right at the beginning. Done it with the coat hanger like I tried to, only Jess stopped us. I mean, what sort of mam am I going to make?'

'You don't have to get rid of it.'

'I can't have it. It's *his*, isn't it? How can I have his kid?'

Niall didn't know how to comfort her. He watched her in silence for a few minutes, wanting to touch her but not daring to, in case she hated him for it and pulled away. He couldn't have handled that sort of rejection. Instead, he just sat there with his insides hurting, bitterly angry towards Zal because the bastard was still making her suffer like this.

'Please don't cry. In the end, it's your choice. I'm sure your mother will stand by you, whatever you decide to do.'

Her voice was agonised. 'She knows about the baby?'

'I had no choice, I had to tell her. She was denying everything, Keely. She even called you a liar. I needed her to understand what her husband's really like.'

'She'll want us dead now for sure. Me and the kid both.'

'No, that's not true.' He risked touching her shoulder briefly. 'Look, if you really want to keep this baby, I'll help you in any way I can. I mean that, Keely, it's not just empty promises. Whatever it takes.'

She looked at him thoughtfully.

'You're sure you don't mind waiting outside?' Mr Swainson asked her again as they walked round the corner towards the school. 'Because I could do this later. We can straight to the police if you prefer.'

Keely shrugged, winding a length of her hair around her fingers and chewing at it. It was much colder now that they were out of the flat and she could feel herself shivering slightly. She didn't really want to go to the police at all. The whole idea made her sick, in case the bastards locked her up for what happened to Rab. But she knew there was no getting out of it, not if she wanted to stop Zal from finding her again.

'It's okay.'

He nodded, watching her face. 'Well, stay right here and try to keep out of sight. This shouldn't take too long. I just need to check what's been happening at school. You know, find out if I still have a job to go back to? Then we'll catch a bus over to the police station and get this whole mess cleared up.'

Once Mr Swainson had crossed the road and turned into the school grounds, Keely took the cigarettes out of her jacket pocket and lit up. Her hands were trembling. The bitter smoke taste going into her lungs made her feel stronger, more able to handle what was coming. But she wished he didn't have to go into the school like this, even if it was only for ten minutes or so. She felt too exposed, standing about on this street corner.

It was lunchtime and there were plenty of kids wandering up and down the road. Keely couldn't see anyone from her year, but some of the older ones looked at her strangely. That made her stomach hurt again. It might be okay to be out on the streets once Mr Swainson had told the police and Zal was locked up like he ought to be, but until then she didn't feel properly safe.

She leant back against the damp wall, turning up her jacket collar against the cold wind. It had stopped snowing, but there was still a grey sludge dammed up in the gutters and around doorways. She was feeling a little bit sick, which might have been nerves about the police, except that Mr Swainson had treated her to a full fried breakfast that morning and the waistband on her skirt was tighter than usual. But having a smoke seemed to be helping her sickness. Keely knew he didn't really approve of her smoking, especially now he knew she was pregnant, but he wasn't there to shake his head at her. It didn't matter about the baby anyway. She wasn't planning on keeping it much longer.

'Hey, Kee!'

Freezing in sudden fear, Keely recognised the voice. It was Eddy, she was sure of it. She swung her head and felt her breath almost stop. He was standing further along the road, just outside the school gates, and as he looked back in her direction she saw that he was talking to someone on his mobile.

Eddy put one hand in the air to get her attention before ringing off and pocketing the mobile. His voice turned threatening as he crossed the road towards her. 'Stay exactly where you are, Kee. Don't move a fucking inch!'

It was hopeless. There was nowhere for her to run. Keely looked quickly along the school fence but there was no sign of Mr Swainson anywhere. She didn't really know what else to do so she just stood there, waiting for Eddy to reach her. He was wearing his usual leather jacket that creaked when he moved, and he hadn't shaved for a while, his chin was black with stubble.

'So where have you been?'

Keely shrugged. 'Don't know what you mean.'

'Don't piss us about here, Kee.' Eddy ignored her cry of pain, dragging her straight up to his face. 'Zal's told me what happened when he went to the squat. I always thought you were fucked-up, but you need your head examining this time. Going up against Zal on your own? That's nothing short of fucking suicide. And what if this teacher tells the police about Rab?'

'Rab's nothing to do with me.'

'Oh, so your hands are clean?'

'You were the one who killed him.'

'I was trying to help you.'

'What?' Keely struggled angrily, but his grip was too strong. 'You were the one who set me up with him that night. You told me I had to play along, do whatever the bastard wanted.'

'But you didn't listen.'

'You're unbelievable.'

'But at least I'm not crazy.' He looked around, frowning. 'Where's Jess then? She's never far behind you.'

'Stuck in a hospital bed with tubes coming out of her. She might even die. That's your fault, Eddy. You did that to her.'

'I didn't hit her that hard.'

'No. But when Jess got home, she was so upset about you laying into her, she dropped most of that gear in one pop.'

Eddy seemed confused at last, his grip loosening.

'Well, that score was meant for your man. There was enough there to kill a horse. She knew that. If the stupid bitch couldn't keep her hands out the sweetie jar, that's her problem. You can't go blaming that one on me.'

'Don't you care?'

'Just one more dead whore, isn't it?'

That was it. Keely broke free and clawed at his eyes. She could hear Eddy shouting something, his hands up shielding his face, but she wasn't listening.

She wanted to hurt him, scratch him to pieces, blind the bastard. Jess had really cared about that little shit but he didn't give a toss whether she lived or died. Keely slashed at him with her nails while he tried to hold her back, grabbing at her wrists. He wouldn't be able to show his ugly face for weeks after she'd finished with him.

Then she heard brakes squealing and a black car pulled alongside them at speed. Eddy opened the back door and dragged her inside by her hair. 'Come on, you crazy bitch. We're going for a ride.'

Keely struggled violently against him, nearly falling and banging her head on the door panel. By the time she'd realised what was happening, the car had pulled away from the kerb again and was speeding along the road. Eddy pressed his arm across her throat like an iron bar, forcing her down against the seats. He was touching his face, as if trying to feel what damage she'd done. There was a long red scratch from the corner of his eye to his mouth, seeping blood. Eddy tasted it with the tip of his tongue. He wasn't smiling anymore.

'Look, I'm bleeding. She's drawn blood on us.' Eddy put his fist down and pushed it up hard under her skirt. It slammed against her insides like a sledgehammer and she yelped at the pain. 'You'll be sorry you did that, Kee. There was no need for that. I'm going to really enjoy hurting you now.'

'Keep your hands off her, Eddy. Leave the little bitch to me.'

Keely stiffened, recognising the other man's voice. Through the blur of pain, Eddy's bruising fingers dragged along her thighs as she stared at the driver's head.

CHAPTER TWENTY-ONE

'That's an incredible story, Niall.' MacFerson shook his head and leant back in the chair, wiping those familiar black-rimmed glasses with a tissue. He resettled the glasses on his nose. 'If everything you've told me is true, I don't know how you managed to stay alive.'

Niall smiled drily across the desk at the head teacher. He could hear the disbelief in his voice, but it no longer mattered to him what the man thought. He hadn't been there. 'Neither do I.'

'You've informed the police, of course?'

'I'm on my way there right now.'

'And the girl?'

'Keely's outside. She's coming with me to the station.'

MacFerson raised his eyebrows. 'Is that really wise? I think you should take some advice on that. I'd steer well clear of the kid until the police have had a chance to deal with the situation.'

'You don't understand.'

'In my experience, teenage girls are notoriously unpredictable. She could just as easily change her mind about what happened and try slapping an assault charge on you. Had you considered that?'

'I never laid a finger on her.'

MacFerson looked at him. 'Do you have any proof of that?'

'That's not the point.'

'I'm sorry to disillusion you, Niall, but that's precisely the point.' The head teacher took a deep breath, leaning forward to put a hand on the telephone. 'Take my advice and don't do anything rash. I'll call the police from here. They can come to the school straight away and you can tell them exactly what you told me. Before this girl has a chance to muddy the waters by accusing you of god knows what.'

'You don't believe a word I've said, do you?'

'That's not the case.'

Niall stood up abruptly, knocking his chair back onto the carpet. He could hardly breathe. After the cold of the streets, he felt almost suffocated by the heat inside the head's blank-walled office with its row of carefully shuttered windows. MacFerson's glasses caught the daylight as the head teacher tilted his head back to stare, blinding him for a few seconds.

There was something unexpectedly sinister about the man and Niall took another step backwards, trying to assess what was going on before any more damage could be done. The situation seemed incredible. He had come here expecting to find support and reassurance, but now he couldn't believe what he was hearing.

'Do I still have a job?'

'Calm down.'

'What are you saying, Jim?'

'I'm not saying anything. We haven't replaced you. But we didn't know what had happened to you, obviously. Why don't you sit down again? You're blowing this out of all proportion.' The head gave him a soothing smile. 'We have got someone else in at the moment, covering your classes, but it's only a temporary arrangement. After a brief period of consideration, you'll probably be allowed to come back to work.'

'Period of consideration?'

'The police will need to be consulted about your story first.' MacFerson shrugged, spreading his hands out in what appeared to be an apologetic explanation. 'Then someone from Occupational Health will have to interview you before you can resume teaching.'

'Occupational Health?'

'It's entirely a matter of routine, I can assure you.'

'Am I being accused of something here?'

'Absolutely not.'

Niall counted silently to ten, trying hard not to lose his temper. 'Well, that's not what it sounds like to me. I tell you what, Jim. I'm going over to the police station now and I'm taking Keely with me, and when I've been cleared of whatever crime it is you seem to think I've committed, you can sit there again and explain to me what exactly you meant by a period of consideration.'

Outside in the cold January afternoon, Niall took several deep breaths and exhaled them with a sense of distaste. He wanted to clear himself of that short interview, as if it had threatened to infect him with something unpleasant. It had lasted less than twenty minutes, but somehow it had changed his perspective forever. He had always assumed that Jim would back him all the way, that he could just walk into that office, explain the situation, and have the school's automatic support. Instead, he had come away from the place feeling dirty and under suspicion.

'Maybe it's time I left teaching and did something less shitty,' he muttered to himself. 'Like being a toilet attendant.'

He walked quickly away from the school buildings, glad to be free of them, scanning the street ahead for some sign of Keely. But the corner where he had left her was empty. He checked the school grounds behind him, just in case she had come inside to talk to one of the other kids, but Keely was nowhere to be seen.

Panic set in almost immediately, but Niall tried to suppress it. There could be any number of rational explanations for her disappearance. The kid had probably slipped off to one of the nearby shops for cigarettes or sweets. Teenagers were like that, they had no sense of time or responsibility. In fact, she could be on her way back to the school right now, unaware that he was looking for her. There was absolutely no reason to believe that she would have run out on him, not at this late stage. They had agreed to stick together until the police were in control of the situation, and she had seemed happy enough with that decision.

Leroy, a sixth-former, was standing aimlessly by the school gates as if waiting for a lift. Niall swung back towards the lad in a moment of inspiration, trying to hide his panic. 'Hey, Leroy.'

'Hey, Mr Swainson. Where you been hiding, man?'

'It's a long story. You seen Keely?'

'Keely?'

'Slim blonde girl, good at art.'

Leroy blinked and fingered his rucksack for a moment as if it might give him the answer. 'She the weirdo who went after someone last term with a pair of scissors?'

'Spot on.'

'Oh yeah, I seen her.' The lad's head jerked casually towards the street corner. 'Few minutes ago. Got into a BMW with a couple of blokes. She didn't look too happy about it neither. Give one of them a right smack.'

'What blokes?'

Leroy sniffed thoughtfully. 'I think it might have been her dad driving, actually.'

'Her dad?'

'You know, that big Greek bloke. Runs a club up town.'

'Christ.'

Leroy looked at him properly for the first time. 'You

okay, sir? Is there anything I can do?'

The stench of cigar smoke inside the car made Keely cough and retch. She thought she was going to puke without the windows open. The ride threw her from side to side, jolting violently against Eddy whenever they rounded a corner.

Zal was driving crazily fast along the back streets of the city, turning to glance back at her whenever they braked for a junction. Keely didn't know where they were headed, but she could tell from his eyes that he was planning to hurt her badly once they got there. She knew a man like Zal expected a certain type of obedience from the women in his family and she had crossed the line when she hit him. It didn't take much imagination to guess what her reward was going to be.

'The police found my car for me last night,' he said, watching her in the mirror. 'It was nice of you to steal it. But did you really think you could just disappear? That was stupid. I was always going to catch up with you in the end. It took a while, but Eddy finally saw the light and told me what you and Jess have been up to at that squat. Handcuffing one of your teachers to a radiator? You should be ashamed of yourself.'

'Fuck you.'

Eddy slapped her hard in the mouth. 'Shut it.'

'I don't know how you managed to swing him to your side, Kee, but I can guess. You can be quite a little slut when you put your mind to it.' Zal fell silent for a moment as he swung onto the ring road. He gripped the wheel and stuck his foot down so the car jumped and accelerated fiercely away. Keely and Eddy were knocked back in their seats by the force. 'But this teacher must be thick or desperate, helping you out when you belong to me. Does the stupid prick know who I am?'

'He knows all about you.'

'Does he now?'

'It doesn't matter what you do to me. He's still going to tell the police everything and then you'll be locked up where you belong.'

'What for?'

Keely wiped her face shakily with the back of her hand. There was blood on her fingers. 'Drug dealing, for starters.'

'Never touch the filthy stuff. Is that the best you can do?'

'Dealing in stolen cars.'

'Prove it.'

'Then what about the prostitutes down at the club? They all give you a cut. Or is that my imagination too?'

'Jesus, what will you come out with next?' Zal was laughing, but his fingers tapped angrily on the steering wheel. She could see the glint of his gold signet ring moving. Keely knew she must be getting closer to the truth than he had expected. Her stepdad wasn't the sort to lose his cool unless he was in real trouble. 'I can't help it if some of the local toms like to drink on my premises. If they pick up a little bit of business at the same time, that's nothing to do with me.'

'Liar!'

Eddy hit her again, only this time much harder. For a few seconds, she could see nothing but spinning flashes of light behind her eyes. His voice came to her through a mist. 'I'm not telling you again. Now shut it, or I'll break your fucking jaw.'

After a few more minutes racing in the fast lane, with Zal checking his mirror constantly as if he was afraid of being followed, the car turned back towards town and began to slow down. Keely struggled to sit up and caught passing glimpses of houses and shops. Her stomach started to hurt again as she realised where they must be heading.

Zal looked at her in the mirror. 'I don't like your fucking attitude, Keely. I've bought you everything you needed over the years, looked after you and your mam with my own money, and this is how you repay me. First chance you get, you run away from home and start lying about me. Talking to your teacher friend about my club, saying there's drugs there and prostitution and fuck knows what else. I think it's about time you learnt your lesson.'

'Where are you taking me?'

'To a very special place, where we won't be disturbed.'

'What place?'

'You know where we're going, pet.'

Leroy's older brother, Christian, pulled the battered old Saab into the kerb and craned his neck past the furry dice to get a better look at the row of terraced houses beside them. His curious eyes rolled back towards Niall, now poised restlessly on the fake leopard skin covering the back seat, ready to leap out of the car as soon as it stopped. 'Here we are then, teacher. You're sure this is the place you want?'

'Yeah, absolutely sure,' Niall said hurriedly, undoing his seatbelt. 'That's brilliant, I can't thank you both enough.'

'It's no problem, man.'

'Okay, I'll probably see you back at school sometime, Leroy. Thanks again for the lift.'

'Hey, hold up a minute.' Christian was looking up at the house with a speculative expression on his face. He ran a hand over his gleaming shaved head. 'So what's the score here, man? You think that girl's in trouble with her people?'

'I don't know. That's what I'm here to find out.'

'You need a hand?'

'I'll be fine. You've done enough, it's okay.'

Leroy leant across, muttering something to his brother. Christian hesitated as if thinking, then nodded slowly. He turned his key in the ignition and the car engine died into silence. 'Yeah, why not? I think we'll hang here for a few more minutes, teacher. Wait and see what happens, just in case you change your mind.'

Niall grinned suddenly. They weren't bad lads really. And if he was honest with himself, he felt a certain sense of relief that he wasn't going to be in this situation entirely alone. He didn't like to admit it, but he might need a little help if things went badly wrong. There was no harm in having a back-up plan, especially since he had no real plan to begin with. Finding Keely had been his main objective back at the school. Niall hadn't really thought past that stage, or about what might happen once he had tracked the girl and her stepfather down. Though he didn't particularly want these lads getting themselves hurt on his account.

'Okay then.' Niall got out of the car and straightened up, feeling the first stabs of apprehension in his stomach. He had no idea what he was about to face, but if Keely really was in that house with Zal, he had no choice but to try and help her. 'You can stay if you want, Leroy. But if I'm not back out here in about ten minutes … '

'Come in and kick the shit out of them, sir?'

Niall managed a laugh. 'I was going to say call the police, but yeah, we might have to play it by ear.'

'There are better people to call than the police, teacher,' Christian murmured, leaning forwards to look at him meaningfully.

'Let's just stick to the police for now, okay?'

The front curtains were tightly closed as always, so Niall rang the bell and then hammered on the door for good measure. He just hoped no one inside had seen him pull up in Christian's car, because he had a shrewd idea they might try and make a getaway from the back of the house. Dusk was beginning to fall now and he was getting cold. Becoming more and more impatient, he banged on the window with his fist. The glass shook but there was no sound from inside. From the parked car, he could almost feel the lads' eyes boring into his back as he stood there waiting.

'Keely?' There was no answer even after a minute, so Niall battered on the door more forcibly, this time yelling frantically up at the first floor windows. 'Are you in there? Can you hear me?'

To his surprise, the door suddenly opened under his fist. It was Anne there, swaying unsteadily in the doorway. Though he hardly recognised her at first because her face was covered in blood. The strappy gold top was stained reddish brown, bare shoulders dark with bruising. Her knees under the short black skirt looked raw, as if she'd been dragged along on them.

She put out a hand and nearly fell. 'Niall?'

'Jesus Christ.'

He caught her in his arms, then heard the car doors open behind him and both lads were next to him within a few seconds, helping to support the woman before she collapsed.

Leroy gently led her back into the house while Niall and Christian did a quick sweep of the rooms. But no one else appeared to be there. There were signs of a struggle, though: a shattered glass-fronted cabinet and a fallen side table in the living room, with coffee cups and several ornaments lying in pieces on the stained carpet.

Christian came back down the stairs, shaking his head. 'If your girl was ever here, she's long gone.'

Niall knelt down hurriedly beside Anne, who was perched on the edge of an armchair with her head between her knees. The blood was still streaming down her face from a deep gash on her temple. It looked as if someone had beaten her about the head with something sharp. Probably one of the table legs lying splintered on the floor. There were no prizes for guessing who'd done it, either.

'It's okay, Anne.' He put a hand carefully on her arm and felt her body jerk in reaction. 'Everything's going to be fine. Leroy's called an ambulance and he's going to wait with you until it arrives.'

'I thought he was going to kill me.'

'Zal?'

She nodded, trying to smile. 'Couldn't let it rest, could I? I said I was going to the police because of the baby. I thought it was about time that bastard got banged up, anyway.'

'So he hit you.'

'Pretty, isn't it?' She wiped some blood away from her eyes with a shaky hand. 'He would have finished the job properly too, except his mobile rang halfway through. I think it was that Eddy he's been hanging round with lately. Then he just left.'

'Do you have any idea at all where he may have gone?'

Anne shook her head painfully. 'Where's Kee?'

'I don't know. That's why I came here first, looking for her. He must have guessed I'd follow him and taken her somewhere else instead.'

Leaning against the wall with his arms folded, Christian shook his head at them impatiently. 'You're wasting time with all this twenty questions shit, man. You've got to think, what would you do in his place? If you're right and he's planning to shut this girl up permanent, he must have some other place he'd take her to do it. But it wouldn't be somewhere like this. He'd want somewhere out of the way. Somewhere real quiet, like.'

Niall looked at him for a moment, then stood up suddenly. 'Leroy, you stay here with Anne until the ambulance comes. I think I know where the bastard's taken her.'

'Stay here until I come back, okay?' Zal said to Eddy, grabbing Keely by the arm and hauling her out of the car. 'Sit up front so you can start the car as soon as I'm out. And keep your fucking eyes open. Give us a call on the mobile if there's any trouble.'

Eddy nodded, glancing quickly at Keely's face as she was dragged away. It was the first time she had ever seen him look scared.

It was getting dark now. The back alley behind the squat was deserted except for the smell of abandoned rubbish, old mattresses, armchairs and dozens of bin bags, rotting somewhere out of sight. Keely felt dizzy, seeing the faded red brick of the derelict row and the high-walled yards behind every house. She thought she had left this place behind for good. They slipped over damp concrete in the dusk, sludge catching the distant street lights and shining. Even the sound of their footsteps in the narrow space was familiar.

She wanted to run but he held her too close, nearly breaking her arm as she struggled and twisted against him. He laughed at her weakness, his breath hot on her throat as he leant over her. 'Behave yourself, Kee. Don't force me to hit you.'

'Christ, why are you doing this?'

'Because I can.'

'You're fucking sick.'

Desperately, she tried to catch hold of the broken gatepost as Zal pulled her towards the back door of the squat.

'I'm not going back in there.'

'Yes,' he insisted, 'you are.'

Zal wrenched her fingers free, and then slapped her face so hard that she staggered backwards.

Her ears were buzzing like a thousand insects. His arm hooked quickly about her waist to keep her from falling. Then he dragged her backwards across the heaps of rubble and decaying wood. Turning slightly, he kicked the chipboard back from the door so they could get inside the kitchen. He was breathing more heavily now, his hair falling into his eyes.

'I warned you. Now stop fighting me or you'll get hurt worse. It's not worth it.'

It was cold and frighteningly dark inside the squat. Even though they had only been gone a few days, the house felt as though no one had lived there for years. She remembered the damp strips of paint peeling from the walls and the missing floorboards near the door, but somehow the place hadn't seemed so bad before.

Panting with effort, he threw her hard against the wall, and then straightened up. He was muttering something under his breath. His boots stuck to the tacky boards underfoot as he felt his way to the table and picked up the candle.

He was mad, she thought, watching him fumble with the candle. Madder than her. And stronger too, which made it unlikely she was going to survive this. Unless she could catch him off guard. Pressed against the wall, Keely tried to stay calm. She heard him hunting through his pockets for a lighter. If she was going to escape, this was probably the best moment to do it. But it felt as though he had cracked her head open on the wall. She was finding it hard even to think, let alone run away from a man of his size.

Then she saw his face lit up by the flame, glancing around the damp kitchen with satisfaction. 'Perfect.'

'For what?'

'You'll find out soon enough, Kee.'

'You need locking up.'

He lifted the candle and stared across at her. 'You started this, sweetheart. You were born to be a whore, you were begging for it from day one. All I did was give you a taste of what you needed. Now you're acting like you didn't enjoy it.'

'Is that what you told my mam?'

'It's not important what that stupid bitch thinks.'

'So why am I here?'

'One last time, Keely. Before I do what I should have done months ago and get rid of you.'

Her belly was heaving. 'You're not right in the head.'

'You love it.'

'God, you're sick. I never enjoyed it. Not once. You make my skin crawl, don't you realise that? Like ants under my clothes. You're nothing but a pervert. I'd rather die than let you touch me again.'

Zal said nothing, watching her face. A trickle of hot wax ran down onto his fingers and he jerked with pain, dropping the candle. It hissed out smokily on the damp floor. 'Fucking hell.'

Keely moved quickly. She ran through the semi-darkness, dragging the kitchen drawer open and feeling for the knife she knew must still be in there. Her fingers closed around its cold handle and then she was back against the wall, edging as silently as she could towards the back door into the yard. Another few inches and she would have to duck her head slightly to avoid the low shelf. Beyond that were two missing floorboards, and then it was the back door. Keely could hear him stumbling about angrily, trying to find the candle he had dropped. He didn't know his way around this room as well as she did. But if he managed to get to her before she reached the back door, she had the knife ready.

Her hands were shaking and she felt sick. But that was only because he had hit her head so hard against the wall. She hated him.

He must have found the candle again, she saw his lighter flare out. The kitchen was suddenly alive with its flame. Her heart going chaotic in case he caught her, Keely ducked under the shelf, jumped across that flickering space where the two floorboards were missing, and reached the back door at the same time as him, struggling with the broken hinges.

He slammed the door shut again and the walls shook. His hands were free, he must have left the candle burning on the table. 'Where do you think you're going, Kee? I haven't finished with you yet.'

'Get back,' she hissed, holding the knife up in the

light.

'Fuck's sake, what's that you've got?'

Keely backed into the corner behind the door, stumbling a little on the uneven floor. There were cobwebs brushing against her face, she could feel them.

'I'm going to cut your balls off.'

'You won't get the chance, sweetheart.'

'Scared now, aren't you?'

He made a quick dash for the knife and she jabbed at him, slicing his hand open. Zal pulled back immediately, yelping like a dog and clutching himself. She could almost smell the blood on his skin.

His eyes glittered angrily in the candlelight. 'You crazy bitch. That's the last time.'

He grabbed her wrist, taking her by surprise when she thought he was turning away. His fingers wrenched her skin and bones. It hurt like fuck. But she didn't drop the knife. They were so close, her face was against his chest and her wrist stretched up high, still pressing the knife backwards into his throat. He was leaning into her, trying to twist her arm aside. But she was jammed hard between the wall and the door, he couldn't shift her position.

Then the soft throat started to give under the blade and she heard his cry. One more little push inwards and she might cut the jugular.

'There,' she said breathlessly. 'In there.'

So many times she had imagined something like this, finally hurting the bastard as much as he had hurt her. Keely held her breath, keeping the knife as steady as she could against his throat though her wrist was aching. But this wasn't how she had expected it to be.

Her head started to hurt. She was remembering how Mr Swainson had scrabbled backwards that time, holding his hands up to protect himself when she came at him with the bottle. The bruising on his face later when she must have hit him without realising. Even the way she had smashed that window with her bare fist and not known what she was doing until he told her. Now the kitchen was so cold, she could hardly keep a firm grasp on the knife handle.

'What?'

She had said something to him. 'I don't have to be like you.'

He was laughing at her because she couldn't do it. His voice echoed around the empty building. 'What's up, Kee? Lost your fucking nerve?'

Keely couldn't think straight anymore. Everything inside was dark and confused. But she knew that she did not want to become a killer. She let him take the knife away and waited silently against the wall for his fist to come down. It didn't take long.

She came round to a familiar glimmering darkness. Her right wrist ached terribly, stretched back unnaturally above her shoulder. Her head was still woozy from the beating and she didn't want to be awake yet. Pain was beginning to throb through her body again. It wasn't fair. She didn't want to feel any of that. She just wanted to slip back into that place of nothingness that was already disappearing from her memory.

Something was burning close to her face and the acrid smell made her nose wrinkle up. She started to cough and choke, her eyes stinging and watering in the smoke, fighting to turn her head away while his hand held her chin completely still. 'I can't breathe...'

Hidden somewhere at her side in the darkness, Zal was laughing at her reaction. But he let go of her chin as she spluttered and struggled helplessly against his grip.

He straightened up and pulled the smoking thing away from her face. She saw then it was a long twist of newspaper he had been burning right next to her face.

'That's better.' He dropped it to the bare boards, stamping the flame out with his boot. 'I thought you were never going to wake up.'

She struggled to get up, but she couldn't move. There was freezing cold metal at her back. Trying to turn her head to stare at her left wrist, fixed painfully above her shoulder, Keely slowly realised he'd used the handcuffs to stop her escaping. She hadn't taken them down when she let Mr Swainson go. They must have been still hanging here, attached to the radiator. But where was the fucking key? She couldn't remember what she'd done with it after letting him go. It could be anywhere in the squat.

It was like one of her old nightmares coming true. She was still in the squat, only now she knew how Mr Swainson had felt. She didn't want to feel afraid, she hated the bastard too much to show him fear, but her lips were starting to tremble and she couldn't stop them. Her brain was starting to work at last and she couldn't get away from what it was thinking. There was only one reason why he would have brought her somewhere like this. He was planning to kill her here before she could shop him to the police. The house was due for demolition any day now. There was never anyone passing, no one would hear what was happening, no one would stop him.

'Uncomfortable?' He bent right down to her eye level and stroked her cheek. She could smell the cigar smoke on his breath. The dark flashed into her eyes at high speed. It was just like before. His hands slowly finding and hurting her. 'You've got no one to blame for that but yourself, sweetheart. You should have thought of the consequences before you started pissing us about, you and that teacher friend.'

'I'm not scared of you.'

'See this?' He pushed aside the thick black hair and showed her a reddish scar running up onto his scalp. 'That was your first mistake. But getting someone else involved was out of order.'

'I'm not scared.'

His heavy black boot took her by surprise, coming out of the darkness without any warning. She felt her face smash sideways into the radiator and tried to lose it, hoping to slip back into nothingness, but the black spots in front of her eyes faded back to candlelight instead. The pain hung about the bones of her head though, humming strangely like electricity.

She hadn't fainted again. She was still here and he was standing above her, watching her face. 'I really enjoyed that. Did you enjoy it, Keely? Would you like some more?'

'Yes please.'

This time the flash was nothing but a blur of rounded light like a breaking-ball. Her belly and ribs exploded, heaving and collapsing back in on themselves. She found herself choking on dust and rubble, tilting her head back to snatch at the higher air. Something was breaking over her stomach in the darkness and pushing deep inside. Keely knew it was pain, but she couldn't feel it properly. Instead there was only laughter and her mouth cracking on the warm trickle which she decided, using the tip of her tongue, must be blood.

'That the best you can do?'

He looked angry, dragging her face up towards him and squeezing the bones until she thought they would break. 'What are you laughing about? What's wrong with you?'

Keely tried to spit at him, but only blood bubbled out. He smacked her back into the radiator, catching her head heavily on the corner.

There was complete darkness for a while after that. She sank into it easily enough but it wouldn't stay. Her ears gradually stopped buzzing. The floor and walls moved gently against her body. Keely was rolling in a long slow wave of the ocean, turning like clockwork under his hands, until her face came up hard against cold metal and she was suddenly awake again. But it still took a while before she realised properly where she was, the place had become so mixed-up in her head with other things. She could hear his quick breathing somewhere above her head and it had confused her. For a moment, she thought they were back in her bedroom at home, with the lights out and her mam watching telly downstairs.

His whisper was so familiar. 'Just one last time. It's a bit late to be shy. Open up for us, there's a good girl.'

The room stank of mould and damp walls and burning paper. Keely was on her knees now, cold bare boards hurting her skin, and her skirt had been pushed up. He was behind her, one arm round her waist to hold her up, the other hand fumbling with her knickers. She was half asleep, running on automatic. But her legs felt like lead weights, they were too heavy to move apart like he wanted.

For a moment or two Keely faded back into silence, then a sharp pain between her thighs brought her back to the dark room.

'Come on, Kee.' His voice was close to her ear. 'I want you to feel this. Don't pass out on us now.'

Niall grabbed Christian's arm. 'There's the car. Pull up further along, we don't want him to know we're coming.'

The lad parked up out of sight just around the corner, then they both walked quickly back towards the derelict row of houses. Neither of them said much. It was darker now and there weren't many street lights on this stretch of road. They could hear a dog barking hysterically in the distance, and somewhere across town the fading wail of sirens. Even though there were a few front windows lit up on the next row of houses, where people were obviously still living, this place seemed to be utterly deserted. It was small wonder no one had ever heard his shouts.

Niall hunched his shoulders and hurried his step. It was bitterly cold tonight. There was a feeling in the air that more snow might be on its way. Inside, his stomach was clenched like a fist at the thought of what that bastard might have done to Keely by now, but Niall knew there was no point losing it. He had to stay calm or he wouldn't be able to help the kid at all.

'You sure you're up for this?'

Christian grinned at him sideways. 'I wouldn't have come if I wasn't.'

'How old are you?'

'What's that got to do with it?'

Niall lowered his voice and spoke hurriedly. They were nearly level with the black car now and he could see Eddy sitting in the front seat. 'Look, I'm not kidding about here. These people are drug dealers, and God knows what else. The bloke in this car's already killed one man that I know of.'

'I'm twenty-two, is that old enough?'

'Okay.'

'You open the door, I'll pull him out.'

Niall looked at him. 'No, you open the door and I'll pull him out.'

'Whatever.'

Leaning back in the front seat of the car, Eddy was obviously doing nothing more sinister than listening to music. His eyes were half closed as he drummed his fingers rhythmically on the steering wheel and nodded his head. When the car door opened abruptly, he only had a second or so to stare up at them both in astonishment. It was clear the lad hadn't been expecting any trouble.

Then Niall had him out on the tarmac, flung face down on the wet surface, groaning as one knee suddenly pressed hard into the small of his back. 'Where are they? Inside the house?'

'Go fuck yourself.'

'Don't piss me about, Eddy.'

'You think I'm going to say a word to you? I don't know why the silly bitch let you go. If it'd been up to me, you'd be at the bottom of the fucking river by now and we'd have...'

Christian trod heavily on his fingers, smiling at the lad's agonised cry. 'Just answer the question, man.'

'Okay, get off my fucking hand. Yeah, they're inside.'

Niall moved away and Eddy rolled heavily to his feet, his leather jacket gleaming with sludge from the wet tarmac. He stood there for a few seconds with a furious expression, nursing his hurt hand, then suddenly belted off down the street. Niall didn't bother following him. He put a hand on Christian's arm when the lad turned to run after him, shaking his head. 'Let him go. Eddy's not important at the moment. He's left his mobile anyway, look. Better get on to the police and let them know where we are.'

'I'm coming in with you.'

'No, you wait here for the police. I don't want Eddy coming back and taking us by surprise.'

Christian looked at him. 'Don't be soft. You can't go in there alone, man. What you playing the hero for? That isn't going to save her, that's just going to get you both hurt.'

'Will you back off for once and ring the police for us?'

'Stubborn bastard.'

'You're my back-up plan, okay?'

The lad nodded. 'Yeah, bollocks. Go on then, you're only wasting more time now arguing. Typical fucking teacher.'

Going back into the squat made the hairs rise on the back of his neck. For a moment, slipping silently through the back door into the pitch-black kitchen, Niall regretted telling Christian to wait outside. Strange though it seemed, he had felt ready for the situation up until that point, but just smelling the musty damp air of the house and seeing these familiar bare floorboards brought everything back in a wave of nausea. He had hoped never to come back to this place.

Niall stood frozen a moment, waiting for his sickness to recede. Then he forced himself to move into the hallway, each cautious step taking him nearer the half-closed door of his former prison. He could hear the girl moaning, but the sound seemed strangely muffled. He pushed the door open wide and stared into the darkened room.

His breath caught in his chest and he needed to retch. But the urge passed as soon as it had come. For suddenly Niall was filled with blind rage, his throat choked with it, hands shaking like an old man's.

Keely was facing away from the door, her face pushed hard against the metal radiator, her skirt up around her waist. Left wrist stretched awkwardly above her head, she had been handcuffed into position. Down on his knees behind her body, Zal had unzipped his jeans and was clearly planning to have sex with the girl.

'Get off her,' Niall yelled, running forward. He kicked the other man hard between the legs, then grabbed Zal by the back of the neck and dragged him away from the girl's trembling body. 'You must be sick in the head. That's your own stepdaughter!'

Zal lurched sideways and tried to crawl away across the floor, groaning and clutching himself between the legs. 'What the fuck?'

'I ought to kill you.'

Panting, Zal held up his hand as if asking him to wait. 'That hurt, you bastard. You got me in the balls. What's this about, man? Don't you ever know when to mind your own business?'

'Keely is my business now.'

'You fucking her too? It's no big deal, you don't have to get so shitty with me. Not over a woman, it's a total waste of energy.' Zal shuffled backwards across the floorboards, zipping up his jeans again with a pained expression. Niall took a few steps after him, ready for a fight. He could almost see the other man's brain moving through the possibilities. 'Okay, you got me. I was planning to show her who's boss. But it doesn't need to be like this. What is it you really want out of this situation? I've got plenty of money.'

'Where's the key to the handcuffs?'

'I can pay you.'

Niall kicked him in the balls again. 'The key.'

'How the fuck should I know where it is?' Zal struggled to his knees, face contorted as if in intense pain. 'Why don't you ask that little whore?'

Keely was crying. 'I don't know where the key is. I lost it.'

'You hear that, man? That's so pathetic.' Zal cradled his crotch with gentle fingers. 'Don't you understand yet? She's nothing special. She's just some stupid piece of shit you've picked up off the street. They're all the same. In the end, you fuck them and walk away. Nice tits, nice arse, but nothing inside worth keeping.'

'Bastard,' Keely hissed.

'Whatever she may have told you, don't waste your sympathy on the lying bitch. There's thousands more like our Keely. They deliberately lead you on. They put it on a plate for you. Then they get themselves pregnant so they can trap you. I've seen them in the club, down the park, on the streets. And it doesn't matter how young they are, all they really want in return is your wallet. You want another girl like Keely? I can get her for you, teacher. Today.'

There was a tide of red rushing in front of Niall's eyes until it was all he could see. Bull-like, he charged forward and knocked the bigger man to the floor again.

There was a ludicrous silence for a few moments, broken only by the sound of their panting and swearing as they rolled across the floorboards. Niall closed his eyes and hung on. His jaw was aching from a punch that must have landed without him realising.

Somehow, he got his hands round the other man's neck and squeezed his thick windpipe as hard as he could. He could smell sweat and cigar smoke and the sickly scent of aftershave right in his face.

Then Zal's knee came up and caught him violently in the stomach, winding him.

For a while, Niall couldn't be sure who was making the thin squealing noise he could hear above their struggling bodies.

He couldn't lose this fight, not with Keely watching. He'd lost the same sort of fight once before in his life and he couldn't lose again.

Struggling to get himself under control, Niall managed to get a firmer grip at last. This was the moment he'd been waiting for. He dragged Zal up by the throat, smashing his head against the brick wall once, then twice, then several more times for good measure until the heavy body slumped against him in what appeared to be a dead faint.

'Mr Swainson?'

Each time it made contact with the wall, the man's head made a noise like raw meat being slapped against a chopping board and suddenly there was blood running down his hands onto his wrists. Below them, his arms were too heavy to keep raised for much longer.

'Mr Sawinson?'

Behind the exhaustion and throbbing pain, there was something like triumph singing through his head.

'Niall?'

It was over. It was all over. He had done it.

'Please. Let him go. He's not worth it.'

It was difficult but Niall finally managed to connect with what the girl was saying. Slowly he unclenched his fingers, one by one, from the thick neck.

She was right. Killing Zal was not worth it. Much as he wanted to murder the bastard, there was no point going to prison for a piece of scum like him. Better to let the police deal with him.

Besides, he had heard that prison was not much fun for child molesters. So it was not like Zal would get off lightly, whatever his eventual sentence.

Groggily, he looked up towards Keely, swaying on his feet like a prize-fighter as he tried to focus on the pale oval of her face which kept swimming in and out of his vision.

'D … Did we win?' he asked.

'I think so, yes.' She was not smiling. 'If you can call this winning.'

EPILOGUE

There was dust spinning everywhere that afternoon. Dust in her throat and hair and clothes and shoes. Dust covering the line of trucks and workmen until they were almost invisible. Dust on the huge breaking-ball swinging loosely at the end of a chain. Dust rising from the rubble of houses the men had already demolished that morning.

Keely dug her hands into her jeans pockets and squinted up through the dust at the winter sunlight. 'How much longer?'

'They're bringing it out now,' Niall said, right beside her ear.

It was hard to see anything with the dust everywhere, but she shielded her eyes and stared along the street.

Four workmen had emerged through the smashed chipboard over the front door. One of them stopped briefly to raise his hard-hat to the man with the walkie talkie, as if that was some sort of signal. Then the four men carried on down the path towards a waiting van with its back doors wide open. Between them, they were carrying the heavy metal radiator that had been attached to the squat wall, chipped and battered now as it swayed towards the van, but still somehow immense in her memory.

'You really bought it?'

'Do you mind?' Niall asked, watching her face. 'Stupid of me. But I thought it might make an interesting souvenir.'

'I don't mind.'

After a short silence, he nodded. 'Better move over here for a moment. I promised the foreman we'd stand well back once they were ready.'

'They're going to knock the whole place down?'

'Flatten it completely.'

They stood together on the street corner, staring back at the long row of houses due for demolition. Some were already in ruins under the dust clouds. Only the far end of the terrace, including their squat, was still untouched. Listening to the shouts of the workmen above the noise, Keely couldn't take her eyes off that breaking-ball. It was swinging closer and closer to the squat as the huge machine came trundling down the street, leaving tyre marks behind in the dust.

She thought of all those dark silent rooms inside, the strange patterns she had painted over the walls.

'I can't imagine ever living somewhere else.'

'You're not having second thoughts about the flat?'

Keely shook her head. 'I promised Jess we'd move in together as soon as she was better. She needs me.'

The workmen had cleared the row of houses and she could hear a crackle of static on the walkie-talkie. Someone was shouting further along the street but Keely couldn't make out the words properly. There was still dust everywhere and she could hardly breathe. She shielded her eyes to see better. Gears crunched noisily on the yellow machine sitting outside the squat and the huge metal ball began to swing and rattle at the end of its chain.

'Do you think they'll ever catch Eddy?' she asked suddenly.

'He can't run forever.'

She shivered. 'Everything feels so different now I don't have to see Zal anymore. It's strange thinking about him and Eddy getting locked up. I never thought anyone would believe me, not even my mam.'

'I'm glad it's worked out.'

'None of this is a problem for you, is it?' Her voice was sharp, almost angry. 'Your life isn't fucked up. You don't have to try and start again now. Whatever happens, you can always go back to work.'

'But I don't want to, Keely. I don't think I can go back to teaching, not after all this. I might try running a gallery instead, or opening an art shop. Perhaps I'll even start exhibiting my own work at last. That's what I wanted to do in the beginning. I never really intended to stay a teacher forever.' Niall smiled. 'That was what my mother wanted me to be.'

'I don't know what I'm going to do.'

'That's easy. Keep painting.'

She looked at him, biting her lip. 'Do you really think I could?'

'Why not?'

'Because of the baby.'

There was a terrible noise and they both looked up. The breaking-ball had swung across the street without warning and smashed the outside wall of the squat into hanging pillars of rubble. As the dust clouds spun on the cold sunny air, they could see the front room with its bizarrely painted walls, red and purple and orange, circles and squares and pentagrams, twisting grotesquely as the walls slowly began to collapse in on themselves and fall.

Keely slammed her hands over her ears and turned her face into his chest. She didn't want to be there anymore.

The breaking-ball hit the squat again with a violent crash. Even the ground under their feet seemed to shake at the impact.

'My pictures have gone,' she whispered.

'You can always paint more.'

'You've got a bloody answer for everything.' Her face flushed. 'Why don't you hate me? I did all that stuff to you, I hurt you so bad.'

'He hurt you first.'

'That's no excuse for what I did.'

'It's enough for me.'

Keely sat down on the edge of the kerb and watched the workmen in their yellow hard-hats directing the last of the demolition from a safe distance across the street. Her legs were shaking. She wrapped her hands around her knees for a minute to steady them. Everything seemed so strange and disconnected these days. Sometimes it was hard even to hang onto the realities around her. She was getting cold in spite of the sunshine, and she still felt a little bit sick. But that was probably because of the baby growing inside her, a tiny secret life she could never completely shake off.

'I may look better on the outside, but am I better on the inside? What if the sickness comes back? What if I hurt people and can't remember what I'm doing? I might even hurt the baby when it's born.'

'You're a different person now, Keely. That bastard's out of your life and you're clear of the shadow. You ought to stop worrying about it and move on.'

'But should I keep the baby? His baby?'

Niall hesitated. 'You have to make that decision on your own.'

'I'm too scared.'

'I said I'd help you and I meant it.'

'But why? This baby isn't your problem.' Keely stared up at him wildly. 'You're not my dad. I don't even know where my real dad is anymore, that's how much he cares about me.' She drew breath. 'Don't you see? It doesn't matter what I do. Everyone leaves in the end, and you won't stay either. But that's not going to stop me loving this baby. It's the only good thing I've got in my life.'

Keely scrambled up off the kerb and stood staring across at the last smoking remains of the squat. Soon there would be nothing left of the ugly old place except dust and rubble.

The sun hit her from above like a ladder dropping rung by rung through the demolition haze, and Keely turned her face instinctively towards the light.

Part of her wished Mr Swainson could be her real dad. Everything would be so simple then. It was stupid and she hated being so feeble about it, but she was frightened of being buried forever under this cloud of dust from the dead houses. The dust of the squat was already inside her, growing bigger with every breath she took. It was like thousands of tiny arrows blinding her eyes, making the tears come at last.

'I'm not going anywhere, kid,' he said, and put an arm around her shoulder.

The squat had almost vanished now. Blackened stone from its old disused chimney crashed down into the back yard. The foreman yelled something into his walkie-talkie, raising his arm at the same time. The remaining walls crumbled and fell inwards at another blow from the breaking-ball. More clouds of thick choking dust filled the air.

Keely looked away, coughing behind a raised hand. When she looked back, all she could see was another row of houses beyond the rubble, red brick covered in a fine white layer of dust.

The squat was gone. Gone forever.

And she thought she could hear a bird singing.

MIRANDA

Jane Holland is also the author of MIRANDA, a new historical novel set in the Isle of Man in 1978.

In the summer of 1978, Lawrence takes Juliet to visit his father in the beautiful and unspoilt Isle of Man. He finds Gil has built himself a haven on the island where the past can be relived rather than forgotten. Relived as it should have been, not as it was. Under the spell of the island, Lawrence believes he can rebuild the magic with Juliet.

But everything changes when the child Miranda goes missing.

To read a free sample, search

MIRANDA on Amazon

or visit

www.thimblerigbooks.com

GIRL NUMBER ONE

Jane Holland is also the author of GIRL NUMBER ONE, a contemporary crime thriller set in Cornwall.

Eleanor Blackwood discovers a woman's body in the same spot in the Cornish woods where her mother was strangled eighteen years ago. But before the police can get there, the body vanishes.

Is Eleanor's disturbed mind playing tricks on her again, or has her mother's killer resurfaced? And what does the number on the dead woman's forehead signify?

To read a free sample, search
GIRL NUMBER ONE on Amazon

or visit

www.thimblerigbooks.com

Available now in paperback or ebook

ABOUT THE AUTHOR

Born in Essex, the middle daughter of romance legend Charlotte Lamb, Jane Holland is a poet, novelist and critic who has published six books of poetry and nearly thirty novels to date, plus numerous novellas and short stories. As a novelist, she writes as Jane Holland, Victoria Lamb, Elizabeth Moss and Beth Good.

She currently lives in the South-West of England with her husband and young family. A keen home schooler, she educates her children during the day and writes in the evenings. (When she's not messing about on social media.)

You can find her on Twitter as @janeholland1

14169504R00172

Printed in Great Britain
by Amazon.co.uk, Ltd.,
Marston Gate.